Typecast

BOOK ONE OF THE

HOLLYWOOD STARDUST TRILOGY

by

Kim Carmichael

Kim Carmichael

Typecast

A NOVEL

Cover Design by JWORX Designs
Book Design by Tamara Eaton

Dedication

To everyone who has ever been forced to play a role.

Acknowledgments

My Husby: Without you, all the happily ever afters wouldn't mean a thing.

C and T: Thank you for always being supportive and for all the hours you let me have so I can create my worlds.

My Fluff Balls: You are happiness personified.

Tamara Eaton: With you, I am a better writer, a better storyteller, and a better friend. Thank you.

Emily Kidman-Smith: You put my name out there and made my vision a beautiful cover. Thank you for the countless hours you spent trying to find just the right couple.

Teresa Neeley-Martin: My comma whisperer. Thank you for perfecting my stories. You are the finishing touch!

Erica Duvall and Summer Clark: Thank you for putting my baby out there for others to critique.

Lia Hearn and Corry Parnese: Always rays of sunshine and positivity, you are what the book world needs. Thank you for always asking the magic words—what can I do?

Michelle Henderson: Thank you for swooping in and helping me. You rock!

Deneale: You are my sidekick—thank you for your unconditional support.

Vicki Rose: You are new to my team and a most welcome addition. Thank you for your enthusiasm.

Chelle: Thanks for your ear.

Joe, Michelle, Alexis, Eva, Kat, Lisa, and Courtney: You take my crazy and accept it. Thank you.

Tabby: You are always there to help. Thank you!

Megan: Thank you for all your support.

Sandra: Thank you for your amazing editing work.

My own instinct: Thank you for stopping me from making a huge mistake. You are living proof people need to go with their guts.

Logan, Erin, Ryder, and Drew: Thank you for coming into my life when I needed you most. I can only hope I do you justice.

Short Glossary of Film Terms

Cut
A change in camera angle or placement, location, or time.

Director
The principal creative artist on a movie set. A director is usually (but not always) the driving artistic source behind the filming process, and communicates to actors the way that he/she would like a particular scene played. A director's duties might also include casting, script editing, shot selection, shot composition, and editing. Typically, a director has complete artistic control over all aspects of the movie, but it is not uncommon for the director to be bound by agreements with either a producer or a studio.

Dissolve
An editing technique whereby the images of one shot are gradually replaced by the images of another.

Exterior
AKA: EXT
Used in a slug line; indicates that the scene occurs outdoors.

Fade
AKA: Fade to Black, Fade In, Fade Out
A smooth, gradual transition from a normal image to complete blackness (fade out) or vice versa (fade in).

Idolized
To regard with blind adoration or devotion. To worship as a god.

Interior
AKA: INT

Used in a slug line; indicates that the scene occurs indoors.

Limelight
The center of public attention, interest, observation, or notoriety.

Producer
The chief of staff of a movie production in all matters save the creative efforts of the director, who is head of the line. A producer is responsible for raising funding, hiring key personnel, and arranging for distributors.

Slug Line
A header appearing in a script before each scene or shot detailing the location, date, and time that the following action is intended to occur in.

Stardust
A naively romantic quality.

Step and Repeat
A term for the backdrop or media wall which typically displays the sponsor's logo or name. A place where notable attendees stop for a photo opportunity. Step and repeats are often found at red carpet events.

Typecast
1. To cast (a performer) in a role that requires characteristics of physique, manner, personality, etc., similar to those possessed by the performer.
2. To cast (a performer) repeatedly in a kind of role closely patterned after that of the actor's previous successes.

HOLLYWOOD STARDUST

FADE IN:

INT. INDIANAPOLIS, IL - HIGH SCHOOL HALLWAY -
DAY

STEVEN - typical eighteen-year-old high school
senior, jerk, troublemaker with the attitude
that the world owes him a living, and of
course, girls flock to him.

STEVEN tosses his books in his locker and
turns to find new student, ROXY, coming down
the hall staring down at her school schedule
and then looking up at the different room
numbers. He hits his best friend, WILLIAM, on
the back.

> STEVEN
> Check this tasty little
> morsel out.

WILLIAM - also eighteen years old the type of
guy who is both the senior class president,
lead in the high school play, and athlete all
in one. The kind of boy every mother wants for
her daughter when her daughter wants STEVEN.

WILLIAM turns.

> WILLIAM
> She's the new one from
> California.

Both STEVEN and WILLIAM watch ROXY walk toward
them.

ROXY - Eighteen years old is not your typical

Midwestern girl, rather she is a California transplant. She is not the cheerleader or student council type, but rather a bit of sparkle and flair in a community that isn't used to her. She stands out though she wants to fit in.

ROXY Looks up and drops her paper.

WILLIAM Runs over and picks up the paper. He holds the paper out.

                    WILLIAM
              Here you go.

                    ROXY
              Thanks, I'm just a little
              lost.

ROXY takes the paper and glances between William and Steven.

STEVEN Saunters over and plucks the paper out of her hand.

                    STEVEN
              I don't think you're lost
              at all. I think you're
              found.

Chapter One

"There is absolutely no way I am going out there and interviewing some B-list has-been bad boy." Julia Davis, the lead entertainment reporter for Chargge.com crossed her arms. "Your little fact finder screwed up again. Seriously, Craig, how can I be expected to work this way?"

Heat encompassed Ivy Vermont, but she met Julia's crossed arms with a set of her own and glanced between Craig Stockton, her boss, and Julia. "Technically, Logan Alexander is not a B-lister. He doesn't even act anymore."

"Your ridiculous details mean nothing." Julia's nostrils flared.

"Ivy, what happened to getting Ryder Scott or Erin Holland from *Hollywood Stardust*?" Shaking his head, Craig approached. "It's a little hard to do a story on the twentieth anniversary of the movie without one of the stars. You told me everything was set."

With facts, rather than stature on her side, Ivy stood up straighter and lifted her chin. "Logan Alexander was as much a star in the movie as the other two of them, well three."

"Last week, rather than getting that little boy in the hot dog commercial with the catchy line, you brought me the dog." Julia stared her down. "How can I interview a dog?"

"The trainer was there. Some say dogs have the mentality of a two-year-old, and it did tricks." No one ever saw the potential. If she could talk as eloquently in front of the camera as behind, she would be the reporter. Actually, she would have been an actress and the interviewee. Even the camera on her phone terrified her, not a flattering trait coming from a family of actors. "A few fetches and atta boys would have been perfect for your report."

"I am not doing this interview." The click of Julia's heels on the wood floor of the conference room grew louder as she approached. "What? Are you scared to face me?"

Though she tried not to look directly at her, Ivy gave in, swallowing back any mention of the tiny mascara smear above her left eye. Julia should meet Mr. Alexander with such an imperfection. "The agent promised me Ryder or Erin. Only, two hours ago, he called to say Logan would be here instead."

"He was one of the major stars." Craig wiped his brow.

"Stop defending your personal pet." Julia turned her back to him.

Ivy held out the note cards she made for the wicked reporter. "Logan Alexander is an excellent person to interview. The villain is always the most interesting. Even after all the scandals, *Hollywood Stardust* is one of the most beloved teen movies ever made, and changed the genre forever."

"I don't need your details. Did you spend your life studying this movie?" Julia grabbed the cards out of her hand and tossed them to the floor. "He was arrested and personally responsible for getting the sequel canceled. He is as bad in real life as he was in the movie."

"Don't forget that I ran off innocent Drew Fulton and no one has ever heard from him again."

At the unexpected male voice, Ivy turned. Her breath caught as her ultimate teen fantasy stood before her.

The heat in the room intensified, but she froze. Mr. Logan Alexander leaned in the doorway—more like filled up the doorway. He lifted a cigarette, twirled it between his fingers, and placed it in his mouth.

Unlike someone who lived the hard-knock life of a disgraced actor, time had kissed him, leaving him looking much like his teen dream self, only a little more rugged. While his other two male costars from the movie possessed more of the good and wholesome image, Logan Alexander personified the conniving character. He was the one who lured people with looks that could only be described as remarkable.

As if this whole thing were nothing but a bother, he pushed away from doorjamb and entered the room, glanced at Julia, turned his back to Craig, and faced Ivy. "So, you think the villain is the most interesting?" The cigarette bounced between his lips.

Interesting? Interesting as in the way he pulled his dark blond hair into a ponytail that hit the nape of his neck leaving one long strand to hang down the side of his face? Maybe interesting in the way his light blue eyes seemed almost translucent, half-closed, and definitely naughty? Of course, also interesting in how the slight bit of stubble highlighted the angles of his face, and the way he managed to keep his cigarette balanced. Then the answer was yes, he, or the villain, was the most interesting.

"The villain always needs to go under the most transformation." She managed to squeak out the words and pointed to his cigarette, unsure if she needed to tell him about the no smoking rule. Did fantasies follow rules?

"Don't worry. I'm not going to light it." His gaze scanned down to her shoes and back up to her face.

Interesting. She licked her lips. The man was more glorious in person than on the silver screen.

"What if the villain hasn't undergone a transformation?" Julia tapped her foot.

Ivy ground her teeth together. If anyone needed to change, it was Julia.

"I suppose I'll get more hard-hitting questions than asking a dog trainer if Rover, the hot dog hunter, is potty trained. You sure know how to dig deep." Though he answered Julia, he continued to look at Ivy. "I liked the dog, a much better choice than the obnoxious little boy."

Transfixed, she continued to stare at him.

"Just because the villain can change, doesn't mean they will." Julia moved over as if trying to get his attention.

He exhaled, but the cigarette stayed in place. "How can I do an interview with you when I know you are team Ryder all the way?"

"*Hollywood Stardust* was the typical love triangle." Julia raised her chin. "Today's teen movies are better developed than movies decades ago."

"Oh, that reference to my age really does pain me." He pressed his hand to his chest. "Tell me, did the villains of your era wear pompadours and leather jackets, or perhaps suits of armor?"

In an effort to stifle a laugh, Ivy bit the side of her mouth. There was something to be said for the villain getting their comeuppance, and she didn't mean Mr. Alexander.

Julia narrowed her eyes and spun toward Craig. "I am not playing her game of bait and switch. If Miss Details loves villains so much, Miss Details can do the interview. Call me when you get a real star." She stormed out.

"Well, that is one thing your runaway hostess and I agree on." Mr. Alexander's smile revealed a perfect set of Hollywood teeth.

"What would that be?" Craig wiped his brow.

"Miss Details should do the interview." In a swoon-worthy move, Mr. Alexander bowed to her.

The spotlight shined down on her and the same stage fright she battled every second of her life took a strong hold over her body, made worse by being presented with her teen idol in the flesh. "Craig." How she managed to utter even one word was beyond her, but she took it as a good sign.

"Oh, no. No, that won't do at all." Craig shook his head. The first and only time she was on camera at Chargge.com, she ended up running off set and throwing up in a trash can. "I am sure Julia will be right back."

"Don't bring her back on my account. I'm Team Details all the way." Logan raised his fist as if he were about to begin cheering and, with a wink, lifted his chin in her direction. "She is clearly an expert on the movie and knows story structure."

His gesture, though probably insignificant to him, served to ignite her courage as well as her body. She chose to ignore them both. All she needed was to throw up on one of the *Hollywood Stardust* stars.

Craig cupped his hand over his mouth. "She is an expert on every movie."

Yes, fine, but she was mostly an expert on *Hollywood Stardust*. She remained silent.

"I refuse to be interviewed by anyone who is not an expert in cinema." Mr. Alexander picked up one of her note cards, gave it a quick scan, and sauntered over to her. Yes, it was a total saunter. His walk may have also included a bit of a swagger as well. "Miss Details is the only one for me. It seems she has found something to talk about other than drugs, Drew, and sequels, since I won't answer those questions anyway."

She fought the need to hug her prepubescent crush, bury her face in his chest, and breathe in what could only be the smell of cologne and cookies. Later, they could go back to her apartment, and she would confess she used to write his name in her notebook and practice kissing him on the back of her hand. In her dreams, she could interview him and then they'd conquer the world together. In reality, she knew he was only playing a role and she would never be able to utter a sentence. Dumb reality.

"Either she interviews me or you can call the company that owns not only *Hollywood Stardust*, but your website as well, and tell them the video blog they expect to make waves won't air today. I'll be in the lounge not lighting my cigarette." He handed her the card and walked out the door.

She leaned forward, bracing herself on her knees. "Oh God, I want to do this."

Her boss paced across the floor. "You would be the perfect person if you could just learn to calm down. It's what we hired you for."

Though Craig never admitted it, she was the bane of his existence. He hired her as a favor to her father, and they gave her the job as a reporter. Technically, her current job as fact-checker and scheduler didn't even exist. The reporters were supposed to do their own research, but Julia sort of snatched her up as a personal assistant. Both her parents who possessed multiple acting awards between them, looked at her with wide eyes and pity every time they discussed her career. Even they weren't good enough actors to hide their disappointment.

She crumpled the note card in her fist and straightened up. "I'll do it. I will interview Logan Alexander." Part of her expected a spotlight to shine down on her signifying her strength of conviction. The other part was thrilled she didn't live in a world where spotlights randomly illuminated at key life-changing moments. She would end up living in the bathroom with the lights off, shaking.

Craig shook his head. His skin had turned the most unusual shade of red.

"This is the movie of a generation, the one that spoke to that specific time. The story should be told by someone who truly loves everything it represents." For once, she needed to be her own spotlight. "This is the movie that pushed the boundaries, didn't rely on the happily ever after, asked the questions." Maybe the movie that meant the world to her could also cure her.

"We need this story, Ivy." He crossed his arms. "Seriously, we need the story. Other sites are competing with us. We need something to go viral. The advertising dollars are not coming in as they should, and you know what that means."

Yes, it meant cuts, starting with the person who technically didn't have a title. She might as well go big or go home, literally.

"Do the interview, but make sure you ask about Drew Fulton and the arrest and the sequel."

"He said he wouldn't answer those questions." The swirl of anxiety circled around her stomach.

"Ivy." He rubbed his hand over his face. "You can do this. You were made for this. Go to wardrobe, ask them for something more contemporary and fashionable, and ask the questions. We need you."

For once she wouldn't disappoint. She stopped herself from saluting and gave him a strong nod. "I got this." As she walked out, she made a mental note to have a trash can put near the set.

HOLLYWOOD STARDUST

                                              CUT TO:

EXT. INDIANAPOLIS, IL - HIGH SCHOOL, BACK OF
DRAMA BUILDING - DAY

STEVEN leans back against his BMW and watches
ROXY run out from the drama building. She
backs up against the wall and puts her hands
over her eyes. Suddenly, she looks up and sees
him. He motions her over. ROXY approaches.

                    STEVEN
               Please tell me you were
               rehearsing a scene where
               your character breaks out
               in tears.

STEVEN puts his fingertips under her chin and
tilts her face up.

ROXY cries and sniffs.
                    ROXY
               I wouldn't know. I didn't
               get a part.

STEVEN shakes his head.

                    STEVEN
               Your acting is too
               sophisticated for this
               town. They're jealous of
               true talent.

                    ROXY
               I just wasn't good enough.

STEVEN uses his fingertips to wipe her tears
away.

                    STEVEN
          Never listen to those
          idiots. They speak to
          empty rooms. You don't
          want to be part of their
          amateur production anyway.

                    ROXY
          I just want to fit in.

Chapter Two

"Do you want the smart suit or the pretty dress?" The woman who collected the props and clothes for the site's photo and video shoots held up a black business suit with a white collared shirt and a red ruffled dress.

"I don't think either of those will fit me." Since the makeup woman held her chin in place, Ivy glanced at the outfits in the mirror. She had enough to overcome without telling these people she didn't care for the clothes or the makeup, but she preferred the 1950s suit she already had on. Her authentic designer outfit was the spitting image of the ones worn by the female leads in those old romantic comedies. Her light makeup and curled hair matched the outfit to a tee.

Craig joined them and rubbed his chin. "Let me think."

"Why on earth do you insist on pigeonholing your hostesses as either smart or pretty when it's more than obvious Miss Details is both?" Mr. Alexander entered the room and the energy in the air changed. What was stuffy and heavy turned electric and sizzled around her. "She's right. Neither of those fit her."

"Excuse me." The wardrobe lady waved to him. "Her name is Ivy Vermont."

"It's him." The makeup lady smiled down at her. "He's so bad."

He chuckled. "Then leave Miss Ivy Vermont in what she's wearing. It's perfect."

Well, he did have excellent taste. At his words, and him using her name, she straightened in the chair, actually more like squirmed, and stared at his reflection as if she were watching one of his movies. The show playing out in front of her, well in the refection of the mirror, was much better than any one of his roles.

"Speaking of pigeonholing. Maybe you can discuss how all four of you were pigeonholed into your respective roles," Craig said. Still studying the outfits, he kept his back to the man.

"Oh, this old song and dance? Yes, the four of us were pigeonholed into our parts. Ryder, the teen heartthrob; Erin, the good girl everyone wanted; Drew, the nerd; and yours truly, the asshole." He counted them off on his fingers. "The world already knows that. I really think this reporter change will do everyone some good."

"Well then, tell us something we don't know." Craig selected the suit and turned to him. "As you pointed out, my website and your movie are owned by the same corporate enterprise."

"Are you giving me a warning?" He bent down, putting his face near hers and staring in the mirror as well. "Funny, this morning after agreeing to do this shindig, the vice president of marketing for our corporation personally asked for me to come do the interview. I swore he thanked me more than once for agreeing to this on such short notice."

The scent of an indefinable yet glorious cologne or soap wafted around her, making her light-headed, and she swore there was a definite cookie undertone. Maybe it was simply the man next to her. How would she ever get through their interview when she felt like she needed to call for smelling salts? She went to lift her hand, but the makeup artist caught her.

"We need to add some color to your cheeks for the camera." The lady picked up a makeup sponge. "Are you all right?"

Now Ivy wanted to thank the makeup woman for drawing attention to her complexion in front of her idol. She forced herself to take a breath, hoping maybe that would bring some life back into her skin.

"We need to get Ivy dressed. We are doing a live feed." The

cords in Craig's neck appeared. "Is there something you needed, Mr. Alexander?"

"Yes." He stalked toward the wardrobe mistress.

The woman stepped back, holding the outfits up as a shield between them.

"Leave her outfit. She's already in a suit." He pointed at the woman and then over to the makeup chair. "Leave her makeup. This isn't a movie or a Broadway play, and she doesn't need it. A natural blush is always preferred to a manufactured one."

If his display was intended to play with her mind and make her forget why she was here, it worked. She swallowed and tried to remember she had a story to get, a job to save. In the interim, she would also try to forget that Mr. Alexander noticed her blushing.

With the entire room quiet, Mr. Alexander's footsteps boomed through the room as he returned to her side.

Her breath caught. Proximity was not her friend.

"Miss Vermont, I suggest you and I get to wherever we shoot these Internet sensations. I am sure we are both on schedules." He offered her his elbow. "Shall we?"

Once again, using the mirror to her advantage, she glanced at everyone. The other women simply stared at them, while Craig returned to shaking his head. Nothing mattered except making it through the next few minutes and maybe taking a few blush-making moments to gawk at the man whose posters once graced her bedroom walls. She slid off the chair and smoothed her skirt down before taking his arm.

He gave her a nod and led her away.

The walk to the small studio took on one of those surreal atmospheres, like a dream where everything made sense, yet nothing made sense.

"So how does this work? This feels more like a television shoot rather than an Internet broadcast."

At his voice, she blinked, willing away the tightness in her chest at the mere thought of entering the studio. "In a way, it's like a television show. We hope that the entertainment we offer goes viral and brings in lots of traffic and then we get more advertisers and such. After we're done, I'll take your answers from the video and couple it with some other research I have done on you and put it up on the site in hopes to keep the momentum going."

"Well, that was quiet an answer, but let's focus on the most important part. You researched me?" He chuckled. "Is there anything personal you would like to know? Perhaps something not relating to the movie or my costars and that cannot be found on the Internet?"

Unless she had her facts wrong, and she never had her facts wrong, his tone definitely said he was flirting with her. If she needed more evidence, the delightful drop in her stomach and the fluttering of her heart concurred. Fine, she had her work cut out for her. She needed to stay strong and on point to make it through the filming. His distraction tactic wouldn't work on her.

"Mr. Alexander." She had nothing planned after she said his name.

"Logan, call me Logan." He guided her into the studio. "That's what I would like you to call me when I take you out tonight. Mr. Alexander is way too formal."

"There's our host with our guest. Perfect." The director of their video productions rushed toward them. "Hi, Ivy. You're going to do great."

She opened her mouth to make the proper introduction, but the director's name totally left her. In fact, every detail in her mind scattered like bugs when someone flipped on the light except Logan's invitation. All he wanted was an easy interview and a quick lay. "I'm not going out with you." At her words, her adolescent self kicked her adult self.

"You say that now." Logan extended his hand to the nameless director. "Hello, I'm Logan Alexander, Ivy's date for this evening. Oh yeah, I'm also one of the stars of *Hollywood Stardust*."

The director, whatever his name was, glanced between them.

"Don't we need to get in position?" Even with the director standing right there, she redirected the conversation.

"You know where." Mr. Nameless motioned toward their

meager set. "We have a clip from the end of the movie with Logan's character driving away, so lead into that."

"Steven." Of all the items she remembered, it was Logan's name in the movie. Though the entire set looked the same as always, nothing felt familiar, not the ultramodern purple chairs, the fern, or the blond wood table to make the setting appear more conversational. No trash can, great.

She let go of Mr. Alexander's arm, sat in the hostess seat, and tried to stop shaking.

"I suppose I will sit here, though it would be a much better shot if we were sitting side by side." The man who made her mind mush sat in the opposing chair.

Rather than more idle talk with the fallen teen idol, she lifted the note cards she retrieved off the floor and tried to study them, but all that ran through her thoughts was how Logan Alexander had asked her out. Yes, he had asked her out, and he would go through with it, if only to get her into bed. Not that being in bed with him would be such a horrible experience. No, horrible wouldn't define sex with him. A more accurate description would be breathtaking, earth shattering, and soul changing.

She exhaled, remembering she needed to ask him what had happened the night that had caused the sequel to be canceled. Craig would be proud, and as an extra bonus, it would render her guest interview speechless. She could make it into a one-two punch and ask about Drew Fulton.

But he had asked her out. One night with a fantasy.

"I was told you need some gloss." Another person she knew trotted over to her.

"That's not what I need." Only last week she'd eaten lunch with the woman barreling toward her. Of course, she couldn't remember what she ate for lunch either, on that day or any other for that matter. The lights flipped on, and each bulb seemed to turn into a super starburst with the rays cutting through her vision. No doubt this is what death felt like.

"Keep your face up and let the camera see you." Her friend went to dab the gloss on her lips. "You'll do fine. Just don't throw up."

Any pride she held on to left, and she glanced over at Mr. Alexander. Though he casually leaned back in the seat, he never took his eyes off her.

"Seriously, I need something." Maybe she needed a small tranquilizer or maybe she needed to ask her guest to ask her out one more time in order to capture it on camera and document it, then she could go in for the kill.

Once more, the woman aimed the gloss wand at her. "Didn't we need a wardrobe change?"

"No, we do not need a wardrobe change or *we* would have changed our wardrobe before we got on a set." Logan remained fixed in his position, but his tone possessed power. "Why is there even a set for this? Couldn't we do this at a coffee shop with a handheld camera? Better yet, we could do it at the restaurant before we start our date."

The woman turned to him. "Excuse me?"

"I believe you heard me." Even without looking in the person's direction, he stared her down. "She doesn't need the gloss."

"Two minutes." The director called out.

"A little late for a wardrobe change." He cleared his throat. "This is a live feed. The pressure is on."

"Break a leg." With her unused gloss clutched in her hand, the woman dashed away.

"Ready?" He shook his head.

"Absolutely." She heard herself say the word, but her voice sounded far away like she was having an out of body experience.

"Good. You can say that tonight. It will be the theme for the evening." He raised his eyebrows.

The lights weren't as hot as his gaze on her. One lone drop of sweat trailed down her back. She shifted in her seat and straightened her note cards.

"One minute!" the director yelled.

As her friend suggested, she raised her head.

"This is all wrong." Logan stood.

"Thirty seconds."

Her heart seized, and going on instinct, she followed his

lead.

In one motion, he slid his chair toward her, sat back down, and grabbed her note cards.

"What are you doing?" Her question came out more like a garbled gasp for air.

"Forget about these formalities." He pushed her back and put a finger on her chin. "No one ever taught you or anyone here about angles, I take it."

His touch radiated through her whole being, causing her to shiver. Though she wanted to protest, once more he left her with no words.

"Keep your chin down and look up at me with your eyes or you'll be showing your nostrils to the world. No one wants to see that." He tilted her face down. "We'll have more time to explore hidden spots later, but not on a live feed. That type of footage needs to be handled with care." He winked.

Sex tapes? He wanted to make a sex tape with her? At least it would give her a memory. She wondered if she would be camera shy in the throes of making love to one Logan Alexander. Wait, she wasn't having sex with him or going out on a date. Shoot.

"Ten seconds."

"My notes." She wanted to celebrate at managing to speak.

"You don't need those. Don't ask what I won't answer and you'll be fine." He scooted even closer.

She smoothed down her dress.

"Don't worry what you look like. These fools wouldn't recognize a vintage designer if it slapped them in the face." Rather than sitting back, he leaned forward. "You look gorgeous."

"Three, two, one . . ." The director pointed.

She said nothing. His designer dress comment finally did its job and rendered her utterly speechless.

Or maybe it was the way he called her gorgeous.

⁓

The joy of being Logan Alexander. He had almost

forgotten. Since the first day he had stepped into the studio with the other three stars, he had been typecast, but of all the roles, his was the most fun.

"Action!" the director with no name called out, and his sassy little reporter found herself with a huge case of stage fright. The introduction music played through the set.

Of course, being Logan Alexander came with its share of crap no one would ever imagine. The side no one knew, and the side he needed to keep on the cutting room floor in order for all of them to live the lifestyle, or appear to live the lifestyle. The godforsaken anniversary of the movie that would never die thrust them all back into the spotlight and him right back into the lead role he never wanted. Over the next few weeks, he would need some distraction to get him through.

However, in less than an hour, he accomplished his goal of distracting everyone away from asking questions he refused to answer. Unfortunately, he managed to paralyze the poor angel who he thrust in the middle of his mess, or maybe it was for the greater good.

The music ended, but she remained motionless, her skin pale, her cheeks glowing brighter than the studio lights.

Good thing for the woman who liked the villain that Logan Alexander would take over, as always. Like it or not, he rescued the world with a sly remark and an insult since he was typecast.

He let out a laugh and grabbed her hand, pulling her toward him and acting like they were in mid conversation. "Yes, I have always lived in Southern California, and to this day, it's hard to drive down Hollywood Boulevard without having flashbacks. Now, Ivy, you wanted to know what my favorite part of the movie was?" His action received the desired reaction and she looked into his eyes.

"Sure?" Her whisper brushed against his lips.

"Hm." He paused and toyed with her fingers, not only to keep her mind elsewhere, but more than enjoying her hand in his. "I have to say it's the scene when we visit my grandparents and she bakes cookies. I remember those were the real deal, fresh out of the oven, because they wanted us to show the joy of a home-baked treat." The mention of the scene didn't naturally lead into questions he didn't want asked.

As if she could see the image in front of her, Ivy smiled.

He started to ask another one of his questions and vomit up another pre-rehearsed answer.

"So, b-b-back on topic, how often do you see your other cast mates?" Still keeping hold of his hand, she sat up. "Are you still friends?"

Well, well, she not only recovered, she got right back on the on-ramp to the questions everyone wanted to ask, shaky voice and all. He had to give it to her for starting with a lead-in question, but the next one would undoubtedly be about Drew, which sped right to everything else.

"Of course we keep in touch." He offered the most benign answer possible.

"All of you?"

At least the woman stayed focused.

He tilted his head and ran his thumb across the back of her hand, wishing he could explore her smooth skin elsewhere. "I would rather talk about what we are going to do tonight to celebrate the twentieth anniversary of one of your favorite films." He smiled the same smile he produced the day the talent scout discovered him and called him a natural. Little did he know back then there was no such thing.

Her eyes widened and her hand trembled in his. "What's the worst part of being the bad guy?"

Not expecting her to keep on track, he responded with the first thing to enter his mind. "Do you know that I never get the girl?" Right as the words left his lips, he wanted them back. Of all the subjects, he needed to leave his love life, or lack thereof, out of the conversation.

"Do you ever wish you would have?"

"Oh, tough question." Again, she surprised him by pressing forward instead of asking if he were attached at the moment, or ever, but he needed a second to reformulate his plan. "What if I tell you after we look at a clip?"

They both stopped and stared into each other's eyes. If they weren't surrounded by a multitude of people and their relationship was more than an hour old, it would be the perfect time for a kiss. He bet her lips tasted sweet with a bit of tang, and was thankful no one put any of that horrendous gloss on them.

"You have ninety seconds and people are online commenting already," the director announced. "Ivy, maybe you should introduce our guest?"

"Oh, man." She shut her eyes for a moment, pressing her free hand to her chest.

Logan knew he played dirty, but even with her stage fright, she threw plenty of mud of her own. In fact, he just managed to avoid the splatter. "You're fine." All women loved the bad boy, even if art imitated life and he never got one long term. No matter, there was always another one, but not many quite like the sultry vine that made up Miss Details. "Take your time and remember to breathe."

When he had arrived at the studio, he'd heard her defend him, and upon entering the room, it had pleased him to find her appearance matched her voice. Dark hair that glowed with a tint of red under the lights framed her face and highlighted her huge gray eyes and perky lips. The second he had seen her, he'd almost expected a cartoon bird to appear and eat out of her hand while she waved her magic wand of facts as her weapon and won.

"Thank you, Mr. Alexander." She opened her eyes.

"Logan." He leaned in even closer, wanting to remind her of the name she would be screaming out tonight in ecstasy. "Keep your eyes on mine, and don't forget to ask me about the new DVD set we still have to sell." Or more accurately, get her to a different line of questioning.

"Okay, we're coming back in five, four, three, two, one."

"Now." He squeezed her hand.

"I'm in the middle with my conversation with Logan Alexander, one of the stars of *Hollywood Stardust*." She nodded. "So, Mr. Alexander, can you give us any sneak peeks to what we can look forward to with the movie's rerelease for the twentieth anniversary?"

His tactic worked and he exhaled. Better yet, the woman took direction, a fact he wouldn't forget between the sheets.

"Was there anything you were hoping for?"

She glanced up at him through her lashes. "How about a little secret?"

Something about her seemed as if she were out of a different time or place, and it wasn't only her chic vintage clothing. He almost wanted to invent a little nugget of juicy gossip to please her, but he would please her plenty later. "I know the DVD package will include the director's cut with some deleted scenes, but I'll have to check about any secrets."

"Maybe you could tell us some secret we don't already know." She licked her lips.

If he answered honestly, he would tell her he never had seen the movie all the way through, but Logan Alexander wasn't about honesty, he was about illusion. "The car in the film is actually mine, and the day after we wrapped shooting, I got a ticket."

"Were you speeding?" She let out a little giggle.

He nodded. "Always."

The director approached the set and held up one finger.

"Before we have to say good-bye, are you going to tell me if you wish you would have gotten the girl?"

Sharp. She got back on point and that made her even more alluring. "Maybe I never found the right girl to get."

At last, she graced him with a smile. "Well, I know we didn't get to spend much time with you today, but we will definitely have some follow-up stories online. I want to thank you for taking the time to talk to me this afternoon."

"My pleasure." Using his character's signature move from the film, he turned his head and pointed to his cheek. Perhaps he needed to act like his character and turn his head and have her kiss land on his lips, but maybe such a move wasn't Internet-show appropriate.

She gave him a slight shake of her head, but finally leaned in and pecked his cheek. "I still have more questions."

At her whisper in his ear, he shuddered. "Sorry, time's up."

"Cut!" The director came forward. "That was sort of different, but on the bright side, you didn't lose your lunch."

"You have to give me more. I barely got anything." She

pulled back.

"You know everything I'm going to put on the record. After all, you studied me. You can fill in. I'll never tell." He kept hold of her hand. "However, tonight you will get everything you want, so no pouting."

She swiped her hand away and stood, but he wasn't sure if this was where the scene should end. Yes, she would make the perfect distraction.

⁓

"Ivy!" Craig ran after her.

Damn, damn, damn. At this point, escape was Ivy's only option, and she rushed down the hallway back toward her office. She didn't even get one of Craig's questions in. Even if Mr. Alexander didn't respond, it would have hung in the air and started chatter. Then after practically having foreplay with Mr. Alexander on a live feed, the second she turned her back, he up and vanished without as much as a good-bye. As she had thought, the entire flirtation had been nothing but a ruse to throw her off the trail, and it had worked. With stars in her eyes, no wonder she was tricked. Now, she had to find him. If she had to tackle him to the ground and straddle him, she would get the damn answers.

"Ivy Vermont!" Craig's voice grew louder.

After basically promising her boss she would succeed, she failed. Her job was on the line and she had to fix the disaster. With no way out, she stopped and spun toward him.

Craig skidded in front of her. "I'm not sure what to say about what just aired on our website."

"Well, we can start with congratulating me for getting through the interview and only stuttering a few times." She gave him a smile and went in for the save. "I think it was very on point and relevant, and it was only the beginning."

"Beginning?" Craig held out his arms and looked around. "What are you talking about? This was an important story for us."

"Yes, and it needs to develop over time. You can't expect

me to meet him and bring up all the tough questions right off the bat." The words spewed out of her mouth in such a convincing manner even she believed them.

"So you are going to bring up the old, tired tomes that have been out there like a bad GIF of some silly animal repeating some inane gesture rather than coming up with something fresh?" Logan made a tsking sound and joined them in the hallway.

How the man continued to sneak up on her was beyond her knowledge, but it was a detail she would get to the bottom of along with everything else. She bit her lip and formulated a plan. Yes, she had to make the situation into a beginning, not an end. "Of course not. In fact, as Craig said, this is an important story, way too important to be told in one afternoon."

Craig exhaled and Logan leaned back on his heels, but she managed to get them both to remain silent and continued. "I mean, we barely scratched the surface with Mr. Alexander. *Hollywood Stardust* was one of those movies that literally changed a generation, so how can we even expect to tell the story in a five-minute video?"

"I am extremely complex." Logan tilted his head.

"I don't understand." A fine sheen of sweat broke out on Craig's forehead. Maybe he needed a trash can.

Somehow, with Logan, she had gotten through the interview—maybe it wasn't great, but it had been better than she had ever done before. She had always been bonded to this movie. It had to be a sign. "I would like to cover the anniversary of *Hollywood Stardust* up until the gala for the new director's cut at the studio. I will interview the other cast members, and I'll uncover the myths and the truths, and see where they all are now." For once, her parents would believe in her. She would keep her job, and if she could cure her stage fright, maybe she could go on to her dream of being an actress.

Craig gave her a slow nod.

Her heart sped and her mind went with it as she practically saw into the future with videos and stories and a world where she went from roving reporter to actress and carried on her family tradition. In fact, the story might even be better than sex with Logan. Maybe. Probably not, but she would have her career. "Since we know the story was important enough for the vice president of the studio to speak with Mr. Alexander, and we are under the same umbrella, I'm sure there will be no problem securing the people needed to pull this off." She held her breath waiting for Craig's decision, but she swore Logan's complexion paled.

"You could be on to something." Craig tapped his fingers against his lips. "Yes, this could be exactly what we need. I'm sure with the magnitude of the story, Julia will be more than happy to work on this project."

Both her heart and her mind, in fact all of her organs, stopped, actually seized. "I did better than ever today. I can do this." Her voice came out more of a pathetic whine rather than a demand.

"Ivy." Craig's tone turned parental.

Her throat dried out, and though she wanted to stand on her own, she turned to Logan for help. Earlier, he was the first to request her and his input had to matter.

"I'm not so sure about this little plan. Stay right there." Without an ounce of snark, he held up one finger and walked down the hall.

As if they both had agreed not to speak until Logan returned, they glanced at each other and then turned away. She watched Logan pace back and forth, hunched over with his phone up to his ear.

Time seemed to halt, and she wondered what caused Logan's sudden change in attitude. She only needed to convince Craig.

At long last Logan returned, his pallor the same. "The execs love the idea, and as luck would have it, I will be your tour guide."

Why did she feel she had betrayed him in some way? "What does that mean?"

"I will introduce you to the people you need to speak to. I will be all things *Hollywood Stardust*." The color of his eyes seemed to darken.

"That sounds like a plan. I am sure once Julia returns we can get this going." Craig extended his hand.

She bit the inside of her mouth to stay quiet. Funny, when the cameras weren't rolling she could speak perfectly fine.

"I made my preferences for a costar clear before, but make no mistake who the star will be." Logan barely gave Craig's offering a glance, but leaned over to her. "You."

His word tingled in her ear. While she wanted to take hold of the man and tell her boss they were an unstoppable team, she needed to win on her own merit.

"This is a huge undertaking. Ivy will be involved, but we need a true professional." Craig kept his hand out.

Before Logan came back with another one of his quips, she thrust herself between them. "No one knows the movie better than I do. I am the only person who can do it justice."

"But you tried before to ask the right questions and froze. This story could save us."

Of course, what her boss left unsaid was that the story could break them just as easy, and she wouldn't allow him to taint her with her own history. She needed to give him some other facts to go on. "I know Ryder Scott wasn't the first person cast for the role of William. I know when Erin Holland dyed her hair for the role of Roxanne and broke out in hives. It delayed production for four weeks. I know the homework that the character Charles was doing on the road was indeed Drew's homework, and it was chemistry." She sucked in her breath to keep going.

Logan tapped her. "What about me?"

"I was going to use the car, but you beat me to it." She swallowed. "But in case you were wondering, I know you were the first cast and I also know you were the first offered a contract for the never filmed sequel."

"And there you have it." He patted her back.

"Ivy, I told you before, we need this story." Craig's voice took on the same tone he used every time he became exasperated with her. Deep down, she knew he wanted her gone, but obligations and friendships wouldn't let him go through with it.

She took a slow and even breath, promising she would utter the next words. "Craig, if you let me be the reporter and I don't live up to everything you want out of the story, I will resign."

Craig lifted his hand to his temple. "What?"

"Let me make it to the gala, and if by that time you don't have everything you want, I will come to your office the next day, hand you my letter of resignation, and you never have to feel guilty."

He furrowed his brow, but didn't fling himself in front of her and tell her not to do it. His lack of action told her everything.

"I never had a woman go to such lengths to be with me. Well, back in the day I did, but those girls did some insane things. I almost expected one to mail me an ear or other body part." Logan looked up to the ceiling and tapped his chin. "Actually, only yesterday, I got comped a turkey sandwich just because I am me. So honestly, I suppose I have women go through great lengths to be with me all the time, but this instance will definitely stand out."

At Logan revealing maybe a little too much, she shrugged and focused on Craig and her fate.

"Just get the story we need." Her boss clasped his hands as if praying.

"I understand." She made her deal and sold herself.

"Well, they say all the best business happens in hallways with ugly linoleum flooring." Logan took his turn to offer his hand for a shake.

"Let me tell production what is happening so we can clear studio time." Craig rubbed his hand over his forehead and walked away, muttering to himself as he left.

"I believe we need to keep business separate from pleasure. Rest assured, when I take you out this evening, I will not put it on our expense report." Like earlier, Logan held out his elbow. "Shall we get started early?"

Alone with Logan, she needed to do some proverbial bud nipping and looked up into his face.

That face was not conducive to nipping, and she lowered

her gaze to his neck. "Mr. Alexander, we are not going out in a social capacity. While I appreciate you offering to undertake this project with me, it will only be for professional purposes."

"No matter what happens, let me make something perfectly clear." His absolutely serious tone made her look into his eyes. "I know you and your idiot boss thought you were speaking some secret language before, but I deciphered it very well." He glanced up and down the hallway and bent down to her ear. "I don't care what you think you'll be getting. I will set up all the interviews, and I will control everything, so don't think you'll be getting some big scoop. I hold the spoon and I do the feeding."

She didn't move, didn't react, and didn't respond. Was he the villain everyone thought or was he only playing a role?

"Promise me we won't have six weeks of arguments when we can make an amazing story." He raked the back of his hand down her arm.

She ignored the shivers he created throughout her body. If she didn't promise, nothing would happen. She would have to get the story Craig wanted a different way, but her specialty was tracking down the facts. Once in the inner circle, she could circumvent him. "I promise."

"I take my promises very seriously."

"I need to go do some research, Mr. Alexander."

"You can meet with Logan tomorrow for our first assignment. Mr. Alexander won't be available." His deep voice vibrated through her.

"Until tomorrow then." Villain or not, his mere closeness stirred every inch of her to life. While she had met stars before, grew up among them, no other held his magic. The man possessed some sort of estrogen magnet, and no doubt his typecast wasn't by happenstance. She needed to go sit under an air conditioner vent.

"Until tomorrow." He gave her a quick peck on the cheek. "I thought I should return the favor. It's purely professional though."

She shut her eyes, again forcing away any reaction. His every move was manufactured to make her forget her name. No matter what, she had to get the story and had to work with Logan. She turned on her heel and walked toward her office, giving a quick glance to her smart 1950s business suit. Maybe for once she would stand out for more than her excellent choice in clothing.

HOLLYWOOD STARDUST

DISSOLVE TO:

INT. BACK OF STEVEN'S FATHER'S RESTAURANT –
DAY – INDIANAPOLIS, IN

STEVEN, ROXY, WILLIAM, and CHARLES sit huddled
together in a booth in the back, working on
their projects due before spring break.

> ROXY
> I want to go to Hollywood
> Stardust.

ROXY puts her elbow on the table and rests her
head in her hand. Looks off far away.

> WILLIAM
> Hollywood Stardust?

WILLIAM takes a gulp of his soda.

CHARLES – seventeen years old the best friend,
the misfit, and the late bloomer, but the one
who will make something of himself one day,
even if no one else sees it.

> CHARLES
> It's a theater in
> Hollywood built in 1927.
> It is built in the art
> deco style and . . .

STEVEN hits his fist into the table, causing
CHARLES to jolt up.
> STEVEN
> We don't need a history

                    lesson. Let Rox talk.

STEVEN motions toward Roxy.

ROXY catches STEVEN'S eye, then looks down,
tracing her finger around the table.

                    ROXY
              Back in the day, everyone
              who was anyone was seen
              there. They're tearing it
              down to make way for some
              multiplex theater with no
              history and no soul. My
              friends planned a trip
              there for spring break. We
              wanted to see it, just be
              around its energy. I'm the
              only one who won't be
              there, and I'll never get
              the chance now.

                    WILLIAM
              Hey, it's okay. You have
              us now. (He puts his arm
              around Roxy.) We'll go
              somewhere, party, get out.

ROXY shakes her head.

                    STEVEN
              I'll take you to Hollywood
              Stardust.

ROXY Looks up at STEVEN.

                    ROXY
              What?

                    STEVEN
              You heard me.

                   WILLIAM
              That's a great idea!

WILLIAM sits up straighter and raises his hand
for a high five.

                   WILLIAM
              Road trip with Roxy to
              Hollywood Stardust.

Once more, ROXY glances at STEVEN.

                    STEVEN
              We will take you to
              Hollywood Stardust.

Chapter Three

The waves crashing, the sea breeze, the seagulls doing whatever seagulls do, and the sun lowering in the horizon provided the ideal backdrop Logan required for his first outing with his new project. He wasn't thinking about the interviews.

Prepared to play tour guide to only one, he put a bandana around his hair and donned a pair of dark sunglasses. With years away from the spotlight, he only needed a slight cover-up to hide in the public. The requests for autographs came in less and less, which was fine by him, but with *Hollywood Stardust* bubbling up to the surface again, he needed to be extra careful if he didn't want to be disturbed, and he didn't.

He walked down the Santa Monica Pier and spotted his leading lady for the next six weeks exactly where he told her to meet him, outside the carousel. Dressed in hot pink pants and a matching sleeveless top with her hair up, she appeared as if she stepped right out of one of those beach movies of yesteryear. The suit she wore at the office the day before did not do her figure justice, but her outfit today might break the law. From his vantage point with her back turned to him, his mouth watered at the sight before him.

It had been way too long since a woman not only created a physical reaction, but a mental one as well. He actually had lain in bed thinking about her, her little pearls of knowledge, the way she forged ahead even under dire circumstances, how her hand shook in his, but she still completed the interview, and best yet, how she looked to him for help. Yes, they would do well together once they got the pesky business of their business out of the way.

He inched up behind her and bent down to her ear. "Do you want to take a ride?"

She jumped and turned to him. "Oh, I'm glad you're here."

The view of her front was more spectacular than the rear. Her breasts filled out the fabric, presenting him with much more than a palm full, and he could make out a little cleavage. Without a doubt, he knew what he wanted for dinner. "Where did you think I would be?" Apparently, he needed to tell her where they could go, or would go.

"I thought you said to meet at four."

He nodded. It wasn't like their arrangement needed a time clock.

"I'm just glad you didn't stand me up." The wind picked up, and she reached into her bag and pulled out a scarf.

"Never worry about that. I'll always contact you, no matter what." He watched her wrap the little bit of fabric over her hair and expertly tie a knot under her chin—a simple act, but old-fashioned, sweet, and most definitely sexy. With the sudden urge to be a gentleman, he held his arm out. "Shall we?"

"Where are we going?" She slipped her arm in his.

"Is there somewhere in particular you would like to go?" Perhaps to the end of the pier, a perfect spot for some kissing before the main event. Making out was a lost art, one he wanted to rekindle.

"Anywhere is fine. I'm pretty portable." Once more, she reached into her handbag. Rather than a scarf, she pulled out a little digital video camera. "Is there a reason you decided this would be the place for our first meeting?" She hit a button and pointed the device right in his face.

Instinct and muscle memory took over, and as with anytime a camera was aimed at him, he struck a pose. "Don't you like the pier?"

"I haven't been in years, but sure. Doesn't it remind you of something?" The camera covered her face.

Apparently, she was fine behind a camera, but that wasn't the behind he was interested in. He held his palm up to the camera, causing her to lower her arm. "Should it remind me of something?"

"Doesn't it remind you of your first major stop in the movie?"

The movie. Yes, the movie. A road trip movie where their characters made their way across the country to the elusive Hollywood Stardust theater, each with their own quest of sorts. He quickly scanned his memories. "The shopping center?" He narrowed his eyes, trying to remember the route. "There are some shops."

"No, the fairgrounds." She let out a little laugh. "Your character was obsessed with Skee-Ball. Did you play in real life?"

"I suppose we do need a photo op." Truth be told, he wasn't bad, and she seemed to want to keep up the sham interview stuff. First, they would do something that smacked of work, and then they could get on to the better part of the day. "Would you like a demonstration?"

"I can't think of anything I'd like to do more." She lit up.

"We'll get to that later." If it weren't for his sunglasses, he would have winked. Instead, he guided her back to the arcade.

Multicolored lights, bells, chimes, and arcade noises assaulted them as they entered, and they followed the lights over to the Skee-Ball machines. Since they were here at an off-hour, only one other older man played. He fished inside his pocket, found a coin, and the balls rolled down the chute.

Ivy raised her camera.

He chose a ball and hurled it up the ramp, using his bank shot.

The ball jumped, ricocheted off the one-hundred-point circle, and landed in the ten-point loser's hoop. He exhaled.

"Has it been a while?" She giggled.

"One could say that." He chose another ball and held it up. "Let's do a retake."

"You got it."

Once more, he threw the ball up the ramp, and rather than a major failure, he got the twenty-point semifailure circle. A couple of tickets popped out of the slot. He bent down and tore them off and handed them to her. "For you."

"Are you going to win me a prize?" She plucked the tickets out of his fingers.

"Can we just buy one?" At this rate, they would be here for days.

"Maybe a stuffed dog, a fifty-cent toy that cost ten dollars, but something a girl has to have?"

"What?" Did they suddenly shift to a different language? "Do you want a stuffed dog?"

"No, what you won Roxy." She shifted her weight from one leg to the other. "You shoved the dog at her and said it cost you ten dollars for a fifty-cent toy. Did Erin get to keep it?"

A slight flicker of some silly stuffed animal went through his mind. "How about we reenact something else out of that scene?" He motioned for her to come over.

She returned the camera to her bag and came to him. "What scene is this?"

After presenting her with one of the balls, he positioned himself behind her and put one hand on the incredible curve that created her waist. At their closeness, her light floral perfume wafted around him, her hair tickled his face, and his body reacted appropriately. He lowered his lips to her ear. "The one where Steven teaches Roxy to play."

"I don't remember that scene." Her voice quivered.

"Then let me refresh your memory." Gently, he pulled her arm back and grazed his lips against her neck. "The secret to Skee-Ball is knowing when to let go."

"Mr. Alexander." With his unexpected move, she practically panted.

"It's Logan." He snaked his arm around her. "I've been thinking about you since yesterday, and I have a suspicion you've been thinking about me."

"Logan," she whispered.

"Did you think about me?" He tucked a little piece of hair that escaped her updo behind her ear.

"Don't ask questions you already know the answer to."

"Then let me tell you what else I know." When she didn't move away, he smiled. "I know that long before yesterday you thought of me. Well, I'm here, ready, willing, and able to reenact any scene your heart desires."

"Logan." Her body stiffened. "Do you know why I don't remember that scene?"

"Because the movie is twenty years old and we have better things to do?" A chuckle escaped his throat.

Without warning, she dropped the ball and pushed him back.

"Don't worry, I'll make sure you have an interview. I have something planned." The ball rolled away, but he ignored it and held his hand out to her. "We can go somewhere more private."

She put her hands on her hips. "I don't remember the scene because it didn't exist. It was William who snuck a kiss when he helped Roxy during miniature golf. Steven kissed her on the Ferris wheel."

"Maybe it needed to be a scene. Those Ferris wheel scenes seem rather overdone." He always knew he should have gone into screen writing, but alas he hated writing.

"I will have you know that both those scenes are two of the most beloved. Many, many other scenes from other movies have used the scenes from your movie for inspiration."

"They should get their own material then." He shot it right back to her. Sparring could be great foreplay.

She huffed. "I would like to continue where we left off yesterday. I have a whole set of interview questions for you."

He needed to remember she had her job on the line. No wonder she was uptight. "Regarding that, I have something for you." Rather than taking her hand, he walked ahead, leaving her to follow.

They returned to the pier. He found a bench, sat, and patted the space next to him.

Once she took her spot, he slipped a paper out of his shirt pocket and handed it to her. "This should solve all your troubles."

She unfolded the paper, sucking in her cheeks as she read. "Why are you giving me this?"

"Here's your first interview. You can do the voice-over and we'll film each other doing Santa Monica Pier things and all your worries will be left behind. As a bonus, I will have Erin and Ryder work on theirs and I'll get you whatever you need. You and I will be in charge of the b-roll." It was simply easier to spoon-feed her whatever she needed and avoid all those messy questions.

"Only yesterday, you told me not to ask the same tired questions, and yet you have broken your rule." Her face went blank, showing absolutely no emotion when she should be thanking him for having helped.

"How so?" He crossed his legs.

"All you gave me is everything I could look up on the Internet minus what you won't talk about. Actually, I can get more on the Internet."

He chose not to tell her he looked quite a few of those answers up on the Internet.

"Also, when you decide to copy and paste from fan websites, you should make sure you have the facts correct. Especially when they are about you." She found a pen in her bag and circled two of his interesting facts. "You were not in *Galaxy Man Four*. You were in *Galaxy Man Three*."

"That was a typo."

"Also, the original name of Steven in *Hollywood Stardust* was Scott, not Sam. The producer's son was named Scott, and he didn't want that connection." She folded the paper and held it out to him.

"Damn that auto correct." He didn't touch the paper. "I was only trying to make things more efficient."

"Maybe it would have been better to let me interview you." Her lower lip made an appearance as if she were hurt or wounded.

He didn't need a guilt trip. The road trip to Hollywood Stardust was enough. "What grand questions were you going to ask?"

"Maybe I wanted to know what you are doing now? Maybe I wanted to know why you don't act anymore? Maybe I wanted to know what truly happened to the sequel?" She crumpled the paper in her hand.

"I'm not answering any of those questions." He lifted his

chin. "Maybe you should answer them. You seem like you know everything else."

"I did more than copy and paste. I need a break. I'll be right back." As she walked away, she tossed the paper into a wastebasket.

A smart and beautiful woman was one thing, but he wasn't going to be put through the grill for all these weeks. He didn't need her. He needed a distraction from exactly what she wanted to do to him.

He put a cigarette between his lips, lifted his phone, and pressed his hand to his temple. Six weeks in Miss Details school of cinema would only amplify his pain.

Much like the movie industry itself, *Hollywood Stardust* possessed its own double-edged issues, but neither of those edges needed to be shoved in his back or through his chest.

Contracts, obligations, and deals made him the only one allowed to handle any publicity with the movie. Though his pay was phenomenal, it came with an equal serving of stress. However, he refused to be tortured or have his time wasted.

He glanced down at his phone and dialed his own personal 911.

"I'm in the car. Speak up." Brian Fleming, his agent, practically screamed into the phone.

"I'm done." Logan rubbed his hand over his face.

"Good, are you going back to her place now?" Brian chuckled.

"I make the rules, and I'm finished with this project. Have the two quote unquote true stars of the movie do some of the grunt work."

"Now, now, you and I both know they are only fit for a talk show appearance here and there. This little thing for the web got you out of a lot of other commitments. Be happy."

"Maybe it's time to get out of the whole thing."

"You should have thought of that before you took action at the hotel, my friend."

Logan tapped his cigarette on his knee. Twenty years ago, he'd manipulated everyone's past, present, and future to get what he wanted and would forever pay the price.

"If you don't want the gig, maybe we can call Drew? Maybe it's time he stepped into the limelight?"

"And there we have it." He threw the cigarette aside. "Don't ever try to negotiate what you know you can't win."

"What's wrong? Didn't your princess live up to her crown?"

He ground his teeth together. Ivy was beyond the crown, almost too much to ask for, and he didn't want to ask for anything. He wanted to have some fun. "The woman knows a lot about this movie. I feel like I'm in a class about myself."

"Why don't you learn from her and then you can teach her a thing or two?" Again, Brian laughed. "The execs like this in-depth look. Just be yourself and she'll be out of your life soon enough. I have to run. Call me when you have a real issue. They own you and you know that."

"I'm done!" Nothing but silence met his ear, and he knew Brian had hung up. He leaned back only to find Ivy standing a couple of feet away holding a bottle of water.

"I thought you might want something cool to drink." She handed it to him.

With caution, he took the beverage, but held his breath waiting for the confrontation over the phone call. "Why don't we call it a wrap for the day?"

"It's probably for the best."

Her issues couldn't be his issues. Once he hauled himself into a standing position, he stood and they walked side by side with the ocean and the sunset at their backs.

"Look." She stopped in front of a sign saying "Route 66." "Interesting."

After a quick glance at the sign, he scanned his memory for any movie trivia. "Did we drive on Route 66 for the movie or something?"

"No, the characters never took Route 66. They took the highways."

"I bet you can name the highways." For the life of him, he didn't understand the interest, but it intrigued him nonetheless.

"I can." She let out a sad sigh. "Not that it matters."

"So, what's with the sign? Would it have been better if we

took Route 66?" He wondered if she had heard the conversation between him and Brian.

She turned to him. "I just thought it was interesting that Route 66 officially ends right there. It says 'End of the Trail.'"

He took her all in. Sharp and sexy, and a definite curiosity. One he wanted to know, but he knew enough to stay away, contract or not. "Yep, end of the trail."

                                    DISSOLVE TO:

EXT. Outside WILLIAM'S house INDIANAPOLIS –
DAY

WILLIAM, CHARLES, and ROXY wait for STEVEN so
they can get on the road.

                    CHARLES
            At this rate, we will
            never stay on schedule.

CHARLES glances at his watch and shakes
his head.

WILLIAM Slaps Charles on the back.

                    WILLIAM
            Seriously, dude, take it
            down a notch. You don't
            need to study every second
            of every day. We're about
            to have an experience of a
            lifetime.

WILLIAM goes to ROXY and puts his arm
around her.

                    WILLIAM
            Wouldn't you agree?

ROXY shrugs WILLIAM off her.

                    ROXY
            We don't want to make
            anyone uncomfortable on

the trip.

              WILLIAM
I thought we were past
trying to hide.

ROXY turns her back to him.

              WILLIAM
Fine then, sometime on the
trip, all right?

              ROXY
If Steven even shows up.

ROXY walks to the curb and looks up and down
the street.

Chapter Four

"Here we are." Ivy pressed her back to the small brick building in the heart of Culver City.

"I feel like we're on a covert mission." Her best friend, Giselle, mimicked her actions.

"One to save my job." She bent down and took a long, slow inhale, one to try to wash away the horrible sinking and twisting sensation in her stomach, as if her middle had become a whirlpool of pent-up anxiety with no drain.

Thus far, she had waited for Logan for three days. Though they reached the end of the trail of sorts, after the Santa Monica Pier, she honestly thought he would contact her or at least formally quit. With her assignment supposedly in the field with Logan, she avoided everyone and no one was the wiser. Of course, the whole ignoring thing would only work until she needed to show up at work with the man who ditched her to do her next report.

"Maybe you need to give it up." Giselle sighed.

Ivy's cell phone vibrated. Maybe she received her long sought after text message from Mr. Alexander, or a call, anything. "I can't. You know that."

She lifted her phone to find two texts, neither from Logan. "Matt and Craig both texted me."

"What does Matt want?" Giselle tried to peek at her phone.

"To help with the story and go out later. He says he misses me." Along with stage fright, she was the only girl she knew who had commitment fright. She and Matt had dated for years, nothing serious and not by his choice. They ended up both working at Chargge.com, but he actually had a real title as a programmer. She put her hand to her forehead.

"Aww." Giselle patted her. "He's such a good guy."

Of course he was a good guy, the best guy. He possessed the big three—stable, smart, and secure. What more could a girl want? She wished she could answer that question. "He wants to help and says I don't need anyone from the movie."

"But the story is about the movie." Giselle reminded her in case she forgot.

"I know. He's trying to help and will come over tomorrow. Craig told me he wants me and Logan in the studio Friday." The whirlpool turned even faster. Somehow, she needed to produce something more elusive than a unicorn . . . a *Hollywood Stardust* star to take Logan's place.

"That's the end of the week, and you don't even know where he is." Giselle slid down the wall.

"That's why we're here." Ivy adjusted her collar and pulled her big girl granny panties up to her neck.

"Then why are we hiding?"

"We're not. We're taking a breath before we walk inside and demand to see Brian Fleming." The same man who handed her Logan in the first place.

"I wonder if I could get him to represent me." Giselle pushed away from the wall and struck a pose. "When I was two, I did that commercial for Dainty Delights toddler couture. Maybe it's time to revamp my career."

Everyone around her had some sort of film or television credit to their name except her, but there was no denying Giselle was a beauty with the complete California wish list— tall, blonde, and thin. "Well, he represents Logan, Ryder, and Erin, and even Drew before he disappeared. Maybe he likes child stars." For sure he didn't like reporters who couldn't get in front of a camera unless Logan Alexander was by their side, especially since she didn't have Logan Alexander.

She pulled on a pair of gloves and tucked her pocketbook under her arm, glancing down at her 1940s black sheath dress with an oversize white collar. "Do I look okay?"

"You look like you're about ready to take over a boardroom in the middle of an old-fashioned movie." Giselle gave her a thumbs-up. "I bet Logan would know the designer."

She pursed her lips.

"I think you should have just let him kiss you. Bet it would have been good." Giselle nodded.

The small sampling she had was amazing. His lips barely touched her neck, and she practically went over the edge.

"Does Matt know the fantasy of your youth made a move on you?" Giselle's tone teased her like they were in the school yard.

"It didn't come up in conversation." She straightened up. After reliving every second of her and Logan's time together, she had finally given up on Logan. He wasn't returning and was volatile at best, and the show must go on. Besides, there was no point in torturing the greatest guy in the world.

"Really? 'Cause it was the first thing you told me." Her friend raised her eyebrows.

"It doesn't matter. We are not an official couple. We're more like friends with benefits without the benefits sometimes." At least, not that often.

"Hence why you should have let Logan do what Logan does best. You need it." Giselle nodded.

"I think I need to get someone from the movie to help me." They had to get to the task at hand. She trudged forward. "Let's go."

"Okay." Giselle followed. "Better than a kiss though, you should have slept with him. I bet it's in his contract he has to create multiple orgasms."

"My guess is he is too self-centered to care about any orgasm but his own." Not that she didn't consider sleeping with Logan many, many times, and in those times, none of them dealt with him being a selfish lover. Logan nailed it when he said she thought about him, and she should have let him nail her. She opened the door.

"He's probably so concerned with his image, he doesn't even bother with an orgasm." Giselle giggled.

The woman behind a sleek white desk leaned around her

computer and barely glanced at them.

Ivy made her way through the office—everything modern, perfect, and streamlined, but with no personality. The space could have easily been an from an upscale medical office. "Maybe we should table this conversation for right now."

"Maybe that should be your story," Giselle mumbled.

"Can I help you?" The woman matched her surroundings with straight, gleaming, dark hair and a matching suit.

Ivy licked her lips, priming herself for a fight. "Hello, I'm Ivy Vermont, reporter with Chargge.com, and I need to talk to Mr. Fleming regarding the story I am working on about *Hollywood Stardust.*"

"I don't know anything about that. You're not on the schedule." The woman's eyes darted between her and the computer screen. "Brian isn't taking new clients, and he doesn't see anyone without a referral."

"Tell her about Logan." Giselle came forward. "He gave her Skee-Ball lessons."

The woman's eyes narrowed. "Logan?"

Leave it to Giselle. "Yes, Logan Alexander referred me." She tried to smile. "We're doing a story together, or were." Her smile faded.

Suddenly, the woman stood. "Honey, I understand. Stay right here."

"Well, it looks like you're in." Giselle elbowed her. "So, about multiple orgasms."

Ivy put her hands on her hips. "No one is going to be having an orgasm. There isn't even orgasm potential. I just need a star."

"Well, that is why they call this place 'Stars R Us.'" A man in a perfectly tailored suit entered the room with the woman trailing behind him. "I'm not sure if I can help with your first problem, but I'll see what I can do about the star. So you're Ivy." He held his hand out.

"Yes." With no use hoping he didn't overhear their talk of orgasms, she shook his hand. "Thank you for seeing me."

"Of course, your conversation is first rate." He laughed. "Is there some trouble with Logan?"

The woman at the desk made a huffing noise.

Ivy wanted to give her a high five. Instead, she swallowed and tried to figure out how to tell the man what had happened without whining. "I am under some pretty substantial deadlines, and since I have not heard from Logan in several days, I have no choice but to assume he is not returning to the project." She used several multisyllabic words—score one for her.

"You haven't heard from him at all?" Mr. Fleming leaned back on the desk. "Did you try calling him?"

Not wanting to tell him everything, she took a breath.

"She was scared to call him, but she texted several times, and then studied all of his social media to see if he posted anything, because he told her that he did all of his own stuff and not some publicist," Giselle filled in.

Ivy held up her hand before her friend revealed her bra size or something equally as mortifying. "It was not my job to keep track of Logan's whereabouts. I had originally asked for Ryder or Erin and would like that promise fulfilled now."

"I see." He crossed his arms.

"Or Logan." She hit her hand against her leg at letting it out. At the end of all the games and banter she wanted Logan . . . for the story. She wanted Logan for the story. "But only with the caveat that we keep in touch. I mean, Logan would be better for the continuity of the story."

"She wants Logan." Giselle cupped her hand over her mouth as if she were telling a secret. "If you can produce him, that would be better. Ever since we saw the movie in sixth grade, I've heard about Logan. He's her favorite."

"I understand." Mr. Fleming cleared his throat.

"At least he isn't a cartoon." Not wanting to go into Giselle's love of an animated dog, Ivy stepped in front of her friend. Maybe she needed to take off her bra and hand it to the man. "Anyway, the bottom line is, I need one of the stars of *Hollywood Stardust*."

"Aka Logan," Giselle interjected.

She tried another smile, but she was sure the one she forced was not camera ready.

"Well, as I explained when we talked before, Erin is on location and Ryder is working on his film, so I'll have to look into this matter." He stood.

No. The man was supposed to snap his fingers and make someone appear. Her lungs constricted. "What am I supposed to do while you are looking?"

"I'm sure there are many other aspects of the story to cover until then," he said. "I have your cell phone."

"Do you find it a bit odd that you are the agent for the three of them?" She couldn't walk away with nothing. "Or are you the agent for all four of them?"

"I am quite certain Logan set the parameters of questions we would answer."

"He would answer," she corrected, and decided to go for everything. "You and I had no such deal, and since we have no such deal, do you think there is a reason Logan seemed to disappear? Do you think it's possible he isn't available or not capable for some reason?" She only went as far as to not mention the word *drugs*.

"Consider your deal with Logan my deal as well." Once more, he held his hand out. "Let me get to work."

"Please." She glanced at his hand but didn't take it.

"I promise I'll call. Texting and social media are optional." He patted her shoulder. "I have to get back to my office."

She watched him leave. Aside from lunging toward him and grabbing his ankles, she was stuck. "What am I going to do?" She might as well start penning her resignation letter.

"Come on. You promised me lunch, and it's practically dinner." Giselle pulled her sleeve.

"I have a place for you to try." The woman behind the desk spoke up. "It's new."

Both she and Giselle faced her.

The woman held up a card.

With both hands, Ivy took the offering and read the card. "Wilson's?"

"It says it's a bar." Giselle pointed to the card.

"The owner is Wilson. Don't tell them who sent you." She winked and returned to her computer.

"I got my first juicy tidbit." Wilson. The name hit a button in her memory bank. Her blood sped, and she tightened her hold on what could possibly be the key to her assignment. "Let's go have lunch."

❧

"I started this last night." Logan closed his eyes and pulled the foil off his masterpiece with the same flourish a magician made when making a rabbit appear out of a hat. Only with his work, there were no tricks or sleight of hand. In the kitchen, everything was out in the open. After marinating, grilling, and resting his flank steak, the meat had to be perfection. The aroma of garlic, wine, and the perfect amount of smoke melded together, and at last, he cut the thin, tender slices then arranged them on the plates over the mashed potatoes and topped them with crispy fried onions for the perfect balance. "I can train whoever we hire as a chef to make this if it works."

"Well, give it. I'm starving." His brother, Wilson, held out his hand.

"Hold on." He wiped a bit of errant sauce off the edge of the plate. "Dig in."

"I'm so glad you took the time to make it presentable." His brother picked a piece of meat up with his fingers and shoved it in his mouth.

"Must you be a heathen?" He lifted up a fork. "My cuisine is art."

"It's my bar, and I'll eat with my fingers if I want to." Wilson repeated his action, chomping down another piece of steak followed by a finger scoop of mashed potatoes. "I only allow you to cook here 'cause it's good." He swiped the fork away.

"And for you." Logan gave the second plate to his friend Isaac. "Ask for ketchup and you will be wearing it."

"I stopped putting ketchup on my food in high school. I opt for steak sauce now." Isaac took his meal and utensils.

"Hey, Mr. Scientist, anyone knows that steak sauce and ketchup are basically the same thing. My steak is perfect as is. I will not allow even a saltshaker near it. Your meal is chemically perfect." Between Isaac and Miss Details, his world was abundant with the scholarly types. He turned to his plate and pierced a piece of his creation. Acting as a gentleman, he took in the food with his eyes first. With the ideal amount of char and pink juicy center, his meal should be the centerfold in a magazine.

"So, what do we owe this impromptu menu tasting to?" Isaac asked.

He chewed with his mouth closed like a civilian, taking the time to savor the flavor, the velvety meat balanced with a kick of spice. However, there was one thing missing . . .

"He decided to make a piece when he didn't get a piece with that chick. Since then, he's been cooking." Always the taller, larger one of the Alexander brothers, Wilson came closer, casting his shadow over the table. "You should have heard the pots and pans banging around. Once we open, the customers will be cramming in here when they find out our mystery chef makes more than chicken wings and fries. If he let me say who he was, we would draw twice the crowd."

"I don't work here, and I don't make guest appearances." Yes, a woman was the only item missing, namely Ivy, which only made his conviction to stay away from her even stronger. Only it didn't stop him from thinking about her. "If you want food for the bar I helped finance, I will remain behind the curtain training the staff."

After Wilson had given up a lot of his time to be with him on set, Logan had invested in his brother's dream. It not only gave him an outlet for his creative cooking, it also gave them both the opportunity to leave their crammed apartments and move to the top floor of the building. The setup was easy and convenient with much more room. Everything would be great if only Wilson would give up on trying to push his ever-dimming star back into the public eye. Though he knew eventually his role at the bar would end up in the tabloids or on the Internet, he wouldn't seek out the attention.

"I remember when I was in graduate school, he showed up at my apartment and made his grilled cheese during finals."

Isaac patted his shoulder. "That was right around the time that one girl he liked dumped him."

"Can you call it a dumping when it's like three dates?" Wilson helped himself to more potatoes. "This is great. Make great big vats of it."

Logan stabbed another morsel of meat. After that rendezvous, he had given up on the notion of someone for more than one or two nights and had made sure he was the person who vanished. The same celebrity that attracted people to him also repelled them.

"When three dates is a record." Isaac inched his hand toward the ketchup bottle.

In a flash, Logan leaned over and snatched the bottle right out from under his suave scientist's nose. "Like you've ever done better." He shook his head at the owner of another one of his investments, Fluent Word Laboratories, Isaac's nutraceutical company. "Don't you have something to show me?"

"We weren't talking about me." Isaac bent down to his laptop case and pulled out a clear plastic bag filled with small plain white bottles, tubes, and smaller individual bags of capsules. "Try the drinks and tell me what you think. They work synergistically with the supplements, and different ones will address different conditions."

"This has to be exclusive. I don't want to ever see these formulations at a drugstore or on television." Already, Isaac's lab was making a name in the field of nutrition and antiaging, a no-brainer for Los Angeles. Add in the upscale clientele and they would have something.

"Nope. No mass quantities. Small custom runs. Now to try another small run." Isaac finally dug into his dish.

Logan waited while Isaac took a bite and chewed. Speed was never his forte. "Well?" While his brother would eat anything practically off the floor, Isaac had a more refined palate as long as the dish didn't involve ketchup. If the dish passed his criteria, they had a winner.

The man chewed and chewed and chewed. At last, he swallowed and looked up to the ceiling.

Logan slammed his fist into the counter. "Speak!"

Isaac leaned back and tapped Wilson. "He's touchy. I think someone needs more than his vitamins. I suppose the vintage babe finally stopped texting."

He took hold of Isaac's collar, pulling him over. "Tell me."

Isaac lifted his chin. "I think if you really wanted to sleep with her, you would have. I think you let her off easy 'cause eventually you will have to see her more than three times?"

"Did you ever think I have to see her more than three times because I'm stuck taking care of everyone, including you?" He made sure to glare.

Isaac smiled. "I think this is one position you want to be stuck in, and remember you created it."

"It's not you." His cell phone rang, and he released his friend.

"I bet she finally built up her courage to call her crush." Wilson gave him a thumbs-up.

"Not even close." Logan shook his head at the caller ID and answered. "Please tell me there will come a day when you and I will never talk again."

"Getting into character I presume?" Brian huffed into the phone. "I hope that is because you are going out on location shooting a webisode, and your absence the last few days has simply been an oversight."

"You're not my babysitter."

"I am when I am the keeper of the contracts. If I have to go with you, to make sure this gets done, then I will."

Logan put his hands over his eyes. His life didn't belong to him. He had sold it. No wonder people ran from him. "Well, it's not like she's knocking down doors to get to me."

"And that is the reason she texted you twice and stalked you on social media."

"What do you know about that?" Did these people resort to putting a tracking device on him?

"She showed up at my office today, begging for help, even asking for Erin or Ryder."

He squeezed his phone. Damn, he should have slept with her and added her to the pile. She didn't care who she had as long as they carried the *Hollywood Stardust* stamp. He wasn't unique. "Maybe we should just let one of them speak already."

"Not without you and not with the questions she threw at me today."

She knew better. He almost laughed. "Well, that ends it."

"It was the deal she made with you, not me," Brian said. "The studio wants this project, and it has to be you. We can't have her or her website poking around without being guided if you want to stay in the lifestyle to which you've become accustomed."

He turned around and looked between Isaac and his brother. Others relied on the lifestyle to which he'd become accustomed. "Fine, I'll fix this."

"Look at all the pay you make, and this is the first time you truly had to work for it in years."

"Yeah, right, don't forget your percentage." He hung up the phone.

Both Wilson and Isaac stared at him.

"I think I'm going to cut our tasting short and playact at being an actor. Hopefully, this won't come up again until the fiftieth anniversary." As if he had a choice in the matter, he kept his tone upbeat.

"All of this will be good for the bar. You'll see." Wilson polished off the last of his meal.

A pounding on the front door interrupted whatever Logan wasn't going to say to his brother.

"I'm expecting a delivery. I'll be back." Wilson put his plate down and left the kitchen.

"Log." Isaac shook his head. "This is my fault."

"No. It's mine and always will be mine." He pointed at his friend. "Don't let anyone ever tell you that you didn't get the best role in the movie."

"How can you say that? You and Ryder had girls practically climbing over each other to get to you. Between my weight issues, the prosthetics they put on me, and my role, I couldn't buy a date. No one would touch me." Isaac held his arms out and glanced down at himself.

"Yeah, but no one knew you either." Logan had to laugh at

the trick. Fake teeth, fake nose, and fake hair had created the character of Charles, the misunderstood outcast of the *Hollywood Stardust* group. At the time, the directors and producers thought it would be a great publicity stunt to have all of them always appear in character. Drew didn't know what a favor they did him. Without the makeup and about fifty pounds, and with a name change, he blended right back into the regular world, and Logan vowed that's where Isaac/Drew would stay if that was what his only friend wanted.

"Still don't. Though I'm still paranoid."

"It's twenty years later, they don't expect it to be you, and you changed your name. No one connects the dots." The conversation of Drew's whereabouts sprang up anytime *Hollywood Stardust* came to the forefront of the media, but he had made it twenty years under the radar. Most thought he had died or moved out of the country.

"Logan!" The door to the kitchen swung open, and Wilson rushed toward them. "What are you doing?"

Once more he lifted his phone. "Nothing." He scrolled through her texts. What he thought was her wanting him was her wanting any star. Though he should be used to being third behind Ryder and Erin, he hoped she might be different.

"Well, if your nothing includes not avoiding Ivy, you're in luck, 'cause she's here." Wilson motioned toward the door.

"What?" He shoved his phone back in his pocket. "She's here?" Here on his turf? His sanctuary? A woman-free, Hollywood-free zone?

"Her and her friend are checking out the front of the house. She tracked you down, or someone gave her this." Wilson held out one of their business cards.

"This is how she wants to play." If she wanted the villain, he would deliver him to her on a silver platter. "Get rid of her."

"I told her you were here." Wilson crossed his arms. "She seems nice."

Nice wasn't the word. "Tell her she will have to wait for my call."

"I'm not your secretary."

"Log, come on." Isaac grabbed his arm.

"Would you like to meet her?" He rubbed his hands together. "She's an expert on the movie. If anyone could pick you out of a crowd, it would be her."

"She didn't fall prey to the great Logan Alexander, and she's trying to save her job. I think more than being pissed, you're fascinated and you hate that." Isaac lifted his chin. "If and when you want me to meet her because you want to show her off, not show her up, I'll meet her."

"Wilson?" A voice distinctively Ivy's rang through the building. "Excuse me, Wilson?"

Wilson turned to the door. "What should I do?"

"She's calling you. Let her interview you." He pulled off his apron and slid the bandana off his hair.

"Wilson!" Her voice came closer. She knocked on the door and it cracked open.

"Stop her!" he spat at his brother and turned to Isaac. They didn't need Ivy's questions about Isaac. The woman was naturally sharp. "Get out of here."

Wilson put his hand on the door, blocking her. "One second!"

"Later." Isaac rounded up his belongings and snuck out the back door.

Once sure that Isaac had escaped, Wilson opened the kitchen door. "Look what I found."

Ivy entered alone, looking right at Logan.

He revved up for the storm to come, but rather than stomping into the kitchen ready to berate him for making her track him down, she tiptoed through the doorway with her huge eyes taking him all in. At the sight of her, he downgraded his storm to more of a strong wind instead of a tornado, but he still raged on.

"Since I didn't give you this address, or indicated a time we would meet, I must ask what you are doing here?" He prepared to hear some convoluted story that held as much resemblance to the truth as Drew in his getup resembled Isaac.

"I didn't mean to come back here, but a deliveryman arrived." She turned to Wilson and back to him.

"Let me go tend to that." Wilson left, making sure the door

closed behind him.

"I'm sorry, I know I must look like a crazy fan, but I panicked when you didn't get back to me. I went to your agent for help." She glanced around the kitchen.

Panic. Help. Trained to show whatever reaction he wanted, he crossed his arms and leaned back on his heels, remaining silent to prod her to continue.

She shrugged. "I know it doesn't matter to you as much as me, but I really want to make this work. When I got a clue as to where you might be, I had to come."

"Because I'm your only option left?" At those words leaving his mouth, his teeth made that horrible scratching that reverberated through his skull and he shuddered. "I know you asked Brian for someone else."

"I wasn't sure if you were still going to do the project with me, and as you know, I have a lot riding on this."

She gave him a standard answer as bland and boring as a frozen diet meal.

"Actually." She shut her eyes for a moment as if trying to collect her thoughts. "I was mad at me and you and I wasn't sure if I wanted your agent to force you to work with me or give me someone else, but on the drive over, I realized that if you aren't going to be my cohost, I'm ready to call cut on the whole project."

"You're willing to lose your job if I don't do the story with you?" He uncrossed his arms.

She pressed her palm to her stomach. "There's something to be said for knowing who you can work with."

He lowered his toes to the floor and stepped forward into her personal space. "You think you can work with me?" It might have been the first time that sentence was uttered.

She didn't back away. Instead, she chose to stand her ground and look up at him. "The stage fright isn't as bad with you."

Funny—he should make it worse, but he liked that he had the opposite effect on her. The storm he had conjured when she'd entered turned into more of a light breeze, one he wanted to brush against those perky pink lips, but he held back. "I don't know. If I even consider this, I would need to set some additional ground rules."

"Good, I can add some of my own to them." She continued to stare right at him.

Her words sent a jolt through him. "They would have to be set tonight at dinner." Yes, he tested her.

"Excellent, I accept your invitation. Now, we can get right to work." A true smile took over her features. The clouds parted around her, allowing in the sunshine.

"First rule, no talk of schedules." He grabbed a bottle of club soda from the fridge, opened it, and offered it to her. The bubbly drink always settled his stomach.

"Then, as an amendment to that rule, don't make me late." She took the bottle.

He pulled a stool out from under the counter. "Why don't you sit here, and I'll go change?"

"Do you live here?" Once she sat, her focus instantly went to the bag of samples from Isaac.

He paused, waiting to see what she said.

As she sipped her beverage, she continued to gaze at the bag as if it were going to do a magic trick. "Do you live here?"

"You are a quick study." He reached over her to take the bag and found himself nose to nose with her.

"Do you live here?" she repeated. "Or am I not allowed to ask?"

Rather than answering, he should give her a guided tour, starting with his new bed. They could break it in. "Yes, I do. Wilson is my brother."

"Oh, you offered something. Though your brother's name is accurate on the Internet and in the teen magazines I used to read."

At last, he retrieved the plastic bag and straightened up. "I need to take my vitamins and get ready." What she didn't know was he was as stuck as her, possibly more, but it did give him the advantage, and she still needed to prove herself.

HOLLYWOOD STARDUST

CUT TO:

EXT. SPRINGFIELD, MO – Farmers' Market – DAY

While WILLIAM and CHARLES get sidetracked
talking to a vendor about video games, STEVEN
and ROXY walk through the Farmers' Market.

>   STEVEN
> Let me know when you want
> to ditch everyone else and
> we can start our vacation.

STEVEN tosses some money to one of the
merchants, grabs a little container of red
grapes, and holds them out to ROXY who plucks
a grape out of the container.

>   ROXY
> You wouldn't leave them
> stranded, would you?

>   STEVEN
> Instead of worrying about
> everyone else, I would
> just like to worry about
> you.

STEVEN chooses a grape and feeds it to her.

ROXY stops in the middle of the thoroughfare.
STEVEN takes a couple of steps past her, stops
and returns to her.

                    STEVEN
          See, I would never leave
          you behind. Don't worry.
          I'll take care of you.

STEVEN goes to feed ROXY another grape. ROXY
grabs his wrist

                    ROXY
          What do you want?

                    STEVEN
          I think I've made that
          crystal clear.

STEVEN bends down to where their faces are
only inches apart. ROXY takes a breath.

                    ROXY
          What about everyone else?

                    STEVEN
          Don't worry, gorgeous, I
          would never leave them
          stranded. I just want some
          time with you to myself.

                    ROXY
          I don't think you're as
          bad as you think you are.

                    STEVEN
          Maybe I can change your
          mind.

STEVEN kisses ROXY. ROXY puts her fingertips
over her lips and runs away.

Chapter Five

The valet at the Grove mall in Los Angeles rushed around to Ivy's side of the car to open the door, but Logan held up his hand. "I got it." He exited the car, handed his keys over for the ticket, and tended to her door personally, offering his hand for stabilization purposes. As a bonus, Ivy's friend was also her roommate and would drive Ivy's car back to their place, thus leaving them together with no worries about odd logistics.

"Thank you." She put her hand in his, got out, and turned back toward the car.

"What is it? Did you forget something?" Following her lead, he also looked at his car.

"No, I wanted to ask you a question." She let go of his hand.

At her breaking contact, he stifled a frown. Minus one for her. "Until we decide our future together, I will refrain from answering any questions." He held out his arm, wondering if she would redeem herself.

Without hesitation, she looped her arm in his, but glanced back toward the valet station once more.

Her gesture was a bit of recompense coupled with some fraction of a point off for her distraction. Still, he had to know what could be more fascinating than him. "What is it?"

"I was wondering if you still had the BMW from the movie?"

Though he was the only one she could ask that particular question, it was still an interview question. "The restaurant is just across the way."

"I've always loved this shopping center." She motioned toward the huge fountain in the center. The outdoor mall located adjacent to the famous farmers' market lent itself perfectly to the balmy Southern California nights. She made a noise as if she were going to say something more but stopped.

He glanced over at her. With questions in her eyes, she bit down on her lower lip. No doubt she managed to restrain herself from mentioning the scene from the movie of them in an outdoor mall with the water fountains and stores and searched for any excuse to draw the parallels. He didn't even bother telling her he remembered the scene. Maybe he never got the girl because he didn't want one. How would he know if they wanted him or Steven?

He guided Ivy around the fountain and through the crowd. Once upon a time, his appearance would have created an avalanche of people running in his direction. However, with the years passing, it happened less and less. At times, he missed it and understood how others in his position became obsessed with finding their way back into the spotlight.

"Oh my God, it's him!"

He only flinched at the woman's shrill voice because Ivy stopped and squeezed his arm. A quick scan landed his focus on a congregation of women charging his way.

"It's Steven!" the intruder yelled again.

"Steven?"

At Ivy's whisper, chills coursed through him.

The woman barreled forward, and he stiffened his spine. Steven slash Logan both played their roles. "Do you have a pen?" He held out his hand, wanting to prevent the great pen search most fans put him through.

In record time, Ivy produced the requested writing implement as the woman and two others caught up to him.

"I hate you." The woman put her hands on her hips and lifted her chin toward him. "I can't believe what you did to William and Roxanne, even poor Charles."

He opened his mouth expecting a comeback to materialize, but he couldn't remember the last time someone yelled at him for being his character. Normally, they hated him for being him and even that didn't happen too often anymore.

"Excuse me, but you do understand that Steven is a fictional character?" Ivy snatched her pen back.

"We were never given an explanation of why Steven drove away." She glared at Ivy. "There was supposed to be a sequel, but he stopped that and we never got any answers."

Any retort he may have come up with disappeared with Ivy's interjection, but he wouldn't stand for the woman's nasty look and opened his mouth to get rid of the battle-ax.

"Do you know that as fact?" Ivy let go of his arm and moved in front of him.

Unsure whose action shocked him more, he allowed her to take over.

"Every report said it was his fault." The woman motioned toward him.

He crossed his arms. Thus far, Ivy had let the matter of the sequel lie, but no doubt with the crazy fan woman it would come up along with his arrest. Any hopes of whatever he hoped for with her faded away now that this woman made the topic bubble to the surface. They would be better off with the stock answers he tried to give her the other day.

Ivy held her hand out as a makeshift shield. "Twenty years ago the media was not even close to what it is now, and you are relying on a few accounts of spoon-fed news to tell the whole story?"

Never, in the twenty years since the day in the hotel, had he ever heard one person try to defend him. He froze. Ivy couldn't be on his side. He went to reach for her but resisted.

The woman's chest heaved. "The sequel —"

"Didn't happen. It will go down as one of life's major mysteries, but many people have addressed this dilemma on fan fiction, some very wonderfully written." She tilted her head. "Sometimes its better to not know the ending."

Fan fiction? He had heard of the stories but had never read any.

The woman glanced at him again. "He's going to hurt you just like he hurt Roxanne."

"I thank you for the warning, and I would discuss the matter with Steven if he existed." She took a step back.

With the admission that she recognized he was not Steven,

he exhaled. While he wanted to wrap his arms around her, he chose to take her shoulders and inched closer, looking down at the top of her head.

"Who are you?" The woman wrinkled her nose.

"A woman who is very hungry for dinner." Evidently done with the exchange, Ivy spun around to him.

"Well, I definitely can't have you malnourished." Rather than offering his arm, he pointed ahead. He nodded at the congregation around them. "Good evening."

"Seriously." Ivy stomped by his side.

Caught in a stare at nothing and struggling to take in exactly what had happened, he put his hand on the small of her back and led her through the large glass doors to his friend's restaurant. Finally inside, he gave a quick nod to the maître d', took her hand, pulled her through the dining room and kitchen, and into the walk-in cooler. The blast of frost did nothing to clear his mind.

Ivy looked around at all the shelves with the restaurant's food, the vegetables, the fruits, and some little baked goods for desserts. "Logan?"

"Did you just defend my honor because you are reenacting a scene in *Hollywood Stardust*?" His voice sounded distant, disjointed, but he needed the answer.

"Considering that was never a scene in *Hollywood Stardust*, I would have to say no." She let go of him and wrapped her arms around her shoulders.

"I have a question for you." He stared into her eyes. Everything about her was beautiful and more importantly genuine. She meant it when she said Steven didn't exist, when she told him she would quit if he didn't do the project with her, everything.

"Is this the start of our meeting?" Her voice quivered with her teeth chattering.

"Are you freezing?" He closed the distance between them and rubbed his hands up and down her arms.

"Is that your question?" she whispered.

"No, this is." Without another thought, he lowered his head and found her mouth with his own.

Most kisses he experienced were forgettable, quick flashes

of fun that might lead to a whole night. Actually, if he dared to be honest, quite of few of his kisses were written into a movie, scripted seconds with no emotion.

His kiss with Ivy possessed many things he had never experienced—passion, truth, and anticipation.

On top of everything, she kissed him back.

No, she didn't stand motionless waiting to be serviced, expecting him to do everything. Instead, she responded, parting her lips, wrapping her arms around his neck. The small coo escaping her throat only fueled the need he had since the day he walked in on her defending him the first time.

Her taste matched her to perfection, sweet with layers and depth, and even the unexpected when she took the lead in searching out his tongue with her own and pulling him closer. Any questions he had left about her were finally answered with two opposing forces, his intense arousal and his alternate urge to simply hold her tight.

She gasped and pulled back, putting her hand to her lips. Her cheeks glowed red.

"Thank you for answering my question." He hooked his fingers under her chin and tilted her face up to him, running his thumb along the outline of her lower lip. "This is one scene I say we reenact immediately."

He went to kiss her once more. In fact, he wasn't planning on stopping anytime soon.

She put her hand to his mouth, stopping him.

He tilted his head.

"This is one scene I can't reenact." She turned away.

Though she trembled in his arms, something told him it wasn't because of the cold. "Maybe we need to let it marinate for a while before we decide if it should end up on the cutting room floor."

Out the corner of her eye, she glanced at him.

"How about we go have our dinner, and I'll make sure you never miss a deadline? Maybe I'll even pick you up in the BMW I drove for the movie." He found himself holding his breath praying she didn't back out.

Somehow, their roles had switched.

HOLLYWOOD STARDUST

                                                    CUT TO:

EXT. GAS STATION - SPRINGFIELD, MO - NIGHT

The teens stop for gas before finding a motel
for the night. WILLIAM and STEVEN have gone
inside to get some snacks, leaving ROXY and
CHARLES in the car.

                                                    CUT TO:

INT. CAR - NIGHT

ROXY bites her nail and CHARLES, in the
backseat, uses a flashlight to study for his
test. ROXY leans over the seat.

                         ROXY
               Will you sleep with me?

CHARLES Fumbles with the flashlight, but
finally catches it and looks up at her.

                         CHARLES
               I don't believe I'm one of
               the choices.

                         ROXY
               What am I going to do?
               William thinks I'm with
               him, and Steven . . .

ROXY wrings her hands.

                         CHARLES
               What do you want to do?

ROXY shrugs.

                    CHARLES
          You are torn between what
          you should do and what you
          want to do.

ROXY looks down.

                    ROXY
          Something like that.

Chapter Six

"I kissed Logan Alexander." Ivy stared at the television even though it wasn't on. She didn't need to watch any reruns anyway. The kiss replaying in her head overshadowed everything else.

Giselle plopped down on the couch and held out a paper bag of mixed nuts. "Are you okay?"

"I kissed Logan Alexander." Ivy reached into the bag and took a handful, popping the salty treat in her mouth. Maybe she needed to join them, because she was most definitely nuts.

"Tell me exactly what it was like." Giselle crossed her legs and faced her. "Those are famous lips."

Tingles took over her body, and she sipped her club soda to cool down. Though never one to drink the mixer straight, she found it quite refreshing. Or maybe she was having a breakdown. "Remember when we used to practice kissing on our pillows?"

"He looks a lot more sturdy than a pillow," Giselle whispered.

"I mean, remember when we would practice and we would picture the most incredible, amazing man kissing us back? One who would make your toes melt?" She put her hand to her forehead.

"No wonder he kissed you in a refrigerator." Giselle grabbed one of the couch pillows and hugged it to her chest.

"You know how unreal those kisses appear in the movies? Like no one could kiss like that because it's all rehearsed, but damn it looks good?"

Her friend nodded.

"Well, Logan kisses better than that." With the same inflection and giddiness of a teenager, she blurted out her confession as if no one would guess her crush would be the best kisser ever. "Oh, God." Somewhere inside, her adult self screamed to be let out.

"It must be something in the genes." Giselle shook the bag of nuts and picked out a few.

For the first time in several hours, Ivy turned away from the blank television to take in her best friend. Giselle was positively radiant and relaxed. Ivy knew that look. "Where did you get those nuts?"

"Wilson gave them to me. Every bar has to have nuts. The salt makes people thirsty and they drink more." Giselle held a sampling of the nuts in her hand. "He said he wanted only peanuts 'cause you can get, like, tons of them for cheap, but Logan insisted mixed nuts were more classy and a conversation starter."

"When did you have this incredibly interesting talk about nuts?" She dug her nails into the couch cushion.

"After we had sex on the bar. I would call it pillow talk, but we didn't have pillows. I was starving, and he got out this huge can of nuts. He wanted to go out, but nuts are sort of fattening and I was full, so we had sex again to burn off the calories and then I came home."

She blinked, wanting to wash away the vision of Giselle and Wilson having sex and go back to the rewind of her kiss. "You had sex twice with Wilson?"

"You should have had sex with Logan. If his brother was any indication, everything we predicted about Logan and his orgasm potential is accurate."

"I can't have sex with Logan!" She jumped off the couch and put her hands over her eyes. "I can't have sex with him and I can't kiss him again!"

Giselle came over and put her arm around her. "Here, have some nuts."

"I can't have any more of your sex nuts." She groaned.

"He gave me a fresh bag. The ones we used during sex, he ate." Giselle patted her back. "I think if you have sex with Logan you'll feel much better. Just think, you will never wonder again what it would be like to have sex with Logan Alexander because you will know."

"How do you have sex with a man whose poster you used to have on your wall?" She walked into the kitchen of their small apartment and leaned over the sink, not sure if she wanted to throw up.

"Well, better than kissing a pillow." Still holding the nuts, Giselle joined her. "So what's next? Is he going to play the disappearing act again or are you going to get your job done?"

The nausea she tried to fight came barreling over her full force. "He wasn't clear on when we would meet again. He only said he would make sure I didn't miss my deadline." Of course, her first report was due was in two days and she didn't know if his plans included her or not.

"Maybe you can interview Wilson. He's coming here."

As if timed, their doorbell rang.

"I'll be right back." Giselle dashed away.

Only her best friend could have a blatant one-night stand turn into a date for the next evening. She stared at the drain, the big black hole to nowhere, or the place where her nonexistent entertainment career and love life would end up.

"Hi, Matt!" Giselle screamed a warning through their place.

She grabbed the edge of the sink and shot up. Matt? Damn her for being disappointed and praying her visitor was Logan instead.

"Ivy!" Giselle yelled.

She shut her eyes and took a breath.

"There's my girl." Matt's voice broke through the all-female energy of their apartment.

Without an escape hatch anywhere nearby, she turned. "Hey, what are you doing here?" She forced her voice to be perky.

"I could have sworn only yesterday I told someone I would swoop in and help." He held up his laptop bag.

She knew his tone, teasing, slightly flirty. He used it ever since they had met in college, only with her it never produced the desired effect. She wanted her heart to speed at the thought of him, or the air to sizzle around him. If only she could think of him as something other than an amazing friend. Other girls would go crazy for his clean-cut good looks, perfectly combed blond hair, and tall, lean physique. Matthew Gentry's persona screamed husband material. The ideal image of a parental dream.

Yes, her assignment. The job she sort of pushed aside to think about Logan and his lip-lock. "You wouldn't believe how crazy things got in such a short amount of time." She widened her eyes at Giselle, giving her the girl signal to keep her mouth shut about a lip-lock with one Hollywood star. Since it wouldn't be happening again, there was no point mentioning it.

"Well, that's why I'm here." He came over and leaned down, giving her a work-safe kiss on the cheek, not a scorching kiss that required refrigeration.

Something about his visit rang familiar. The memory lived way off in the distance, a time before Logan Alexander kissed her. Like nothing but a fan girl, she barely wanted to brush her teeth for fear she would lose his taste, but she already knew nothing about Mr. Alexander was forgettable. She swallowed and focused, needing Matt and his expertise more than ever.

"You can make this work, even if you don't have a *Hollywood Stardust* star." He settled down at the dinette table and patted the chair next to him.

"Well, about that . . ." She sat. How did she explain she wasn't sure if she had one or not without mentioning some inappropriate behavior?

"I planned for this exact contingency. You can get everything you need on your own." He pulled out his laptop and turned it on. "I've helped you by putting together some preliminary ideas. It may be even better not to have anyone from the movie. That way you are not bound by any promises you made to that guy you're crushing on. I say, good riddance."

"Craig only let me do this because I had a star." Rather than tell Matt everything, she chose to find out the reasoning behind his words. A twinge hit her in the heart. Yes, they kissed, and she swore he said they would work together, but she still hadn't heard from him. She picked up her phone, pausing before hitting the button and finding out if his message graced the screen.

"That was just the in you needed. What you're going to do is much better than interview a star from twenty years ago." He turned his computer to her. "This is why I love technology. If you know what you're doing, you can find out anything, and now you shall benefit. I'll be helping you and Chargge at the same time."

She took in the spreadsheet he presented her. Everything focused on the sequel, the night at the hotel room, and speculations about Drew Fulton's whereabouts. If she filled in the squares, the story would go viral and she would save her job and answer questions that had plagued fans of the movie for two decades.

"This is the hotel they were at." He pointed to the first entry. "The Beverly Garland."

"Right." Although she knew every detail by heart, she tried to take in the data with new eyes.

"Look, if you click this, it's everything we know to date." He selected the box, and the screen filled with images taken from the destroyed hotel room and the original newspaper article.

"At the heart of the controversy is the arrest of *Hollywood Stardust* star Logan Alexander. In a tale told way too many times among the Hollywood elite, Alexander was apprehended at the Beverly Garland hotel after engaging in a drugged-up brawl that destroyed one of the suites." She read the words aloud and flinched at the photo of Logan in handcuffs, remembering the day she had seen the picture for the first time and how she had cried. He supposedly went to rehab after and came out clean. A flash of his unlabeled vitamins went through her mind. Was he still clean? Maybe that's why he didn't text or call. Though she had read the story a million times, the words still stung.

She continued, "Sources say that Alexander had been on a rampage stemming from an initial conflict with Drew Fulton. Famously friends on-screen and off, Alexander's costars, Erin Holland and Ryder Scott, rushed to the hotel to calm the situation. By the time they arrived, police were already on the scene, and Alexander was taken into custody."

"We should go to the hotel. It's been privately owned for over thirty years. Someone must remember something." He clicked another button. "Look at the people we can delve into."

"The original screenwriter, the reporter from the *LA Times*, studio people." She took in his list and sighed. These were the ideas she should have come up with rather than fooling around with Logan. "You thought of it all."

"See? We have everything we need, so you can even interview the agent again. It's not like he's making any money off that guy. This will be much more newsworthy." He typed a couple of notes into the computer.

Though the excitement consumed her, the simple act of reading what Matt had produced seemed dishonest, as if she had stepped into a pool of slime. She promised Logan not to go here. Why didn't he call? She squeezed her phone, and it vibrated in her palm. Unable to resist, she pressed the button and glanced down at the screen.

Good afternoon. We must get to work. Tell me I should be on the way, and I'll come and get you. You can thank my brother for speeding up the process and giving me your address.

She gasped and stopped short of hugging her phone, but couldn't cease the shivers he created with a simple text.

"Is everything okay?" Matt bent down to get into her field of vision.

"Yes, this is for work, one second." At least she didn't lie. Logan mentioned work in his message. Was she or wasn't she upset about the acknowledgment of work but not the kiss? *Be on the way.* She hit "Send" and stared down at her phone, waiting for a response.

"Ivy?" Matt waved his hand.

"Sorry." She resumed staring at the computer, but the

words blurred together.

"I'm thinking you need to pose the questions and offer some theories. Make it like an expose," he said. "If we go down to the hotel, maybe we can get someone who was there that night to appear on camera. Even filming in the room would be a coup."

"That would be amazing. We could even compare and contrast it with the old pictures." Would delving into some of the forbidden without Logan constitute a breach of his trust on her part? She promised from the beginning she would get the answers her own way.

"See." He nodded. "Maybe we can even stay there."

Did Matt just invite her for a hotel rendezvous? Before she had time to digest his words, the phone vibrated once more.

As Steven once said . . . I'll be right on time as long as it's my time.

She giggled. *Actually the line was . . . I'll be right on time as long as you don't waste my time.*

"That's some work conversation." Matt cleared his throat.

"Well, I work in the entertainment department, and you work with data. It's very different." Though she tried to look at the real person sitting in front of her, the phone demanded her attention.

What? Did you study this movie for school or something?

"You caught me," she said the words and typed them to Logan as well. She supposed she couldn't hide it much longer.

"What are you talking about?" He snapped his fingers.

Ha! I'm not crazy! I didn't know they had a major in . . . me.

She couldn't stop her smile and didn't really want to try. *It's actually a master's degree in cinematic arts, but part of my thesis was movies that changed their generation.*

"Ivy, are we working or what?"

At last, she pried her phone away from her face. Matt was here. He showed up, didn't toy with her, or make her wait. "You know, maybe we can make this work. I did my graduate work in movies like *Hollywood Stardust.*"

"Of course, we can do this together." He reached over and

took her free hand. "You can't quit just because you hit a rough spot. Life is like a stage. It can be scary, but you can't hide."

His words sunk in. "You don't know what it feels like." Strange, Logan never mentioned her stage fright like Matt. She slid her hand away from his as Logan texted again.

Well, with a pedigree like yours, I will allow you to choose what we do for our project tonight.

Our project. He called it "our project." Together. An idea entered her mind for their project. *I know just the thing.*

"I know when you get scared, you hide. That's why we aren't further along in our relationship."

Her screen flashed with a response from Logan, and her heart jumped.

"Ivy, I've told you many times how I feel about you." Matt's gaze traveled down to her phone.

She turned the phone over, forcing her focus on the man in front of her. "Matt." How many times did she have to tell him it wouldn't work? While his friendship meant everything to her, she couldn't conjure magic feelings for him.

He reclaimed her hand. "I wish you would stop letting fear get in your way."

She gave Matt the requisite nod anyone received whenever they gave her advice about her life. All she wanted was her hand and to know Logan's reply. She gave in to one need and flipped the phone over.

You can be the boss . . . tonight. I'm on my way.

A quick calculation in her head told her it would take Logan no more than twenty-five minutes to arrive. Nothing on Matt's spreadsheets could be accomplished instantly, and she couldn't have their paths cross. "I'm doing better."

Matt moved his chair closer. "I know it was a blow to have that man disappear. You know more about the movie than anyone. Bring something new to the story and don't be scared."

"I'm not scared." Her gaze fell back on the screen with the spreadsheet of every one of Logan's sins. She jumped out of the chair and shut the laptop. In the process, her phone fell and skidded across the floor. "This story is meant for me to tell, but right now I have to tend to something."

Before she could get to her to her phone, Matt retrieved it. He peeked at the screen and placed the phone in her palm. "Now I understand. Be careful, Ivy."

"I'm not in any danger." She peeked to make sure Logan hadn't texted again.

"Everything about him is manufactured, remember that." He packed up his equipment. "He's designed to make you see stars in your eyes, and when this is over, don't expect to see him again."

Deep down she knew Matt spoke the truth. "I do want to work on the story with you. What you created is exactly what I need."

"When you need it, then it will be here." He walked toward the door.

She scurried after him, passing Giselle in the living room and opening the door to find Logan standing there. "Oh my God!" Her heart seized, and she pressed her hand to her chest to keep the poor organ in place. He never ceased to surprise her or sneak up on her, and the air sizzled with his mere presence. "What did you do, fly here?"

"I texted you while I was getting gas. I thought you might want to take a ride." His signature unlit cigarette dangled from his lips, and he stepped away from the door.

At the sight of the car—*the car*—she shook her head. "Logan."

"There's no way I can compete with that." Matt gave her a kiss on the cheek and, without a word to Logan, left.

"Matt!" she called after him.

Her friend simply waved.

As if under a spell, she looked up to Logan and her knees weakened. Only yesterday she had kissed him. She had kissed Logan Alexander.

"I would kiss you hello, but we are still marinating." He bent down as if telling her a secret. "See how I took what could potentially be an uncomfortable situation and turned it around?"

At his comment, her only choices were to laugh or kiss him. She hated herself for choosing to laugh. "I need to ask you something."

He nodded.

"Do you have any advice for my stage fright?" Why did she ask him? He had known her for three minutes, and he was the personification of confident. "Why haven't you mentioned it?"

"You know you have it. No need to mention it. When you need me, I'll be there, and FYI, I don't give advice. I'll tell you what to do."

A pure Logan Alexander answer. A pure answer. She couldn't stop her smile or the way her eyes darted toward the magnificent car once more.

He motioned toward the vehicle. "Go ahead. You know you want to."

With his permission, she rushed toward the jade-green 1984 BMW coupe, ran her fingertips over the lines of the car, and stuck her head inside the open window to breathe in the scent of vintage leather and Logan. The car from the movie was more than a prop. It was a character. Sales of vintage BMWs skyrocketed the year the movie came out.

"What do you think?" Logan took her by the waist and pulled her out of the car only long enough to open the door.

She slipped in the driver's seat and put her hands on the steering wheel. Twenty years ago, the actors did the same thing and took off on a journey unlike any other. Closing her eyes, she tried to transport herself to that magic time.

"I can't remember what my character would have said at this moment." He kneeled down by her.

"That's okay. After tonight, you'll know." With her resolve set, she faced him.

"Oh, are you going to feed my lines to me?" His eyebrows rose.

"No, before we do anything else, you need to see your movie." She made sure not to break eye contact. "I thought we could go back to Chargge's office. We have a video room there. You need to see it on a real screen." Though the thought of taking him back to watch it in her bedroom did cross her mind, she had to keep her resolve.

As if needing a moment to process her words, he stood,

walked around in a circle, and returned to his position next to her. "I've never seen my movie."

"I know." It took all her strength to hold back a laugh at his admission.

"If we are going to see it, we will see it my way." He offered her his hand. "Starting with me driving."

She took his hand and let him lead her around to the passenger side.

While he got settled in the car, she took her time to truly look at the man, an easy yet difficult task. His words said everything. With him, everything would always be his way. He would tell her what to do, he would drive, and he would be the one to drive away after he was done.

No matter what she couldn't kiss him again.

HOLLYWOOD STARDUST

CUT TO:

INT. CAR ON THE ROAD IN KANSAS - DAY

The drive is long, the road desolate with
nothing to see. CHARLES is not feeling well.
Both WILLIAM and STEVEN are upset after all
four of them shared a room the night before,
and ROXY opted to share CHARLES'S bed.

> ROXY
> Do you ever feel torn?

From the front seat, WILLIAM and STEVEN both
shoot her a look.

> WILLIAM
> I'm not sure about torn,
> but I'm sick of people
> thinking they always need
> to hide.

ROXY looks down.

> STEVEN
> Maybe sometimes people
> hide for a reason.

> WILLIAM
> Yeah, what good does it
> do? It always comes out
> anyway.

> STEVEN
> How do you know?

> WILLIAM

Know what?

          STEVEN
Know if someone is hiding
something. Maybe sometimes
it comes out, but what
about all the things that
never do?

Chapter Seven

"Ivy?" Logan entered one of the studio's private screening rooms. Every once in a while his name held some clout after all, or at least a threat. After Ivy let her activity out the bag, he wanted to argue, then he wanted to sit down on what appeared to be her comfortable couch in her apartment and stretch out while she watched the movie and he tried to ignore the travesty.

However, when he looked down at those pristine pink lips he got to play with the night before asking him to see his own movie, and she coupled her request by pleading with her huge gray eyes, he knew he could deny her nothing, even if it meant two hours and four minutes of torture. He did want to remind her there were far better ways to spend two hours and four minutes.

"Over here!" She twisted around in her seat and waved to him as if she were guiding him through a crowd.

He wrinkled his nose at the tiny mock theater boasting about ten plush, oversize, royal-blue velvet chairs, a huge screen, and some of the best projecting equipment money could buy. In these rooms, executives could make a star, or snuff one out, without ever leaving the studio lot. Thankfully, tonight he and Ivy were the only ones here.

As they had taken the car for a little joy ride, he had made his plans with the studio. They had chatted about the project and shot a little video. Though he'd wanted to ask who the clean-cut gnat was who had decided to show up on his turf,

Logan had held his tongue and planned to allow Ivy to make full use of the organ at her earliest convenience. His tongue and mouth happily remained open 24-7 for her to use as she saw fit.

Once at the studio, Ivy went to the commissary to get some treats and he received a much too detailed lesson of how to use the controls in the room. With the remote created straight from the depths of hell, or some overactive technology hormones, clutched in his hand, he took his seat next to her.

"Look what I got." She opened her purse.

"As long as it's not nuts, I'm good." What his brother did to those nuts was, well, envious. But he took the opportunity to do as she asked and look at what she had. On tonight's menu were her legs, highlighted by her 1960s simple, but sexy, emerald-green minidress and knee-high go-go boots. The peek he got of her thigh might rival her breasts, but he didn't know why he had to choose.

With a little giggle, she pulled out some red licorice and opened the package. "Would you like some?"

The answer to her question was a resounding yes. Well, he wanted some, but not licorice. "Sure."

"Here you go." Her manicured fingernails slowly peeled off a piece of the treat, and she handed it to him. The simple act of candy sharing shouldn't arouse him, yet he needed to shift in his seat.

As she crossed her legs, the already short hemline of her dress rode up her leg to an almost inappropriate level.

He shoved the candy in his mouth and ran his hand through his hair. Her telling him things needed to marinate did throw a monkey wrench into his plans. Of course, they could have sex and not kiss. Problem solved.

Wait. He was going to be a gentleman and wait for her to make the next move. Gentlemen sucked.

"Are you okay?" She put the licorice between her teeth and pulled. The red rope extended until it broke, and she smiled as she chewed.

Good thing they were going to watch a teen movie, since his body decided to behave like an adolescent. Rather than speak, he gave her a thumbs-up.

"Well, then. Are you ready for your first time?" At her

words and the blatant double entendre, she covered her mouth with her hand.

"Most definitely." Hell, she opened the door. He merely walked through it. He offered her the remote.

"I'll let you do the honors." Instead of taking the device most women longed to control, she motioned for him to go ahead.

He lowered the lights and put his finger above the play button, but went no further.

"Logan?" Her voice came out as a whisper as if she needed to be quiet for the audience.

"Yes?" His finger remained in the air.

"Are we going to watch the movie?"

"That's why we're here." He didn't move.

"Logan?" She leaned over, her arm brushing against his.

"Yes?" Thus far, he'd made it twenty years without seeing the movie. Even at the premiere he'd managed to dodge the entire film. Between the behind the scenes drama with the four of them, and being distracted by the entire fanfare of the whole thing, he never screened the movie all the way through. Now it seemed like he shouldn't watch it.

"Are you nervous?"

"No." His throat dried out and he swallowed. "Yes."

"I get it. It has to be weird to watch yourself, especially with this kind of movie." Without him instigating, she hooked her arm in his. "I think you may like what you see."

He patted her hand. "Is it weird to see this with me?"

"I don't know. We haven't seen anything." She put her finger over his. "Ready?"

Seriously, a simple touch shouldn't turn him on, yet here he was. "Absolutely."

She pushed his finger down on the button. The studio logo flashed on the screen, the telltale alternative rock music filled their small space, and Ivy gasped.

Suddenly, the trip to Hollywood Stardust came alive.

For the first bit of the movie, he fidgeted and got caught up in watching him and his friends, not as William, Steven, Roxanne, and Charles, but as Ryder, Logan, Erin, and Drew. Memories of what happened on set and how their real lives intertwined with the story distracted him.

As if she inherently understood, Ivy patted him or squeezed his arm at just the right times, and he cocked his head to watch her.

The flickering light from the screen illuminated her pristine profile, her eyes wide, watching the movie she loved enough to work into her graduate degree. But she didn't know about the days he was on set with the stomach flu, and how behind the scenes the love triangle depicted in the story played out in real life—but it was more of a square and almost ended all of their friendships. She wasn't there the day Drew slammed his hand in a door and how he went with him to the hospital to be the buffer between his friend and his parents. She didn't get that the movie was shot out of order. Combine that with the fact he was teenager himself, plus all the years that passed since then made him forget the plot she knew by heart.

All she saw was a story she loved.

He wanted to see the movie she did, and he refocused his attention back to the screen and allowed the story to absorb him.

Four friends were on slightly different quests, but traveled on the same road. In the BMW he and Ivy drove to the studio, the characters took a trek from Indianapolis to Hollywood, encountering their trials and tribulations, a carnival, a bad hotel room, a car breaking down, lack of money, infighting, even an impromptu visit to his on-screen grandparents for some comfort.

One hundred and twenty-four minutes of teen angst—the struggle to break free but the need to go home. The search for love and acceptance, not only by one's peers, but internally.

By the time Charles flew home to make it back in time for school the next day, William and Roxy had kissed outside the theater to go fulfill their destiny and Steven had driven away. Logan finally understood.

Steven had driven away.

Steven, not Logan, but Logan wasn't ready for the story to end.

A hollow sensation took over his chest. He watched the screen while the credits rolled and the music resumed.

Everything made sense. The fans, their reactions to him and his character, why Ivy needed to correct him at every turn. At last he understood why the film had such a following, why they begged for the sequel, and why no one would ever forgive them for not finishing the story.

No one would ever forgive him.

Not Steven, but Logan.

He would forever be responsible for Steven driving away and the world not knowing what happened when Roxy opened her eyes and watched him go.

Lost in the world of *Hollywood Stardust*, he finally realized Ivy hadn't moved in quite a while, and he turned to her.

She simply stared straight ahead with the light flickering on her face and tears twinkling down her cheeks.

He opened his mouth, but then closed it, turning away to give her a moment. After what seemed like much longer than necessary, he faced her again.

The tears continued, accompanied by little sniffs.

Her reaction was bigger than the movie. The last few days had to take a toll on her. They had had more twists and turns than a ride across the country in a BMW. "Ivy?"

She closed her eyes and shook her head, grimacing as if something hurt.

Not sure what action to take, he slid up in the chair. "Are you all right?"

A squeak left her throat and she swallowed.

"Speak to me." He got on his knees in front of her and took her by the shoulders. "Ivy."

She inhaled, her breath hitching. "He just drives away." With the words out, she lowered her head. Her whole body shook as she let the emotion out.

A crying female, more accurately a crying Ivy, ignited a primal instinct he didn't know existed, and he pulled her into his arms. "Come here."

"Logan." With a sigh, she gave in and hugged him.

"I'm here." He ran his fingers through her hair.

"Every time I see it, though I know how it will end, I think he'll turn around." Her fingers toyed with his shirt collar. "I wanted Roxy and Steven to be together."

"You did?" He tilted his head. Did they watch the same movie? Still, he pulled her a tad closer. "Why?"

"I don't know. Steven needed someone, and no one understood him like Roxy. I think she was scared to love him." She looked down.

"I was such an asshole." He hooked his fingers under her chin and raised her face to his.

"You're not Steven. You're Logan."

"Steven follows me everywhere." Though he played the role twenty years ago, the hype and the scandal never let the movie die. Every woman wanted Steven, not him.

"Then maybe rather than trying to outrun him, or forget him, you need to embrace him." She pressed her palm to the side of his face.

He moved his face down close enough to feel her breath puff against his lips. In every movie ever written, now would be the time to kiss her, but he resisted. "I don't know if I can."

"I know you can. You watched it tonight, and you're fine." Her fingers danced along his stubble, giving him the shivers.

"Only because you were here." He stared at her. With her looks, she should have been an actress or a model, or maybe she was destined to be the smart girl who wanted to believe a villain could be redeemed. She believed in him, and he had to have her, be with her. "I don't want to be the guy who drives away."

○‿‿‿○

At Logan's words, Ivy held her breath, and as if on cue, the small bit of illumination from the projector turned off, leaving them in utter darkness, yet neither of them moved.

She forced herself to inhale, exhale, and inhale again. Everything about him pointed to him using her and having his fun while giving her the ultimate fantasy. In the end, he would do exactly what he said he wouldn't and drive away.

"Logan." She wanted to push him away, but with the way he held her, dried her tears, and whispered those incredible words, she didn't have the strength. No, in truth, she didn't want to. She wanted to stay right here in the little screening room with Logan, and not because he once played a role in a movie she loved, but because he was amazing all on his own. Strong enough to admit he was nervous watching his own image on the screen and man enough to tell her he didn't want to drive away.

Without answering, he reached down and took her hand.

Her stomach bottomed out at the simple act. No, she didn't push him away, but instead, she gave into her need to touch him and traced her fingers over his jawline. Sharp, Hollywood perfect.

In turn, he raised his knees and cradled her to him, encompassing her.

She caressed him down to the slight divot in his chin. He gently took her wrist and moved her hand up to his mouth, kissing her fingertip, but doing nothing more.

Her heart swelled, while her skin heated. "Logan?"

"Kiss me." The words as simple and as deep as telling her he didn't want to be the guy who drove away. "Now."

Unsure what took over her, she obeyed and, even in the pitch black, found his mouth with her own.

Rather than a soft kiss, one that would grow slow and steady, the second their lips touched it unleashed a pent-up urgency within her, and she opened her mouth, giving him a deep kiss, taking in his taste, his tongue, anything he offered.

He held her tight, putting one hand on the back of her head to keep her in place, and matched her actions, with a long, drawn-out kiss that only served to inflame her skin.

She gasped, but without losing any momentum, wrapped her arms around his neck and guided his tongue into her mouth, sucking along its length, taking in his taste, a sweet yet savory combination belonging only to Logan.

"Um." He moaned. Somehow without interrupting them, he managed to lower her to the floor with him on top. Only then did he break the kiss. "Ivy," he panted, but before she answered, he kissed her again.

She gave in to one of her fantasies by reaching back and freeing his hair of the rubber band holding his signature ponytail in place. His locks fell down around him, tickling her face.

She never remembered anyone taking the time out to simply kiss her without rushing to whatever came next, but Logan seemed to relish in the act.

The man may not have been a classically trained actor, but he could give lessons in the fine art of arousing a woman. He nibbled and sucked his way down her neck and to her ear, while his hand roamed, traveling first to the side of her breast, then down to her knee. His every touch created a need within her she didn't think possible.

She took her turn to study him, the way the muscles in his back flexed as he tended to her, how his arms seemed to tremble with restraint, and yes, she copped a quick feel of his backside.

With no light to face reality, they laid together on the floor exploring one another, again finding their way to one another's mouths. The kisses increased in intensity. The light fondles that toyed with their nerves turned into grinding their bodies together to rouse every one of their senses.

She worked the buttons on his shirt, snaking her fingers inside to finally touch his skin. He slid his hand up the hem of her dress, cupping her bottom.

"God," he growled.

"Logan." She twisted his hair in her fist.

"I need you."

His voice came out strained as he reached behind him to get what she assumed was his wallet for a condom, and she wasn't going to stop him.

A jangle of the doorknob rattled through the room right as he pulled off his shirt.

She grabbed his shoulder, and they both froze.

With shallow breaths, they waited.

A slice of light cut through the space, but vanished as fast with the click of the door closing once more.

Even shrouded in darkness again, she hid her face in his chest, breathing in the delicious aroma of his soap, his skin, and his cologne.

In an unexpected move, he tucked his shirt under her head and laid down next to her, taking her into his arms. "I need a second."

"Okay." She raked her nails down the inside of his arm.

"That's not helping." Nuzzling her neck, he let out a groan. "Don't stop."

"What's wrong?" His feather-light kisses created a cascade of shivers throughout her.

He rolled to his back, taking her with him. "Maybe we should have gone to a drive-in."

At his joke, she let out a giggle.

"Don't laugh. They still have them." After a quick peck, he got them both standing.

Her legs wobbly, she held on to him for any sort of stability. "Logan?"

"Let me turn the lights on." Though he kept hold of her, he rustled around. "I need to find the stupid button."

In a flash, the lights blared down on them, and she winced at the sudden brightness.

"Lord." He shielded his eyes, but found his shirt in a crumpled heap and put it on.

While he undid all her hard work and buttoned his shirt up, she peeked at his chest. What she saw was as magnificent as what she touched.

"While I think the last part of our work needs a definite repeat performance, I don't think it needs to go in our broadcast tomorrow." He pulled back his hair and took her hand.

"Darn, you just took my whole story." They weren't going to even go back to one of their places and finish? Unsure if she was relieved at their coitus interruptus or not, she shook her head and gathered her purse and their candy. "So, what now?" Maybe she needed to give him a hint without saying, "Your place or mine?"

"Now, I will bring the princess back to her castle and return her carriage to its garage." He gave her a wink. "Do you have everything?"

Really? They were done? What the hell happened? With a quick scan, she took an inventory of the room. "Do you have your wallet?"

"Yes?" He put his hand on his back pocket. "I never took it out."

"Oh." If he never took it out, he was never getting a condom, which meant he wasn't planning on having sex with her. She wrinkled her nose. Did he simply want to find out if he could make her crazy? With a sigh, she shrugged. Not having sex with him had to be better than doing the walk of shame over hot coals coated with shards of glass after sleeping with him. What did she expect to happen?

"May I interrupt the conversation you're having with yourself?"

"It wasn't that great anyway." She smoothed her hair down. Even in a wrinkled shirt, he looked amazing, but she couldn't say the same for her.

"First, you look gorgeous. The way your lips are all swollen from kissing me only makes me want to kiss you some more." He pulled her closer and bent down to her ear. "I am so damn turned on from you that I'm never going to be able to sleep. Tomorrow, when you see me, remember the pain you are going to put me through tonight."

Wishing for fantasy in the darkness again, she shut her eyes and willed away the flutters. Logan would make her forget her name if she allowed it. What she wanted to happen and what would probably happen were two different things entirely. Maybe the man wasn't the villain everyone made him out to be. Or maybe he was screwing with her. No matter what, she had to find out.

HOLLYWOOD STARDUST

                              DISSOLVE TO:

EXT. SMALL TOWN — KANSAS - DAY

The four teens walk through the small town
looking for a restaurant.

WILLIAM points across the street to a
pizzeria.

                    WILLIAM
          Here we go.

                    CHARLES
          That's good, nice and
          fast. We can get back on
          schedule.

                    STEVEN
          We can't take Roxy there,
          not looking as gorgeous as
          she does.

ROXY turns away but still smiles to herself.

WILLIAM leans over to STEVEN and talks low.

                    WILLIAM
          If you would've gone and
          found a hotel with
          Charles, I could have
          taken her out on a date.

                    STEVEN
          If the two of you would
          take a hint, I would be on
          a date.

STEVEN and WILLIAM face each other, inching
closer as if goading the other.

                    CHARLES
          Guys.

ROXY turns back.

                    ROXY
          What's wrong?

WILLIAM stares at her with his mouth open.

                    STEVEN
          My best friend and I were
          just discussing why you
          torment us with your
          beauty.

WILLIAM shakes his head.

                    ROXY
          I like torturing you.

ROXY points to the pizzeria and walks across
the street.

Chapter Eight

"Okay." Logan paced the length of the kitchen, stopped in front of the stove, lifted up the lid on his pot, put it back down, and spun on his heel. He retraced the same steps he'd made for the last sixty-seven minutes, ending up back in front of the refrigerator. Though not a walk-in, the appliance reminded him of Ivy. He pressed his forehead to the cool stainless steel of the appliance and stared down at his phone. "Okay."

Again, he read the texts from his woman. The morning after their make out presented him with a girl who decided to go all business on him. While she suggested doing their shoot from the bar, she also prodded him on making good on his promise to get Erin and Ryder. Well, he didn't need anyone else in their twosome. In fact, he and Ivy did quite nicely all on their own. Something he wanted to continue, like right this moment.

Once more, he paced back to his simmering pot, lifting the lid. The escaping steam brought with it the aroma of wine, spice, fresh vegetables, and chicken. Something cooked with emotion, yet not too heavy. He didn't want Ivy too full to participate in any physical activities or to know the identity of the chef yet. "Okay."

"Okay what?!" Wilson came barreling into the kitchen.

"Don't lift the lid off this pot." Logan slammed the top back on.

"What is your deal?" Wilson came over and hovered his hand over the lid of the pot before he flicked him on the forehead.

He shoved his brother away.

"You may as well tell me." Wilson went to the refrigerator and opened it.

"Don't look in there." Logan rushed over and slammed the door shut. All refrigeration units seemed sacred. At his own thought, he rolled his eyes. When did he turn into a lovesick teenage girl?

Wilson put his back to the appliance. "Speak."

He pressed his lips together.

"Now." Wilson grabbed him by the sleeve. "You may have gotten the looks of the two of us, but I got the strength and I'll use it."

"I think Ivy is angry with me." He brushed his brother's hand off him and returned to the stove.

"Gee, I don't know why she would be. You only left her basically panting for you and then dropped her off at her doorstep."

"You know, that is absolutely untrue. I walked her to the door, I kissed her good night, and then I did the total guy-loser move and texted her three times afterward." He also did something else three times, but in the privacy of his bedroom and shower. At least he didn't lie when he told Ivy he wouldn't be able to stop thinking about her.

"You could have gone inside and done the deed, and she would be all happy now." Wilson gave him a wide, toothy grin. "Instead, she thinks you're a jerk."

Logan crossed his arms.

"Actually, she probably thought you were a jerk before, so you really lost nothing." Wilson opened the refrigerator and got a bottle of water.

At his brother's words, he ground his teeth together. "I was trying not to be a jerk."

Wilson shrugged.

"I was showing restraint and consideration."

His brother took a sip of his drink and looked up at the ceiling.

"I'm not like you. I can't just go making love to Ivy hither and yon like you and Ivy's friend. Then she'll think I'm that guy." He pointed to himself.

"You can't go *making love* to Ivy?" His brother's tone taunted him.

"Whatever." He lifted his phone. What he wanted to say was he couldn't mess up with Ivy. Wilson didn't understand. He didn't have the reputation. Girls didn't run after being with him. Wilson had to work to get a woman, while he had to work for a woman to stay. Ivy needed to stay. "I need to make a call. Go away."

"Aw, did I hurt my baby brother's feelings?" His brother used a mock baby tone and went to his side.

"I need to get some work done before she gets here to do some work." He scrolled through the contacts on his phone. "I am in charge, and I have to deliver."

"What does that mean?" Wilson leaned over his shoulder.

"I can't just have Ivy interview me, and I can't just recreate scenes. I have to make good on my promise." His chest constricted. "I have to give her someone else. Her job is on the line."

"Seems like you like to do things to save other people's jobs." Wilson grunted.

"Been nipping into the bitters you use to make that specialty drink of yours?" He glanced at Wilson out of the corner of his eye.

"Well, at least Ivy cares enough to try to promote the bar. Do whatever you need to keep her happy."

"I need to pick between Erin and Ryder." He spat out the sentence.

"Oh man, you must have it bad if you're going to break the seal." Wilson chuckled. "Who gets the gig?"

He considered his options. Ryder, the personification of the teen heartthrob especially to a woman who studied the movie, or Erin, the . . . well, the female. Too bad he couldn't pick Drew. "Who would you choose?"

"They both sort of suck ass."

"I'm just going to pick the lesser of two nightmares." He resumed his pacing and dialed. The phone rang once, twice, and a third time, and he squeezed the device. No matter what, he had to have something for Ivy when she arrived, and he didn't want to leave a message.

"No one ever calls anymore, everyone texts, so either I'm special or you want no proof you talk to me." Erin used her actress voice, the smooth tone trying to tell him she didn't care an ounce if he called or not when he knew the truth.

"Maybe because I don't need you having a record of anything I say to you." He squeezed his eyes shut.

"If you want to do things off the record, I say we both put our phones aside and focus on something much more interesting and fulfilling." She let out a low laugh.

"Not tonight." He opened his eyes and stared at nothing.

"By not tonight you mean not ever, right?"

"Something like that." He turned to his brother.

With narrowed eyes and his arms crossed, Wilson stared at him.

"That's not what you used to say." She gave him an overexaggerated sigh.

"Well, in the spirit of rehashing the past, I need to set up a time for an interview with Chargge.com." He grabbed the edge of the counter.

"Logan." At last her tone changed. She turned into Erin the girl, the one who always hated her hair, who wanted to hide behind him or Ryder when faced with fans, who couldn't make a decision or stand up for herself.

"You'll be fine. I'm sure Brian explained the project." He would give her only enough nurturing to appease her. In a snap, she could turn on him, as he had found out too many times. "The woman in charge of putting the piece together is really smart, brilliant actually. She has a degree in cinematic arts, and not any old degree, but a master's degree, and she is a huge fan."

"Are you sleeping with her?" Erin whispered.

For a moment, he lowered the phone. How did they have the same conversation for over two decades? They were stuck in a time warp. He lifted the phone again. "That's none of your business."

"You don't usually recite someone's resume. You barely

remember their name," she countered. "I thought with our arrangement I wouldn't need to do this. Isn't that what I pay for?"

"More than that." He smiled at her comeback. "You haven't spoken about *Hollywood Stardust* in twenty years, so everyone will be hanging on your every word. You were the one every girl wanted to be."

"That is true."

Erin's vanity always worked to his favor. "Fine, so it's settled. I'll text you a time so you do have a record."

"At least I get to see you." She paused. "Logan."

"Don't." Now she would ask about Drew.

"Have you seen him?"

If he didn't know she had the ability to cry on a director's cue, he would have sworn her voice cracked. Erin only wanted what she couldn't have, and she wanted to see Drew and hurt him again.

"Doesn't matter." Her voice lowered. "Text me and I'll be ready."

"Fine." With too much force, he pressed the button to end the call and had the overwhelming urge to take a shower. Ivy would be here soon.

"You are a wimp." Wilson stood with the exact same expression on his face.

"I set up the interview. That's the last thing I wanted to do." He shoved his phone into his pocket.

"You chose Erin for you, not Ivy. I guess you only want to be the gentleman when it suits you. Though honestly, I would have banged her and given her Ryder." Wilson waved his hand as if trying to make him disappear. "Scared of a little competition?"

"He's nothing." After a quick check of his watch, he headed toward the door. "I need to make sure the place looks presentable."

Wilson caught him by the sleeve. "Just because he's the one who looks like he made it, doesn't mean he did."

"I guess the movies and television sort of gives that impression." He snapped his arm away.

"If Ivy is who you think she is, she won't be swayed by the pretty boy." Wilson opened the door for him.

He stomped into the main room, the heart of the establishment. Rather than a typical bar, the place was unique. At his urging, Wilson designed something different, part old-world library where gentlemen would sit with a book and a brandy, part hipster cocktail lounge rolled into one. Aside from the long antique bar with every available type of glassware and a display of backlit vintage alcohol bottles, different seating configurations dotted the large space—tables for two, areas for a larger group, and even a couple cozy little alcoves for something a bit more intimate.

He set his focus on a curved black leather booth in a corner. "That's perfect."

A quick glance at the time told him she should be here. "I should probably be ready for her." He scurried around the bar, collecting some glasses and a bottle of wine and a candle, and set them up on the table. Maybe they could use the wine later. He played his gentleman card last night, but now they could cement their relationship.

"How pretty." Wilson joined him with the video camera. "I thought I would take some establishing shots for Ivy."

"I'm going to get some air before she gets here." He would tolerate Wilson wanting to plug the bar since he agreed to shoot the footage and they didn't have to have a camera crew come here. His brother might be a good elixir to her stage fright, but he would like his starlet to show on time.

"Okay, go wait for her. She's like a minute late." Wilson set up his gear.

Ignoring his brother, he walked out the front door, grabbed his pack of cigarettes out of his shirt pocket, and placed one in his mouth. He shielded his eyes from the midday sun and checked out their corner, a little off the beaten track in Hollywood, but still close enough to be relevant.

Where was Ivy anyway? Once again, he looked down at his watch. The one-minute acceptable grace period turned into five and then ten. His chest tightened. Why didn't she call? Wait. Maybe she couldn't call. Driving in Hollywood could be a challenge—narrow streets and a lot of tourists who didn't know their way around.

The adrenaline surged through his muscles, and he ran back into the bar, right past Ivy and some blonde.

Wait.

He skidded to a stop, inhaled, and turned only to have the breath knocked out of him.

Thus far, Ivy had given him quite a sampling of decades with her unique style choices, but hands down, no holds barred, he would say with absolute and complete certainty that her 1980s black lace bustier and black leggings layered with a matching blazer, spiked heels, and a contrasting string of white pearls had to be his favorite. His girl gave new meaning to the trend of lingerie as outerwear. With her underwear in full view, what was she wearing underneath?

He put his cigarette behind his ear. "I have wine." Those three words were the best he could do at creating a coherent sentence, since his blood supply had been diverted elsewhere.

"And good afternoon to you too." She licked her perfectly pigmented lips.

He wasn't going to make it through their interview. Maybe they should test-drive her outfit first and then do the taping. He blinked and swallowed in an effort to get himself together and took his time approaching her. "How did you sneak past me?" With the urge to kiss her too great to deny, he bent down. "I thought you were late."

"We came in through the kitchen. There was a little traffic down Melrose." Ivy stepped back and motioned toward the blonde. "I don't think you ever formally met my best friend, Giselle."

With nothing but air meeting his lips, he glanced at the woman boffing his brother. "Hello."

The woman elbowed Ivy. "It is Logan Alexander."

He sort of wondered who she was expecting. He turned his attention back to the right woman and went to greet her with a proper hello once more.

She put her hand to his chest and leaned back. "Don't you think we should get started?"

He never thought he would receive the cold shoulder, or in her case, the cold lips, for not making love to her, a situation he would not repeat. "First, why don't I give you a tour, and we will have ourselves a little chat?"

"I think I pretty much got the lay of the land. Wilson gave me a little tour while we were waiting for you not to smoke your cigarette." She pointed to his ear.

"Let me show you something in the kitchen." He narrowed his eyes at his brother. Any dealings with Ivy should go through him.

"If you insist." Her voice came out nonchalant, as if nothing was all too special.

"I do." He put his hand on the small of her back and guided her away, taking a brief second to take in how the leggings clung to her form. No, he was never going to make it.

"Something smells great." She entered the small kitchen he had designed when they were completing the build-out.

Without a word, he went to the stove, retrieved a plate, took his time portioning out a bit of his treat, and returned to her. Steam rose from the dish. "There are too many things in this room that are too hot to handle."

Though her expression didn't change, her cheeks took on a bit of color.

He cut a piece of the chicken and made sure to get a representative sampling of each vegetable to make the perfect bite. "So, while you were making yourself even more luscious than ever, I got a bit of work done on our project."

"What would that be?" As she leaned against the small island, her cleavage came into clear view, making his mouth water.

With his focus solely on her, he lifted the fork and blew on the food to cool it down, but just to make sure, he pressed the bite to his lip before holding it out to her. "Open."

After a brief pause, she opened her mouth.

"My mother used to make this dish. It sort of tastes like home." He fed her the bite.

Her eyes widened as she chewed and swallowed. "Who made this?"

"So, as I was saying, I did a little work and called one Erin Holland." He prepared another bite, making sure to go through the same ritual as the first.

"You called Erin?"

With a bit of flourish, he placed the next bite on her tongue. "Yes, and tomorrow you and I will go interview her if that is acceptable with my cohost?"

Upon swallowing, she opened her mouth for more and nodded.

Once more, he repeated his actions. "I think maybe a wardrobe change is in order. You are so gorgeous, I think I may be jealous of the entire world seeing you."

"Logan." The color on her cheeks deepened.

"I suppose we should get to work. You have a deadline to meet." He placed the dish aside.

"Logan." As he turned, she caught his arm.

"You paged?"

"I thought you might want a taste." In a sudden move, she pulled him down and kissed him.

His body reacted instantly. The combination of his food and Ivy created an insatiable combination, but rather than a full course, he got merely an appetizer when she broke the kiss. "Ivy."

"Okay, let's get to work." With one last peck, she walked back into the main room.

He watched her leave and shut his eyes. Without a doubt, he had to have her, and without a doubt, he couldn't screw up. At least he chose Erin rather than Ryder.

HOLLYWOOD STARDUST

CUT TO:

INT. CAR ON THE ROAD- DAY

The four pass the time by playing traditional road games.

> WILLIAM
> All right, let's play a new game. What are you most scared of?

WILLIAM twists to look around the car, pointing, trying to find a player.

No one speaks.

> WILLIAM
> Come on. Charles?

CHARLES puts his book aside.

> CHARLES
> I guess I'm afraid of not making it, not being successful, and relying on others.

The car becomes silent.

> STEVEN
> What about you, the question man?

> WILLIAM
> (Pauses.)
> I'm afraid of not being

noticed, fading into the
background.

WILLIAM hits STEVEN in the shoulder.

                    WILLIAM
          Now you.

                    STEVEN
          (Sarcastic tone.)
               I'm terrified this highway
               will never end.

                    WILLIAM
          Seriously.

                    STEVEN
          I'm afraid that nothing
          matters.

STEVEN clears his throat.

                    STEVEN
          Let's hear from our
          resident female.

                    ROXY
          I'm afraid I'll never find
          my place.

Chapter Nine

"While I appreciate the infomercial on Logan's brother's business, I would like to know where we stand on something more substantial." Even through the phone, her boss's voice came out strained with stress or the need to yell.

"Craig." Ivy winced. It was probably a good idea she chose not to mention that while he may not have liked the story, Wilson's place was receiving a ton of calls to reserve a spot for the grand opening.

"I got the scoop on how Logan never saw his movie all the way through." Again, she went with not telling Craig she also got the scoop on how he kissed or that he felt her up. Some things were better left off the record. "I also think I'm doing much better in front of the camera." With Logan holding her hand under the table and playing with her fingers, she sort of forgot about the camera.

"All right." Her boss's tone was completely flat.

"The story is building. I'm seeing Erin Holland in a few minutes." She looked up at the hotel where the meeting was set. Since she'd lived in Los Angeles her whole life, she never needed to stay in a hotel, but the one for their interview had a definite reputation for being a Hollywood hangout. Her chest constricted, and she inhaled as Logan taught her. Holding Logan's hand in his brother's bar and an interview with Erin at a famous hotel were two different things.

"Well, let's dig a little deeper than movie screenings and bar openings."

"I need to go in. Everyone else is already here." The cameraman had showed up a while ago to set up the shot and Logan had texted saying he'd arrived early. When he met her he was late, but she wasn't Erin Holland, the superstar. She wished Wilson were filming. At least he fit in her comfort zone . . . sort of.

"Go break a leg and maybe dress a bit more conservatively."

"It wasn't underwear." She waved her hand in front of her face in an unsuccessful attempt to cool down, then hung up and straightened her outfit. In keeping with her 1980s theme, she opted for a dark gray power-skirt suit, complete with a bow at the collar and shoulder pads. Her cell phone vibrated, and she glanced at the messages, expecting to find Logan. Instead, she got two texts from the two big M's in her life—her mother and Matt.

Confirming you and Matt are coming to the Palm Springs house for the weekend.

She wrinkled her nose. In all the insanity, she had sort of forgotten about the weekend, and Matt had neglected to remind her like normal, or maybe he had. Since he'd left her apartment, she and Matt had texted, but not much else. Logan seemed to take over everything, oozing into each one of her pores. At her parents house, only talk of her career and stage fright would ensue unless she took a man with her, in which case the discussion would turn to settling down. The entire visit would consist of her ducking and dodging from the onslaught of questions, and she never looked good in sporting attire. Rather than answer, she clicked on Matt's message.

Good luck with the big interview today. Let's have dinner tonight and talk about moving forward.

She bit her lip. With Logan and her interview, she couldn't go look at spreadsheets later or have a talk about moving forward.

Who was she kidding? She was hoping Logan asked her out. The same reason she conveniently forgot the trip.

For the better part of the night, she had tossed and turned thinking about the interview, but mostly about Logan. After their so-called infomercial, Giselle and Wilson had disappeared while she and Logan had shared another helping of that delectable chicken. They had ended up pretty much making out in the little booth, after which, only to prove her point, she'd ended it and had gone home, leaving him glassy eyed and in need. Maybe points weren't meant to be proven. Even an icy cold shower didn't help her.

Out of time to stew about her stalled sex life and with the shakes starting, she lifted her head. With the influence and history her power suit demanded, she marched through the huge glass doors of the hotel, allowing the staff to bow in her wake. She made her way out to the huge pool where she would meet Erin in a private cabana.

She spotted one among the matching yellow-and-white-striped tent tops with people gathering, and Ivy made her way around the pool.

The actress's distinctive laugh echoed out from the curtains and a smile took over Ivy's face. While Logan may be the crush, Erin represented the aspiration, the star, the success, the personification of the woman every other woman wanted to become. She tiptoed over to the cabana and peeked inside.

"There she is." In a plush yellow chair, Logan let go of a woman's hand and stood.

Wait. Stop. Rewind. He let go of Erin's hand. A burning nausea rolled through her. Why was he holding it in the first place?

In what Ivy would describe as a chaise lounge, Erin reclined like an old-fashioned Hollywood starlet in a sheer white robe, showing off her legs and her curves. Her blonde hair was pulled back to highlight an elegant face with big blue eyes, heart-shaped lips, and a perky little nose. Twenty years might have passed since the movie, but her age didn't keep up with her. Even poolside, she came complete with every accessory, including stilettos, a pair of well-known designer earrings, and a glass of water in her hand with floating fruit.

Suddenly Ivy's suit and the shoulder pads squeezed in on her, as if she had become bloated in an instant, and she longed for some of the water sans the macerated fruit. She swore the small space shrank further.

He reached his hand out to her, the same hand that had held Erin's. "Ivy, I would like you to meet someone who needs no introduction."

Her cheeks heated to the point of blistering, but she cemented a smile on her face nonetheless. In all truth, she had no right to be jealous. "It's an honor to meet you." She came forward, but caught her shoe on the edge of the chaise and tripped.

"Oh!" Erin let out a little squeal.

Logan caught her. "Careful, babe."

She found her footing. "Thanks." In case Erin didn't hear, Logan had called her *babe*.

Still keeping hold of her, Logan placed her in the seat he'd previously occupied and went and sat at the other side of Erin.

"Wren, I would like you to meet Ivy Vermont from Chargge.com." He motioned toward her and winked.

Wren? A nickname? Ivy tried to show no emotion. She didn't have a nickname. Well, he did call her babe. It would work for now. She held her breath, waiting for Erin to acknowledge her.

After not only a pregnant pause, but a pause that definitely needed to take a trip to the maternity ward, Erin turned to her. "Logan told me you studied us in college. Isn't that interesting?"

"Well, I did study *Hollywood Stardust* as part of my master's thesis." She sat up as straight as she did the day she sat among her professors defending her work.

Silence.

Both she and Erin turned to Logan.

He reached into his shirt pocket and pulled a cigarette out of his pack. After taking his time to put the cigarette in his mouth, he motioned for them to go ahead. "Don't think about the camera." She knew he said that for her benefit. Erin lived in front of a camera. "Just talk, make conversation—the video will take care of itself."

He never lit the damn thing. The man didn't smoke. He

simply carried cigarettes around with him. She promised the next time she saw Logan with a cigarette she would pull out a book of matches and call his bluff.

"I'm not saying a word on the record until someone adjusts that light." Erin pointed to a lamp in the corner. "It's in my eyes making my pupils look small."

The cameraman reached over and turned the light. Nothing changed, but Erin gave him one nod.

"Okay." Erin lifted her glass. "You know I specifically asked for raspberries, not blueberries."

All Ivy wanted was to give her a raspberry, but she held her tongue, not wanting to insult her favorite fruit.

"I think you'll live through it." Logan patted her leg.

"I suppose I have no choice." The star sipped her drink and slowly faced her.

Like the first time she'd interviewed Logan, her throat went dry, but rather than try to rush, she took a breath and sat back. "You haven't spoken about *Hollywood Stardust* in twenty years. Why not?"

Erin didn't as much stare at her, as she stared beyond her. "I didn't want to only be known as Roxy. When you play such a role, it's easy to never escape it."

With no point asking about the sequel after Erin's answer, she continued wondering what it would be like to be able to pick and choose roles, and have the world at her beck and call. "So both you and Ryder made the conscious decision not to talk about the movie, ever?" Her voice came out much terser than intended.

Erin jutted her jaw out. "We share an agent, so it's not strange we received the same advice."

Logan narrowed his eyes.

"I guess that it must be nice having Logan as the spokesperson for you all." She swallowed to hold back the rest of the statement. Of all of them, Logan, the one who was arrested, the one who was blamed for the cancellation of the sequel, even the one who never saw his own movie, was the least likely choice for a mouthpiece.

"Well, he offered the most controversy and has the most to

say. I think it's perfectly fitting." Erin smiled and gave a quick peek back at Logan.

Logan didn't move, his stance tight as if ready to spring into action at any second.

"Then you have all remained friends all these years?" Her voice shook. Every word she spoke seemed like it was undergoing microscopic scrutiny.

Erin's complexion paled. "Logan, Ryder, and I have always been close."

The moment naturally opened up for a question about Drew. Her body mimicked her voice and she trembled.

Logan sat up.

She played with the bow tied way too tight at her neck. One decision ahead of her with two outcomes—go to work tomorrow or basically quit tonight. If she asked the question, she would lose Logan for sure, but if she lost her job, Logan would probably go with it. Still, she needed Logan if she kept her job. Actually, she wanted Logan, or maybe she needed him.

She sighed and wiped her brow. "Tell us a juicy tidbit. What was it like to be the center of affection between those two costars? Was it only on-screen?" Though she asked the question, the sick, sinking sensation in her chest told her she didn't really want the answer.

"It was magic." Finally, Erin looked her in the eye. "When you're so young and there are all these beautiful almost-men around you, it's magic."

Logan turned away.

Erin reached forward and grabbed her hand. In fact, her whole demeanor changed. "I was the only girl on the main cast, and sometimes when we were shooting and on tour, it was hard to tell where the movie ended and where our real lives began."

Back in the day, rumors of hook ups and break ups peppered the tabloids, but the confirmation made a vile metallic taste take over her mouth.

Out of nowhere, Erin's eyes glossed over with tears. "Everyone but Drew."

Drew? Ivy froze, bit her tongue, and waited. Out of the corner of her eye, she saw Logan squeeze his hand into a fist.

"Drew always knew where everything stood. Knew I would never choose him because I couldn't." Erin put down her glass of water and dabbed the corner of her eye. "I miss him. There was so much pressure to choose."

"Choose?" Her voice came out ragged, and her word hung in the air.

The cabana fell silent.

Erin inhaled. The faraway, mournful expression vanished as she transformed into cunning actress Ivy walked in on. A smile grew across her face. "Through the years, we tried, but it was never right. They wanted me to be with the good boy and we never overcame it. Don't let anyone ever tell you different. The bad boys are the most fun."

Logan crossed his arms.

Everyone's life had one of those moments. The second one thought they would be chosen for an award, or won something, and then realized they'd lost, yet they still needed to keep a straight face. With sweat running down her spine and nausea creeping up on her in record speed, this was one of her moments. She would label it the time where she found out her crush slept with his costar and continued to for twenty years. At least her stage fright had been replaced with something much more useful . . . anger.

Maybe they lived out the sequel every day and laughed at how they had turned her into a pile of mush. Maybe that's why he didn't make love to her. Actors lived in a different world. While kissing might be fine as long as they were playacting, sex was not an act.

"There's probably a reason no one is ever with the bad boy." The word's exited her mouth and hung there like a cartoon bubble.

Logan turned and stared her down.

"So true." Erin laughed. "So true."

Only sheer will and the fear, not of the camera, but of utter embarrassment, forced her not to stand up and leave. But she could end the fiasco. "Before we end, tell me, since this is the first time you are talking about the movie in public, what is something you have been longing to tell us?"

Erin leaned forward. "I loved Roxy and I envied her. I'm thrilled another generation will get to watch her."

"Cut!" Logan shot up out of the chair. "Ivy, there are some things we need to review."

"I can't thank you enough. I've always wanted to meet you." She let go of Erin's hand and got up as well, but didn't acknowledge her cohost. "I need to leave."

"That's it?" Erin looked between her and Logan.

"I have to run, but I'll make sure Logan tells you when your interview goes live." Any excuse would be a lie.

"Wait." Erin held one finger up and took a little card off the table. "Here's my e-mail. Logan always forgets to call unless he wants something."

"I understand." She took the card. "You have a Chargge e-mail." Long ago Chargge.com became one of the go-to email providers for those on the go. Just about everyone had one or ten accounts to their name, why not Erin Holland?

"That's my personal e-mail. Had it for years. Don't share it." Erin picked up her glass. "I should have offered you something to drink."

"Ivy," Logan growled.

"Thank you anyway. I need to get back to the office. I have to leave to go out of town." She picked up her bag and rushed out, pretty sure she would end up right in the swimming pool.

Pure dumb luck on her side, she managed not to trip on anything, knock down anything, or destroy anything on her quest to get out of the hotel. Her heart throbbing from exertion and disappointment, her throat on fire and needing moisture, she made it all the way into the lobby before she had no choice but to stop and take a breath. She braced herself on her knees.

"Ivy!" Logan yelled.

She straightened, looked around, and hid behind a huge palm tree. While she pressed her back to the wall, she smiled at one of the porters watching the scene.

"Ivy." Logan rushed by her.

She actually felt like cheering, but chose to stay silent and perfectly still.

He scanned the area, stared right at her, and then marched

over to the tree. "Ivy!"

Fine, she didn't win. No surprise there. "I did the whole interview. I think you can do the establishing shots alone or with Erin." At letting that last part out, she ground her teeth together.

"You and I have a lot of establishing yet to do." He reached out to her.

"I have established plenty, too much, in fact." She pulled down a leaf to shield her. "I need to go home. I have company coming over and then I am leaving for my parents' this weekend." With her words, she officially closed the door on any excursions with him. Good. Well, not good, but smart.

"I wasn't informed of a weekend outing."

"I don't have any obligation to let you know of my whereabouts off hours." She lifted her chin. "Now please let me pass."

"That's what you think." He moved aside.

With the branch still between them, she walked forward.

"I like your jealousy. Very hot." He peered over the huge leaf.

"I am not jealous. I'm just an intelligent woman." She let go of the plant, and the branch snapped back, slapping her in the face.

"Ivy. Come on." Logan wrangled the foliage for her.

"Let me go." She managed to hold her head up high. No wonder she wasn't an actress. He saw right through her. She retrieved her phone and texted Matt. *Great. See you at seven.* All she needed was a white flag to signal her surrender.

HOLLYWOOD STARDUST

CUT TO:

EXT. OKLAHOMA CITY, OK - STREET - NIGHT

With CHARLES back at the hotel, WILLIAM, ROXY,
and STEVEN explore the town. ROXY walks ahead
of them to look inside the window of a
clothing store.

> WILLIAM
> What are you doing?

> STEVEN
> Hmm, let's see.

STEVEN looks around as if searching for
something and pats down his pockets.

> STEVEN
> Walking around in this
> mall in the middle of
> nowhere. Funny how all
> malls look alike no matter
> where you are.

> WILLIAM
> You know what I mean. I'm
> talking about what are you
> doing with Roxy?

STEVEN stops and faces WILLIAM.

> STEVEN
> What are you doing with
> Roxy?

WILLIAM lifts his chin.

                    WILLIAM
          We're together.

                    STEVEN
          Are you so sure about
          that?

WILLIAM crosses his arms.

                    STEVEN
          If you were so sure, you
          wouldn't be asking what
          I'm doing.

Chapter Ten

Ivy dashed around her bedroom, throwing clothes into her suitcase, not caring what mixture of styles and decades she tossed together. Palm Springs boasted plenty of vintage shops, and she could fill in any gaps. All she knew was she had to get the hell out of Dodge, Dodge being anywhere within a one-hundred-mile radius of one Logan Alexander.

Done. She was done. Done with the games, the flirting, the amazing swirl in her stomach anytime Logan decided to gift her with a glance. He needed to stay a fantasy. In reality, she only had jealousy, despair, and disappointment waiting for her. Why she was even surprised at the turn of events was beyond her.

She caught her reflection in the mirror. "What did I expect?" The man could have Erin Holland and had indulged on multiple occasions.

In less than ten minutes, Matt would be there. Unlike her teen dream turned nightmare, Matt showed up when he said. Always punctual, to the point, and predictable. Yes, he was Old Faithful. She never needed to worry as long as Matt was there.

Maybe it was time she considered Matt. He wouldn't wait forever for her. She marched to her closet and put on a modern, conservative tan dress, something smacking of this decade and of a woman who possessed a graduate degree.

With a nod of conviction, she went to her dresser, opened her lingerie drawer, and peered inside. Unbeknownst to him, Matt was getting some on their trip. If nothing else, she was getting some. She assessed her options: 1950s long, flowing nightgown or 1960s baby-doll?

At the knock on the door, she scooped up a pile of the pieces, dumped them in her bag, and closed her suitcase. Matt hated being delayed, and she rushed to open the door.

Rather than a person, a huge bouquet of flowers greeted her. Did Logan come here? She pressed her hand to her heart and leaned over the threshold. "Hello?"

"Here's to the start of our weekend." Matt peeked his head around the flowers.

Her heart fell, and at the moment, she wanted to grab the damn organ and kick it for overriding her good sense. Of course Matt brought flowers, not Logan. The movie star believed his mere presence was good enough, and it was true.

No! She shouldn't settle for a man who would show up when he pleased. Matt wanted to be here. "I didn't realize visiting my parents was a special occasion." Over the years, they had visited her family's little retreat in the desert many times.

"Well, you never know what life can hold for you." With his still hand behind his back, he finally approached.

In her questionably cute dress, she leaned against the door in an attempt to be seductive. Matt never became overcome with passion. He was more of a planner right down to their almost nonexistent sex life. "What do you mean?"

From behind his back, he revealed a box of candy. "For you."

Flowers, candy, a man on time. What more could she want out of life? She refused to answer her own question under grounds she might incriminate herself. Still, she assessed the situation: flowers, candy, a man on time. What the hell was going on? She broke out into a sweat. "What's all this for?"

He smiled. "I should have taken a stand long ago, but seeing you with that has-been actor really put things into perspective."

Funny for her, Logan made everything cloudy.

He came closer.

Maybe she only needed to open her mind and be receptive

to all Matt had to offer. She licked her lips in preparation for his kiss.

He leaned down and gave her a peck on the cheek. "Are you ready to go? I checked the traffic reports. We should get going while the going is good."

"Are you sure?" She glanced at him out of the corner of her eye.

"Did you pack?" He gave her the chocolate.

"Yes."

"I also brought my laptop. We can make a plan to get the story wrapped up without any more surprises." He kissed her again in the same spot.

With a sigh, she opened the box and spied the maple cream. "Do you want a piece?" She waited for the suggestive reply.

"That will ruin dinner. Save it for later and we'll share it with everyone." He walked inside. "Let me get your bag, and we'll be off. You should put the flowers in water."

She put the lid back on the candy and gazed out at the street. With the sun setting and the sky darkening, the drive to Palm Springs could be really boring or really sexy. If they got right on the 10 freeway, it would be a straight shot. If they took the 60 freeway, the road would take a few turns before leading to the 10. She always preferred the turns even if it was a bit out of the way. Would being with Matt condemn her to always taking the 10?

Right as she went to pick up her posies, a set of headlights came down the street—more like careened down the street— and screeched to a stop in front of her apartment building. Logan's car.

She straightened up and held her breath.

Logan got out of his car, slammed the door, and basically sprinted over to her. "If I were to ever bring you flowers, I would bring you a red rose. It's timeless, beautiful, and tells the receiver exactly what the giver wants."

"Well, these are what were given to me." She held her head up high.

"The night is not even close to being over. You never know

when you may get a different opportunity." He reached behind him and held out one long-stemmed, deep red rose tied with a matching ribbon.

Her hand seemed to move on its own to take the token. "What are you doing here?"

"I wanted to ask the same question." Matt returned with her suitcase.

Logan didn't bother even glancing in Matt's direction. "I'm taking you to Palm Springs. I thank you for offering a bellman, but I have it covered."

"We have our plans set, and we have to get on the road." Matt attempted to walk out the door with her bag.

Logan stretched his arm out and put his hand across the doorjamb, essentially blocking Matt's way. "Only if I get to ride shotgun."

Every muscle in her body tensed and tightened to the point where she started to shake.

"Listen, I don't know what kind of game you are playing with Ivy, but it's stopping right here and right now." Matt put her bag down.

"If I'm playing a game, which I assure you I'm not, then I will win." Logan faced him.

"Wrong. I will because I am the one seeing clearly, not through some haze." Matt stepped toward him. "You know how she feels about the movie, about the characters. What are you, the villain come to life?"

Her breath quickened, her heart sped, and she put her hand over her mouth. In the movies, having two men fight over a woman seemed romantic, but here on her porch, it was horrifying, especially since the men were her crush and her friend. Her friend. Not a man she had sex with. What was she doing?

"You don't give Ivy enough credit. She knows the difference between fantasy and reality." Logan's tone remained perfectly calm, and he glanced at her.

For less than a second, their gazes locked but spoke volumes. A moment only two connected people shared. Everything had changed between them once she'd told that fan woman he wasn't Steven.

Then there was her friend, the man who proofread her thesis, the man who brought her orange juice every time she got sick even though she hated juice, the man who she could count on, but who didn't make her heart sore with want.

The man who brought her the most beautiful bouquet of flowers when all she wanted was a single red rose.

"I give her plenty of credit. I also help her. You ditched her before, but we don't even need you. We have everything covered for your so-called story." Matt set his jaw. "We don't need some backstabbing drug addict who destroyed his own career."

"Matt!" She thrust her hand out to stop him from going too far, and she wasn't sure if it was for her or him or Logan.

They both turned to her.

"Ivy, we need to get on the road." Matt's voice shook in restraint.

"Why don't you ask her who she really wants to get in the car with?" A seasoned actor, Logan's tone remained calm. "Unless you're scared she may answer the backstabbing drug addict who destroyed his own career?"

She looked between them. How could she answer?

"You don't even know her. What on earth do you want with her?" Matt crossed his arms.

"I know more than you think, and I don't know enough." For the first time since he'd arrived, his voice wavered. "That's why I'm here, but if she thinks I only rushed here because I'm playing some game, then I will go and leave the two of you be."

Tears distorted her vision, and she found herself shaking her head. Nothing Logan did made any sense, yet it made perfect sense.

"I am going to make this easy, not for you but for Ivy." Matt put his hand on her arm. "I am going to leave and let her live out whatever fantasy she has going on with you. Rest assured, I will be back the second she realizes where her future lies."

"Fantasies that seep their way into real life are the best ones." Logan lowered his voice.

"They are called fantasies for a reason." Like before, Matt

gave her a peck on the cheek. "No matter what, your parents are expecting you."

Both she and Logan stayed still and quiet until Matt started his car and drove away.

"Ivy." Logan broke the silence.

Holding up her hand, she walked inside, placed the chocolate on the coffee table, but kept hold of her rose.

"What are we doing?" After closing the door, he came up behind her.

"I need to ask you something." In an effort to collect her thoughts, she stared at the petals.

"Anything." He put his hands on her shoulders.

"If I leave and go to my parents alone, are you going to follow me even if I tell you not to?"

He turned her and stared into her eyes. "Absolutely."

Did she cheer at being left with her crush? Did she cry? Did she try to push Matt away because he was the real deal and she knew he wanted more? In the end, was Logan the safer choice because he was unattainable? Deep down she knew the truth, but couldn't face it or herself. She lifted her phone and texted Matt. *I'm sorry.* "Then get my bag and let's go."

HOLLYWOOD STARDUST

                                    CUT TO:

INT. HOTEL ROOM — OKLAHOMA - DAY

The four are getting ready to leave and head
back on the road. CHARLES is in the car, antsy
that they are not keeping the schedule.
WILLIAM is on the phone.

                                    CUT TO:

EXT. HOTEL PARKING - DAY

STEVEN and ROXY lean on the car, waiting.

                    ROXY
              Don't you need to call
              home or anything?

                    STEVEN
              I don't see you running to
              the phone.

STEVEN puts his sunglasses on.

                    ROXY
              I think they were thrilled
              I found some friends to
              play
              (She makes air quotes)
              with.

                    STEVEN
              Anytime you want to step
              into my sandbox, just say
              the word.

ROXY shakes her head.

                    ROXY
          Is there anyone you miss?

STEVEN shrugs.

                    STEVEN
          I don't know. Maybe my
          grandparents, been a while
          since I saw them. They
          live in Arizona.

                    ROXY
          Maybe you should call
          them.

                    STEVEN
          If I had someone to
          introduce them to, maybe I
          would.

Chapter Eleven

A little oasis in the middle of the desert, Palm Springs always screamed vacation to Logan. The hotels built around the hot springs, the casinos, and the midcentury cool vibe of the town lent itself to a different sort of lifestyle, one more relaxed than Los Angeles.

With little traffic, they made good time down the freeway. They barely spoke, but when he reached the twists and turns of part of the 60 freeway, at last Ivy smiled. He knew he had a little inner daredevil.

From the time she ran off from the interview with Erin, to getting her to agree to let him tag along, he thought his chest was about to explode. He didn't put up such a good performance in *Hollywood Stardust*, but he knew he had to buck tradition and, at least in this scene, end up with the girl. However, even though she didn't voice it, her fears came through from her friend, the guy he wanted to punch across the jaw and tell to keep quiet. Deep down, she doubted him, but he was never more certain about anyone. He needed to figure out a way to prove his intentions.

She directed him into the residential area, the kind once frequented by the more hip to the jive stars of yesteryear. They glided to a stop in front a single-story modern masterpiece with a palm tree in the front yard and Wilson's car in the driveway.

Wilson's car?

"What is my brother doing here?" He pulled in behind his brother's truck.

Ivy opened her mouth and faced him.

Before he repeated his question, a gaggle of people, including Giselle, his brother, two people he assumed were her parents, and another couple with a baby, charged out the front door holding balloons and some sort of banner. As speechless as Ivy, he pointed.

She turned back. "Oh my God! What does that thing say?"

The wave of people thundered toward the car, but as if working with one collective mind, stopped.

"I'm assuming they noticed a slight change in plans." He squinted to read the metallic letters. "Happy Engagement."

"What do I do?" She didn't move.

Engagement? "Were you in some sort of relationship with that person?" He tightened his hold on the steering wheel.

"What?" She spun around back to him.

"What the hell am I, if you were on the verge of an engagement?" He spat the words at her. They were beyond some fun make-out sessions and exchanging entertaining quips.

"You?" She put her hands over her eyes. "You?"

He remained silent.

"I don't know! You are a cross between a fantasy and a nightmare. Most definitely you are the man who is going to stomp all over me, break my heart, and leave me a blubbering idiot on the side of the road." She put her hands down and glared at him. "But if you think I was in some sort of relationship while I panted after you, then I want you to be the guy who drives away."

They stared at each other.

While he wanted to either drive away or yell back, he took a breath and analyzed her words. Broken heart? Panting after him? With her outburst, she handed him the road map on how to prove himself to her. He only needed timing on his side. "You better go meet your public." Chaos consumed the crowd. The parents motioned toward the car, and even with the windows rolled up, he heard the baby crying. Baby? He wasn't even going there.

She huffed and opened the door.

"Ivy Raleigh Vermont!" A woman suspiciously resembling Ivy let go of her balloon, and it soared off into space. "What is going on?"

Raleigh? Interesting. He got out of the car and walked around to Ivy's side, holding out his hand. From this second on, no one, not Ivy, not the parents, not even the baby would question his intentions.

"Why don't you tell me?" She put her hand in his and used him for leverage to stand up.

"Oh, God! It's him!" Another woman, this one younger than the first, jumped up and down and dashed toward them.

"Mom!" Ivy thrust herself as a human barrier between him and the woman.

Thus far, he had done essentially nothing and Ivy had her back pressed to him—bonus.

"Fern, calm down!" A stylish woman in a white button-down shirt, jeans, and boots shooed Fern back and turned to Ivy. "I ask again, what is going on?"

"Yes, missy, please explain." A tall man who appeared as if he were ready to put on a robe and smoke a pipe came over. "For someone who never liked improvisation, I have to say you have thrown us for a surprise."

Giselle came over. "This isn't Matt. Um, we may be a bit premature on the engagement."

For once, Giselle said something that made sense. No, he wasn't Matt, but nothing about him was premature. Nothing. Zero.

"Matt was premature on the engagement. We weren't even dating. We barely had sex!" Ivy stomped her foot. "Where did you get the idea he was proposing to me?"

Her mother and sister both gasped. The man who he assumed to be the father hardened his jaw, the younger man holding the baby smiled, and Wilson gave him a thumbs-up.

"I waited until our wedding night to have sex." The one named Fern turned back to the guy with the kid.

"Right, of course you did, which is why Rose was born at full term six months after your wedding." Ivy practically growled. "Stop living in the movies with convenient math."

Laughter not an option, he bit the inside of his mouth.

"Fern has always created her own reality." The older man nodded.

"Matthew told me he felt this was the perfect way to make you closer. That you would grow to love him once he committed himself to you." Her mother shook her head.

"I think by the time someone gets engaged they should already be in love." Ivy softened her voice. "I always pictured that if someone asked me to marry them that by the time they did, I would be so anxious wanting that ring that I almost couldn't function."

Her tone came out almost ethereal, dreamlike, and he fought the need to put his arms around her.

"Oh, your Raleigh side is showing." Her mother sighed. "Life isn't a silver screen fantasy."

He held his breath. Not two minutes ago she'd called him a fantasy.

"Why not?" Ivy shook her head. "Why would I want to grow to love someone? Don't you think it just happens and sometimes there's no explanation? You spent your life up on stage performing some of the most classic tales of love. Love is nuts and random, and it may grow, but I don't think getting engaged in hope it takes root is the answer."

He exhaled. No better words were ever uttered on the subject. No, she wasn't the type to get engaged because she wanted to be married. She wanted to be with the man she loved. Her actions made him want her all the more.

"He was perfect for you," her mother whispered.

"He was perfect for you," Ivy countered.

He ran his fingers down her arm and let his hand settle in the perfect indent of her waist. The pieces fit into place, and he looked down at the top of Ivy's head. They both had their doubts they needed to work through.

"I just want you to be happy and have a stable life." Her mother focused on his hand.

Ivy shook her head. "Is anything really stable?"

He needed to be the personification of stability.

The women stared at each other.

"Excuse me," the sister practically yelled, jolting everyone out of the moment. "Love or not, engagement or not, I think we are all forgetting the sheer fact that Logan Alexander is standing on our driveway."

The entire entourage turned to him. He put his hands on Ivy's shoulders.

"And you didn't believe me." Giselle leaned over to Fern.

"You didn't believe this was an engagement party until you saw the cake." Fern shook her head.

"You didn't tell me until I saw the cake." Giselle pursed out her lower lip.

"We should make the introductions." The older man cleared his throat and ran his hand through his perfectly styled and swooped-back hair.

"It's just an amazing coincidence with how Ivy loved the movie." The woman extended her hand. "Fern Vermont Paddock. Is it strange knowing she was such a huge fan?"

Ivy stiffened.

"No, it's usually strange when people come barreling toward me yelling, 'Oh, my God, it's him.'" He kept his hands where they needed to be, on Ivy.

Fern put her hand down and backed up toward the man with the baby. "This is my husband Robert and daughter Rose."

Fine, they had a little botanical theme going on.

"Logan, this is my father, Dennis Vermont." Ivy motioned toward him. "And my mother, Cecelia Vermont."

"I've watched your film. You were convincing." The father held his hand out.

Logan shook the man's hand and put on his best smile. For the mother, he took her hand and bowed his head. "Pleasure to meet you."

"Did you ever study acting? Film? The dramatic arts?" She pulled her hand away.

"Mother," Ivy growled.

"I can't say that I have." He had to give it to the woman for throwing him a zinger of a question first thing.

"Are you still acting?" She crossed her arms.

"Some would say everyone is acting." He waited for a

spotlight to be put on him and squeezed Ivy a bit tighter.

"You still have an agent, right?" She pursed her lips.

"Yes."

"I need to check the roast." Her mother spun on her heel and stomped back into the house.

All right, her mother wasn't a fan of the actor, but didn't Ivy say something about her parents being on stage?

"I'm going to help." Fern ran after her.

"I'll get our bags." He didn't expect such a tough audience.

"I think this is about the time for some drinks." The father nodded and walked away.

"Give me that." With her hands out, Ivy stomped over to the man with the baby.

"I think she needs to be changed." Robert handed over the baby.

"I'm on it." Ivy gave the baby two kisses and, with a quick glance in his direction, walked away. "Come on, Giselle."

"Play nice, boys." She wrinkled her nose and followed her friend.

Logan popped the trunk open, but before grabbing their luggage, he took a breath and stared at the house. "I love this kind of architecture."

"You don't know where you're at, do you?" Robert approached.

He supposed Palm Springs wasn't the answer. "Enlighten me."

"This is Curtis Raleigh's home." Robert swiped his hand in front of him.

"Raleigh." Ivy's middle name. Out of the corner of his eye, he glanced at Robert. "He starred in some of my all-time favorite movies." People prayed to be compared to Curtis Raleigh. He had it all, from the swagger, to the lines, to the looks.

"Well, Cecelia is his daughter." Robert reached inside the trunk and took out Ivy's suitcase.

He looked up to the desert sky. The stars plentiful. At some particularly dark times right after *Hollywood Stardust* wrapped and everything imploded, he used to study the stars.

He pictured each flickering light as one of the many actors or actresses that left before their time. Curtis Raleigh was up there. A star that shined bright enough to go supernova, but exploded with the all too familiar story of fast fame, fun, and fortune. All the trappings and downfalls.

"What do you do for a living?" The gears meshed and began to turn.

"I teach drama and act." Robert chuckled. "I'll save you the trouble and fill in the rest. Fern works for a theater. Cecelia and Dennis are classically trained actors."

He nodded and lifted his duffel bag. Though he was racked with more questions, suddenly Ivy made complete sense. The attraction, the mystery, the choice of profession, even her mother's reaction to him.

"We should get inside. The faster we eat this dinner, the faster we can get to our own rooms." Wilson came over and elbowed him. "I got the tour, brother. This house is incredible, and everything is nice and spread out."

"You are a traitor." With newfound focus, he solidified his plan. He slammed the trunk shut and took the handle to Ivy's suitcase. Before he worked on Ivy, he needed to work on her mother.

⌒⌒⌒

The house was spectacular, truly and utterly spectacular. In fact, spectacular didn't quite describe the home of Curtis Raleigh. Designed as a hexagon, each of the four bedrooms looked out into an amazing outdoor space with a hexagon-shaped pool and even a hexagon hot tub. Except for the modern electronics, every painting, every bit of furniture, every accent in every room was exactly right for the period, absolutely perfect and authentic, a decorator's dream.

Also, it was solid proof that an actor's life could be a nightmare. Even with everything perfect on the surface, underneath the world could crumble. All around the home were little artifacts from Curtis Raleigh's career intermixed with pictures of Ivy and her sister and the rest of the family, a sad reminder of what the grandfather had missed by leaving the world too early. No wonder her mother wanted a stable home.

With Ivy and Giselle still gone with the baby and the mother and the sister tending to dinner, he had been relegated to sitting in the swank living room with the men talking about sports, electronics, and video games, none of which he knew much about.

"Here you are." Dennis Vermont held out a glass to him. "Is it true you were discovered on a street corner?"

"Something like that." He lifted the drink, allowing the liquid to catch the light. Long ago did Curtis Raleigh drink from these glasses? Did one of those drinks lead to the downward spiral? Ivy already defied her mother once by not going with the stable man. Could she do it a second time by choosing him, the antithesis of what her mother wanted? Not needing to even give a hint he ever lived up to his reputation, he held his hand up. "If you don't mind, I think I'll take a rain check and be right back."

"The bathroom is that way." Mr. Vermont pointed.

"Thank you." Before he worked on Ivy, he needed to get Mrs. Vermont on his team. Stability could be illustrated in one simple act, and he took the opposite route and headed for the kitchen.

"Oh!" Hunched over some clearly overcooked carrots, Fern straightened up as if she were part of a marching band.

"I can't seem to get any liquid from this pan to make the gravy." Mrs. Vermont studied her roasting pan.

"Mother, Logan is in the kitchen." Fern pointed at him.

Mrs. Vermont turned and motioned with her pot holder. "The bathroom is that way."

Well, he supposed eventually he would find that information useful. "I appreciate the map, but that's not what you need."

"What is it you need?" The smile the woman tried to force on her face turned more into a line.

"I'm fine. You need me." He strolled through the kitchen, first pointing at Fern. "Stop touching the carrots. You've hurt them enough."

Fern backed up.

"I don't need anything." Mrs. Vermont crossed her arms.

"Yes, you do." He joined her at the stove and inspected the shriveled piece of dried meat. After spying a few available necessities and scanning the area, he made a plan. "Please get me a decent bottle of red wine, some beef broth, flour, and butter."

Her mother stared at him.

He rolled up his sleeves and chose a whisk from the canister of tools on the counter. "Look, I'm not going to make it worse."

While Mrs. Vermont walked around the kitchen and collected the requested items, he moved the massacred meat to a cutting board and covered it with foil.

"Mother," Fern whined from behind him.

He turned to her. "You are not cooking and you are not taking care of your child, but I can guarantee you will be quiet."

"It wouldn't have been dry if we didn't spend so much time out on the lawn when you arrived." Ivy's mother placed the ingredients next to him.

"And you think congratulations on a forced engagement would have taken less time?" He put the roasting pan on the stovetop and began to make a proper sauce.

Out of the corner of his eye, he caught her watching him while he continued making his roux.

"Where did you learn to cook?" She stepped closer.

"Well, I'm not classically trained. I first learned from my mother, but then I had to learn on my own." He gave her a short sound bite to pull her in. The sauce bubbled and began to thicken.

"What does that mean?" Again, she inched over.

"My mother passed away when I was sixteen, right after I got scouted by my agent. She was ill." No matter when he spoke of it, his chest still constricted. "You know, I almost quit the movie. At the time I thought it was a bad omen. All my agent and the director seemed concerned with was that I could play the part, not the fact I had lost my only parent. Do you have a spoon?"

"Those dirty bastards." She shook her head and opened a drawer for him.

"But thanks to the movie and the people around me, I got to stay with my brother. They really helped when I needed it. I think they're used to dealing with children in bizarre situations." He grabbed a spoon and took a taste of his impromptu wine sauce. The right bit of earthiness from the meat and acid from the wine danced over his palate. In need of the ultimate approval, he dipped a second spoon in the sauce and held it out to her mother. "Always taste your food. That is very important."

"I'm sorry about your mother." She patted his arm and opened her mouth, a genuine smile gracing her face. "That's delicious."

"I'm sorry about your father. He was an incredible actor. I am more than honored and humbled to be staying in your home." He set the burner to simmer. "My mother always said there was nothing you can't do with wine and broth. Why don't you slice the meat really thin while I tend to the root vegetables?"

"Logan." She went about her task. "May I ask you a question?"

Fern backed up when he approached and took the poor side dish. "You may ask me anything you wish. There is trust among cooks." He found some cream in the refrigerator, then took the blender and moved next to Mrs. Vermont.

"Are you the reason my daughter didn't get engaged tonight?" As if she didn't want to ask, she lowered her voice.

He proceeded to make a carrot puree. The blender's buzz took over the room, and he waited until shutting it off to speak. "While I'd like to think I am, I am not. I made my intentions very clear to Ivy before I even knew someone else existed."

She tapped him to show him the fully sliced roast. "What are your intentions?"

Before answering, he took the meat and slipped it into the

savory sauce. "I want to be with your daughter. I've never known anyone like her. She's exceptional. You did a magnificent job."

Much like her daughter, Mrs. Vermont's cheeks reddened and she put her hand to her chest. "What do you do now?"

"I invest, and I work with my brother in his bar, but my specialty is taking care of others." He winked and motioned toward some dishes. "Why don't we plate everything up in here, then no one will know our secret?"

She nodded. "Fern, go get everyone gathered around the table while Logan and I finish up."

With a huff, Ivy's sister barged out of the room.

He put all the food into an assembly line and began to plate the dishes with a splash of carrot puree over the roast slices and then topped it with the sauce, wiping drips off the rim before handing the completed creations to Mrs. Vermont. "I am a much better cook than I am an actor."

She stood up on her toes and gave him a peck on the cheek. "Thank you."

Right as they finished filling the plates, the kitchen door swung open. "Mother, I can't find Logan." Ivy skidded to a stop the second she saw him and glanced between him and her mother.

"I would never be too far away from you." The way his blood sped through his veins at the sight of her told him again how much he wanted her.

"Oh, I'm glad you came back here." Mrs. Vermont held her hand out.

Ivy went to her mother and took her hand. "What's going on?"

"You were right. I want you to be happy. I'm sorry we blindsided you with all this hullabaloo, but it got you here and Logan here and that's what matters." She leaned in and hugged Ivy.

"Thank you?" Ivy patted her mother. "What's going on?"

"Logan helped me with dinner. It was almost a complete disaster." She held Ivy at arm's length. "You look beautiful."

With wide eyes, Ivy took in the scene.

He had noticed her more conventional dress before, but with everything, forgot to mention it. "She always looks gorgeous, though I must say I prefer the vintage look."

Through her lashes, she peeked over at him, her cheeks glowing.

"Sometimes you just have that spark." Her mother beamed. "I'm very happy for you. I don't want you to worry about us at all, and now that I know the two of you are together I'll tell Daddy not to worry about you and Logan sleeping in the same room."

The color in Ivy's cheeks vanished. In fact, her complexion change startled him and he stepped forward.

"I'm not tired at all." She backed up and turned away.

"Don't be embarrassed. It's not like I wasn't young once." Her mother returned to her plates.

Apparently, the sleeping arrangements hadn't occurred to his bedmate. He kept his eyes on Ivy. Somehow he needed to prove he was worthy of sharing her sheets.

❦

With the covers pulled up to her chin and in the most unsexy, unrevealing sweatpants and sweatshirt she could conjure from her suitcase of lingerie, Ivy stared up at the ceiling waiting for Logan. Well, not waiting, more like dreading his arrival.

A true gentleman, he allowed her to use the bathroom first, and now she had ample opportunity to listen to his nightly ritual, complete with humming, tooth brushing, and running water. The man made enough noise for everyone here.

She squeezed her eyes shut trying to figure out exactly the point where she ended up waiting for Logan to join her in bed with no intention of having sex with him. In fact, she shouldn't be waiting. They should have run in here and thrown their clothes off and done the deed.

No. Again, she needed her own dose of reality. The man was created to be alluring. How many times did she have to be reminded how he would break her heart? Hell, if it weren't for him, she would be engaged.

No, she wouldn't.

After dinner, in keeping with their family tradition, they all made their way out on the patio for dessert, drinks, and music. In a strange moment, her mother and Logan redecorated the cake, or more accurately, stripped it free of its engagement embellishments, all after having served a meal that left her wanting to lick her plate. Since when did the bad boy of Hollywood, the one solely responsible for destroying the sequel to her most beloved movie, learn to cook?

The door clicked open, and she caught sight of him in a pair of lightweight navy pajama bottoms and a matching tight T-shirt. Double damn her for leaving an accent light on for him to navigate his way to the bed. She practically laid out a trail of bread crumbs.

"Well, isn't this cozy?" He peeled off his shirt.

Though she tried not to look, there was no choice. He presented her with a perfect chest to match the rest of him. Smooth, wide, a perfect landscape to dig right in. She ground her teeth together. The last person her teenage self would have thought she would truly be in bed with on a warm Palm Springs evening at her grandfather's home was Logan Alexander. Or was this the moment she had dreamed of?

The last few weeks upped the strange ante of the evening to surreal, but having Logan on her home turf amplified her foolish behavior.

He pulled the ponytail out of his hair and slipped into bed. "Shall I turn off the light?"

"Sure." Heat overtook her. They didn't call her clothes sweats for nothing.

The bed bounced as he turned off the light and got comfortable. "Are you all right? Can I get you anything?" He patted her arm.

Even through the thick fabric she made out his searing touch and she tensed. Of course he wanted to get her something, and they were in the perfect place for that special something. Honestly, she wanted to blame the entire situation on Logan, accuse him for manipulating the situation to such a point that she had no choice but to bring him along, but she made it all too easy for him to get here. With her mother glowing and declaring them together and her sister seething, there wasn't any way she could go sleep on the couch. In an abrupt move, she turned over with her back to him.

They lay in silence for several minutes, and she balled her hand in a fist. Only men could sleep through anything. There was no way she would sleep. Between the outfit and Logan, the room had to be over 100 degrees.

"So, I am going to assume that the answer to my question is no. No, you would not like me to get you anything, and no, you are not all right." Logan turned over and put his hand on her shoulder. "If the issue is us in the same bed, trust me if I'm not one hundred and ten percent certain you want me, I'd never touch you."

The issue wasn't not wanting him—it was wanting him too badly. With too many questions building like the heat through her body, she flipped over. "What do you want?"

Without a word, he took her into his arms.

"What are you doing?" Though she didn't resist, she put one hand on his chest in a sad mock show of defiance, but she gained the opportunity to take in his smooth, tight skin.

"Answering your question. I want to hold my lady in bed." He pulled her closer.

"Your lady?" What did he mean? His arms suffocated her, but she couldn't leave. Instead she gasped for air.

"Yes." He rubbed her back. "In case you're wondering, in my definition of the word, it's not an English title."

She refused to react, refused to acknowledge how her stomach fluttered, refused to take in the scent of his soap. "What do you want, Logan?"

"For someone with enough smarts to earn multiple degrees, I thought I made my intentions very clear." His breath brushed against her lips. "I want you."

"Logan." Unsure if she wanted to slap him or grab him, she opted for feeling his chest again. How could he want her? "When you were a teenager, what did you want?"

"A motocross bike and a naughty magazine." He let out a

laugh.

"You don't understand." She shook her head.

"Yes, I do. What I'm trying to tell you is the boy that wanted a bike and naked pictures is not the same man who met a woman and now wants her." He moved her bangs off her forehead. "The girl who saw a character in a movie and had a crush is not the same as the woman who met a man years later."

Could she let go and be with him and not worry every time he wasn't in her sight? "What's your fantasy, Logan?" All her cards were faceup on the table. He knew everything, and they needed to even the odds.

"Not Erin, if that's what you're worried about."

"Logan."

"I want to kiss you until neither of us can breathe, and then I want to take my time and explore every inch of you until you're writhing beneath me. Then, I want to make love to you until you have no choice but to dig your nails into my back and scream." He took her chin in his hand.

The heat amplified, but her mind yelled out a warning. Sex. He wanted sex with her when he could have anyone. His definition of lady and hers weren't the same after all.

"But that's not my fantasy." He lowered his voice.

She held her breath.

"Then, I want to do it the next day and the next, until I lose count of the days." He pulled her flush against him.

"Start today, right now." All her strength left, but her heart grew along with the desire that followed Logan everywhere, and she wrapped her arms around his neck and kissed him.

He tightened his hold and continued to kiss her, alternating between soft, sweet kisses and deep ones filled with passion.

Even in the dark, she shut her eyes, allowing the sensations Logan created throughout her body with a simple kiss to engulf her. She caressed his back, his arms, and his shoulders, taking in the way his muscles flexed beneath his skin.

With a moan, he slid his lips to her neck giving her a series of openmouthed kisses down to her collarbone. His hands wandered, traveling over her hips, down to her legs, and then over her breasts, teasing and taunting her on the outside of the too thick fabric of her shirt.

Craving more, she squirmed under his touch, trying to direct him to what she really wanted.

Rather than give in, he returned to her lips, kissing her, taking his time to tangle their tongues, run his fingers through her hair, move against her.

The heat from earlier burned. Every bit of her seemed enflamed, and she broke out into a sweat and gasped for air. "Oh, God, I'm hot."

"I know it, baby." He went to connect their lips once more.

She kicked the covers off. "No, this shirt, these pants."

"I was getting there." He pushed her back on the bed, straddled her hips, and snaked his hands up the bottom of her shirt until he reached her breasts. "Yes."

The moment his fingers found her already tight nipples she sucked in her breath.

"I can't wait any longer to take a taste." He made a little noise of satisfaction and at last rid her of the torture device, her clothes.

The cool air helped her temperature, but once Logan lowered his face to her chest, the heat rose again. He paid equal attention to each of her breasts, massaging, tasting, and flicking his tongue over each tight peak. With agonizing slowness, he slipped her pants down and used his foot to fling them off the bed, leaving her in nothing but her panties. "Logan."

He moved to one side and silenced her with a kiss, while his hand slid between her thighs.

She held her breath. No doubt he felt the extreme reaction she had to him.

"Now that is hot." He crushed his lips to hers and snuck his fingers inside her panties.

With each passing minute, her arousal amplified, coaxed purposely by the man in bed with her. She needed him now. For what seemed like eternity, he would give her a bit of satisfaction, only to take the relief away, leaving her panting for more no matter how she tried to contort her body to take a little extra.

Even in her state, she managed get her panties off and to move to her side to take her turn to reciprocate. Never before had the simple act of touching a man thrilled her to such a level, but with Logan everything was different. Again, she took in his chest, but then delved lower to his stomach, to the waistband of his temperature-appropriate pants, and finally, inside.

No underwear gave her instant access to what she witnessed as only an oversize bulge in his pants. Solid, thick, and pure man, he lived up to everything she had already envisioned. She treated him to a few soft caresses.

He moaned and took his pants off. While she tended to him, he kissed down her arm and back up to her mouth.

She couldn't take anymore and, trying to give him the hint she was more than ready to make love, returned to her back and opened her legs, the universal sign to any man with an erection. In fact, the point of longing had passed and discomfort was fast coming up on her. "Logan."

He answered by palming one breast and nipping at the other.

"Logan." She arched her back, and he reached between her legs again, lightly circling her most sensitive bundle of nerves with his fingertip. "Please."

"What?" He dipped a finger inside her.

Her heart accelerated, every part of her seemed sensitized, and she had to resist pulling him on top of her. "Make love to me, now."

Instead of giving in to her, he kissed her once more and abruptly flipped over and hung over the side of the bed.

"Logan!" What the hell? She pounded her fist into the mattress.

"One second, baby."

At the distinctive crinkle of a condom wrapper, she took a breath. She scratched her nails down his back and leaned up to kiss his arm.

"Damn, I want you." He turned over and gave her a long

kiss as he got her on her back and moved on top of her. Without any more delay, he entered her in one smooth, gentle motion.

"Oh." She grabbed his shoulders and bit her lip. Though her body stretched to accommodate him, she obtained the sheer gratification in being filled.

He lowered his face to the crook of her neck. "Perfect."

She practically purred.

As with his foreplay, he never rushed, choosing instead to lavish attention on her in every way possible, with his mouth and hands, while he made love to her. He found his momentum with slow, even strokes down where he would add the extra pleasure of rubbing his hips to hers, and then a torturous egress where she writhed to have him deep inside her.

Though he set the pace, she moved with him, kissed him, and fondled him in return. The yearning he created by simply being him and being here with her built in intensity. She needed more and wrapped her legs around his waist.

"Like that." He hissed and sped up. His thrusts came a bit harder, his kisses more erratic.

Her body's demand swelled, her carnal need consuming her as he inched her closer and closer to her release. "Logan."

"Come, baby." His voice enticing and tempting. "Let go for me."

She wanted to obey and tensed. Her climax was right there, almost, and she had to have it. "Please."

"Let go." As if sensing her need, he drove into her.

One hard thrust finally sent her careening over the edge. As the most exquisite rush of ecstasy and bliss took over every part of her, she held on to him for dear life for fear she would float away. "Logan!"

Without a word, he continued, propelling into her. "Baby." He reached back and pulled her leg up farther. "Damn."

At last, he lost control, and shook, plunging his body to hers at a rapid rate.

She moved his hair back from his face, wiped away the sweat on his forehead, and made sure to move with him to give him maximum enjoyment. The sheer act of watching him get closer and closer and knowing he used her body to get there served to arouse her. "Come on, Logan."

He shut his eyes as his body trembled. "So good."

"You're there." The sounds of their bodies connecting echoed through the room.

His body stiffened as he throbbed inside her. "Ah!" He let out a yell, pulled back, and thrust once more, repeating the action twice more before lowering himself on top of her. "Oh, God."

They held each other, and he ground his hips in a circle as he settled down.

"Um." She scratched her nails down his back, and her breath quickened with her desire growing. "Don't stop." Until the words left her mouth, she didn't realize how close she was to another orgasm.

"Come again." He pressed down even harder.

"I can't." Though she couldn't stop.

"Yes, you can." He remained embedded deep within her. "Take your time and let me feel it."

Her body belonged to Logan. Beyond her control, the ripples reverberated through her body once more. Her breath caught and she leaned up.

"That's perfect." He held her while the pulses morphed into a warm afterglow, leaving her weak, but satisfied.

Without a word, he swept his mouth across hers and moved off the bed.

Once more, she listened to Logan in the bathroom, but rather than irritating her, she smiled.

He returned to the bed and scooped her up in his arms. "Come here."

"I'm right here." She cuddled up to him and rested her face in the crook of his neck.

"Doesn't feel close enough." He pulled the covers up over them. "I don't need to state the obvious and tell you that was incredible."

She laughed and tried to move closer. "What do we do now?"

"We're going to live out my fantasy." His voice came out

heavy with sated exhaustion.

"What's that?" Though the woman who made love to Logan wasn't the girl who hung his posters on her wall, he lived up to his reputation on both counts.

"Do it again until we forget how many times we've done it and then do it some more." He combed his fingers through her hair. "I can hardly wait until we get through this godforsaken project and the anniversary is behind us and we can just live our lives. The only good it's done is bring you to me."

Logan settled down, and she lay awake rewinding his words. More than ever she needed to find out the truth about what happened all those years ago if they were going to be together until they lost count of the days.

CUT TO:

EXT. CONVENIENCE STORE - AMARILLO, TEXAS - DAY

The heat is killing them. They stop at a convenience store for something to drink and for ROXY to use the ladies' room.

> CHARLES
> At this rate, we'll never make it back by Sunday night. We aren't even close to being there.

WILLIAM holds up map.

> WILLIAM
> No look, Texas, New Mexico, Arizona, California. If we take two states a day, we'll be there by tomorrow.

> CHARLES
> Texas is huge. You don't just drive across it. You can't count states. You have to count miles.

> STEVEN
> Charles is right.

With wide eyes, CHARLES stares at STEVEN.

> CHARLES
> I am?

STEVEN pats CHARLES on top of his head.

                    STEVEN
          Yes, you are. You need to
          count miles and then you
          need to have a contingency
          plan. None of us ever
          planned for any delays or
          emergencies.

CHARLES puts his hand to his head.

                    CHARLES
          Oh my God, I made a
          mistake. What if something
          happens?

                    STEVEN
          I suppose we just have to
          wait and see.

Chapter Twelve

She had sex with Logan Alexander.

Really amazing, mind-numbing, multiple-orgasm-type sex.

Not only did Ivy have sex with him, she had sex with him multiple times and in multiple locations. The ride from Palm Springs back to Los Angeles would never be the same.

On top of everything, pun intended, he spent the following night at her place, and rather than using her name, he decided to call her babe, baby, or his lady the whole time. Privy to the fact Logan, or her guy, cooked, she wrangled him to make breakfast, and then they christened her shower.

Only after Logan had left her apartment to get some camera-worthy clothes did she really reflect on all that had happened and still she couldn't wrap her head around it. Her stomach twisted as she relived some of the highlights. Not only had she practically begged her teen dream to make love to her the first time, but she even allowed him to pick out her outfit for the broadcast.

She glanced down at the little early 1980s alternative-styled outfit with skintight black pants and a fitted tweed blazer, showing a work-appropriate amount of cleavage. But then she shivered with another realization.

If she were sitting here in her office rewinding every moment with Logan, what was he doing? Was he recalling her making some weird orgasm face? What if, besides the begging, she had made a strange noise? Did she do something that maybe wasn't a turn-on?

Adrenaline coursed through her, and she shot up out of her desk chair and put her hand over her mouth.

"Did the footage of your last interview spook you?" Julia entered her office with Craig at her heels.

"Julia." Craig's tone let out a halfhearted warning.

"What? I just want my assistant back." Julia motioned toward her.

Right now would be the perfect time for Logan to show up with one of his lines. A quick glance at the time told her Logan was running late, or maybe he'd decided he needed to get a better gig. In all the research she had conducted on him, he had never been linked to any woman. He always said he didn't get the girl, but maybe he ditched the girl instead.

"I got the first interview where Erin Holland spoke about *Hollywood Stardust*." She focused on Craig. Something had to be said for the mention of Drew and the confirmation of the off-set love triangle everyone speculated about, though the thought of Logan and Erin together wanted to make her ill.

"You did well." Craig squeezed past Julia.

Ivy exhaled.

"I need you to dig a little deeper." He put an art board on her desk.

"I would have had all the questions out there by now." Her nemesis put her hands on her hips. "Are you too scared to ask what the world wants to know?"

"There is something to be said for letting the story unfold. What about some buildup? We have plenty of time." She glanced down at the graphic. "Between the Vines?"

"That's the name of your show." He cleared his throat. "The art department made an animated version of it."

"My show?" She stared at the black piece of cardboard with the name of her show written in ivy tendrils.

"You need to get Ryder right away, no more delays." Craig leaned over. "I need you to push, Ivy, really push. You can make or break it now."

Julia crossed her arms. "Now she's getting a show? She does a handful of interviews without running off set and she gets her own show?"

She propped up the art on her computer, hoping Logan arrived with enough time to show it to him. Where was he anyway? She couldn't lose. Since Logan entered her bed, her mind was cluttered, but she also knew that no matter what, she had to get to the bottom of all the mysteries surrounding him. The Logan who spoke of losing count of days with her and the Logan who played the sharp-edged mouthpiece for the movie were two different people.

"She has a few more weeks before the anniversary, and the show needs some consistency." Craig tapped the art board.

"Thank you." Once more, she stared at the piece, the sensation weighing her down in the pit of her stomach. Not because of Craig or Julia or her job, but because of Logan's obvious tardiness.

"Your numbers are up." He finally smiled. "People like you with Logan. They like the banter and the fact you're a fan of the movie."

"At last, the public has some taste." Logan's voice interrupted the conversation.

She took a breath before turning to catch sight of the man who matched the voice. Damn, if he didn't make her heart and everything else flutter. He wore a pair of dark jeans and a sky-blue button-down and entered still wearing his sunglasses.

Craig turned. "Mr. Alexander."

"Pardon me." He glanced at Julia and didn't even bother acknowledging Craig as he made his way around to her side of the desk.

Her breath caught. They never really spoke about how to act in her office, but with the way she needed to grab on to the edge of the desk to keep standing, she knew she wouldn't refuse if he kissed her. Of course, he didn't acknowledge her either.

"They made a graphic for the show." She pointed behind her, not sure if she was upset or relieved there was no kiss or anything else.

He nodded. "At least they didn't do a play on your initials, but the vine reference is pretty obvious."

"Mr. Alexander." Craig tried to get his attention.

"Please don't interrupt when I'm studying something

important." He stared at the graphic a bit longer and straightened up. "Now, what is it?"

"You're almost late for your broadcast." Craig tapped his watch.

"It's not like they're going prime time." Julia spoke through clenched teeth. "My numbers are still larger."

"Almost is only good in horseshoes and hand grenades." He sat down in her desk chair. "I guess that could also apply to your other reporter there. She almost got the gig. Thank God that was 'almost' averted."

Well, at least Logan came through with his line for Julia.

"I need to prep for my report, now that I don't have anyone to help me with research or scheduling anymore. I guess I'll do everyone's job." Julia spun on her heels and walked away.

"I don't know what the fuss is over. She didn't take advantage of Ivy's skill set." Logan rocked the chair back.

Craig crossed his arms. "Speaking of which, we're hoping for some more meaty interviews."

"Good. The next interview Ivy and I do will be at a steak house." He chuckled. "If you don't mind, I need to talk to my cohost alone before the broadcast."

Her throat constricted at his words. In an attempt to show no reaction, she bit the inside of her mouth.

"All right, you have about five minutes." Shaking his head, Craig left.

She faced Logan, wanting him to spit out whatever he had to say.

"May I?" He reached for the bottle of water on her desk.

Almost beyond her control, she nodded.

Without saying a word, he reached into his pocket and took out a tiny plastic bag full of white capsules.

"Logan?" She balled her hand in a fist. The night at his brother's restaurant she had spied a similar bag. One that he had scurried away rather fast.

Right as he opened his mouth, a buzzing from his other pocket interrupted them.

In all the time they had spent together, she had never heard his phone do anything. He retrieved his phone out of his pocket, held up one finger, and answered. "Yes." After he took two pills out of the bag, he popped them in his mouth and swallowed with a swig of her water. "Yeah, I wanted to make a quick drive-by, but I ran out of time, between getting a late start and having to get to my so-called job."

Well, she supposed she was sorry for being a time waster. Last time she checked, he had joined her in the bathroom for a little fun.

Still speaking into the phone, he strummed his fingers on the desk and looked over at her. "Yeah, I need some more of my fix. Come by tomorrow. I have enough to get me through today."

With narrowed eyes, she stared back. Who the hell was on the phone?

"I need to run. See you tomorrow." He furrowed his brow and hung up. "Everything okay over there?"

It took great effort not to look at the baggie full of capsules. Maybe part of her was in denial, but she didn't want to believe he had any sort of issue in that arena, at least not anymore.

"Ivy." He stood and returned everything to his respective pockets. "I am going to ask you again, are you all right?"

"Did you call Ryder to set up that interview?" No way would she tell him her concern and chose to redirect his question. "I don't want to lose my job now that they gave me a graphic and everything."

"Didn't I tell you only yesterday that I would be calling Ryder sometime today?" With a bit of swagger, he leaned back on the desk.

She shrugged. The statement sort of stuck in her mind. "I'm just nervous about being on set and interviewing Ryder."

"Did I not say that later tonight we would go to the bar and practice with Wilson?"

Well, for a man who was going to ditch her, they sure had a lot of plans together. "You did."

"Then why do you doubt me?"

Doubts seemed to round every turn with Logan.

"However, I can promise you that I will not call anyone or step one foot on any set until I get an answer to what's going on."

"I . . ."

Apparently, he wasn't in a rush now. He simply stood there tapping his foot waiting for her answer.

"I mean, like, I know you . . ." She huffed. Nothing she said would make any sense to him. "I don't know."

"I think I know." A smile grew across his face. "It's like the morning after."

"Logan." Sort of like avoiding looking at an accident or eclipse, she decided not to look directly at him.

He came over, standing right next to her. "I got caught up running an errand. I apologize if I was late."

"It's fine." Unable to meet his eyes, she decided to study his shoes.

He hooked his fingers under her chin and tilted her face up to his. "I went to the drugstore to make sure the two of us were well stocked, and after I made my purchase, I got to thinking about the last couple of days and got a little riled. By the time I walked in here, I contemplated throwing you over your desk and having my way with you, but there was an entire entourage of garbage in here. I didn't think it in your best interest to do this in front of everyone." He treated her to a soft but lingering kiss.

She held on to him, her body relaxing after getting the acknowledgment she wanted.

"So, I see my lady requires lots of reassurance," he whispered in her ear. "No worries. I'm up for the job."

"Speaking of jobs." Though it would be much easier and more satisfying to stay here with Logan, eventually they needed to get back to real life and get to the set.

"Yes, let's go report some *Hollywood Stardust* news." He motioned for her to walk ahead of him.

Yes, the news. The news she should be getting instead of kissing Logan and thinking about him. But with all the smooth words still came the doubts and questions. Her family went through the same thing with her grandfather . With stars it was sometimes hard to pry and ask the hard questions, but someone had to or it could end in tragedy.

"We have enough time between our broadcast and Logan's school for broadcast arts to test-drive what I bought at the drugstore." He winked. "Say, 'Yes, Logan, I would love to.'"

Like she had done many times, she turned and took him in. "Yes, Logan, I would love to." She might as well enjoy him while she had him. Somehow though, something told her she would be able to keep count of the days.

❧

"All right, babe, we have this all set up like the set if the set were decorated." Logan paused and guided her to one of the chairs. "Well, if it were decorated by me."

Ivy had worried about him not paying her enough attention at the office, but after their quick taping, where he had done most of the talking, he had let the floodgates burst forth.

After going by her apartment and test-driving his drugstore purchase, they went to the bar. He and Wilson set up their classroom, while she and Giselle caught up on some gossip. As a bonus, she now knew way too much about Wilson. She wished she knew as much about Logan's baggie of capsules.

He kissed her twice, held up one finger, and dashed over to Giselle. "You'll be our interviewee."

"I didn't act in *Hollywood Stardust*." Her best friend smiled at him.

Logan narrowed his eyes. He stared at Giselle and blinked a couple of times before answering. "While I thank you for clearing that up for me, this is just a practice round, you can pretend."

"Can I be Erin?" Giselle took her seat.

"If you like. There's nothing like getting into a role." Logan glanced over at Ivy.

She bit the side of her mouth not to crack up.

"Oh, then I'm a bitch." With a bounce, Giselle crossed her legs and faced her. "Isn't that what you called her?"

Before she could go in for the save, Giselle finished her off.

"No!" Her friend pointed at her. "You called her a hussy first and then a bitch."

Ivy put her hand over her mouth.

"What's a hussy?" Wilson called over.

"An immoral woman." Logan let out a laugh.

"No, she can't live forever. Ivy was trying to call her loose," Giselle clarified.

"*Immortal* is when you can live forever." Ivy's elementary school self bubbled to the surface, and she stomped her foot. "And you should talk—you slept with Wilson on the bar only two hours after meeting him. Twice!"

"And last night." Giselle giggled through her words.

Logan turned to his brother. "Is nothing sacred? You already defiled the nuts."

"Gee, I'm sorry. Gorgeous blonde with big boobs gets left here, we hit it off, and I'm not supposed to be with her?" Wilson motioned toward her. "To date, you have defiled Ivy's grandfather's home, your car, and the BMW because you knew Ivy wanted to make love in that car."

"They also did it in both our kitchens—at the apartment and the one here because Logan wanted to compare and contrast appliances." With a huge grin, Giselle nodded.

Silence took over the room, and they all looked at each other.

"For the record, the appliances here are better." Logan took his seat on the other side of her.

"That's because you picked them." The laugh Ivy held back before came to the surface.

They all cracked up. The language of couples was unique unto itself, a unique bond. Did she have it with Logan? For how long? What happened after Wilson's opening? Her chest tightened.

"Are you okay?" Logan grabbed her hand.

His touch jolted her out of a mini panic attack. "Yes."

"The way the color left your face tells me different." Taking her chin in his hand, he turned her toward him. "This is nothing to be nervous over."

She stared at his face. How on earth did anyone end up looking like him?

"I think it's time we start our lesson, but before that, there is something I must do." He leaned in and kissed her hard, opening his mouth and really giving her a good one.

In an instant, her mind hazed, and all her attention diverted to Logan's lips and what they did.

He pulled back and smiled, a little starburst practically flashing on his perfect teeth. "Now that you are focused, there are five rules to interviewing someone on camera."

Focused? If he meant focused on how bad she wanted him, she was a laser beam. "Five rules."

With his thumb, he wiped her lower lip. "Yes. Now, when you approach an interview with a celebrity, or someone who thinks they are a celebrity, they are not your ally. You're not playing for the same team. You have to keep your eyes and ears open for their tactics so you know how to proceed. Watch as I demonstrate."

They both sat up in their chairs, and he turned to Giselle. "Erin, on the set of your last movie, I was told you got in a fight with your leading man costar."

Giselle twisted to look behind her. "Erin's here?"

"Sweetheart, you were Erin." Wilson waved his hand.

"Oh, yeah." Giselle twisted back around. "Well, I'm a bitch, so of course I was in a fight."

Logan held his hand up to her. "Take a break and let me work with Ivy." He huffed. "I will interview you. Ivy, when you used to hang my posters on your wall, did you ever think about what would happen if we actually met?"

Her cheeks heated. "Logan, I was twelve."

"Were you always a fan of *Hollywood Stardust*?" He tilted his head.

"Since the day Giselle and I saw it in the theater." She nodded. "We stayed and saw it a second time."

Giselle clapped.

"You naughty girl." He moved his hair out of his eyes. "So, of all the stars, who was your favorite?"

"I was a sucker for the bad boy." Where was this going? "I suppose one could say that now I'm sleeping with him."

He raised his eyebrows. "Did you ever think you'd be doing that when you would gaze longingly at my posters on your wall?"

She opened her mouth, but had nothing to say.

"Oh my God, you answered anyway!" Giselle moved her chair closer.

"Lesson. You have nothing to be afraid of if you keep the tone conversational and ask the questions naturally. I used two techniques there. First, I redirected you into talking about what I wanted you to talk about. Second, I prodded you until I got the answer." He lifted his chin.

Redirect and prod. She nodded.

"Wilson, move the camera so Ivy can see it." Logan motioned behind him, and Wilson moved the tripod.

She faced her tormentor, the lensed demon.

"Unless you are directed to break the fourth wall, never look at the camera. Look at the person you are interviewing. In the case of reporting, pretend that lens is an eye." He leaned in. "You're one of the smartest and strongest women I know, if not the smartest and the strongest. I've watched you fight for what you want and win. That camera has nothing on you. You stare it down and make it your bitch. Do you understand me?"

His words wrapped around her, enveloping her in strength. No one ever explained it that way. They simply told her not to be scared.

"Pretend the camera is Erin," Giselle whispered.

"Ivy, you have an interesting background. While you were growing up, how did you handle being Curtis Raleigh's granddaughter?" Logan went on with his interview.

Wilson slid the camera closer.

She peeked over at it and back to Logan.

"Everyone wants to know what you have to say. They wouldn't have tuned in otherwise." Logan sat back.

"It's weird because so many people watched his movies and identify with his characters and they feel like they know him so they come at you with preconceived notions." She had wondered when he was going to ask about her grandfather, but if anyone understood, it would be Logan. "Even though I never met him, I always felt his presence, but still . . ."

"It always felt like something was missing?"

"Yes. I felt cheated."

Rather than prodding her, he sat and waited.

"I think that's why my mother went the stage route. She wanted to be connected to him, but a little distant. I think my wanting to go in film was my way of being closer to him." She shrugged.

"Maybe then part of the stage fright is fear of failing him."

Pressure built behind her eyes, and she looked down at her lap.

"I think no matter what, he would have been really proud of you." Logan leaned in, took her hand, and kissed it.

Giselle sniffed. "That was the best interview ever."

Interview. Right, they were play-acting.

"Ivy." Logan lowered his voice. "Are you all right?"

Still digesting her revelation about her grandfather, she nodded.

With her hand in his, he led her over to the bar and got her some club soda, even bothering to put a lemon wedge on the edge of the glass. "I didn't expect the interview to go quite that deep, but along with learning about the magnificent woman in front of me, I wanted to teach you about getting to your subject's soft side, asking direct questions, and even using silence to get your guest to continue talking."

"I think I needed it. In all these years, I never thought about my grandfather that way." She took a sip of the bubbling water she had come to like quite a bit. Logan seemed to use it as an elixir anytime things got rough. "Why is this your go-to drink?"

He retrieved a glass for himself and took a drink. "You don't find it refreshing?"

"It's not that. It's just an odd choice. Did you always drink it?" The liquid did serve to cool her down. She plucked the lemon wedge off her glass and dropped it in Logan's.

"My mother always gave it to me to settle my stomach." With a tilt of his head, he lifted the glass.

She watched him watch the bubbles.

"When my mother was sick, I used to bring it to her." After a pause, he put the glass down.

They stared at each other.

"You are a quick study, my dear." He gave her a wink.

Well, they both seemed to open up today. She tapped her glass against his. "To your mother and my grandfather, something tells me they are both proud."

"Come here." He leaned over the bar and kissed her. "I think I need to call Ryder, and I also wanted to ask you to come here for lunch tomorrow and meet my friend Isaac."

"I would love that. Is there a reason?" Her lips grazed his as she spoke, and the tightness in her chest lifted. At least she knew who he had spoken to at the studio, and meeting the friend was a definite milestone.

"I just want to show you off." He treated her to another kiss.

If only this could be the first of many milestones.

HOLLYWOOD STARDUST

DISSOLVE TO:

INT. CAR — AMARILLO, TEXAS - DAY

They are driving, trying to make up some time.
CHARLES and ROXY are asleep in the backseat.

STEVEN hits WILLIAM'S shoulder.

>   STEVEN
> The check engine light
> just came on.

>   WILLIAM
> I think we should check
> the engine.

STEVEN pulls car to the side of the road.

>   STEVEN
> Sometimes, I think you're
> as smart as Chuck.

CUT TO:

EXT. CAR - DAY

STEVEN and WILLIAM get out of the car. STEVEN
opens the hood and steam erupts from the
engine. They both jump back.

>   WILLIAM
> The car is overheating.

STEVEN rubs his hand over his face.

>   STEVEN

                    I hate this trip! Nothing
                    ever goes as planned!

STEVEN kicks the fender.

The door to the car opens and ROXY steps out
and stretches.

                    ROXY
               Is everything okay?

WILLIAM rushes over to her.

                    WILLIAM
               Totally fine. We are just
               having a minor car mishap.

                    STEVEN
               Don't lie to her!

STEVEN kicks the car once more and joins them.
                    STEVEN
               There's no need to
               sugarcoat this because
               she's Roxy and she's
               fragile.

STEVEN stares ROXY down.

                    STEVEN
               We are stuck in the middle
               of nowhere with an
               overheated car and no help
               in sight.

ROXY reaches up and presses her hand to
STEVEN'S cheek.

                    ROXY
               Thank you.

                    STEVEN
          (Relieved.)
                For what?

                    ROXY
          Not lying.

Chapter Thirteen

"Ivy's favorite is raspberry, and she has a little bit of a sweet tooth." Logan topped his sorbet with fresh raspberries and a mint leaf and put the filled glasses back in the freezer. "Also, I noticed she doesn't like raw tomatoes, so I didn't put any in the salad."

"How did you notice that?" Isaac reached for a raspberry.

"Notice what?" Logan swiped his dish of berries away from his friend. He meant to put them up in his place later and feed them to her. They hadn't christened his bed yet.

"Tomatoes and her lack of like."

"Well, at her parents', she put them on the edge of her plate, and when we stopped for dinner on our way back, she left them untouched. Then yesterday at lunch she pierced the tomato wedge and put it on my salad." A warm feeling encompassed him, the same one he got when his sheets were freshly dried on a cold night. Little things like knowing about the tomatoes built a connection to the other person.

"So you are at the point in your relationship where you share vegetables?" Isaac asked.

He went to the oven and checked his chicken. "She doesn't care for extra things on her plate. The tomato, the lemon, the parsley, the piece of kale. When we went out to get some groceries after . . ." He stopped talking and let his brain catch up to his mouth. After their lessons, they went back to her apartment and decided the drugstore items definitely needed further investigation. "Because we were starving. We got some iced tea, and she dropped her lemon slice into my drink, and she did the same thing when I tried to give her some with her club soda."

"Oh, I get it, you are the human garnish disposal." His friend burst out into a round of laughter.

Once he dubbed the chicken perfect, he turned down the heat, crossed his arms, and faced Isaac. "Well, I guess I'll suffer since no one ever lasted long enough to give me their garnish before."

The smile faded from Isaac's face. "I know. No one ever lasted long enough to have you want to show off before."

"I know I sort of sprang this meeting on you." He went to the refrigerator and grabbed some small grape tomatoes. "You cool with this?"

"I look at it this way." Isaac gave him a thumbs-up. "With her background and standing next to you, if she doesn't connect who I am, I know I passed the test."

"What if she puts the dots together?" He put some tomatoes on the salad.

"I think if you care enough for her that you are putting those tomatoes on so she gives them to you, she would be the type of person I could explain my situation to." Isaac plucked one of the tomatoes off the salad and popped it in his mouth.

"I agree." He nodded. Though given the task of finding out about Drew and the sequel, something told him if he asked her to keep certain things private, she would. They were a couple.

A couple.

At the thought, he stared straight ahead, only to be jostled by a knock at the back door. "I should get her a key." He sprinted over and opened the door.

The afternoon sun backlit the other half of his couple. "My lady." He took her hand and guided her inside. The sweet coral-colored circa 1950s dress with a flared skirt fit her figure to perfection. "You look lovely."

"So do you." She giggled.

Not wanting to make the same mistake as yesterday at her office, and needing to taste her coral-colored lipstick, he bent down and gave her a bit more than a peck. "Delicious." He straightened up and motioned toward Isaac. "Ivy, I would like you to meet one of my closest friends, Isaac Abrams. Isaac, this is Ivy."

Isaac held his hand out. "Apparently, in order to hang with Logan, your name has to start with *I*."

In search of any reaction, he kept his focus on Ivy and held his breath.

"Then thank God my parents didn't go with Wisteria or Hydrangea." She flashed Isaac a smile and shook his hand.

Both she and Isaac laughed.

He exhaled, pulled out the stools from underneath the kitchen island, and returned to the stove. "Well, the two of you get the chef's table for lunch, so have yourselves a seat while I get the food."

"Let me help." Ivy came up behind him.

Help? No one ever offered. Most anyone he cooked for sat while he served, but together they got his meal on the table and it was a welcome change of pace.

At last, they joined Isaac.

"So you and Logan are tearing it up online." Isaac dug into his food.

"Maybe just a little ripping." Ivy picked the grape tomatoes off her salad and, without a word or permission, snuck them onto his plate.

He swallowed, the whole action riling him up a bit, and he couldn't stop from staring at her profile.

Isaac coughed to cover a laugh. "What's the most interesting thing you've done so far?"

"I loved taking a ride in Logan's car and going to see the movie with him." She quickly glanced at him and then back to her plate, eyeing her next victim, the grilled green onion he put near her chicken. "Are you a fan of the film?"

Logan noted she didn't mention meeting Erin, but then again she thought the woman was a bitch, and he wondered what she would think of Ryder later this week. Either way, he had to wonder what she would think if she knew she was having lunch with the elusive Drew Fulton.

He tore his gaze away from Ivy long enough to glance at Isaac. They rarely spoke about the film. It wasn't the best time for his long lost costar.

"It's been a long time since I've seen it, but I'll say it was interesting." His friend lifted the onion on his plate. "Didn't you study the film for your degree?"

He returned his attention to Ivy.

"I finished my master's thesis on films that changed their generation." She scooped the onion up on her fork.

He held his breath.

"You never wanted to go on and get your doctorate degree?" Isaac asked.

With her fork in midair, she answered. "I thought about going on, but I wanted to work in the industry."

"Well, I predict that soon all entertainment will be on the Internet." Isaac nodded.

"That's the forecast." In one smooth move, she smuggled the onion over to his plate.

"Look!" Logan yelled.

"Logan!" She dropped her fork. "What?"

"I'm sorry." Not meaning to scare her, he caught her hand.

Isaac cracked up.

"What's wrong?" With wide eyes, she looked at him.

"Ivy." He took her other hand. "I need to tell you something."

"What is it?" She furrowed her brow. "Logan?"

He leaned in to her ear. "I like the way you put your garnishes on my plate."

"Are you talking about sex?" she whispered.

Isaac stood from the table and bent over in a round of silent laughter.

"Not quite. I'm talking about your tomato and your onion."

"Maybe we should save this conversation for later, then we can experiment." Her voice lowered even further.

Well, one thing he adored about Ivy was her willingness to be a little experimental. "I was talking about food and the way you put your tomato and your onion on my plate."

"You like that?"

Isaac straightened up and returned to his seat.

"Yeah, only couples do that."

"Oh." A smile took over her face, outshining her already reddened cheeks, and she returned to her plate but scooted her seat a little closer to him. "Does that mean you would rather me not give my garnishes to anyone else?" Without skipping a beat, she took a bite of her meal.

The direct question. He had to give it to her for heeding his lessons and going for what she wanted. "I think we should only share our dishes between us. Does that sound all right?"

"Especially since your cooking is so delicious." She tilted her head and peeked over at him.

"Eat up and enjoy." He winked.

"So." In an abrupt move, she turned back to Isaac.

"I swear I wasn't trying to even look at your garnishes." Isaac held both hands up. "Now if Logan would have served like an edible flower or something, it would have been a game changer."

"Well, Mr. Abrams, now that you know probably more about me than you wanted, are you going to tell me what you do?" Rather than slipping an errant piece of food on Logan's plate, she reached down and put her hand possessively on his thigh.

As strange as it seemed, he was never the man who had the woman at the table. Somehow he was destined to be the one who watched others, but for the first time, he got the girl and a spectacular one at that. Everything about her amazed or enticed him, especially their private conversation they had in front of his friend and how she seamlessly went back to her other conversation as to not make Isaac feel uncomfortable.

"Logan didn't tell you?" As if he were telling a secret, Isaac cupped his hand over his mouth. "I own a laboratory."

"A laboratory?" She used one nail to trace the inseam of his jeans, down to almost his knee and then up to his midthigh. "Like with beakers and Bunsen burners?"

"I even wear a white coat." His friend puffed his chest out. "It's a lab plus a small, boutique manufacturing plant."

"What do you manufacture?" Her fingernail traveled up and down its chosen path again.

Between talk of garnishes and her passive yet sensual

attention, his body reacted. Wanting to lead her up the right path, he spread his leg slightly.

"Nutraceuticals." Isaac dropped the word that usually no one understood.

"Oh, like nutritional supplements?" Ivy took direction well and raked her fingers a little higher, discovering almost instantly what he wanted her to find.

"Yes, I am fascinated by all-natural remedies. It is amazing what we haven't tapped into what nature provides for us."

"I agree." Without a hitch, she continued the conversation.

He stifled a moan as she brazenly ran her hand over him, and he put his hand on her back, treating her to a more PG-rated massage.

"Exactly." Isaac beamed at her. "In fact, I can tell you two secrets about your chief chef."

"Really? Do tell. I have a few of my own." She rubbed her hand over his every contour.

He shut his eyes. All he wanted to do was get her up in his room and consummate their couple-ship. Though at first, he wanted to find out how far she would take it. He didn't think he could be aroused to this level with just some simple touching.

"First, Mr. Alexander invested in my laboratory after I finished my doctorate program." Isaac's voice broke through his desire. "Second, I am his supplier of vitamins. In fact, I custom blend his myself."

"Really?" Ivy gave him a squeeze.

"Yes." Logan hissed. "Like that."

"I like to think I am the reason for his vitality." Isaac laughed.

"That's funny. I was thinking I might be the reason." She removed her hand.

"Ivy!" He gasped and opened his eyes, blinking several times to focus.

"Fine, she's the reason, but maybe she'll thank me for your stamina later." Isaac got out of his seat, walked over to his bag, and tossed him several baggies of his beloved white capsules. "I think I'll take a rain check on dessert. After committing to only share forks with one another, I think the two of you need to be alone to conduct your own experiments."

"Thank you." In no shape to stand, he pointed at the door. "I'll call you later."

"It was an amazing pleasure meeting you, Miss Ivy." Isaac shook her hand. "Feel free to swipe a couple of those vitamins from him. He says they give him plenty of energy." With one last wave, he let himself out the door.

They turned to each other, and as if acting with one mind, both left their seats.

In an instant, he pulled her into his embrace and crushed his lips to hers, backing her up to the far wall. His kiss was hard, deep, telling her how bad he needed her. "Why did you stop?" He tore open his jeans and snaked his hands up her skirt.

"Because we couldn't do this right in front of your friend." She twisted her fingers in his hair.

"I never wanted someone like I want you." Again, he kissed her.

Once more, her hand found him. With nothing in her way, she gripped him and gave him several satisfying strokes.

"Damn." No longer possessing any fine motor skills, he shimmied his wallet out of his back pocket and pressed it into her free hand. "I need to make love to you right now. I can't even get upstairs."

"I suppose those vitamins do work." She let go of him to get the condom.

"You work. You're my IV." He managed to get one chuckle out. "Hurry, baby, I'll make it up to you later."

"I'm just so relieved they're vitamins." She dropped his wallet to the floor.

Even in his sensitized state, he not only heard her words, he understood her meaning and he lifted his head. "What do you mean by *relieved*?"

"Nothing." She shook her head. "I've seen you with those baggies of pills before and wondered about them."

"Then why didn't you ask me?" The arousal fading fast, he pushed back. "They're not pills. They're vitamins. You would've known if you'd asked me."

Her complexion paled, and she pressed her lips together.

"Why would you be with me if you think I'm doing something like that?" He fastened his pants and turned his back to her. "Did you just expect it?"

"Logan—"

"I don't know why you would even want to be with me, let me drive you around, let me make love to you, if you thought I was sneaking drugs behind your back." He turned back around. "Hell, I'm so good I didn't even bother hiding my phone call yesterday. Who knows, maybe I only brought my friend here to throw you off the trail."

She wrapped her arms around her shoulders. "You don't understand."

"I know I'm not as smart as you. I don't even have a degree behind my name, let alone two, so why don't you explain it to me." Rage heated through him and he raised his voice.

"I . . ." Her breath caught and she swallowed. "I wanted my chance to be with you."

"What?" He stepped closer. "I must be stupid. What does that mean?"

Again, she didn't answer, only lowered her head.

"You didn't think this was going anywhere." He filled in for both of them. "You wanted your fun and were ready to go back to Mr. Reliable once the curtain closed on the anniversary party. What did you think? I would reveal some big secret if you mastered the trick to getting me hard?"

"You know, I don't think it's too difficult of a thing to master." Without looking at him, she collected her purse and walked to the door. "I think I should leave."

"You're smart. Do what you think is best." He ground his teeth together. "Don't forget we are meeting with Ryder this week. Aside from that, I assume I'm off the clock."

"How could I forget? That's the only reason you think I'm here." She slipped out the door.

He stood, watching the door close and hearing her car engine start. She proved to be no different than any other woman who wanted to add a notch to her bedpost with his name on it, but in a strange twist of fate, he wasn't the one driving away.

                                    CUT TO:

EXT. SERVICE STATION - AMARILLO, TX - DAY

The four wait for the verdict on the car.

                    CHARLES
          We're never going to make
          it back in time. We're
          using the whole week just
          to get there.

                    STEVEN
          That's not even the half
          of it. Who here wants to
          call home and tell them we
          failed?

CHARLES puts his hand to his head.

                    CHARLES
          Don't say the word *fail*.

                    STEVEN
          Why not? Everyone has to
          fail at some point.

                    WILLIAM
          Way to look at the bright
          side, dude.

                    ROXY
          Steven's right. We all
          have to fail sometime or
          how do we ever know if
          we've won?

Chapter Fourteen

At the beginning of the week, the idea of going up to the mountains with Logan to the location where Ryder was producing and directing his movie seemed really romantic.

Of course, the romantic notion also included Logan driving up the two-lane mountain road, then stopping for breakfast, and maybe taking in a little of the San Bernardino Forest. The area was rife with Hollywood history and used for location shootings for decades, including one of her grandfather's films.

Instead, she woke up before the sun rose and made her way alone with only the *Hollywood Stardust* sound track as her companion. First, it seemed fitting, but once the chart-topping, penultimate song boomed through her car stereo, the song where Steven and Roxy danced, the tears she refused to let fall for two days overcame her.

One second she was Logan Alexander's girlfriend. Though they had hidden the true meaning of their conversation with fruits and vegetables, the message was clear. The next, she not only let her dumb words about the vitamins escape, but as the cherry on top of Logan's sundae, she revealed she really never thought they would stay together.

The look on his face told her everything. Even he wasn't a good enough actor to hide his disappointment. If she wasn't stupid and hadn't doubted him, she would still have him.

As she finally made her way to the small main street in the mountain town, she stopped in a little clearing, pulled down her visor, and took a look in the mirror at her makeup-smudged face complete with blotchy complexion. She would forever go down in history as the woman who tossed Logan Alexander aside. Lest she forget, she could add to her list of accomplishments that she chose Logan over her steady and stable friend who somehow got the idea he should marry her, and she never even bothered to call.

Without second-guessing her next move, she dialed Matt.

"Hello," he answered on the second ring.

"It's Ivy." Poison Ivy. She grabbed her makeup bag out of her purse.

"I'm aware. I've had your number programmed in my phone since we sat together in undergrad chemistry."

"Matt." She wiped the smeared black mascara from beneath her eyes.

"I'm sure by now, you know the big fool I was going to make of myself in front of your family. Do you think we could not mention it?"

"But—" She fixed her eyes and added a bit of lip gloss.

"Please don't say you're sorry." He cut her off. "I wouldn't have wanted you to say yes because you felt you had to, and I'm glad I didn't get to hear you say no. In a way, your boyfriend did me a huge favor."

"He's not my boyfriend." Not anymore. She looked up to the ceiling and blinked. Matt didn't produce tears, Logan did, and she had no right calling Matt to make her feel better.

"Whatever. If you don't mind, I'm not quite ready for the 'we're still friends' line. I'll e-mail the files to you if you want to use them to help with your research."

"Thanks." She started the car and glanced at the directions Logan gave her.

"I have to get to work."

"Okay, I'll let you go." The phone went dead, and she continued her journey, making the final turn onto a dirt road.

Her car bounced over the uneven road, but with a little more force on her accelerator, she made it up the ledge, slamming on her brakes at the sight of Logan standing right there. She tried to remind herself Logan was the fantasy, part villain, part superstar all rolled into one scrumptious package. The only problem was that he was more magnificent in reality.

With a shake of his head, he guided her to a parking place under a tree, keeping up with her car the entire time.

Her heart sped to such a point she had no doubt she would pass out, but she managed to get the car in park. For a second, she waited to see if he would open the door for her, but out of the corner of her eye, she saw him standing there with his arms crossed.

She opened the door.

"The crew is already here." He jutted his jaw out. "I was waiting for you."

"I'm right on time." Her voice came out weak.

"Do you have everything you need?" He fired the question at her.

Fine, they had disposed of the niceties. "Give me a second to collect my things."

"Well, hurry, people are waiting. I want to get this done with and get out of here."

She grabbed her mess of a purse and got out of the car.

Even with his sunglasses on, she could tell he stared at her. Though she wanted to ask what was wrong, she knew the answer and simply stood without moving. She supposed flinging herself at him and asking him to forget what she'd said was also out of the question.

"Is that what you're wearing?" He tapped his foot.

His question came out more as an accusation. She licked her lips and swallowed. "I suppose so." After trying on about five different ensembles, she had opted for a high-waisted, black formfitting skirt with a white button-down, fishnets, and heels. Fine, she went for an outfit to show off any curves she possessed, hoping he would miss her. Maybe she was only good at getting him hard. Well, not anymore.

"Stay right there." He stomped to his car.

Logan opened the trunk, pulled out some fabric thing, and then went to the passenger side to grab something else. While she waited, one of her heels sank into the dirt below her. Fine, heels weren't the best option in the middle of a national forest, but they fit the outfit perfectly.

He returned and thrust a stack of papers to her. "Hold this for a moment."

"Shouldn't we get to Ryder?" She took the pile, glancing down at what appeared to be his mail.

"You don't need to be doing anything but what I say." He shook out the huge black piece of fabric and held it up to reveal a long black trench coat. "Put this on. It's much more appropriate."

Spring in Southern California wasn't exactly long black trench coat season, even in the mountains. Actually, she wasn't sure if any time in Southern California was long black trench coat season. She looked up at the clear blue sky. The birds literally sang around them in this little piece of wilderness. With him in his normal uniform of jeans and a button-down, she didn't think he feared for her getting chilly.

Apparently, he didn't even want to look at her, and not wanting to make any more of an issue, she allowed him to put the coat on her.

As she went to adjust her purse and his papers into the other hand, he took her purse, but notably did not take his items.

"I can't have you dropping things all over." He put her bag under his arm, slipped the garment over her, and came around her front where he proceeded to tie the belt, taking special note to cover her neck.

"Logan." In the lined coat a sick heat overtook her, made worse by the way he walked away the second she said his name.

"Come on." He pulled his hair out of his ponytail.

She followed, and he seemed to slow down enough for her to catch up.

"Take care of this." He put the rubber band on top of the mail.

While she wanted to drop everything and shoot the rubber band at him, again she chose to remain silent and not take in how his hair wafted around him as he walked.

In an attempt to prevent her heels from sinking into the ground, she tiptoed and let Logan lead her through some trees.

"There they are." A familiar, yet unfamiliar, voice greeted them.

Logan stopped at her side.

Ryder Scott.

Right in front of her stood Ryder Scott.

Her heels sunk, but for one shining moment, her troubles vanished.

Logan exuded gorgeous bad boy, but Ryder dripped Hollywood star. Dark, wavy hair framed a face that almost couldn't be real. Every angle, every line, every curve of his features were perfectly proportional, as if he were created from some master plan and not born like the rest of the human population. As a teenager, his dimples had caused more than a stir, but today, with a few years behind him, they served to accentuate a gleaming smile and equally sparkling deep blue eyes.

By now, she thought she was beyond being starstruck, but then again she never stood less than two feet away from Ryder Scott.

Tall, lean, and dressed in jeans and a red T-shirt, he closed the distance between them. "How are you?" He gave Logan a pat on the shoulder before turning to her with his hand outstretched. "Hello, I'm Ryder Scott."

A giggle escaped her throat. Yes, a full-fledged giggle with heated cheeks and everything. "I see that." She put her hand in his. "I'm Ivy Vermont."

"Ivy Vermont." He kept hold of her and put his other hand over hers. "Ivy and *I.V.*"

"I have already discussed her unique initials with her at length." Logan cleared his throat.

More like he said she was his IV. Rather than remembering that, she focused on Ryder.

"Maybe you discussed it, but I haven't quite scratched the surface yet." Ryder raised one eyebrow in her direction. "I have heard a lot about you."

"You have?" Though no one had told a joke, and she didn't really wanted to know what Logan had said recently, she giggled again.

"I suppose I don't need to ask if you know about me." He pulled her toward the chairs set up in a little clearing. "But I do have some new things that may surprise you."

Logan walked between them, causing Ryder to let go of her hand, and took the middle chair. "Come sit down, Ivy." He patted the chair next to him like he was calling his dog. "You look a little pale. Maybe you're coming down with something. "

With no choice left, she took her seat. She was only coming down with a case of wanting to slap Logan across the face.

"Hold on." Ryder held his hands up as if framing the scene. With a shake of his head, he took the empty chair, moved it to the other side of her, and sat down. "This is much better. Do you feel all right, Miss Ivy?"

The entire crew made their adjustments.

"I do feel as if I'm burning up." She lifted Logan's papers and used them as a makeshift fan.

"Do you think you have a temperature? Maybe we need to do this another day?" Logan thrust his hand onto her forehead. "You do feel a little warm."

She opened her mouth to protest.

"Of course she does, she's wearing the trench coat you insist on carrying with you everywhere like you're waiting for some monsoon." Ryder stood up and motioned for her to do the same.

She got up along with Logan.

"It's very cold out here in the wilderness," Logan noted.

"It's at least seventy-five out." Ryder wrinkled his nose and untied the belt. "You consider anything without room service the wilderness."

The coat opened, bringing with it a waft of cooling, soothing air. "Oh, that's better."

"Yes, much better." Ryder took the coat off her and returned it to its owner. "You have great style. Don't cover it."

She glanced between Ryder and Logan. While Ryder smiled, Logan glared at her.

"I think we should get to the interview." An emptiness took residence right in the center of her chest.

They all returned to their respective seats.

"Do you need anything in your bag, notes or anything?" Logan held her purse up.

"You told me to keep it conversational." Why he insisted on holding her bag when he wouldn't hold her hand was beyond her.

"You're right. I'll keep this just in case." He returned her bag to his lap and leaned over to Ryder. "I've been coaching Ivy. She suffers from stage fright."

"Logan." Well, until this moment, she was suffering from heartache and didn't have enough room for stage fright. Now that he mentioned it, she ground her teeth together.

Logan motioned forward. "You bugged me incessantly to get his interview for you, and I pulled many strings to block out this time with Ryder, so get to your questions."

Ryder pursed his lips.

"Fine." In an attempt to take a breath, she bought some time by fiddling with his paperwork.

"She likes to hold on to my paperwork." Logan nodded. "Get to work."

"Since when?" She turned to him. "Only two days ago it was garnishes."

"I thought you were interviewing Ryder." He sat back.

"Are you taking too many vitamins today?" Fine, she hit below the belt.

"Are you trying to imply something, Ms. Vermont?" Without even making eye contact, he countered. "If you are, speak up, and we'll address it right on camera."

"Why don't you speak, since you never gave me a chance to the other day?" She threw his papers to the floor. "Maybe we can use some of your techniques."

"There was no explanation needed. I think everything you meant was right out in the open. No subtitles necessary." At last, he turned and stared right at her. "What could you have said anyway? Didn't you say it all?"

"I'm not sure all of your personalities heard me." Her whole body shook. No way could she interview Ryder when all she wanted was to get away from Logan. "If you would have let me breathe, I would've told you that you were right. I am sorry about"—she stopped, not wanting to say anything that would end up on tape—"even hinting at that."

At last, he looked at her.

"And about the garnishes, I was scared. Maybe I'm too scared of everything, but let me tell you, it's terrifying when you get your dream. Where do you go from there? All I could think of was losing it." Taking a breath, she forced herself to keep going. "But I did, and I'm not dead. Score one for me."

"Ivy." He stood.

"Do the interview yourself. I'm done with all of it." Unable to turn and face the crew or Ryder, she walked straight toward the trees.

"You have my rubber band," he called after her.

She rolled the accessory off her wrist, stopped, pulled it out, and shot the damn thing away. At one point, she would have kept it for a souvenir, but he had already left her with a broken heart.

⁕

"You always were an ass when you weren't the center of attention." Ryder elbowed Logan. "Maybe you should go get your girlfriend."

"Maybe you should get her. Just follow the trail of bread crumbs and giggles." Logan kept his focus on the trees but lost sight of . . . well, lost sight of his girlfriend.

"Next time, rather than wrapping her up and giving her your overdue bills, just lift your leg on her to mark your territory." Ryder exploded into a round of laughter.

"It was never my bills that were overdue, lest we forget." He crossed his arms. "Plus, no matter if I fenced off my territory, you still honed in." Maybe his friend needed a little reminding of the past and the Erin fiasco.

"She understood us. Sucks being us sometimes, doesn't it?" Ryder shook his head. "All the questions, the speculation, the accusations. Erin didn't have an issue 'cause she was one of us. Plus, she was a good teacher."

"Well, everything I know about fashion I know from Erin." He tilted his neck from side to side, trying to stretch his tense muscles. Of anyone, his costar understood, but Ryder usually got the girl. However, neither of them got Erin. In his case, he was thankful.

"She gave the best lessons, with every piece of clothing she took off, she would tell us the designer." Ryder broke out into chuckles. "Every girl I'm with thinks I'm a god for knowing such things." Ryder's laughter died down to knowing chuckles.

They glanced at each other.

"So." Ryder leaned back on his heels. "Can I get my crew back to filming my movie?"

"Remember who helped finance your crew and your movie." He ran his hand through his hair, wishing for his rubber band. "Get them working and stop wasting my money."

"Well, in a way, your financing is my money recycled. Plus, I had other help financing. It's good to be me." Ryder patted him on the back. "If you're going to keep staring, I can get you a part as an extra."

"I need to do something." Since the door closed at his restaurant, he wanted to call her, see her, be with her, but he didn't want to explain himself and didn't want her questions. Again, he allowed something that happened twenty years ago to affect his life. If he didn't act, it could cost him Ivy for sure.

"I gather she delved a little too deep into stuff that isn't her business?"

"It would be her business if we were still actually together." Did he blow up because it gave him an excuse not to have to answer for what happened?

"Yeah, well, it's also my business, and Erin's business, which affects your business even more."

"I hate you, always have, always will." He rubbed his hand over his face. Everything he touched turned into a disaster. Maybe it was better if he let Ivy go and not get her in the middle of the mess. One day she could look back and maybe smile that she was with the guy from the movie she loved. As for him, he was done with women. He only wanted her anyway.

"Yep, one day we can talk about it in therapy or in a reality show." Ryder stepped in front of him. "But for now, go get your girl."

"No point." Why see her if he couldn't have her?

"Do you want her?" Ryder looked him in the eye.

Without pause, he nodded.

"Then you are missing the obvious solution to your problem."

"The last time you gave me a solution to a problem we ended up having to chase down three cameramen to get back one of your inconvenient private tapes." He raised his eyebrows. "I'm still scarred from watching you in the footage, and you still owe me for that one."

"You were the one who said you had to see what you were paying for." Ryder smiled the smile that made him famous, part innocent, part knowing.

"I'm looking at him."

"In a way, isn't it the other way around?" Ryder gave him a knowing nod. "No matter, you got an amazing deal."

More like ripped off. He exhaled. Where the hell was Ivy? Shouldn't she be coming out from the tree line about now saying she saw a bug or something?

"Even though you're an arrogant ass, I'll impart this tidbit on to you." Ryder returned to his side and put his arm around him. "Throw her a bone and then give her a boner."

Out of the corner of his eye, he took in the guy he hated, but his friend nonetheless. "That's your advice?"

"It's one of my better ones. Only good can come from here." Ryder motioned toward the front of his own jeans. "It gets everything moving again, releases endorphins and all that, creates a bond."

He continued to stare into nothing.

"Here's the deal. The clock is ticking. Your girlfriend is walking in stilettos through a forest with no purse and no sense of direction." Ryder reached into his pocket and held out some keys. "But this next tidbit is good for all kinds of bones. She's walking toward my cabin. Keep going straight."

If he went to get her, he had to have her back. He swiped the keys and went in the direction he had watched Ivy leave.

Once he got into the trees, he scanned the area. They really were in the middle of the wilderness, and he had allowed her to walk through here in heels without him. Some boyfriend he turned out to be. His chest tightened at the image of her traipsing about out here where there could be a bear or worse. "Ivy!"

Nothing.

Not knowing which way to take, he ran forward. "Ivy!" The blood coursing through his ears made it hard to hear. "Ivy! Where are you?" Maybe he needed to call a ranger. No, he had to be the one to find her.

"Ivy, please let me talk to you." He turned around once more. "At least let me get you out of the forest."

"I'll take you up on getting me out of here." Her voice echoed from the right, but something seemed off.

"Ivy?" He sprinted toward her voice to find her sitting on the forest floor with one shoe missing, a rip in that form-hugging skirt, and some leaves in her hair. "What happened to you?"

"I said I'm up for you getting me out of here, not for talking." She put her hand over her eyes.

"Ivy." He knelt down by her and picked a leaf out of her hair. After everything, he only wanted to take her into his arms. Somehow he had to fix them.

She flinched. "Don't touch me."

"Are you hurt?" He forced himself not to walk away, and at least give her a chance, give them a chance.

She shrugged.

"Are you scared?" He used her words on purpose.

After a pause, she lowered her hand. "I don't know. For the first time since I met you, I'm able to breathe."

What was she trying to tell him? She was better without him?

"I'd rather not breathe." She looked up at him through her lashes.

Unable to stop himself, he bent down and kissed her.

"I'm sorry." She wrapped her arms around him and whispered in his ear. "I should have come to you, but I didn't want you to be upset. My mother always said she wished someone had talked to my grandfather, but everyone was scared."

Her grandfather—he should have remembered how her family's situation was practically embedded into her DNA. "I shouldn't have let you walk out the door. It's only normal you're going to have questions. But promise to come to me, and I'll answer them. Don't assume the worst." He stared into her eyes trying to make sure she heard him and to send her a message. If they were as connected as he thought, she would absorb his words.

"I promise." She tickled her fingertips over his jawline.

"We need to get out of here. Ryder gave me the keys to his cabin. We can regroup." While part of him wanted to simply stay in their little woodsy retreat, he needed to make good on his promise of getting her out of there. He scooped her up, stood, and walked in the direction Ryder had told him to take. With a film crew nearby, they didn't need any errant cameraman taking any liberties.

She allowed him to carry her out of the forest. Her focus wasn't on her surroundings, but on him. The woman could arouse him with only a look. Once he spied the cabin, he sped up.

He leaned against the wall as he opened the door. "You know what's strange?"

"What?" Her gaze traveled over different parts of his face.

"The last few days without you I couldn't breathe, and now I can take a breath." He barely finished his sentence before she pulled him down.

They kissed, completely surpassing the slow, soft, playful tastes and heading straight toward an intense melding of their mouths. The couple of days apart melted away, and they landed back where they were before, but stronger, with more passion and a deeper bond. Still keeping hold of her, he got them inside, kicking the door closed.

As if needing to take him in, her hands traveled over him, skimming his shoulders, arms, and chest. Everywhere she touched left his skin electrified and aching for more. In turn, he slipped his hand up her skirt, rubbing over those sexy fishnet stockings, cupping her round bottom.

Lost in her and their reunion, he stumbled into the bedroom and got them both on the bed. Their hands and minds working in unison, they rid each other of the inconvenience of their clothes while they continued to kiss.

"Logan," she gasped.

He opened his eyes, the world around him hazy except for the woman writhing beneath him. "I need to make love to you." He skimmed his hand along the bed and found his wallet, flipping it open and retrieving one of the requisite condoms he kept at all times.

"No." She pushed him over to his back and crawled on top

of him. "I'm going to make love to you."

The sheer image of her on top enflamed him further. Unable to wait, he snuck the condom into her hand and grabbed her hips. "Now, baby."

She put her hands over his. "I said I'm making love to you."

No one ever took the lead with him. No one. Without moving his hands, he looked into her eyes. In the bedroom, he always played the role of director.

She slid up his body and skimmed her lips over his. "I promised myself that if we ended up back together, I would make love to you."

Though it would take all his strength not to take over, especially in his state, he swallowed and forced his hands under his head. "Make love to me."

At first, he closed his eyes, took in the way she kissed down his neck and over his chest, and relished in how she skimmed over his skin.

She worked her way lower, and he let out a moan when she took him in her hands. His flesh seemed tuned to respond to every one of her caresses and soaked up every bit of attention she doled out.

In a move he didn't anticipate, she took him into her mouth. Her warm, wet mouth overtook him, and he dug his fingers into the pillow the moment her tongue swirled over him. "Oh, man!"

All too soon, he found himself moving with her, the way she sucked, licked, and nibbled, a perfect combination. It would be easy to let go. Since their separation, he had been wound tight with emotion and pent-up arousal, but with her here with him, he had to have more. "Ivy."

She didn't let up. Instead, she brought her hands back into to play to edge him closer.

Any second he could easily go to the point of no return and he had to stop her. "Baby, please."

Still keeping hold of him, she straddled his hips and didn't delay in sheathing him with the condom. At last, he opened his eyes in time to take in the most glorious sight of her up on her knees, followed by lowering her body down upon him.

Nothing in the world compared to being inside her, except

for maybe the way the sun came in through the window, giving him the perfect lighting to watch her do as she wanted and make love to him. "God, you're beautiful, baby. Lean back a little." He lifted his knees.

She bit her lip, but did as he requested and gave him the most exquisite view of her breasts bouncing every time she impaled herself on him.

His gaze traveled from her face to her body to the area where they were joined, and he couldn't take his focus off watching her engulf him, relishing in the way he disappeared deep inside her. "Faster." The throb began, the distinctive pleasure-filled burn that resonated through him as his need climbed, his climax on the horizon.

Again, she obeyed, but added gyrating her hips to his to stoke her own desire. "Um." She took hold of his leg to use him as leverage, yet her rhythm wavered as she prepared for her own release.

"That's right." His breath quickened and he swelled—any second he would have to let go. Not waiting for permission, he reached between them, rubbing his thumb over her and nudging her toward her end.

"Oh, oh." She bucked her hips and gasped.

The instant she clenched around him, immersing him in primal pulses timed to spur him on, he couldn't hold back. He had to come. "Come here, baby." He pulled her down.

"Logan! Harder." She tightened her hold on him. "Logan."

"Yes!" Again and again, he drove into her until his final thrust sent him flying. Ecstasy flooded through him, and he remained buried inside her, drawing out every last drop of satisfaction.

They both lay there, panting in unison, their bodies relaxing and melding into one another.

"Logan." Her voice vibrated on his chest.

"One second." He kissed her and gently moved her off to one side, wincing as their bodies separated. As fast as possible, he dealt with the condom and returned to her.

"Come here." He took her into his arms. With her, the sex was more than simply getting his rocks off. He wanted to be with her. They had made it through a rough patch and found

each other again. "You can make love to me anytime you want."
Actually, he wished he'd lasted a bit longer, but his passion got
away with him. Having her want to please him was its own
turn-on. He was usually the one who always had to perform.

"Does that mean that nothing changed about us sharing
our garnishes with others?" She raked her nail lightly over his
chest.

While the same question ran through his mind, he was
more than happy to answer. "I think we should cut to the chase
and just say we are a couple."

She looked up at him. "A couple?"

He nodded and went to kiss her, but stopped short. "Is
there something I need to do to make it official?" ID bracelets
and letterman jackets seemed like the wrong decade on a
number of different levels.

"The kiss would be good." She pursed her lips.

Maybe he needed to do a little more. He lowered his face
but didn't make the connection. "Ivy."

She groaned.

"Seriously." He stared into her face. "I want to tell you
something."

Her eyes widened. "Okay."

"I was the first person to sign the contract for the sequel."

She didn't speak, didn't move, and her expression
remained exactly the same.

"I signed for the sequel first and then Erin and Ryder, but
Drew didn't sign." He swallowed, trying to make sure nothing
he said was a lie. "They decided Drew was expendable."

Her complexion paled, and her eyes glossed over.

"You can't just replace twenty-five percent of the cast."

She shook her head.

"I thought the three of us could band together and convince
Drew to come on board and the producers would reconsider."
Flashes of the night haunted him as if he were still there
walking into the hotel room. All he had wanted to do was
discuss the sequel and see if they could talk to Drew, but Drew
hated acting and loved Erin and didn't want a part of either
one.

Still, she didn't utter a word.

"Instead, after the incident at the hotel room, they canceled the movie. I was blamed for breaking my contract. The movie couldn't go on without me." He sat back and stared up at the wood beam ceiling.

Rather than speaking, she moved closer to him, gave him a light kiss, and then rested her head on his chest.

"Ivy?" He combed his fingers through her hair.

"We are a couple." She hooked her leg over his and yawned.

"But . . ." He let his voice trail off. They could do a whole report on what he told her. Nothing he said matched the media.

"You know, I think the fake story about drunken fights and threats and you asking for more money to support your habit is much more exciting, but I'm glad I'm one of the only ones who knows the truth." She grabbed his hand.

The truth was a relative term. While he didn't lie, he didn't exactly tell the truth. Maybe one day he could tell her, maybe. "We are a couple."

⌒⌒⌒

"I'm thinking that next time we take an overnight trip, we maybe should pack some things." Logan ran his hand through his hair, gave a halfhearted attempt to smooth out his shirt, and leaned over. "Are you wearing underwear?"

"To be honest, I never put panties on to begin with. I only wore the fishnets." Ivy glanced down at her wrinkled and ripped ensemble. "I didn't want panty lines."

He rubbed his hand over her bottom. "Nice." With a low chuckle, he sidestepped behind her, took her by the waist, lowered his face to the crook of her neck, and kissed her.

Shivers ran through her. "Logan."

He moved his hands up and cupped her breasts. "I see we found our bra. Too bad."

"Logan." Though she really didn't want to tell him to stop, at the moment they had no choice.

"Oh my God, I just realized something horrible." He moved them over to the mirror and put his hands over her boobs.

"What would that be?" Yes, they were having a conversation looking at one another in the mirror.

"I'm hungry and horny, and I'm not sure the male body was meant to be both at the same time." He moaned. "Also, I can't be horny, because we used the last of the condoms. Once we get rations, I can be horny again."

"Let's go." Truth be told, while also hungry, she would rather be in bed with him as well, but in the course of the afternoon and evening, they had made a complete mess of each other.

"All right." He took her hand. "Off to market we go."

With one shoe dangling on her fingers, she let him lead her the three steps to the door and stopped to reconsider the normally innocuous errand of going to the market with the other half of her couple. In her case, one Logan Alexander, bad boy celebrity at large.

"What's wrong?" He turned back to her.

While the man could never possibly appear anything other than gorgeous, like her, he appeared as if he had spent the last several hours having sex, because he had. Running through a grocery store in Los Angeles was one thing, but a small town in Big Bear was completely different. "I'll go into the store. You can wait in the car."

"That's a good one. I'm not allowing you to walk through anything in the middle of the night without me. Just to cover our bases, I'm not leaving you in the car and I'm not leaving you here, so it's both of us or none of us." He gave her a light tug, and they walked through the cabin. "Plus, Ryder's here, and I would never leave you alone with him."

From the couch in the main room, Ryder saluted them using her missing shoe.

They both skidded to a halt, and she made a halfhearted effort to hide the rip in her skirt. If he were here for any length of time, he heard them.

"What are you doing here?" Logan's voice rumbled through her.

"Well, since it's my cabin, I think the answer is obvious. The sound effects in here were extremely entertaining." Ryder let out a laugh, his overall demeanor much more jolly than Logan.

Fine, he had heard. At least they tackled the

embarrassment head-on. Still, her cheeks heated as she wondered what all he had heard.

"I figured eventually you'd emerge, so I waited. Your cars are still at the set. I'm starving, and if nothing else, you owe me food."

"You waited here all this time for a meal?" Logan growled.

"Aww, we barely spend any time together anymore, and I really want to get to know Ivy now that she's part of the Stardust family." He stood.

Her heart warmed at being called one of the family.

"I don't do granola and organic, Mr. Scott." Logan tapped his foot.

"Well, I can cheat for your patented pancakes." Ryder approached them. "Miss Ivy, I bet someone would like to know that when we used to go on location, we used to have the grips go get us ingredients, and your man would make everyone pancakes and bacon. I swear I've never had better."

She smiled at the image.

Ryder looked her up and down. "Rather than a reporter, you should've been an opera singer. Those were some amazing notes you hit."

Instead of cowering, she stared him straight in the eye. "What? You've never made a woman hit a high note before?" Something told her she needed to give him exactly what he doled out. "You better step up your game."

Logan put his arm around her shoulders and nodded.

Ryder's leading man smile lit up the room, and he didn't need a spotlight. "You're a cool cat." He raised his palm to her.

Yes, she high-fived him. Why not? In her surreal life, she should talk about her sex noises with Ryder Scott after having sex with Logan Alexander.

Logan cleared his throat. "In addition to this interesting, yet inappropriate, conversation, you want me and Ivy to traipse around a grocery store with you and then you want me to come back here and make you pancakes?"

"That pretty much sums it up." Ryder handed Logan her missing shoe.

Logan glanced down at her.

"Pancakes sound amazing." Though not starving before, a

homemade pancake made by her boyfriend definitely whetted her appetite.

"Fine." He bent down and helped her with her shoes. "At least we don't have to get you grocery store shoes."

"Let's go." Ryder motioned for them to leave.

She put her foot down and pain shot through her. "Oh."

"What's wrong?" Logan held her at arm's length.

"This morning these shoes seemed like a good idea." She hobbled a few steps. Somehow the footwear seemed to have shrunk.

"Well, they are lovely." He supported her as they followed Ryder.

The mountain air chilled her the moment they stepped outside.

"Well, now we could use my trench coat." Logan rubbed her shoulder.

"No one in this decade should use that trench coat unless they're planning on getting arrested for showing off their nether regions to unsuspecting folks." Ryder unlocked the door of a vintage, yet pristine, pickup truck. "Girls in the middle."

She bit the inside of her mouth to not state the obvious. While Logan still owned the BMW used in the movie, Ryder's truck was similar to the one used in the scene after the BMW breaks down and the guys jump-start a truck to get Roxy to the hospital after being stung by a wasp, except this one was perfect. She guessed all of them had different ways of holding on to the movie.

"Nice." Logan held the door, helped her inside, and took his spot next to her. "When did this replace the Ferrari?"

Ryder got in on the driver's side and started the car. "Not a replacement, an addition. Ferrari is all cozy in the Bu, compliments of my most recent benefactor."

She peeked over at Logan for a translation.

"The car is in a garage in Malibu thanks to the latest woman who has succumbed to his charms." He wrinkled his nose.

"Oh, I see." Sort of. She wasn't sure. The vintage truck rumbled along, and the comforting aroma of old car filled the air.

"It's been quite a while since we had a girl between us in a truck." Ryder gave her a light elbow.

She smiled at the movie reference.

"Well, at least this girl made her choice in men early on and stuck with it. May I also add, that was the perfect decision?" Logan nodded.

Along with smiling, she swooned.

"What are you talking about? Roxy clearly chose William." Ryder slowed down for a stoplight and strummed his fingers on the steering wheel.

Again, she found herself holding back her words. She had to know what Logan would counter.

"That's absolutely inaccurate. Though she's with William at the end, she most definitely opens her eyes and watches Steven's car drive away, thus showing her indecision."

She took hold of Logan's hand. He nailed it, and whenever he wanted, he could nail her too.

Ryder pulled into the parking lot of a twenty-four-hour market. "Well, whatever interpretation you want to use, at least we're not driving Ivy to the hospital with a bee sting."

"Wasp." Both her and Logan blurted out the word at the same time.

She turned to him.

"I'm also a quick study." His smile boasted a bit of arrogance.

"You are." She had no choice but to lean in and kiss him.

He wrapped his arms around her and opened his mouth.

"Pancakes!" Ryder got out of the truck and slammed the door.

"I'm never on the receiving end of PDA." He gave her one last peck, tangled their fingers together, and helped her out of the car.

Late in the night, the store stood empty except for a few employees. Nonetheless, the moment one of the workers spotted Logan and Ryder, the points and whispers started.

"Ryder gets to push the basket." Logan motioned to Ryder and pulled her toward him.

She twisted around to find two box boys leaning over.

"Pretend they're the sun and don't look directly at them. It won't get too bad here. They know me." On her other side, Ryder waved. "We'll just be a few minutes."

The two men made it down one of the aisles while she limped. As Logan chose his ingredients, she dared to peek around. It seemed as if the onlookers took Ryder's hint and left them alone.

"Ry, go get some milk and a dozen eggs while Ivy and I get a couple of things we need." Without waiting for a response from Ryder, Logan continued past him and led her through the store. "They're after Ryder, not me."

Rather than watching where he took her, she glanced at him, unsure if she sensed a bit of regret behind his voice. While he was pegged the villain, the public had loved him until the scandal. What was it like to have the world turn on him in an instant?

"Do you have a preference?"

Logan's question cut through her thoughts, and she turned finding herself face-to-face with a display of condoms. "What?" She could go for that trench coat right about now—or not.

"I just want to make sure there's nothing you request in this arena." He swiped his hand in front of them.

"What's your preference?" In her whole life, she never bothered to talk about condoms once she started using them. Before that, she didn't really know what she was talking about.

"I don't know. I've always bought these." He pointed to one of the familiar boxes. "Wilson handed them to me the first day on set and said never be caught without one. The strategy worked, and I never questioned it."

"Pick whatever you want." She shrugged. Maybe they shouldn't be having an entire conversation in a public place about their condom usage, especially with these shoes on her feet. The act of stopping to put a condom on and having to deal with the thing after was a bit of a buzzkill, especially with Logan who tended to want to hold her. "The whole thing is just a necessary evil when you're dating."

"In case you haven't noticed, we're not dating anymore." He squeezed her hand. "We are a couple."

"We didn't date that long." Actually, they didn't really date at all.

"We didn't need to."

They looked at each other.

"Since we are only with each other, did you want to use a different method?" He lifted his eyebrows.

"I'm on the pill." She wrinkled her nose at telling him such a detail, but she supposed he had the right to know.

For the first time in their relationship, Mr. Alexander did not have a quippy comeback or a command. He simply continued to gaze at her.

Her core heated, radiating out through her body.

He leaned down to her ear. "Before you, it was quite a while since I was with anyone, and I've always listened to my brother."

"What would he say if you didn't listen to him now?" She swore she might have to tackle him right here in the aisle with condoms on one side and feminine protection on the other, but she didn't want to use a condom.

"I'm pretty sure he would say it's the natural order of things when you're in a relationship." He kissed her ear.

"All right, guy and gal, I am ready for my pancakes!" Ryder rushed down the aisle and stopped, taking his time to look at the more than obvious display. "Here is your brand, buddy. Stock up so you can work on composing more of your operas."

"We're good, thank you." With her hand firmly in his, Logan walked toward the front of the store.

"What does that mean?" Ryder rushed after them.

Logan held his head up high but didn't answer.

"If you're embarrassed to buy them, I'll do the deed for you." Ryder continued to prod.

"Never be embarrassed to buy condoms. Everyone should be jealous." Logan chuckled.

"Are you saying you don't need them because you remembered a secret stash or did you just decide you didn't need them?" Ryder came up beside her.

"Let's check out." Logan pointed ahead.

In an attempt to alleviate the strangling shoes, she tiptoed to the checkout stand and supported herself on the counter.

Ryder unloaded the basket onto the conveyor belt.

"I forgot something. Come on, Ivy." Logan pulled her.

She tripped, her heel hit the ground, and she moaned. "You want me to walk more?" Men should have to wear heels.

"Dude, what is going to happen? I can watch her for one second." Ryder nearly dropped the eggs, but managed to set them down.

"Don't break anything. I know how many hairs she has on her head, and I expect them all there when I return." Logan walked away, turning back twice.

"You don't think he actually knows that, do you?" She watched Ryder complete his everyday task of unloading the grocery cart.

"He may. You never know. He takes his role as rescuer very seriously." Ryder finished and grabbed one of the entertainment magazines off the rack. "Look, they are making a sequel to that sci-fi flick all the teen girls went crazy for. I guess when something makes mega bucks they will recycle any plot."

Ryder handed her the perfect lead-in to the questions she needed answered. The pain from her biting her tongue outweighed the pain in her feet.

"With our sequel, Logan actually had a clause added to his contract that he would be allowed to approve the final script. He didn't want a crappy sequel." Ryder shook his head. "He always protected us, even when Erin and I wanted out."

She froze. Erin and Ryder wanted out? Only a little while ago she lay in bed with Logan while he told her they all wanted to do the sequel except Drew and Logan got blamed for the cancellation. Something didn't add up. She wanted to ask questions, needed to, but instead searched the store for Logan, exhaling when she spied him walking toward them.

He headed for her, leaned over as if inspecting her head, and nodded. "I suppose she's no worse for the wear."

"Who would have thought I could keep a woman alive for five minutes?" Ryder slid down while the checker scanned their order.

"Not me." Logan tossed a pack of cigarettes in with the rest of the groceries.

She picked it up and put it off to one side with the gum and mints.

"Is that your way of telling me you want me to quit?" He

retrieved the pack.

"No." Before he put it back with their order, she caught his arm. "It's my way of telling you I know you don't smoke."

"I think the cigarettes would say otherwise." He tilted his head, and his eyes sparkled in amusement.

"I have never seen you light one up, and you never taste like an ashtray." She straightened up.

"Are you trying to take care of me?"

"Dude, she has you pegged." Ryder laughed.

"Be quiet or there will be no pancakes for you." Logan flipped off Ryder and returned his attention to her.

The banter between the two men was first class, born over years of knowing each other and keeping in contact. Hell, Ryder even knew Logan's condom brand. If Logan had told the truth and Erin and Ryder had wanted to do the sequel, how could they have remained even acquaintances if and when Logan managed to ruin the movie?

But what if Ryder had told the truth, and he and Erin had wanted out? Along the way, did Logan try to rescue them? For her and for Logan, she had to find out. Maybe she could be the one who cleared him and maybe he could have the career he seemed to want.

She looked him in the eyes. "Someone needs to take care of you."

Logan set the cigarettes aside. "You've got the job."

HOLLYWOOD STARDUST

                                    DISSOLVE TO:

EXT. MOTEL - AMARILLO, TX - DAY

WILLIAM and CHARLES are in the room sleeping
while STEVEN sits beside the half-filled pool
staring out at nothing. ROXY joins him.

                    ROXY
          Can't sleep?

STEVEN doesn't glance her way.

                    STEVEN
          With my side of the bed
          empty, it was the perfect
          time to sneak in with your
          man.

ROXY takes the chair next to him.

                    ROXY
          Who said he was my man?

                    STEVEN
          Some things don't need to
          be said.

                    ROXY
          Whatever, I just came out
          here to check on you.

                    STEVEN
          Why do I need checking on?

                    ROXY
          I just woke up and you
          weren't there.

ROXY stands.

                    ROXY
               Never mind.

STEVEN gets up and takes her by the shoulders.

                    STEVEN
               If you're with William,
               why worry about where I
               am?

ROXY looks up at him. STEVEN bends down and
kisses her. ROXY wraps her arms around his
neck. Suddenly, STEVEN pulls back. ROXY gasps
and puts her hand to her lips.

                    STEVEN
               Maybe a better question is
               why are you kissing me?

STEVEN walks away.

                    STEVEN
               I feel a scandal coming
               on.

Chapter Fifteen

Logan's cell phone rang.

In all the time they had been together, Ivy rarely if ever heard it ring. Actually, she had only heard him talk on the phone one time and he texted only once in a while.

Even Logan seemed surprised by the noise, first turning his head and then wrinkling his nose before lifting his phone to his ear. "This is Logan."

She tried not to appear as if she wanted to eavesdrop and continued to look through her closet for an outfit. They had stayed at Ryder's, and true to his word, Logan had made the most scrumptious pancakes. Afterward, they had tried out their new and, as both she and Logan would call it, much improved birth control method. The way they weren't interrupted with condom etiquette and the way Logan held her tight while they slept would stay in her heart forever.

Unfortunately, morning reality had set in, and after Logan had bribed one of Ryder's production crew to drive her car home, they'd traveled back down the mountain together. As Ryder had told her, a man liked to take care of things, be the protector. In the course of their travels, he'd arranged for Wilson to deliver some of his clothes to her place and had decreed that once they got cleaned up and changed, they should go into her office.

"What is that?" Still on the phone, and in nothing but his towel from their shower, Logan turned his back to her. "Oh, I see."

Still in her bra and panties, she put her hands on her hips. His one-sided conversation gave her no information, and it seemed to her as if he purposely metered his words.

"Can you please e-mail me the information? Thank you for calling."

All the outfits in her closet blurred together. Maybe she needed to go shopping, since clearly she had nothing to wear. Or maybe she needed to find out who was on the phone.

"Do you need some help?" After hanging up, he sauntered over to her side, riffled through her wardrobe, and pulled out a late forties fitted jacket and a flared skirt.

"Is there something you need to work on?" Unsure how he managed to pick the perfect attire, but not really caring, she slipped on the outfit he chose. "The call sounded official."

He chuckled and opened up the suitcase Wilson had left for him. "Last I recall, someone promised me she would ask me if she had a question."

Biding her time to conjure a question that didn't make her sound like a nutcase, she licked her lips and took a breath. "Do you have a job?"

"A job?" With slow, thoughtful movements, he laid his clothes out on her bed.

Rather than looking at him, she glanced at the contents of his luggage, the copious contents. Suddenly, her bed was filled with shirts and pants, all on hangers, a ton of underwear and socks, as well as several pairs of shoes and a bag of what she assumed to be toiletries.

"Why do you ask?" He grabbed a handful of hangers.

"Well . . ." Before she had the chance to ask her question, she watched him walk over to the closet, carefully move some of her clothes aside, and place his hangers on her rod.

"I'll save you the trouble and tell you." He gathered up his shoes and took his time lining them up with hers at the bottom of the closet. "I invest, and sometimes I dabble at Wilson's, and in case you forgot, I work with you."

"Oh." She wanted more information, but didn't really know what or how to ask.

"But that's not what you wanted to know anyway." With a

handful of boxer briefs, he approached her dresser.

She rushed over, opened one of the drawers, and moved her underwear over.

"You wanted to know who called." He placed his underwear next to hers and then added his socks to her sock drawer.

She peered inside the drawer. When he dubbed them a couple, he obviously meant coupling up in her drawers as well.

"Brian called to give me the heads-up on something he read today."

At finding out the answer she had wanted, she turned to find him standing buck-naked in her bedroom. Why the hell was she dressed?

Rather than do the guy thing of showing off his package, or the Logan thing of making love to her or at least giving her a naughty look, he retraced his steps through her room and put his clothes on.

While fascinating to watch, something was wrong. "Logan." Her chest tightened.

Fully clothed, he sat on her bed—or was it their bed? "Come here." He opened his arms.

She crossed her arms. "Just tell me."

He rubbed his chin. "You know, with the anniversary of the movie and of course the project we are working on, I've been in the media a little more than I'm used to the last few weeks."

A numbness took over her body, one where she could only stand in the middle of her room, stare at Logan, and listen to her own heartbeat throb through her ears. The man never prefaced anything he needed to say.

He stood, went to her, and stared straight into her eyes. "The *National Reporter* ran a story about the two of us and our love affair today."

They were in a tabloid magazine? The world's most disgusting tabloid? Though she wanted to speak, she had no words, and her throat dried to such a point she couldn't talk if she tried.

"We are not going to be upset." He gave her a smile.

Maybe he wasn't going to be upset, but she was definitely traveling down that path. "What did it say?" she managed to squeak out.

"Let me take a look." He picked up his phone and wrapped his arm around her. With one finger, he navigated around his screen until the e-mail from Brian popped up.

"All right." With her in his grasp, he sidestepped over to the bed and sat, placing her next to him.

Not sure if she wanted to throw up or cry, she put her head on his shoulder and awaited the verdict. Across the room, she spied her own phone light up. "Logan, hurry." No doubt any phone call, text, or e-mail had to be about the story.

"Stop shaking, I can't read." He rubbed her arm.

After what seemed like the longest pause in modern human history, he put his phone down.

"Logan." She turned to him.

He stared straight ahead, and she watched his Adam's apple travel up and down his throat twice as he swallowed.

She dug her nails into his jeans.

Finally, he cleared his throat. "Well, it seems as if you and I are popular enough to have people following us full time, not simply taking a well-timed photo."

"Just tell me."

"The *National Reporter* took it upon themselves to chronicle our time in the mountains together, including our argument, our makeup in the woods, me carrying you to the cabin and being unavailable for quite some time, and lastly standing in the condom aisle of the market kissing. But the upside is they now have a poll on what birth control we are using on their website."

"Upside?" She found it hard to catch her breath.

"They are giving away a *Hollywood Stardust* prize package to the winner."

"Logan!" The numbness left to be followed by a burst of angry energy, and she grabbed his collar, pulling him down. "What happens now? People are going to be watching us! What if I'm alone and someone comes here?"

"Impossible." He shook his head. "In case you didn't realize, I moved in with you this morning."

Well, her first clue was the fact they now shared an

underwear drawer.

"At least I planned it before we knew about the tabloid." He lifted his eyebrows. "I want to be with you, and we end up together every night anyway."

At least his point had logic behind it, but she wouldn't allow him to make it better with a suitcase and a smile. "Logan." She lowered her voice. "We're in a tabloid known for smut. Right about now my mother and my boss are catching wind of this story."

"Then they will also be able to read a rehash of the infamous night at the hotel room, including a photo of me being taken away in handcuffs and a retrospective of Drew Fulton's career with another poll asking if he's living or dead." The calm, joking demeanor he put on for her sake melted away. His eyes darkened, filled with shadows of the past. The smile he tried to maintain vanished. "The first time this happened to me, the director of *Stardust* told me to be flattered I was tabloid worthy."

"I'd rather them talk about our birth control." One tear escaped her eye, and she ground her teeth together.

"I'm not going to allow them to make you cry." He captured her tear with his fingertip.

"I can't believe they dug up that old garbage. Anyone can look that up online." The words left her mouth, and they looked at each other.

"God, I'm in trouble." He grazed his lips over hers in a light kiss.

"Logan?" She gasped. "What's wrong?"

"I don't know how I could want you more, and yet I do." He pulled her into his embrace.

She closed her eyes and breathed in the clean scent of his freshly pressed shirt and of Logan.

"I'm sorry. I never thought I would be the one they were after. It was always Ryder." He tightened his hold. "I got lazy. With you, I get to forget all those times and focus on the good. There's so much more to the story than what happened for a few hours one night."

She nodded. Every cell in her body told her there was more

to the story, and somewhere in there, Logan wasn't the villain. She just needed to figure out how to prove it.

⁓

"Craig, I have the Ryder Scott interview." Ivy held up the video card containing the middle of the night breakfast they had shared with Ryder, though she didn't hold out much hope of redirecting the conversation. She and Ryder had took turns recording while Logan cooked. At the end, they'd ended up with an amazing segment, complete with Ryder and Logan sharing a couple of fun stories about being on the set of *Hollywood Stardust*. Her favorites included Ryder revealing the time Logan nearly broke his neck running away from a cat on location in Arizona. Not to be outdone, Logan one-upped his friend by telling how Ryder delayed a shoot because he got sick after challenging someone in Texas to a steak-eating challenge. She also managed to get Ryder's dissertation on health food, gluten-free eating, and becoming a vegan.

"Is that your secret to overcoming stage fright?" From the seat next to hers, Julia swung her leg and held her pen up high as if ready to take notes. "Sleeping with your cohost?"

"Practice and coaching." She didn't glance in Julia's direction.

"I didn't know that's what they're calling it now." Julia let out a low chuckle.

"Maybe we need to save the Ryder interview for later in the week, and today Logan and I should address the tabloid head-on." She and Logan had discussed some strategy on their drive over.

Craig rocked back in his chair. "I don't think I've ever been involved in anything like this."

"I sincerely doubt that." From across the room, Logan interjected one of his Loganisms.

She shot Logan a look only a couple shared. The wide eyes should tell him to remain quiet. He'd promised to allow her to take the lead before they'd ever walked into Craig's office.

Logan crossed his arms.

She bit her nail. At this point, her job held little hope. The sheer fact she was escorted to Craig's office the moment she'd entered the building gave her all she needed to know. She and Logan should have brought a box with them. Along with Logan moving in, they could also move the contents of her office. Good thing Logan's brother owned a restaurant, since waitressing was the usual career for those who didn't make it in the entertainment field. "While we were not hiding our relationship, we never planned on it being revealed this way."

"You never planned on this?" Craig stood and tossed the freshly minted tabloid in front of her. "I doubt anyone plans on this."

"Watch it." Logan stepped forward.

"It looks like you forgot a detail." Julia reached across the desk and lifted the magazine.

"Why are you even here?" Logan made a noise of disgust. "You're like a cockroach. If I turn on a light, will you run away?"

Julia shook her head.

"Logan." Ivy went with a more sinister narrow-eyed look. Maybe the act of squinting would focus her energy to shut Logan's mouth.

"You let a questionable publication scoop your story." Craig shook his head. "Everything you wanted to do you failed at the second you got in bed with him. Cora Caine called this morning asking what was going on."

At the mention of the Chargge CEO, her chest tightened. She needed to continue her quest to find out the truth, not for Chargge.com, not for her, but for Logan. The man with the sarcasm and sneers was not the man who invested in his friends' businesses or who held her at night.

Rather than speak, Logan came up behind her.

"Craig, while I know that I am a public person now, this is my choice. I feel simply addressing the situation head-on will calm everyone." At least she hoped.

"Sounds like more self-serving publicity for you," Julia interjected.

"Your personal life ended up as a four-page spread in one

of the nation's top-rated trash cans," Craig said. "How can we even continue with the story now?"

Though her mouth dried, she forced herself to continue. "As you know, I'm the one who has the exclusive access to the stars of the movie. The story is viable and needs to be told. The numbers are there and growing."

"Maybe this was simply a little stunt to make sure your numbers continue to grow." Julia put the magazine down. "Maybe it was planned after all."

Logan put his hands on Ivy's shoulders.

She swallowed. "Craig, I assure you nothing is further from the truth. I still have to call my mother back after this."

"Another has-been Hollywood child." Julia muttered under her breath.

"If you would've done your research, you'd know that my mother hates Hollywood and anything to do with it. She's a woman who lost her father." For the first time, she glanced at the witch.

"I wouldn't need to do my research if certain people remembered their place," Julia shot back.

"My place was never to be your gopher." She faced Julia head-on and made sure to speak slow and clear.

"Who better than the girl who can't speak unless her big, bad villain is there for moral support?" One side of Julia's mouth curled up in a smile. "Is he going to play the role of permanent cohost so you can do your job?"

"If I have to." Logan squeezed her shoulders. "I will do whatever Ivy needs, as she would with me."

She found herself nodding.

"I don't know what game you're playing." Her boss stared Logan down and then transferred his glare to her. "I'm a friend of your father's, and I have to say this—what are you going to do when this is over and he's not there?"

"That's it!" Logan let go of her and rushed to the side of Craig's desk.

Though Craig's words stung worse than a slap in the face, her own instinct fired off and she jumped up. "Logan!" She managed to capture his arm. Under his shirt, his tense muscles trembled.

Craig raised his hands.

"Ivy, why don't you step out and let Craig and I settle this like men?"

"Logan, please go take a breath and let me talk to Craig." She swallowed back the sour taste creeping up from her throat.

"Ivy." Logan said her name through clenched teeth.

"Logan, please, this is my job." While she appreciated he didn't want to leave her, if she went down, she had to be the one responsible. "I need to take care of it myself."

"Fine." He practically shook her off his arm, then turned on his heel and walked out.

Every part of her wanted to run after him, but she couldn't simply quit. The stakes were too high. "Craig, may I talk to you alone?"

"I think I should stay. I need to know what's going on when I take over this story." Julia softened her voice as if she were innocent and only trying to help.

She wished she had the guts to slap Julia across the face.

"Julia, don't you have a location shoot?" Craig returned to his seat.

"I always end up the human mop when she can't hack it." Julia motioned toward her.

He gave Julia a look, an all too familiar look, and Ivy's stomach churned at the image entering her mind. She just shot Logan a similar look. Were they together?

"I'll see you after my shoot." With a huff, Julia left.

"If you tell me you planned this to create exposure and unearth some amazing detail that would answer so many of the unanswered questions, I may be able to breathe." Craig wiped his brow.

"Maybe you should have some respect for me and trust the fact I won't lie to you and tell you that fractured fairy tale." She crossed her arms. "Or, maybe you should have some respect for me because I'm diligently doing my job."

"Are you any closer to finding out anything of any merit?"

"I can feel it."

"Are the two of you really together?" He furrowed his brow.

"We are."

"So, if you had to make a choice, would you choose him or the story?"

"I'd like to think I wouldn't have to make a choice."

He glanced over at his computer screen. "What about your duty as a reporter?"

"If the story is what my gut is telling me, it's going to be incredible." She would clear him of the burden of his past across every media platform.

He glided his mouse around. "Your damn numbers are through the roof. They were before the story broke, and now they're off the chart."

"I know." She sat up straighter. All media worked the same way.

He balled his hand into a fist and lightly pounded it on his desk. "We can't have this getting out of hand. It's Chargge.com's story. Watch who you tell things to. Maybe use a different e-mail."

"I will."

"Go film something. Keep your momentum." He turned to her.

Before she had the chance to celebrate her mild victory, the door to Craig's office shot open.

"Ivy!" Logan rushed inside. "We have to go right now."

"What's wrong?" His stark white complexion set off every alarm bell throughout her body. She nearly fell trying to reach him.

"Wilson called. The bar's been vandalized. Goddamned story. We have to get there now." Without waiting for her, he stomped out of the room.

"I have to go. Filming will have to wait." She headed for the door.

"Well, at least I know the answer to my question." Craig called to her.

"You'll still have a story." She ran after Logan.

HOLLYWOOD STARDUST

                                              CUT TO:

EXT. GAS STATION - AMARILLO, TX - DAY

They are given the bill for the repairs.
Steven's parents' credit card doesn't work.

STEVEN steps away from the counter and joins
the other three.

                    STEVEN
               Hey, I need some help
               here.

STEVEN holds his hand out.

WILLIAM reaches into his pocket and hands
STEVEN some crumpled-up bills.

                    WILLIAM
               I'm almost all tapped out.

CHARLES takes a step back.

                    CHARLES
               I'm only allowed to use
               the credit card in a grave
               emergency.

                    STEVEN
               What do you call this?

ROXY holds her wallet out to STEVEN)

                    ROXY
               Here.

STEVEN shakes his head.

STEVEN
What is wrong with you
people? Do I always have
to carry everyone?

Chapter Sixteen

Feeling like he was trapped in some alternate universe, Logan had to wonder if certain events in his life were on an endless loop doomed to repeat themselves over and over again. Twenty years ago, his car had been slashed multiple times, and he had lost count of the windows broken in the middle of the night.

Construction was causing an unusually heavy traffic jam in Hollywood, and the six-mile drive might as well have been one hundred miles. On the plus side, he had plenty of time to reflect.

He tightened his hold on the steering wheel in an attempt not to drive like a maniac with Ivy in the car.

"Logan," Ivy whispered. The entire ride to the bar she fiddled with her phone, probably searching for a way out.

"I shouldn't have brought you with me." Maybe situations like these were why he never got the girl, because all he brought was danger and destruction. He played his role in life like an Oscar contender, taking responsibility for everything and everyone.

"Don't say that." Her tone businesslike and curt, she continued plunking away at her phone.

"I can say whatever I want as long as it is a fact." In an attempt to find out what held her interest with such intensity, he leaned way over.

"Logan!" Her eyes wide, she pointed straight ahead.

He looked up with enough time to slam his brakes at the red light. The car skidded to a stop in the intersection and lurched both of them forward.

"Oh my." She pressed her hand to her chest.

"Damn it!" Frozen, he simply stared at her.

From behind them, a car honked.

"Fine!" With the light green and no other choice, he drove forward.

"It's going to be all right." Her voice took on a soft, soothing tone, and she put her hand on his arm.

"You don't know what this is like." Though he wanted to grab her hand and never let go, he flinched away at her touch.

She returned her attention to her phone. "Then tell me."

"Why don't you tell me what you and your boss needed to talk about in private?" His teeth scraped together, and a horrid screech reverberated through his skull. He shuddered.

"I needed to prove I could stand on my own two feet."

"You don't have to. You have me." He kept his eyes on the road and spotted the bar up ahead. From his vantage point everything seemed normal, but Wilson said the damage was in the back.

"I'm sorry." Once more she went to reach for him but stopped herself.

"Don't be sorry for what you did. If you don't need me, that's fine." He turned the corner. "Your instinct is probably right. I hope whatever you were doing on the phone involved getting 'old faithful' back."

The moment he turned into the back parking lot, she gasped.

Every muscle in his body tightened.

Across the back wall of the business he had bought his brother were the words "Hollywood Stardust" in black, with the "Star" crossed out in red. Next to that literary masterpiece someone had scrawled in blue "go back to rehab." At the sight, his head began to throb. His brother and Giselle were already outside waiting for him. "Maybe I shouldn't have moved in with you. This is what you have to look forward to."

Without as much as a word, she opened the car door and stepped out.

He got out of the car and stared at the damage.

Rather than going to him, his brother and Ivy's friend ran to her.

Wilson gave her a hug. "We got what you told us to. I didn't call anyone for help like you asked."

"There's already too much media attention on us. We'll fix it." She shook her head and headed for the door. "Let me change and we'll get started."

"Ivy," he called to her. When did she take charge? He would fix the situation once he assessed everything. How did she tell them what to get?

She tilted her head. "Elle, do you want to snoop in Logan's closet?"

"You don't have to ask twice." Giselle ran after Ivy, and the two women disappeared inside.

Wilson approached the car. "Your girl is incredible."

"We need to get someone down here right away." He took his phone out of his pocket.

"Ivy said no outsiders." Wilson held his hand up. "She said we couldn't take the chance with the tabloid."

"Then how do you suppose we get that off your wall, or are you planning on leaving it there as some sort of reminder of who your brother is? Do you think it will bring in more business?"

"Ivy gave us a list of things to get while you were driving here. The area is not that big, and we have some cans of the original paint."

"Since when did she become the boss?" He returned his phone to his pocket.

"Since you needed her to."

As if her entrance was timed, the back door to the bar opened, and Ivy reappeared in a pair of his shorts and one of his plain white T-shirts that she tied at the bottom. The sun hit her in exactly the right way for him to tell she ditched her bra along with her clothing.

"Well, well. At least we get a little eye candy." Wilson patted his shoulder.

"Stop looking at her." Apparently they needed to have a little discussion about her wardrobe.

"I'll look at my girlfriend if I want to." Wilson went and joined the girls. "You have it bad, if you didn't even notice Giselle's short shorts."

Logan shrugged at most of Giselle's bottom hanging out of her almost pants and went to Ivy. "What're you doing?"

"I'm going to fix the wall." She kept her back to him and bent down to read the instructions on one of the bottles she had Wilson get.

"How did you become an expert on graffiti?" He peered down at her and managed to get a small look inside her shirt. Well, his shirt.

"Well, rather than contacting geysers in Yellowstone, I searched how to fix the issue." She stood and motioned for Wilson, pointing to the back label on the jug of some chemical designed to make everything better. "Never was much one for Old Faithful."

Wilson took the container, and Giselle laid out some tarps.

Ivy picked up a bucket and turned.

He caught her arm. "You don't have to do this."

"I have work to do. I'm not going to do that to your brother." She jerked her arm back and walked away with her bucket.

For a few minutes, he simply watched her as they used her magic solution to scrub the spray paint off the wall. The three of them worked together with Ivy leading the pack.

"What are you doing?" Wilson yelled. "You're making a lousy director in case you wanted to know."

He blinked, snapping himself out of his stare, then stomped by them. "You're a terrible actor."

Once inside, he went straight up to his room. Not too long ago everything had been new. With no one to impress, he had bought furniture he'd settled for, nothing special. Then Ivy had appeared. While she had been up here with him a few times, he tended to prefer her more lived-in space. Still, they hadn't broken the bed in yet, but now the whole place seemed tainted by the vandalism.

They had started here free of his past, and then it had barreled toward him, picking up speed, and threatening to destroy everything.

He sat at the edge of the bed and glanced into his closet. While his past might linger around him, a little sparkle of his future hung on a hanger on the right side in the form of Ivy's outfit with her shoes neatly placed alongside his. He supposed turnabout was fair play, and the way she changed into his clothes like she owned the place warmed him. She belonged here, and she cared, and he tried to push her out because he didn't want her to see him in this state. He didn't want her to view him as the villain.

Rather than sit in self-loathing, he needed to help. Finally, he jumped up, changed into sweats and a T-shirt, and rushed downstairs. Going with his own strengths, he darted around the kitchen and threw together some simple sandwiches then collected some bottles of water for his brother and Giselle and iced tea for him and Ivy. Fine, he put her drink on a saucer and added a slice of lemon before joining them.

Three things struck him once he walked outside. First, a quick assessment of the wall told him whatever product Ivy researched seemed to work. Second, Ivy was up on a ladder with a metal brush scrubbing away the paint, and the ladder was rather high. Third, the fumes in the air instantly made his eyes water.

"Why don't you all take a break?" He doled out his waters and went to the ladder. "Baby, why don't you get down from there?"

"I'm fine." She cleared her throat and coughed.

"I brought you something to drink."

"I'm fine, thank you." Without even peeking at him or the drinks, she continued her work.

He glanced over at Wilson, who only shook his head. "Ivy."

No answer unless he wanted to count another round of coughs with the addition of an eye rub and a sniff.

"Ivy." He set the drinks down and got up on the ladder with her.

"I'm not sure this ladder supports two people." She punctuated her statement with another cough. "Why don't you go see how much paint we have?"

The blow off. Maybe one he deserved. He climbed up a couple more rungs. Her backside was now right in front of his face.

What should be a sexy moment or perhaps even the opportune makeup time quickly became marred when another round of coughs overtook her, bad enough to cause her to drop her brush and to gasp for air.

"Ivy!" He went up another rung and wrapped his arm around her waist. "That's it. You're done."

"I said I was fine." She lowered her head.

"I say you're not, and I say you're done." Not wanting to take the chance of them falling, he tightened his hold on her, hoping she would acquiesce and come down. "The fumes are making you sick."

In a defiant move, she gripped the ladder. "I say you need to decide if you want to be with me or not. Until then I can take care of myself."

Before simply answering, he scanned the area, the graffiti, the mess, and him and her on the ladder arguing among the fumes. They had been together much longer than he had ever been with anyone else. It had been almost a month, most of his flings barely lasted a week. "Maybe I don't need to make the decision. Maybe it's you."

"Get down." Her voice came out cracked as she held back the coughs.

"Let me help you." He moved down a step.

She put her hand on her forehead. "Logan, get off this ladder right now."

The edge in her voice made him do as she asked. He jumped to the ground and refrained from helping her. Their position was ripe for her to get hurt.

Even with her coughing fit, and the sweat breaking out on her pale face, she rushed off the ladder and toward the restaurant. "Stay away from me."

Close at her heels, he followed. "So, now you just walk away?"

"I wasn't walking away. I wasn't driving away. That role has been filled." She threw the door open and disappeared inside.

With heat consuming his body and his muscles tense, he kicked the door before going after her. "There's a reason I need to drive away." He glanced around the empty kitchen and almost charged for the upstairs when he heard a whimper coming from the front of the house.

"Ivy?" Rather than storming over, he walked into the large room and found her slumped on a barstool with her hand over her eyes.

"What's the reason?" she mumbled.

"It doesn't get better." He went behind the bar and took down one of the glasses.

"Please don't play games with me, Logan." With her hand still on her face, she peeked at him through her fingers. "Just be straight."

"People talk, rumors start, one day . . ." He turned his back to her and scooped up some ice into the glass.

"One day what?" More coughs.

He filled the glass with club soda and turned to find her resting her head on the bar. "Drink this."

"One day what?" Her voice came out muffled, yet stern.

"Do we have to do this now? Why don't we get you fume free first?" He set the glass down next to her.

"No!" She raised her head and slammed her fist on the bar. The glass of soda water teetered. "We can't do this later. We do it now. I'm not going to live every day wondering when you are going to drive away or force me in my car."

They stared at each other.

"One day what?" She stifled a cough and spoke through her teeth.

"What if I don't force you in your car?" He crossed his arms and turned away. When other women left after a couple of dates, it didn't matter, but with Ivy, everything mattered. "You don't even need me." The words left his mouth before he could stop them.

"Oh, Logan." Her voice hitched, and she went into a round of coughs, deeper than before.

"Ivy." He rushed over to her, once again taking her into his arms, and shuddered. The fumes seemed to settle in her clothes. "We have to get you into different clothes."

"Lo–" Her coughs rattled through him.

"Baby." He gave her some of the water, set the glass aside,

and lifted her up. "Come on."

She held on and lowered her head on his shoulder. "I don't feel so great."

"Yeah, I figured that out." He made his way up the stairs, into his room, and headed straight for the bathroom where he turned on the water. "That chemical leached everywhere."

With no resistance, she allowed him to undress her. He took her in as he held a washcloth under warm water and wiped her face down. "You're really beautiful."

She shook her head.

"Don't contradict what I know." He guided her over to his bed. While she sat at the edge, he dug one of his old *Hollywood Stardust* T-shirts out of his dresser drawer and slipped it over her head. At least she cracked a little bit of a smile at the black oversize shirt emblazoned with a large gold star. "Lay back."

"You're not getting this shirt back." She reclined on the bed.

"It looks much better on you." After helping her slip under the sheets, he changed his clothes and gathered up all the laundry. "I'll be right back." He made a quick dash downstairs and dumped the contaminated clothes in the hamper before returning to her.

The glorious sight of her curled up in his bed on her side hugging a pillow, both comforted and aroused him. "Don't ever tell me you aren't beautiful." He joined her and pointed down at the pillow. "Do you mind if I take its place?"

"Only if we decide we're going to carpool instead of taking separate cars," she whispered. "I don't want to play this game where you shut me out every time someone or something hits a nerve with you."

He nodded.

"Things happen. You can't go from moving in with me to shoving me out the door in an instant."

He paused and tried to absorb her words. There would always be bumps in the road, and yet she wasn't running from him, she was here. "I moved in with you because I want to walk into our bedroom and always find you waiting for me. I want to be with you."

She lifted the sheet, giving him an invitation. "Say it again."

"I want to be with you, Ivy Raleigh Vermont." He removed the pillow and slipped into the bed with her, moving down until they were nose to nose. "Thank you for trying to fix the mess. You did amazing."

"Maybe every once in a while, you need someone to take care of you." She traced his lips with her fingertip.

"Do you need someone to take care of you?" He kissed her finger and pulled her closer.

"No. I need *you* to take care of me." Her finger traveled over his nose and outlined his eyebrows. "I would have suffocated if you didn't save me."

"That's my job. I prefer you breathing. I will always nurse you back to health." He combed his fingers through her hair. While he thought he would be breaking in his bed differently, having her here was perfect.

"See? You're a hero." She smiled. A slight smile, a small upturn of her mouth, but her eyes really expressed her emotion. "Not only am I breathing because of you, but I would've never been able to be in front of a camera without you."

At the moment, her smile said she saw him as a hero. Some sort of knight in a vintage BMW who swooped in and saved her from the fire-breathing camera on set. "Only for you."

"So, I guess I'm lucky I'm the only woman who gets the Logan who cooks and covers me up at night and makes sure I buckle my seat belt." A small laugh escaped her throat. "You're not the bad guy everyone wants you to be, or that you want to be, Mr. Alexander."

"Again, only for you." He gave her a light kiss, something he should have done instead of yelling at her and trying to push her away.

"Do you ever wish the world saw what I do?" She took her turn to kiss him and let her lips linger against his.

"I don't know. Being the bad guy has some advantages."

"But in my heart, I know you're not the bad guy." She pressed her palm to his cheek. "It doesn't add up."

Rather than shutting her out at the mention of the past, he

needed to allow her to address it and not react like a lunatic or a bad guy. "Once the fanfare of the anniversary dies down, it won't be as bad. It's part of being with me." His chest tightened.

"I know." She gave him another kiss. "I'm fine. I just wish you didn't have to go through it."

He put his hand over hers. "I'll live with knowing the one person who matters doesn't think I'm the bad guy. Maybe it just doesn't matter anymore. All right?"

She blinked.

"There's a reason I asked you to let things be. It doesn't affect us anymore." While he may be the protector, she was the crusader. "All right?"

"All right." Her answer was more of a sigh.

"Good." Once more, he kissed her. If she went looking into the answers she wanted, he wouldn't be the redeemed villain, and he needed to be her hero.

                                        CUT TO:

EXT. GAS STATION - AMARILLO, TX - DAY

WILLIAM, CHARLES, and ROXY sit at the gas
station waiting for Steven to return.

                    ROXY
              Where do you think he
              went?

                    WILLIAM
              Who cares? He's been an
              ass this whole time.

                    CHARLES
              He probably didn't want us
              to see him groveling to
              his parents.

                    WILLIAM
              He's a jerk. We should've
              just taken this trip by
              ourselves.

                    ROXY
              Don't say that.

ROXY turns away.

                    WILLIAM
              Why not? It's the truth.

                    ROXY
              At least he's trying to
              fix it.

                    WILLIAM
          He makes the messes and
          then makes you grateful
          when he cleans them up.

Chapter Seventeen

"This hotel has completely been remodeled." Matt lifted his phone and took a couple pictures of the lobby.

"They redid the whole place after the fire ten years ago." Ivy wrapped her arms around her shoulders to stop the shudders. The Beverly Garland hotel might have been redone, but decades' old ghosts seemed to linger. Once the apex of Hollywood glitz, the place to be seen, the hotel had also been the hub for many scandals, not the least of which included Logan Alexander. After the fire involving yet another celebrity, the place had closed down and reopened with the old Hollywood glam replaced with Italian villa décor. The place instantly lost the "it" factor.

"Didn't you tell me they filmed a scene for the movie here?" Matt snapped a couple more pictures.

"Yes, one of the hotel scenes had to be redone when the original place in the valley wouldn't let them in, and they used this hotel." She sighed. "Thanks for meeting me."

"I'm glad you finally decided to do the right thing." Once more, he scanned the room and shrugged.

"Matt." She put her hand to her forehead. "I shouldn't have called you about this. I'm sorry."

"No, I'm glad you did." He put his arm around her shoulders. "You've always relied on me, and I'll always be here for you."

Her chest constricted. If Logan knew where she was and whom she was with, he would flip, and he would have every right. Yet the moment he had announced he needed to go with Wilson to some restaurant supply shop, she had taken her first opportunity to put her plan into action. "I told you on the phone I'm not trying to frame him. I'm trying to clear him."

"Are you prepared to find out things you don't want to?" Matt led her over to a small couch in the lobby.

A flash of Logan's expression when he saw Wilson's bar nearly destroyed by graffiti gave her every answer. Even after the wall was painted, he still stared at it as if he could see the slurs. Later, she heard him ordering security cameras for Wilson's place and a security team for both the bar and her apartment—actually their apartment. "I have to do this."

"Then what?" He pulled his laptop out of his case.

"What do you mean?"

"What are you going to do with the information?" The ding of the computer powering up echoed through the quiet space.

"Prove he's not the villain." Her throat dried out.

"How?" He continued to fire questions at her.

"Matt, I need to know." She powered up her own computer. "He deserves better. I'll figure it out."

"Okay, let's do this." He turned the computer toward her. "Sometimes the best way to go back is to look at what happened since the incident. We have to be able to find something. Let's start with the charges against him."

In coordinated clicks, they both typed on their respective machines. "Disturbing the peace, disorderly conduct, assault and battery, possession of drugs." She didn't need the Internet to recite the laws Logan had broken.

"What drugs?" Matt scrolled down his screen.

"Marijuana and other drugs." The words left her mouth, and she stopped. "Wait."

"Well, that explains a lot." Her cohort laughed. "No wonder he loves to cook—constant case of the munchies."

"Matt." Their first breakthrough couldn't be this simple.

"What's wrong?" He turned to her.

"Logan doesn't smoke."

"Maybe he did before." Matt countered. "Not that it matters. Just because someone doesn't smoke cigarettes, doesn't mean they don't smoke pot."

"I don't know, but it seems off. He barely takes an aspirin. His cure-all for everything is soda water." She returned her focus to her computer screen.

"All right, let's table that for right now. What did he do right after he got out of rehab?"

"After rehab and pulling out of the sequel, he tried some acting jobs." She recited his history from memory.

"Okay, after *Hollywood Stardust* there're like two bit parts listed on his résumé, all within the first couple of years, then nothing." Matt hovered his fingers above his keyboard. "What does he do now?"

She licked her lips.

"Ivy," Matt prodded.

"Well, he cooks . . ." She hooked her hair behind her ear. "And he does a lot of investing, like in the bar and in his friend's lab and in Ryder's movie." Of course, she enjoyed his new career of being in front of the camera with her.

"Where did he get the money for all this investing?" Matt shut the computer.

Her first instinct was to shout out *Hollywood Stardust* or an inheritance, but she knew he didn't have any family money. "The actors on *Hollywood Stardust* were all unknowns at the time and famously did the movie for ten thousand a piece."

"Unless he invested every bit of that money in a really awesome stock, he either has more to do with marijuana than you think, or he's getting it somewhere else."

"Matt." She barked out a warning.

"Fine. I'm sorry, but seriously, haven't you ever heard the saying 'Follow the money'?" he asked.

"Follow the money," she repeated.

"His car alone is close to six figures and new."

She gazed out at the lobby, but her vision blurred. Logan never mentioned money, and his answers about work were nebulous at best.

"I don't think being a sometimes cook at a bar will pay his bills," he added. "What kind of investing does he do?"

Her phone vibrated, and she slipped the device out of her

pocket.

The alone thing isn't working for me.

No matter how many times Logan texted, her heart fluttered all the same. *You aren't alone. You are with Wilson.* She hit "Send" and giggled.

"Okay, I know I can't compete with the sexy texts." Matt patted her back.

Logan's next message appeared on the screen. *Fine, then the without you thing isn't working for me. Come home and we will get some work done together.*

"I'm sorry." She wrinkled her nose.

"As I told you before, I'll always be here for you." Matt packed his items, stood, and saluted her. "Follow the money first. I have a feeling it may lead you somewhere."

She gave Matt a quick hug and immediately returned to her phone. *What are you going to do when we don't work together anymore?*

We don't need to work.

As she typed her next message, her heart seized. *Why not?*

I'll provide for us. Don't worry.

She toggled between wanting to hug the phone and smash it. Instead, she answered. *On my way.* She needed to follow the money.

<hr />

"Ivy?" Logan took silent steps down the stairs. "Ivy?"

The banging together of pots and pans reverberated from his kitchen.

He tightened his hold on his laptop case, pressed his back to the wall, and slid toward the door. "Ivy?" With one eye closed, he tried to peer into the room. Nothing. Though he promised he would stay out until she called him, he couldn't resist.

As Wilson's opening neared, they had stayed at the bar the last few nights to help get ready for the big event. When they had woken, Ivy had announced she would make them breakfast. Even with his protests, she'd insisted, telling him she wanted to take care of him. He had caved, and she'd bounded into the kitchen.

Yes, she might want to take care of him, but he wanted to reciprocate. Well, not exactly. What he wanted was to show her he had them covered. Since the vandalism, she seemed overly concerned about his money situation or his job. While she did not come right out and ask him, he heard the true questions behind the ones she masked with nonchalance, and he somehow needed to give her some security without telling any semblance of a falsehood. Women craved security. They also hated lies.

Breakfast was usually the fastest meal to prepare, but she had been down here for over an hour. He looked at his watch and nodded. "Ivy, I'm starving."

"All right, hungry man, come on in." Her voice came out strained, followed by another clash of metal on metal.

He rushed through the swinging door and stopped. Nothing was currently on fire, but there seemed to be a definite potential for combustion. A quick glance at the sink filled with almost every cooking utensil he owned told him she might have had some difficulties, and the charcoal aroma and haze in the air confirmed his suspicions.

She lifted two plates off the counter and approached. "I made French toast."

He only prayed she didn't put egg-soaked bread actually in the toaster, and he couldn't stop from looking over at the little chrome appliance. Adrenaline coursed through his veins, and he fought the urge to clutch the toaster to his chest and run for safety.

"Don't worry. I'll clean up while you get to work." Her weapons at the ready, she stalked closer.

Ah, another one of her little comments about work. At last, he would call her bluff. "In fact, I have some personal work I need to get done now. Why don't we eat in the main room?"

"Okay! Can you grab the coffee?" Her face lit up with a smile, and she lifted her chin in the direction of the coffeemaker.

"Sure." He retrieved the two mugs, and unless she decided

to use a chicory blend, he discovered one of the sources of the charcoal aroma stinging his nose. "Let's go to the big booth."

"I already put the syrup and butter on your plate for you." She leaned over the table and arranged her dishes.

Well, his mouth watered at her rounded backside in her jeans. Maybe a diversion was in order. "Why don't we take a break and go back upstairs?"

"I made breakfast, and you said you had work?" She spun toward him, her brow furrowed.

"I know, but you just look so luscious, I can't help but to want to feast on something else." He slipped into a booth, pleased he managed to save the situation and tell the truth.

"Oh, well later." She took her place next to him.

Before tackling the food, he took his time setting up his space. Nothing spoke more of production and work than office supplies, and he neatly arranged a yellow pad, pen, pencil, calculator, and his mail out in front of him. As a grand finale, he took out his laptop and powered it up.

"Are you going to eat?" She scooted closer to him.

Oh yes, eating. Out of the corner of his eye he caught sight of the plate of food. Three bloated yet charred pieces of what he assumed was French toast floated in a lake of syrup and melted butter with crispified bacon creating a border.

No way could he eat the food. He didn't even like syrup that much.

"I know this isn't close to your pancakes, but I didn't want you to always have to cook for me." She leaned over and kissed his cheek.

Damn it. Why couldn't she be a taker like everyone else? He lifted the fork, pried off a piece of the French toast, and shoved the tough triangle in his mouth.

Equally important to food taste was texture. As far as the taste, his mouth was overtaken by sweet to such a point where he welcomed the bit of burned to cut the sugar. However, the chewy, gooey, squishy texture almost did him in.

Almost.

Until he looked over at Ivy staring at him with a slight smile on her face. Whatever agents turned her down in the past due to a little stage fright had no vision, because the sight in front of him was nothing short of magnificent. She could sell anything. He swallowed and raised his eyebrows.

"You have a little syrup on your lip." Once more she kissed him but took her time to run her tongue over his mouth.

"You make the world's best napkin." Rather than take another bite, he pulled her in.

"Do you like it?" She giggled.

"I like you more." Again, not a lie. He dipped his head down.

She snuck her hand between them. "I thought you had to work."

The work. The work she didn't believe he did. With one peck on the tip of her nose, he pushed back and turned to the computer. "Yes, let me get everything fired up here."

"We must keep you in top shape." She nudged his dish over to him and dug into her own plate.

Somehow he needed to eat the food or hide it. Damn him for never getting a dog. "I want to savor every bite." As he chiseled off another piece, his cell phone saved him. "Work call." Without even looking, he dropped the fork and answered. "Logan Alexander."

"I remember the days you used to call me first." Erin breathed into the phone.

"Hold on to your memories." He returned his attention to his laptop and brought up one of his spreadsheets. "What do you need?"

"I had two reporters call wanting an interview about the anniversary," Erin whispered.

"Handle as you normally do. What's the issue?" Though he pretended to stare at the screen, he kept his eyes on Ivy and his ears on his words.

"They said I spoke with your girlfriend, so why couldn't I speak to them?" She sighed. "We have an arrangement."

He shook his head. Erin didn't make mountains out of molehills. No, she made them out of anthills, but never missed the chance to remind him he was bought and paid for. "E-mail me the information and I'll take care of it."

"Fine."

"Do you need anything else?" He strummed his fingers on the keys of his laptop and ground his teeth together at the loaded question.

"I need a lot of things, but I did want to tell you that Brian made your deposit. I added extra for the anniversary gala."

"You didn't have to do that." After the whole spectacle was over, he wanted to work on ending their connected lives completely.

"Yes, I did. I ruined your career."

With her years of acting experience, he wasn't sure if the break he heard in her voice was real or not. "Guess we'll never know."

"How's the bar?"

"The opening is in two days. Why don't you see for yourself?" He almost laughed. Erin would never show, especially with Ivy in his life.

"You don't need a date, but I'll see. Good-bye."

"Thank you for calling." Rather than making the phone call mysterious, he decided to treat it as any sort of work. "Well, I got that out of the way. That was one of my funding sources." No lie in his statement. He was on a roll.

"Funding?" Ivy lifted his fork and aimed it toward his mouth.

"Yes." He barely got the word out before she fed him. Using every ounce of strength, he swallowed.

"What kind of funding?" She curled up next to him in the booth. Booths were so much better than tables.

Finally, they would get to the work. For two days, he had practiced how to explain without any untruth. "Look here." He pointed to his computer screen, mostly to direct her to the amount of money he had. He never wanted her worrying about him not being able to provide. "Many years ago, I ended up with a settlement that is paid to me monthly."

"Were you in a lawsuit?"

At not having rehearsed that answer, he ground his teeth together. "No."

"So how did you end up with a settlement?"

His phone chimed off, saving him. He held up a finger and answered. "Logan Alexander."

"Ryder Scott." He chuckled. "I think I would make a better voice-over artist than you."

"Good to know." Logan put his elbow on the table and rested his forehead in his hand.

"I just got off the phone with Erin, and it reminded me to tell you I made your deposit," Ryder told him. "I also have a list of media that's been hounding me, Mr. Mouthpiece."

"Fine. Send it to me and I'll deal with it." Logan wondered which one of Ryder's women would make the deposit for him this month.

"Seems as if the interviews with Ivy opened the door up to everyone thinking we could talk. Questions about our missing fourth is making louder than normal waves. I think he's doing it as a publicity stunt, and if that's the case, the time to come out is now where he would make the most of it."

Everything in Ryder's life barreled down to dollars and cents, but how could Logan judge. His did as well . . . until Ivy. "Leave it be. You know the drill."

"I'm not bound by any contract from talking about it with you," Ryder huffed into the phone. "Watch Ivy. The paparazzi is hot for her, especially after that story in the *National Reporter*. Careful at the opening."

Instinct caused him to wrap his arm around her. No one would get near her on his watch again. "I have to go. Thanks for the update." He tossed his phone across the table. "Busy morning."

"I've never heard your phone ring so much."

"I prefer it being just you and me." Of all the things he said thus far, that sentence was the most true.

"You were explaining how you ended up with the settlement." She tilted her head up at him.

Along with everything else he needed to remember, he could never forget Ivy's intelligence. A scholar at heart, her mind remained focused on every last detail.

However, he was an actor, taught to improvise and make due even if he didn't have the lines. When in doubt, the best way to get through a situation was to buy time by using a prop. He grabbed one of the strips of bacon and shoved it into his mouth. The petrified pork crumbled and the flavor of "burned and salt" replaced "burned and sweet." By only a miracle, he managed to chew and swallow. "Payback for a long-term loan and it compounded over time." He wasn't sure if he'd lied or not, since he didn't even understand what he'd said.

She nodded.

"Anyway, enough of this. Long story short, over time I invested the money and it grew. So today I wanted to check the numbers, and I thought later we could go take a drive and look at a couple of properties and have lunch out." If the thought of eating ever appealed to him again.

"I would love that."

"My work this morning entails researching the area and the opportunities." Between the bacon, the French toast, and the phone calls, his palate needed to be cleansed. He reached for the coffee and took a sip. "Oh my God." The taste bore right through him.

"What's wrong?" Ivy straightened up.

"I didn't know coffee had a texture." Without spilling or dying, he managed to get the cup back on the table.

"You like your coffee strong." She winced. "Is it too strong?"

"Baby." It was time to face the truth and her head-on. "This coffee just took me out."

She put her hand over her eyes. "I'm not a good cook."

"No, you are not." Gently, he moved her hand away. "But lucky for us, I am."

"But—"

He cut her off by putting his finger over her lips. "I would eat your cooking every meal, every day if it meant keeping you happy."

"I don't really enjoy cooking." She wrapped her arms around his neck. "I just wanted to do it for you."

"You do enough."

"I don't think so."

"Just being with you is enough." At his admission, his true

admission, he also knew his true feelings.

"Logan." She brushed her lips over his and moved over to his jaw and ear. "I'm so hungry."

"How about I make breakfast?"

"Okay, how about I play assistant and research where we're going today?"

He pulled back and took her all in, something he found himself doing quite often. "That sounds like a deal. I really hate working on the computer."

"I love it." She gave him a huge grin.

"Then we're a perfect match." Before retreating to the kitchen, he set her up on his computer. In truth, he rarely used the thing, preferring to keep all his personal information on his phone.

"I didn't realize all about your job." She typed away on the computer.

In truth, no, she didn't realize about his job. The investments served as a distraction to his babysitting role, one he didn't audition for or covet. But now his past was on a straight collision course with his future, and he didn't want any casualties.

HOLLYWOOD STARDUST

CUT TO:

INT. STEVEN'S GRANDPARENTS' HOUSE — FLAGSTAFF
AZ. — NIGHT

All four, plus the grandparents, are sitting
at the dinner table enjoying a home-cooked
meal and the feeling of home.

>   STEVEN'S GRANDMOTHER
>   I think this adventure is
>   good for you.

>   CHARLES
>   You do?

CHARLES shakes his head.

WILLIAM, ROXY, and STEVEN look up from their
plates.

>   STEVEN'S GRANDMOTHER
>   I do. It's part of growing
>   up.

With a bowl of mashed potatoes in her hand,
GRANDMOTHER stands up and makes her way around
the table, stopping first at CHARLES.

>   STEVEN'S GRANDMOTHER
>   You will live if you ever
>   get a B on a test, and
>   you'll be better for it.

GRANDMOTHER doles out a spoonful of potatoes
and moves on.

WILLIAM leans back to allow her to serve him.

                    STEVEN'S GRANDMOTHER
          I think you're finding
          that not everything in
          life can be
          solved with a smile.

GRANDMOTHER pats WILLIAM'S shoulder, gives him
another serving, and continues on.

ROXY puts her hand over her plate.

GRANDMOTHER moves ROXY'S hand away.)

                    STEVEN'S GRANDMOTHER
          One day you will regret
          the serving of mashed
          potatoes you didn't take.
          Make sure you always look
          at all your opportunities.

ROXY smiles at the pile of potatoes on her
plate.

STEVEN pushes his plate over.

                    STEVEN
          What about me, fortune-
          teller?

GRANDMOTHER leans down.

                    STEVEN'S GRANDMOTHER
          First, never assume.

GRANDMOTHER squeezes his cheek.

                    STEVEN'S GRANDMOTHER
          Second, always take the

opportunity to tell
someone how you really
feel, not how you think
you should feel, but
what's in your heart.

Chapter Eighteen

Ivy made her way down the stairs and peeked out at Wilson's bar. The low mumblings of the freshly minted waitstaff and the clinks of glasses and dishes over the light jazz music in the background all made the establishment come alive. For the last few days, the place had buzzed with activity and it finally all came together. The retro speakeasy was completely on trend.

Though they had all tried to keep the vandalism out of the media, both she and Logan knew no matter how fast they dealt with it, the story would leak. They had taken to their own show to discuss the situation. In a twist that had warmed her heart, they'd received an outpouring of support from their fans, or as Logan called them, her fans. Either way, after the opening for the VIPs, the reservation list was positively packed. Still, she had her objective. Somehow she needed to figure out the mystery that was her man.

Once spying Wilson, she headed toward the bar. A couple of servers stopped to let her go by, making her feel more like a princess than the investor's girlfriend.

"Can I help with anything?" As of yet, she had never gotten the chance to talk to him alone.

He gave her a slow shake of his head. "Not looking like that."

"Do you like it?" She glanced down at the 1950s form-hugging black satin strapless gown. After three different tries, she had finally found the right bra to give her cleavage the *vavoom* she wanted.

"Every man likes that dress, trust me. How about while we wait for our other halves I make you a drink to match your outfit?" Like any good barkeep, he lifted a glass and held it up to the light. "Plus, I have a question for you."

While not normally a drinker, she nodded and perched at one of the barstools. "I may have an answer for you."

He opened a bottle of champagne. "How did you sneak away from my brother?"

"Oh, yeah." Once more she glanced over her shoulder. Logan didn't lie when he said being away from her wasn't working and decided it would be much more efficient to do everything together. Not that she minded in the slightest, but it was making her research extremely inefficient. After being with him for a full day of his work, she knew something wasn't right, but her instinct said he wasn't trying to hide as much as he was trying to protect her, especially since he didn't seem to want to let her out of his sight. "He takes longer to get ready than I do."

"It's the hair." With a little bit of flourish, he dipped a sugar cube in some liquid and put it at the bottom of a champagne flute and poured in some cognac. "Also, he's probably trying to look pretty for you."

"I'm glad he decided he wasn't going to cook tonight." However, she had been privy to watching Logan train the chef and staff as if they were going to be defending the country. The man was sexy when he was stern. Hell, the man was sexy when he wasn't stern. He was just sexy.

"One champagne cocktail for the lady." Wilson topped his concoction off with the champagne, put a black napkin on the bar, and presented her with the drink. "Between you and me, I think I may have lost my special guest chef."

"What makes you say that?" The bubbles trailed up from the sugar cube in a little line, their goal to reach the top of the glass. Like the bubbles, she had her goal. She smiled, tilted the drink in his direction, and took a sip. A bit of sweet and a bit of tart.

"I think he likes his new career with a special lady in a slinky dress much better."

"You mean the show?" She took another sip of the drink.

"Just you." Wilson wiped down the bar.

"What did he do after the movie wrapped?"

He shrugged. "Some bit parts, then he just did what he always did, but whenever *Stardust* bubbles up to the surface, his job is to be the mouthpiece for the rest of them."

Never an actress, she tried to be nonchalant and ran her finger along the rim of the glass, but her mind skidded to a halt and replayed Wilson's statement. Why didn't this occur to her before? When she had scored the first interview with Ryder and Erin, she had assumed they didn't want to speak, but Logan coordinating everything had been deliberate. Maybe a paid position? Why?

"Hey!" From the back, Isaac entered, waived, and joined them. He handed Wilson a bottle of extremely expensive wine. "I'm not sure what you get a bar owner, but congratulations."

The men shook hands.

"I better get everyone in position to open the doors and find my woman." Wilson gave them a thumbs-up and walked away.

Isaac turned to her. "So, are we at the shy smile, handshake, or hug stage in our relationship?"

"Relationship?" She took her time to study the man. Last time they had met, she'd barely noticed anyone was in the room but Logan. Unlike her bad boy, Isaac was the perfect representation of a clean-cut professional. He was more likely to be Matt's best friend rather than Logan's with his tailored pants and white button-down and his brown hair neatly parted and combed off to one side. Isaac could blend in anywhere— put him in a suit, he would be a banker or a lawyer, or give him a white coat, the owner of a laboratory.

"The relationship between the friend and the girlfriend is extremely important." He put his hand to his chin. "If we don't start off right, I could be kicked to the curb in a second."

"No way, both our names start with *I*. That binds us." She held her arms out.

"Excellent deduction." He gave her a hug. "And may I say you look quite lovely?"

"I will take your compliment and return it." Though she had only met him one other time, he felt like an old friend. Like she knew him before.

"Well, it took me a while to get my hair and outfit just so, but it came together." He leaned on the bar. "Of course, nothing compares to your Mr. Alexander trying to get ready."

At realizing another opportunity, she polished off her drink. Suddenly, her whole world felt like it was leading toward the truth. Everyone was suspect. "Did he always take this long when the two of you would go out?"

"We tried it a couple of times, but we are not each other's types." Isaac laughed. "Actually, we don't really go out where we have to get ready. He doesn't like going out that much. It's a pain."

Fine, fair answer. She needed to dig deeper. How did Logan Alexander, the actor and investor, become involved with Isaac, the chemist? "Did you know him before he was a pain?"

He opened his mouth but paused, a slight yet noticeable break in the rhythm of the conversation. "Logan has always been a pain."

Of course, there was always the possibility she wanted to read too much into his actions. She tried one of Logan's tricks. "So the movie didn't change him much at all."

"I met him right before he started filming, but I think he has mellowed over the years." Rather than staying in his relaxed pose, he moved closer and leaned in. "I have to say that of anyone I met from the film, he was the true actor, the one who cared about the craft and telling the story."

The passion in Isaac's voice made her eyes well up. Still, Logan had never seen the movie all the way through until her. Maybe it was somehow too painful?

"However, that wasn't your question. You wanted to know what happened when we would go out, as in searching for women. And only to show my loyalty to you, I will let you in on the secret." Without her prodding, he continued. "We both rarely went into that scene. He hated the whole game of it and thought women only wanted him to say they scored with a star, and I was too much of a Poindexter to get anywhere without him."

Poindexter. His word choice reverberated through her like when someone hit her funny bone. A unique term for the geek or nerd, one not used often, but one used in *Hollywood Stardust*. She stared into his eyes. His expression didn't change, but something was there, deeper.

"Not that anything we talked about matters. Your date is here." He lifted his chin.

Instinct caused her to turn, and her breath caught.

How, where, and why did the man coming their way end up with her? Dressed in dark pants, a gray shirt, a tie, and a vest, and his hair pulled back with one naughty lock hanging down, only Logan Alexander could pull off such a look.

Like the superstar he should have been, his mere presence owned the room.

He kept his focus on her, but slowly sauntered across the room. By the time he reached her, trembles had taken over her body.

"Gorgeous." He held out his hand.

"You are." Grateful for the support, she put her hand in his and managed to get off the barstool without falling over.

He shook his head and held her arm out. "When I'm with you, I don't need anyone else's company, but damn if I'm not proud to show you off tonight."

Unable to help herself, she closed the small gap between them and kissed him.

His lips caressed hers, and he smiled. "I taste we already sampled the bar?"

"Just a champagne cocktail." She wiped a bit of lipstick off his lower lip.

"I don't want you to leave my side."

Funny, she wanted to say the same thing to him. "I won't."

"Good, because that's where you belong." He brushed the back of his hand against her cheek.

"Logan." She tilted her face up to him.

"Excuse me!" Isaac came over and put his arms around both of them.

"What do you want?" Still, Logan didn't take his eyes of

her.

"I wanted you to pay attention to me." Isaac stuck his face in with theirs and laughed.

"I believe when I came down here I caught you paying enough attention to my girl for all of us. Your attention quota is full." Logan pushed him back.

"Ivy and I need to bond in our own special way." Isaac gave her a wink.

"Well, you're done now, and Ivy and I will go bond in our own special way." In a possessive move, Logan slid his arm around her waist.

"Hey, we need to open the doors." Wilson rushed out and snapped his fingers.

Ivy tore her focus away from Logan to find the staff members waiting, and Giselle standing alongside Wilson. She waved to her best friend, and Giselle blew her a kiss.

"Well, you've been talking about this forever. Open the door." Logan backed them up toward the side of the bar.

With a final inspection as he walked across the room, Wilson opened the doors.

The light from the street illuminated the entry, and people began to stream in.

Wilson went into proprietor mode, shaking hands, hugging, introducing Giselle, and making small talk. The servers and rest of the staff scurried around them as the place filled up with well-wishers.

"I hate big crowds of people." Logan tightened his hold on her and motioned to the bartender. "Champagne cocktail and a soda water with lemon."

He didn't need to tell her twice since they hadn't moved from their spot since the doors opened. While people gathered around Wilson, only a few came over to Logan with a quick hello, maybe a handshake, but mostly waves and smiles.

"Here we are." He handed her the drink and tapped his glass against hers. "Thank you."

"For what?" She waited to take a sip.

"Being here, being with me." He stared into her eyes. "For the first time I've been at one of these events, I feel normal."

For as many questions as she had about the man who stole her heart, at last she received some answers with his simple admission. "Well, I'm going to toast to Mr. Logan Christopher Alexander, who finally proved beyond a shadow of a doubt that reality can be so much better than fantasy."

"I love you."

The words left his mouth with such ease that she would have missed them if they weren't three life-changing words. For the second time since he had joined her at the opening, her breath hitched. She opened her mouth, but what did she say? Did she return the sentiment? What if he didn't even realize what just happened?

"Shh. This is my turn." He smiled and put his finger to her lips. "I believe we have a toast to finish."

Caught in a daze, she copied Logan and put her glass to her lips.

"Come here." He took her glass, placed it on the bar, and pulled her close.

Never needing his kiss more, she lifted her face to his.

"Hey, the place is really on fire!" Isaac came over.

"I'm glad. That's what my brother wanted. I guess we're all getting what we want tonight." Logan raised his eyebrows at her. "What do you say, Ivy?"

Somewhere, she needed to find her voice. "Best party I've ever been to."

"All right, I don't need a doctorate to take a hint that this is a party for two, but before I let you stare at each other until it is socially acceptable for you to sneak away, I need to show you something." Isaac elbowed him.

"Make it fast." Logan took her hand, intertwining their fingers.

In a useless attempt to focus, she blinked.

Suddenly, the low constant hum of the people amplified as if someone had hit the ball out of the park, and as far as she knew, no one heard their conversation.

"Unbelievable." Logan tensed.

At last she tore her gaze away from the man who only minutes before had said he loved her and turned to the crowd.

No wonder the crowd went wild. "Ryder and Erin are here." Along with them came Brian the agent.

"What are they doing here?" A bit of excitement laced Logan's voice.

"You haven't all been together in one room since—" She stopped herself from going too far.

"Since that night." His voice cut through her. "Let's go say hello."

As he guided her away, she stopped. "Wait." She turned back to wrangle Isaac. He must want to at least watch the spectacle, especially since he knew Logan through the filming.

"What's wrong?" He gave her a little tug.

Isaac was nowhere to be found.

She followed Logan. "Nothing."

Hushed tones and whispers took over the place as Logan guided her through the sea of people toward his unexpected guests, and she found herself holding on to the man who loved her like a life preserver. All eyes were on them.

"Isn't this different?" Logan gave Erin a chaste kiss on the cheek and shook both Brian's and Ryder's hands. "What are you doing here?"

She detected something behind Logan's voice, a mixture of surprise and annoyance.

"You came to my set. I thought it only fair I show up to your digs. Plus, Erin called saying we owed you one." Ryder patted Logan's shoulder and turned his attention to Ivy. "And there's the real reason I came."

Ivy wondered if she would ever get used to talking to Ryder like a normal person.

The once teen idol grabbed her hand and pulled her into a hug, causing her to let go of Logan. "I haven't seen a better interview of myself in twenty years. I wanted to talk to you." Ryder wrapped his arm around her shoulders and took a couple of steps away from the rest.

She opened her mouth and glanced over her shoulder.

Though talking to Brian, Logan kept his eyes on her.

With her head held high, Erin held on to Brian's hand and glanced around.

Wait, Brian's hand? Strange.

"Seriously, I loved my interview, and after all this fanfare with *Stardust* is over, I want you to come and spend some time on location with me, covering the movie." He moved them closer to the wall. "I think it would make a great follow-up to your story with Logan. Maybe we can even find you a small part."

Once more she glanced over at the others, who were pretty much in the same position. The fact Erin seemed to be standing closer to Logan was probably a figment of her imagination. Maybe Logan was right about the constant together thing. The few feet separating them seemed like a mile or two.

"You told me you wanted to be an actress." Ryder waved in front of her face. "I'd love to give you your big break."

She forced her focus on him. "I'll have to check to see what mine and Logan's schedule will be, but of course we'll do something." If she had a job and if Logan still went to work with her. Her stomach swirled with nausea.

"If Logan's busy with all his money laundering, you can always cover me solo." Ryder winked at her.

A cold chill ran through her, yet she broke into a sweat. The urge to run overtook her, exactly like any time a camera was aimed at her. Well, until Logan.

Left without a comeback, she almost gave in and dashed to her rightful man, but was saved by the most unlikely source of them all.

Erin.

In a shimmering gold, figure-hugging cocktail dress, she joined them. "I didn't get a chance to say hello before."

"Hi." Ivy forced a smile on her face. "You and Ryder showing up was a huge surprise to Logan."

"It's been too long since we were seen together." Erin moved her hair away from her face. "But it feels as if change is in the air."

"Well, there's a lot going on right now." In search of Logan, she peeked around, finding him still talking to Brian.

"You seem to understand." Erin held out her hand.

With no true choice in the matter, she took it.

Erin pulled her closer. "The only thing that would have made this night perfect would have been Drew. I almost thought he'd be here."

"When was the last time you saw him?" She dared ask the burning question.

Ryder crossed his arms.

She glanced between the two of them and swore they had a silent conversation. Erin even went as far as to shoo Ryder away with a slight lift of her chin.

"I never get to talk to anyone." Erin turned away from him. "I saw him right after, then I saw him a year later, and he looked so different. The last time I saw him, he wouldn't talk to me, but I swore I thought he'd be here. I almost felt him here."

Ivy took a breath. The woman in her, not the wannabe actress or reporter, caused her to ask the next question. "Were the two of you together?"

As if she were on fire, Erin let go of her.

Ryder went to Erin's side, bent down, and said something in her ear, and Erin nodded.

Unsure of how to handle the situation, she scanned the room for Logan only to be blinded by a flash and another uproar of the crowd. She really wished Logan, the man who wouldn't normally leave her side, would do one of his amazing appearing acts right now.

She blinked away the stars in her eyes.

"There they are!" Several men holding up cameras charged inside.

Both Ryder and Erin struck a pose.

"Tell us, is this an unofficial reunion?" one of the photographers called out.

"Are you all here?" shouted another.

Neither answered, and it seemed as if the three of them were caught looking for the one man designated as the mouthpiece.

After what seemed like years, Logan dashed across the room with Brian right behind him.

"Ivy!" He headed toward her.

"Logan, now that you're here, can we get some answers?"

the first photographer yelled.

Before he reached her, Logan stopped, glancing between her and the other two. "I don't remember hiring any photographers for the event."

The crowd rumbled with a low laugh.

"He was always the natural." Brian came up beside her. "Quite a few of his lines in the movie are ad-libbed."

"I know." She wrapped her arms around her shoulders. Of all of them, he should have been the breakout star.

"Can we get a picture of the three of you together?" The man gave Logan a thumbs-up.

"Do you promise to send me copies?" He joined Erin and Ryder.

Again, laughter.

"Of course." The photographer raised his camera. "I'll even frame them."

The flashes went off as the three posed. Around the room the guests raised their cell phones to snap a shot.

"Got my story snaked again." She sighed and watched the flashes pop around them, little stars bursting with light, but the fan in her wanted to savor the moment, forget the backstory, and simply enjoy.

"You got the interviews, and you got Logan." Brian patted her shoulder.

"If we ask nice, can we get you and Erin?" the second photographer asked.

Even though Ivy knew he loved her, the request still made her chest constrict.

Ryder stepped back.

Erin slid closer to Logan, and Ivy swore the woman looked back at her with a slight smile.

Were they in some competition she didn't know about?

"This is good for him." Brian leaned back on his heels. "He always fit in the spotlight."

"Then why was he pulled out of it?" She balled her hands into fists. Anyone could see where he belonged.

"He chose to leave," Brian countered.

"I think you and I both know that's not true." She refused

to allow the man next to her, or anyone else, to tell her different.

"How about we make tonight really special and recreate the scene everyone wants to see?" The photographer stood on one of the chairs.

"The dance." Fan or not, she couldn't watch, but she refused to be one of the many that ruined Logan's chances. She tiptoed into the background.

⤶

"They want us to do the dance." Still staying in a pose, Erin faced him.

Logan held up his hand in an attempt to stop the scene before him. He scanned the area. Every person's face blended together, but one would stand out. Where was Ivy?

All eyes were on him. For the first time in twenty years, he wasn't the man responsible for getting the sequel to a beloved movie canceled. He wasn't the bad guy. His woman was responsible for the tide turning.

"Did you ever wonder why one of the most memorable scenes was between me and the villain and not me and the hero?" Erin produced one of her smiles, a mixture of sexy and sweet. She tilted her head slightly, knowing exactly how to catch the light to show off every asset.

"You do know you are not Roxy, and I'm not Steven." The rhythmic clapping of the crowd beat in time with the reverberating through his body.

"You know that's not true. We should have been together. That's why this is the scene everyone comes back to time and again." She reached up to get in position.

"Let's see it," a photographer yelled out. "The world is waiting to see the famous couple."

Only one person's arms went around his neck. "Then let me get the right girl." He backed away from Erin. "Get the music on."

A collective gasp went through all the guests, and Erin's expression went from her model-perfect smile to wide-eyed and unrehearsed. Without caring if he remained the villain for the rest of his life, he rushed through the bar and headed straight for the kitchen.

The chef and one of his assistants both pointed, showing him the way.

With a slight nod to the staff, he made his way around the far side of the refrigerator to find Ivy holding a glass, complete with a lime wedge as a garnish. "I believe this is mine." He approached and plucked the unwanted citrus off her drink.

"It got a little warm out there. Please, do whatever you need to do. Maybe it was all those champagne cocktails." Rather than turning, she remained facing the wall.

After putting the lime in his mouth, he called her bluff. "So you decided to chase it with a vodka on the rocks?" At least whoever served her gave her the good stuff.

"Logan, you need to go back out there. Didn't you see how they want you?"

"I don't care who wants me as long as one person wants me." He set her glass aside.

"Logan, you know I want you." She stared down at the floor.

"Plus, they want the two of us anyway." He put his hands on her waist and pulled her closer.

At last, she lifted her head.

"If they want me to recreate a scene from the movie, they're going to have to do it with the woman I'm in love with, not some actress playing a role." His admission earlier had come unexpected to both of them, yet he had meant every word. For a second, he paused, not realizing until that moment that even though he'd told her to wait, he had wanted her to repeat the sentiment. "Will you dance with me?" Rather than wait for an answer, he took her hand and led her back out to the main room.

Among the applause from the patrons, the penultimate song from *Hollywood Stardust* began.

Ivy's trembling resonated through his hand, but he wouldn't allow her to succumb to stage fright. He guided her right into the middle of the room, but rather than melding into him, her body was tense, wound tight. "Look up at me."

She did as he asked.

"It's just you and me." He stared into her eyes. "Come on, you know you dreamed of this."

A hint of a smile twinkled on her face, and at last she wrapped her arms around his neck.

"Those are the right arms." He pulled her flush with his body and started by swaying to the music.

"That's her, the one from the tabloid." The photographer's statement was followed by a series of flashes.

The song boomed through the speakers, the music that followed him for two decades. Every time he heard the familiar tune, he took pause. It brought him back to a specific moment to being on set, being with his friends, and thinking he was on the verge of something spectacular. He wished someone would have told him the something spectacular would happen decades later and not with some movie contract but with the woman in his arms.

He treated his audience and his girl to a bit more sensual version of the dance he and Erin had shared on set and wondered if anyone would guess that for the first time tonight he had told someone other than his mother that he loved them. All he could do was pray she returned the feelings and hope his little display fulfilled one of her dreams.

In *Hollywood Stardust*, the song served as a turning point. It cast a doubt on Roxy's love for William and made her realize she could have feelings for the manipulative Steven.

He glanced around the room at the guests gawking, the photographers taking advantage, and his big brother, who had the smarts and the ingenuity to find a video camera to capture the moment. Lastly, Ryder and Erin stood on the sidelines with twin scowls at not being the ones in the spotlight. As he and Ivy danced, a different turning point barreled down on him, but nevertheless one of change.

When at last the music ended, Ivy hugged him tight.

Applause vibrated the room, and she pulled him close. "I love you too, Mr. Alexander."

Along with never having told someone he loved them, no

one sans his mother had ever said the words to him. Unable to resist, he turned his head and kissed her, a true kiss, not a camera kiss, complete with opening their mouths and tangling their tongues and leaning her back. Only the whistles and catcalls stopped them, and with reluctance, he pulled back. She hid her face in his chest.

"What did she say to you?" the more boisterous of the two photographers asked.

"She loves me." He had to let it out. "But it's all good, because I love her too."

Again, the guests applauded.

Exhibition time was over, but contemplation and alone time with Ivy was upon him, and he lifted his hand toward the photographers. "Thank you."

One photographer saluted, while the other gave him a thumbs-up. "Good luck."

He leaned down to her. "How about we disappear?"

She nodded and cupped her hand over his ear. "I want you to make love to me. I can't wait."

His body jolted at her words. Though no one else could hear her, her admission in a public venue still aroused him. "We're out of here." He assessed the room, making an exit strategy and seeing nothing but unwanted commitments, connections, and favors he needed to repay laid out before him.

The first rushed over to them.

"This is for Ivy." Wilson held up the data card from the video camera. "I didn't want you not to have your own story."

"I appreciate that." She took the card.

"Good work." Wilson held out his hand.

"Hey, we're going to head up. You have it covered. This place is going to be a great success." He shook his brother's hand.

"I knew planning the opening around the anniversary was smart, but I'll never know how you managed to get Ryder and Erin here. It was brilliant, brother, brilliant." Wilson leaned in and hugged them both. "I always told you that *Hollywood Stardust* would continue to make us money. You just didn't want to listen."

He took a breath and pushed back. Ever since the day the agent had spotted him, Wilson had played his second banana, and Logan had spent the rest of the time trying to make it up to him. Try as he might to get away from the movie, everything in his life revolved around it, down to Ivy.

"Go on, you two lovebirds. You deserve the night off. Wonderful performance." Wilson gave him one last pat and walked away.

He glanced down at her. If he ever needed to be alone with her, the time was now. "Come on."

They no sooner turned, than Ryder, Erin, and Brian appeared, almost causing him to jump back. Both his former costars appeared as if they recently had a root canal.

"Ivy and I have an early shoot tomorrow for Chargge and have to go, but I want to thank you for coming." The urge to push Ivy behind him to shield her overwhelmed him. Instead, he wrapped his arm around her shoulders.

"Well, that's a brush-off if I ever heard one." Ryder chuckled. "Maybe this will be the jumping-off point to a new career. Just don't forget where you came from."

Apparently, he wasn't the only one who found Ryder's remark cutting. Though Ivy didn't speak, she dug her nails into his side. He stared right at his friend. "I don't need a career. I'm independently wealthy, in case you forgot."

"Nope, it's always important to protect your money at all costs." Ryder raised his chin. "As I said, we just wanted to come by and show you our support."

"And it was appreciated." He returned Ryder's gesture and heard the real message behind his words. They were checking up on him.

"As for Miss Ivy"—Ryder gave her a hug—"my offer to make you a star still stands."

Logan clenched his jaw. What was Ryder hatching? Twenty years wasn't enough time to go by to allow him to forget that the second he and Erin had gotten together, Ryder had come in offering bigger and better things.

"I'll have to take that up with my agent." Ivy pressed her body against his.

"I'd sign you in a second." Brian stepped forward.

Why did every termite suddenly crawl out of the woodwork and offer the woman he loved her dream?

"Thank you, but I'm already represented." She looked up at him.

He fought a smile.

"Oh, well, I didn't know Logan was opening an agency, but maybe I'll give you the couple price since I represent your agent." Brian gave him a thumbs-up. "Just get through the anniversary party and then we'll talk. I've been watching the numbers."

He needed to give it to Ivy for not even responding to the man.

Erin glanced at him.

"Good night, Erin." He knew he better play nice with Erin while she licked her self-inflicted wounds.

"I never thought that out of all of us you would find love first." She shook her head. "I always thought things would be different."

"So did I." On purpose, he gave her a cryptic answer, but one she would understand.

Her eyes widened, and without another word, she headed toward the exit.

Brian followed, and Ryder saluted and left, stopping to sign an autograph on the way out.

"Can we go?" Ivy stared straight ahead.

"Yes." Keeping hold of her, he made a beeline for the back, nodding to people who wanted to stop him on the way. All the conversations replayed in his head, and in the background, everything told him he needed a change.

They went up the stairs and down the hall to his room and he retrieved his key from his pocket. "Should we go back to the apartment?" Originally, they had decided to stay at the restaurant.

She stood next to him simply looking down at the floor.

"Ivy." He needed to get this off his chest. "I don't know if you realize this, but most major deals come from the small chance encounters that happened tonight. If you want to talk to

Brian about representing you or you want to be in Ryder's film, I'll set it up for you."

"When I saw them come tonight, I was happy. I thought that's what you wanted. I thought they wanted to be there for you, but you were miserable, and they only showed up to make sure you weren't stealing their limelight." She shook her head and turned toward him, tears twinkling in her eyes. "You were the one who should have been the star."

"Ivy." He took her shoulders and pushed her back against the wall. In a million years, he would never be able to take her all in.

"What?" Her eyes searched his.

"I am a star with you, and that's all that matters." Love, desire, and the need to be with her drowned out everything else. Erin, Ryder, even his past didn't matter with Ivy. When she looked at him, she saw only the mislabeled villain, the proverbial bad guy with a heart of gold, and he never wanted that to change. He took her face between his hands, dipped down, and swept his mouth across hers.

Her lips upturned in a smile.

Rather than rush, he repeated his action, taking time to truly kiss her, taste the way her lip gloss blended with the alcohol giving him his own kind of high.

Deepening the kiss, she wrapped her arms around his neck and opened her mouth.

He pulled back slightly. Lately everything seemed fast and out of control. Vandalism, events, paparazzi, parties literally under their feet. Their lives zoomed at record speed, and he practically threw her in bed every night and made love to her at the same velocity. Though magnificent, he needed to focus.

She gazed up at him.

Once more he kissed her, feather light, teasing her by taking her bottom lip between his, and then moved back to look at her, to notice the flush on her cheeks, her swollen lips, how it took a moment for her to open her eyes.

A moan escaped her throat.

He skimmed his hand down her side, admiring her curves.

"Logan." Her voice came out breathless.

Rather than answer, he trailed his fingers up her arm and over the graceful swoop of her shoulder. Keeping his gaze affixed on her, he unlocked the door and took her hand, guiding her inside where at last he gave in to her, pulled her in tight, and crushed his lips to hers.

In unison, their mouths opened and their tongues found each other. As with any time he kissed her—hell, as with any time he simply looked at her—his body reacted.

Her hands snaked their way under his vest, down to his waist, and traveled toward their goal where, if he let her continue, she would find him already inflamed and ready to satisfy them both. If he could get her out of the dress, he could be inside her in an instant.

No. Not tonight. Not the night he told her he loved her. For this night he needed to show it as well. He caught her wrist before she reached her destination and kissed across her jaw, her ear, and made his way behind her to the back of her neck.

She shuddered. "Oh."

"Do you like that?" He closed his eyes and breathed in, her perfume swirling around him.

"Every time you touch me." She tilted her head.

He took her hint and gave her an openmouthed kiss at the juncture between her neck and shoulder. "Every time I touch you, what?"

"I just want you."

Though she went to turn, he held her steady and found the zipper on the back of her dress. "What do you want me to do?"

"Make love to me." Her voice changed, now dreamy as if under a spell.

"I'm making love to you right now, and I'm going to spend the night making love to you." He inched the zipper down, exposing her back. First, he traced the skin he revealed, then kissed the same spot. "Don't move. This is my show."

She whimpered, and the signal let him know she needed more.

He slid the zipper down a little more and unhooked her bra. Every bit of skin he revealed he fondled and kissed until he found himself on his knees.

"Logan." She breathed his name and braced herself on the dresser. "Please."

From his vantage point, he studied her, her pale skin almost glowing against the open dress she held up by draping one arm over her breasts. At the sight, his mouth watered. He pulled off his vest and loosened his tie. "Drop it."

Without question, she obeyed and the dress fell, pooling at her feet.

In keeping with her tradition, she wore no panties as to not create any lines to ruin her outfit. Before ravishing her, he lifted each of her feet to free her dress and placed it on the nearest chair. Finally, he turned her toward him.

Any remnants of shyness she possessed around him needed to go, especially since they loved each other. Even now, she had her hands over her breasts and legs pressed together. "When are you going to realize how much I love looking at you?"

Her lips parted, but she didn't speak. Instead, she put her hands back on the dresser.

Damn, if her breasts weren't magnificent, made only better by the fact they were au natural, with some sway and bounce as she breathed that no surgeon could duplicate. He couldn't resist and reached up to graze his fingers over her already tight nipples. "So perfect."

At his words, her cheeks reddened.

He made sure to not break eye contact as he skimmed his hands down her sides, working his way down and nudging her legs apart.

She bit her lip.

He held her gaze a moment longer before moving in and going after what he really wanted.

The second his mouth connected with her most intimate area, she gasped.

Better than any delicacy he could conjure in the kitchen, her taste filled his mouth and his erection swelled. He treated her to what he knew she loved most, and alternated between flicking his tongue over that all too sensitive bundle of nerves and sucking on her.

"Logan." Arousal blunted any embarrassment, and she spread her legs to give him plenty of access.

He continued, teasing and tempting and then lavishing her with the attention she craved. With ease, he added one finger and a second. His love was more than turned on, and he loved bringing her to this point.

"Oh." She twisted her fingers in his hair and moved with him. "Oh, God."

His own desire growing to a painful point, he unfastened his belt and practically tore his pants open, but didn't stop. When he entered her, she would definitely appreciate the moment.

Carefully, he used his teeth, edging her closer, and thrust two fingers inside her.

"Logan." Her muscles contracted around the source of pleasure. "I'm going to come."

He let up, his fingers retreated, and he barely allowed his tongue to make contact.

"Ah!" Her thighs trembled. She couldn't take any more. "Please!"

"Do you love me?" He straightened up and kicked his pants away.

"So much." She basically fell into his arms.

"What do you want?" He held her close and got them both on the bed, taking his position on top of her.

"For you to make love to me."

"That's what I want." He slid inside her. Slick and ready, her body opened right up, but still kept a tight hold on him. "'Cause I love you."

She sucked in her breath and instantly wrapped her legs around his waist.

Though he could simply bang into her and bring them both to an amazing end, he resisted and chose to treat both of them to a series of slow, metered strokes. "How's that?"

"Umm." She arched her back. "More."

"Take a breath." He kissed her and closed his eyes, taking in the fact he was making love to the woman he loved. Their bodies joined, moving together to literally bring the other to a climax, the ultimate bond. "God, you feel good."

She pulled her legs back farther and undulated against him, working to drive him as deep as possible.

"That's right." With the way she writhed and squirmed beneath him, he had no choice but to speed up, thrust harder.

"Yes." She found his mouth and kissed him deep. Her hands roamed over his back and took in his backside.

Talk subsided, the world faded into the background, and he lost track of how long they lay on the bed, kissing, making love, and admiring the other's body. Only with Ivy could he let go and be free.

The pressure built, the distinctive throb that forced him to move faster in demand of being let loose. "Ivy." His control waned and he called out her name. "I'm there."

She dug her nails into his shoulders, her muscles tightening. "Please."

Unable to stop, he plunged into her. They both needed the release. "Come, baby."

As if her body was trained to obey him, she cried out. The ripples of her orgasm gave him the last push he needed to achieve his climax. In a rush, the surge of his release hit him. His body pulsed in time with hers, giving her everything he had and blanketing him in the most exquisite ecstasy.

Exertion and exhilaration leaving him light-headed, he closed his eyes and tried to catch his breath. Beneath him, she panted, her heart nearly vibrating. There was no one else he ever shared so much with, no one else he wanted to share with. "I do love you, Ivy." He pressed his lips to her temple and held her close as he moved to her side. "I do."

She cuddled up next to him. "It's unbelievable."

Though her tone came out dreamy, he glanced down at the top of her head and considered her words. "Why is it unbelievable?"

At first she didn't answer, but then turned up to him. "Because when you want something so bad and you finally get it, it can seem unbelievable."

"Believe it." He scooted down until they were face-to-face.

"I do, but it's scary."

"Don't be scared. Love shouldn't make you scared. I wouldn't say the words if I didn't mean them."

She pressed her palm to his cheek and kissed him. "Then I'm a very lucky girl."

No, he was the lucky guy. The one who finally got the girl, the one he wanted and the one he most definitely loved. Though Ivy didn't say the words, he knew why she was scared. Way back in her mind, the villain and the rumors existed. She simply chose to not acknowledge them.

He never lied when he told her the rumors weren't true, but she didn't realize the truth was worse than the fables the media made up. If she wanted a real villain, she needed to look no further.

Adrenaline shot through him and he sat up.

"Are you okay?" She reached up to him.

He captured her hand and kissed it, staring down at her. How did he tell her what was truly unbelievable was not his love for her, but what he had done? "Tell me you love me, Ivy."

A smile taking over her face, she pulled him down. "Damn you, Mr. Alexander, I couldn't love you more if I tried."

He gathered her up in his arms and lay back down. In his case, the truth wouldn't set him free, but he needed to make some changes and make it disappear.

                                        CUT TO:

EXT. STEVEN'S GRANDPARENTS' HOUSE — DAY

WILLIAM convinces ROXY to take a walk with
him.

                    WILLIAM
              It seems like forever
              since I've spent any time
              alone with you.

WILLIAM grabs ROXY'S hand and pulls her
closer.

                    ROXY
              Well, we are on a group
              trip.

                    WILLIAM
              Still, we were supposed to
              be together, make it
              official before
              graduation.

WILLIAM wraps his arms around ROXY. She looks
up at him.

                    ROXY
              Will.

                    WILLIAM
              Where there's a will,
              there's a way.

WILLIAM kisses ROXY.

ROXY pushes him back.

                    ROXY
          William.

                    WILLIAM
          Come on, Rox. What do I
          have to do to prove I want
          to be with you?

                    ROXY
          Exactly what you are
          doing.

WILLIAM stares at her. ROXY gets out of his
arms.

                    ROXY
          Before we are together, I
          need to tie up some loose
          ends.

Chapter Nineteen

Out of the corner of his eye, Logan spied his enemy. Well, one of many, but today's sampler plate came in the form of the makeup woman from Chargge.com.

Though pretending to read the latest issue of *Celebrity News Magazine* with the four-page spread on *Hollywood Stardust* featuring him and Ivy as the centerpiece, he waited until the woman stepped within his firing zone.

He drew his imaginary line and waited.

At last, she crossed over the cord he dubbed as the boundary into his space. "No makeup, no wardrobe change." He turned the page.

Right in his crosshairs, she stopped. "Logan."

"Mr. Alexander." He corrected.

"Mr. Alexander." She tiptoed toward them. "I was told Ivy seems a bit pale."

He glanced at his girl. Rather than acknowledge their conversation, she sat completely consumed in the task he had given her of organizing his wallet. Her nerves had started before their morning coffee, but once Wilson had presented him with a stack of papers and magazines with the story of their dance, she had panicked. By the time they had made it to the Chargge studio, her anxiety had bested her and he'd used an old trick he'd learned on the set of his movie: he offered a distraction. Apparently, his wallet held endless fascination for her.

"Her complexion is not pale. It's ethereal and matches her

ensemble perfectly," he growled.

Luck have it, Ivy wore a midcentury kimono-inspired dress with her hair up and no panties. He would make use of that last fact later. Making love offered amazing anxiety relief. All the pent-up energy needed to go somewhere—may as well be an orgasm.

The woman looked between him and Ivy. One false move and the blush brush would need a rebristling.

He narrowed his eyes, daring her.

Craig entered the studio, trailed by Julia. "Kathy, the star is fine."

Ivy raised her head and clutched his wallet to her chest.

"Julia said to fix her." The woman turned.

"She looks as if she's ill." Julia snarled. "Did stage fright get the best of her even with her man in tow?"

This was a whole new enemy to snare. Logan tilted his head from one side to the other to stay loose for the kill.

"She's fine," Craig repeated.

The makeup maven huffed and scurried out of the studio.

"So, what is the plan?" Craig joined them and sat at the edge of the coffee table.

Julia remained off to one side, her arms crossed, and her lips pursed, resembling a part of the anatomy he would rather not mention—but he was sitting on it.

"First, I'm going to ask why someone who is not your top-rated star is here." Logan leaned back and crossed his legs.

"This was originally my spot. I want to know what happens with it so I can salvage it when I get it back." The battle-ax crossed her arms.

"Let me ask you something." He leaned forward to Ivy's boss. The man had to be sleeping with Julia to allow her behavior. "Is she really *that* good?" Talk about pent-up energy—the woman had the power of a stink bomb.

Craig widened his eyes.

"Why are you here?" Logan went right to the source.

Julia cleared her throat. "Like the rest of the world, I wanted to see the two of you together. Her grandfather was known for media stunts."

"Then you should watch the story unfold like the rest of the world." He stared her down.

"Julia." Craig spun toward her.

"I will get ready for my broadcast." As if to check the time, she lifted her wrist to her face and backed out. "Do you think this whole thing will be over in about fifteen minutes?" She left without waiting for an answer.

Craig faced him once more. "So, what is the plan?"

"We're going to address the story, be honest, and give our fans something they won't find in any of the other media coverage." He grabbed Ivy's hand. More like pried it away from her.

"Excellent. I was a bit concerned when the story came out. I didn't want the carpet ripped out from under us." Craig nodded. "You've been trending all morning. The timing is perfect. I'm going to stay for the filming."

Once more, he took in Ivy. Her ethereal complexion turned pale. "Before we get started, I'm going to give our gorgeous star a pep talk."

Craig took the hint and stood. "I would say break a leg, but I think Logan would kill me." He patted Ivy's shoulder and left.

"Here's your wallet." She thrust it at him. "I never knew anyone to take a good driver's license picture, but here we are."

"Baby." He returned the wallet to his pocket and reclaimed her hand. "Why the sudden bout of nerves? I thought we were past this."

The director walked to the edge of the set behind Ivy and held up three fingers.

Logan gave him only a slight chin lift. Under the guise he needed some water, he spoke to the man and told him to begin filming without his skittish love realizing it.

"That was before—"

"Before what?" He slid his chair closer to hers and, with his free hand, gently prodded her face to an ideal position to catch the light.

"Before you said you loved me and before our story was plastered all over every piece of printed and electronic matter in the world." She furrowed her brow.

"Oh, but that should make this even easier. Anytime you are with the one who loves you, nothing horrible can happen."

Her first smile of the day lit up her face.

The director gave him a thumbs-up telling him they had started filming.

"You know, we never really talked about it, but what did it feel like dancing with me last night?" He made sure to keep his tone conversational.

The color the stupid makeup woman wanted to artificially apply to her cheeks appeared in its natural glory in a perfect pink glow. "Logan."

"Come on, tell me."

She bit her lip and toyed with his fingers. "Well, it's so weird because part of me was, like, I'm here dancing with Logan Alexander to *the* song. That's sort of all part of the fairy tale, especially for my inner teenage fan girl."

"What did the other part say?"

"That I'm dancing in front of a million people, but I'm with the man I love and nothing else matters." She turned his hand over and traced her fingernail over the lines in his palm.

A shudder tickled its way down his spine, and he arched his back. Before he had the chance to ask another question, she continued.

"You know, once we started dancing and the music took over and my body was pressed up against yours, I was so aroused by everything I could hardly wait for us to go be alone." Now she stroked one of his fingers. "I think someone else felt the same way."

His mouth opened, but his words left him.

She leaned over. "I love when I can feel how turned on you are when we are in public. It's so naughty."

Redirect. He needed to redirect her. Maybe he needed to devise a better plan on a live feed.

A wicked chuckle escaped her throat, and she lifted his finger to her lips, giving the tip a combination of a chaste, but erotic kiss. "How are we doing now?" Her gaze fell to his lap.

He glanced over at the director. The man had his hand over his mouth and made a motion to cut.

Before Ivy decided to use his finger to demonstrate what she did to him on their second round of lovemaking, he squeezed her hand. "Why don't we cut and take a look at what is now going to be the second most infamous moment of our Chargge.com interview series."

"What?!" Ivy jumped out of her seat. "What do you mean cut?"

"It's okay." He stood and held his arms open for her.

"Oh my God!" She put her hands over her eyes. "Did I just speak about your erection to the entire world?"

"It's a natural human body function, especially around you." He took her by the shoulders.

Eyes wide, she looked up at him. "I almost gave your finger a blow job."

"I saw where it was going and stopped it." He gave her a toothy grin.

"And now, I just spoke about giving you a blow job in front of everyone here." She groaned and hid her face in his chest. "Why didn't you tell me we were filming?"

"Because you were so terrified and I had to fix it."

Tears twinkled in her eyes only adding to her already ethereal look. "I want the world to see you the way I do."

"What do you mean?" He pulled her in closer.

"I love the fact that one minute you will be giving me club soda to settle my stomach and the next terrorizing the makeup lady." She wrapped her arms around his neck. "I love that you wait for me to put my garnishes on your plate, but will then stomp into a restaurant's kitchen to tell them how to season things properly."

"Ivy."

"I guess I just love you and that's what I want the world to see." She stood up on her tiptoes and gave him a sweet kiss on the lips.

Before her fear of cameras took center stage, he had toggled about how to deal with the Erin and Ryder situation. With her words, her honest words, he had his answer. "I love you, baby." Unable to resist, he gave her a real kiss, then reluctantly interrupted them prematurely and pulled back. "Maybe we should finish the segment. I need to go get something done."

"Don't worry. We took care of that." The director came to the set. "We got everything sans the blow job talk and up to you saying you loved her. It was raw and real, and nothing anyone else has. Good work." He gave them a quick salute and walked toward the back.

"Well, now I know exactly what we can do later to give me a reward for my good deed." He raised his eyebrows.

"What else do we need to do?" She smiled up at him.

We. Oh, no. While he didn't want to be apart from her, he couldn't take her on this errand. In an effort to buy some time before he answered, he slid his phone out of his pocket. As if their ears were already burning both Ryder and Erin texted him. He quickly typed a mass message back asking them to meet right away.

"Well, it was different, but it was great." Craig approached. "Ivy, I want to go over some reports with you before you leave."

Reprieve. Her boss handed him the perfect excuse. At his phone vibrating, he glanced down to see they both accepted. Their anxiety must be getting the better of them. "You know, I need to go have a really fast meeting with Erin and Ryder, so why don't I leave you here to do your reports and then I'll come and swoop you back up."

She wrinkled her nose. "The reports won't take long."

"If you can use it for the story, the reports can wait," Craig offered.

Ivy nodded.

Damn. "No, no, there are a few business things we need to discuss. Let's do it this way, then we have the rest of the day and evening together." He tried his best to make it sound enticing.

"Oh, okay." Though she put a smile on her face, the paleness returned. "I should get my work done anyway."

"I'll be fast." He leaned down and gave her a kiss on the cheek. "I love you, baby." In an effort to make the whole thing sound as benign as possible, he waved and walked away, turning back twice to get a look at her before exiting. He didn't remember the last time there was this amount of distance between them and shook his head.

"Wow, you're letting your precious little protégé out of sight." Julia sauntered down the hall.

"Maybe you need to find a mentor because you need an

acting class or a million." He reached for a pack of cigarettes, but then remembered he didn't smoke.

"I need to land some of her luck. Only she can end up in the tabloids and have her story stolen from under her nose and still end up on top." The viper let out a nasty chuckle. "I should have taken the story when I had the chance."

He forced himself not to skip a step at her words, but a chill ran through him. At one point, he thought it had to be Ryder leaking the stories to the media, but now he knew better. Once more, he texted his former cast mates changing the location of their meeting.

"Thank God for small favors." He had one more villainous act in him before retiring that part of his persona, but right now, he had to deal with his original sin.

I got a little detained. Are you all right? I'll be there as soon as I can and will spend the night making it up to you.

Ivy narrowed one eye at Logan's text. His really fast meeting she couldn't attend turned into not quite that fast.

She swiveled her chair toward her computer and stared at the screen. With Logan constantly with her and his whirlwind of activity, she never had the chance to really sit and think, only react. With some time on her hands, she rewound the last day from the moment Logan had said he loved her to the shoot this morning.

"It's okay." She didn't want to read too much into Logan's actions, or wonder what he had to hide by not having her there, or try not to focus on how both Erin and Ryder seemed conveniently available within a moment's notice. Instead, she decided to indulge a little and clicked on the video Wilson filmed of their dance. As of yet, she hadn't gotten the opportunity to watch it all the way through.

Fine, she couldn't stop the flutters in her stomach. She leaned in and studied Logan. The man possessed the most amazing aura. Everyone in the audience stared at him, captivated, and she didn't blame them.

In what seemed like a lifetime ago, she would hear that

song and a pang would ring through her chest at thinking about *Hollywood Stardust.*

The video panned over the spectators, pausing at Ryder.

Yes, the man was insanely good-looking, but nothing like her Logan. A slight snarky grin on his face, he leaned back on his heels and watched. Though she didn't know him all too well, her instinct told her he was pissed.

Next, the camera paused at Erin. Where Ryder seemed to be able to hide his emotions, even Erin's extensive training in acting couldn't mask her feelings. She stood with her arms crossed and her head tilted away, but with her eyes on the action, her expression nonexistent.

At one point, Erin must have loved Logan. It was no secret they had their so-called connections over the years. While Ivy wanted to believe they only came together out of mutual need and shared history, the way her chest tightened told her things were different for Erin.

Maybe that was why she couldn't go with Logan.

"You will always have your little dance."

At Julia's voice intruding into her thoughts, Ivy hit "Pause" on the video and squeezed the mouse. "Do you need something?"

"I thought since you were abandoned by your boyfriend, I could get you used to the idea of returning to your real job, and had some items for you to research." Without an invitation, Julia entered, took the chair on the opposite side of her desk, and leaned over. "Oh, maybe you are already doing some research, perhaps on your competition?"

Ivy swallowed and, after taking a breath, faced her nemesis.

"You know they were together before." Julia put some files on the edge of the desk.

"Oh, really? That's news to me and the rest of the world." She balled her hand in a fist at the way her voice shook. "Do you have any evidence?"

"Maybe you lost your touch." Sighing, Julia sat back in the chair. "Try a search engine, or just look within your gut. You know I speak the truth. The look on your competition's face is enough anyway. Not that it's any competition."

Her heart sped, thumping a warning not to listen, but the bitch managed to articulate every one of her fears. Rather than continue on, she decided to combine two of Logan's tactics: the redirect and the direct question. She always was a fast study. "What is your problem with me?"

"Do you really want to go there?" The woman narrowed her eyes.

She had to give it to Julia for at least not trying to say she didn't have an issue. "I wouldn't have asked if I didn't want to know." Another Logan lesson: goad them and prod them into giving something away.

Almost like she was cocking her weapon to fire off the next round, Julia pursed her lips. "You don't know what it takes to make it in this business."

When all else failed, stay silent. In truth, it took her a little off guard that Julia didn't have something bizarrely inappropriate and cutting to say.

The tactic worked, and Julia continued. "You grew up all around the industry, your family is practically considered Hollywood royalty, you could have any job you wanted, and you chose to come here? Why?"

"I thought this would be a good place to start my career, learn how to get over my stage fright. Plus, the wave of the future is streaming and live feeds, and this is a great place to learn."

"Don't you understand?" Julia shook her head. "What you see as a stepping stone, a means to an end, I see as my career. I fought for this job. Your family was your résumé. You didn't even audition."

"Every industry is all about connections." She gave an attempt to defend herself, but she had also been bitten before by someone she or her family didn't know when someone pretended to be a friend but they only wanted to pry into personal business.

"At the end of the day, you couldn't even do your job and you were given to me so I could take up your slack, and then—"

"Then?" Ivy needed to hear the rest.

"Then you take what's supposed to be an interview and make it into a career-changing assignment." Julia stood. "Only for you, it's another stepping stone. You won't get the true story because you get a man out of the whole deal."

"Julia." She held her hand up to stop her from leaving. Maybe the woman was nasty, horrible even, but it made sense.

"What?"

"I'm sorry." Maybe everyone dealt with jealousy a different way.

"Don't be." Julia put her hands on her hips. "He's probably using you. The man is a villain, you know, on screen and off."

At having broken one of Logan's rules, she pressed her lips together. She should have never allowed her enemy to see her softer side.

Julia sauntered to the doorway, turned, and pointed to the computer screen. "From one woman to another, I would find out what's going on behind the scenes. I think you know anyway." With her final blow dealt, the woman left.

Ivy returned to study the image of Erin, now blurred from the tears in her eyes. If Logan could have the beautiful starlet, why was he with her? Of course at the moment, he wasn't—he was at some quote, unquote meeting. She clicked on her Internet browser and typed in Erin's name. The typical websites popped up.

She returned to the search bar, added the word *relationships*, and hit "Enter."

The second image to pop up was Erin and Logan, clearly years after *Hollywood Stardust*, holding hands. She had seen the image before, but right now it mocked her.

What did she know about Erin Holland? She strummed her fingers on the computer keys. Not much after the movie. The actress didn't really interest her once she typed the last word of her thesis.

Unsure where to start, she returned to the Chargge.com home page.

Chargge.com. The neurons in her mind connected. She reached over to her bag and pulled out Erin's card from her wallet.

Erin's card with the Chargge.com e-mail.

E-mails were a living history, one most people didn't bother to purge, especially someone with the attention span of an actress. Beyond a shadow of a doubt, Erin's e-mail held many secrets. Hell, in those little messages were probably the keys to whatever had happened that night, why Logan had served as the mouthpiece, and her relationship status.

Once more, her phone announced a text. She lifted the device.

I'm sorry baby. I'll be there in a couple of hours. You okay?

She chewed her lower lip and read the text twice before responding.

Do what you need to do. I'm just doing some research. She hit "Send" and turned back toward the screen and Erin's card.

Unsure of what to do with the time, she typed Erin's e-mail address into the log-in bar.

If she only knew the password, she could find out everything.

Someone like Erin wouldn't have a complicated password. The woman said herself she had trouble remembering things.

Ivy pulled her lower lip. Maybe Matt would know how to crack the code.

At her own thought, she winced. Breaking into e-mail would be wrong, illegal.

Her cursor flashed in the password box, beckoning her. On a lark, she typed in the word *password* into the box.

An error message indicating the wrong password came up in red.

Well, the woman was smarter than she thought.

She almost clicked the *x* in the corner to close the window, but almost as joke her herself, she decided to try once more and typed in *12345678*.

For the second time, the error message came up with a warning. She would get one more try before she was locked out.

Always one for a riddle, she shut her eyes.

Seconds later, she opened her eyes and glared at the password box. Would serve Erin right always having to go to Logan for everything. They did one movie together so it wasn't like they had a relationship. With a lift of her chin, she typed in *Hollywoodstardust*, lifted her finger high, and pounded the "Enter" key with conviction.

The screen changed and in a flash she was gazing at a list of Erin's e-mails.

"What?" She gasped and held her hands back away from the keyboard.

After catching her breath, she slid her chair closer to the computer. Did she dare? What if her actions could be traced?

Her body shook, and she scrambled to pick up her phone, scrolled past Logan's and Giselle's texts, and found the master of all things electronic.

You in the building?

She tapped her foot waiting for the answer.

Only if you're buying the candy bars and have time for a chat.

She bit her lip at Matt's message and typed back. *How about a candy bar, my treat. A chat and some computer expertise, your treat?*

What's wrong in the digital world?

Having some e-mail issues. It wasn't really a lie.

I'm on my way, cape and all.

Thanks. She hit "Send" and turned back to the screen. What had she done? Could she go through with it?

❦

"Is there a reason we are in the middle of nowhere?" Ryder stomped to Logan's side.

"I hardly consider a piece of land in Los Feliz the middle of nowhere." Logan continued to stare out at the view of downtown Los Angeles. The little upscale town, close to Hollywood but far enough away to have a life, always held appeal for him.

"This is not cool in heels. You should have warned me." Wearing a scarf around her head, sunglasses, and a cross between an overcoat and a cape, Erin clutched Ryder's arm and put her hand above her eyes as if she were trying to see something way off in the distance. "What is this place?"

"This is my land." He swiped his hand in front of him.

"You own a piece of land here, but you live above your brother's bar?" Erin shook her head.

"After I got out of rehab." He made the quotation mark sign around rehab. "I used to drive around up here. It was my first investment."

"So, we bought the land." Ryder motioned between himself and Erin.

With slow steps, he circled his friends or his enemies. Their status toggled through the years. He stopped in front of them. "I earned every cent."

"Speaking of which, this is why we called this meeting." Ryder lifted his chin.

"Correction." He held up one finger. "I called the meeting."

They stared each other down.

"It doesn't matter who called the meeting." Erin wedged herself between them. "What matters is Ryder and I spoke after yesterday's little gala, and we want to make sure that your end of the bargain is being held up."

"While I'm not surprised you asked me, I am disgusted." He put his hands in his pockets. "Let me ask you a question."

When they both stayed quiet, he continued. "Do you ever wonder what it would be like if we woke up one day as totally separate entities from each other? No strings, no contracts, no payments, nothing."

"What do you mean?" Erin turned to Ryder.

"Although I think I understand, why don't you elaborate?" Ryder glared at him.

"I want to set you both free. I want to set myself free." He swore the lump he had carried in his stomach since he'd realized he wanted Ivy lessened some. It allowed him to take a full breath. "We need to separate our lives if we are ever going to have lives."

Though he didn't expect cheers and a band to start playing, he did expect smiles and possibly a handshake. Instead, Erin turned paler than Ivy at the studio, and Ryder turned away.

"Don't you understand?" He walked over to them. "We are finished. There's nothing more owed. You can do your own thing."

"That night, you told us our lives would be forever intertwined," Erin whispered. "You said you would take care of everything."

"I did take care of everything. Both your careers flourished in their own ways. I became a businessman. But I think twenty years is enough. You can't say you don't agree." What was the issue?

"So when you decide the time is right, you can drop us and go on with your life?" At last Ryder faced him. "Did someone offer you some money for finally telling the story?"

He stomped up to Ryder. "I have been offered money too many times to count, and though some of the sums were better than what I was paid for not telling the story, I never said a word."

"He wants to tell his girlfriend. Maybe he already did." Erin put her hand to her chest.

"No." Ryder squared his shoulders and looked him in the eye. "He got offered a movie deal and forgot that at the end of the day we own him."

Each one of their accusations piled up on one another, a wall of bricks between him and his love. He lunged at Ryder, grabbed his collar, and pulled him up to his face.

"Logan!" Erin jumped back.

Ryder tensed, but didn't struggle, almost daring him to do something.

"Listen here, both of you." First he stared down Erin, then Ryder. "I have no need to rehash the past. I need to have a future."

"You're masterminding this, just like you masterminded that night." Ryder grabbed his wrist.

"Listen here." His heart threatened to leave his chest, his muscles begged for him to act, but he tempered himself and gave Ryder a tug. "Never forget that yours truly covered for you. Yours truly sacrificed himself so you didn't have to do the sequel. Yours truly allowed you to go on with your careers. Remember, I had offers too."

"You got paid much more for covering for us than you would've ever made on that independent film." Ryder hissed at him. "We had real deals."

"It was what I wanted to do, and I didn't do it. I got fired." He thrust Ryder away from him.

Ryder stumbled but caught himself.

"You canceled the sequel because of Drew." Erin's voice cracked. "You took him away."

"You nearly killed him and then you decide you want him?" He stepped toward her. "You slept with me, you slept with Ryder, you slept with Brian, and the only man you claim you wanted, you never even touched?"

She pressed her lips together.

"He worshiped you. You broke every promise you ever made to him and left me to mop up the mess as usual." He leaned forward. "You don't want him. You never did. You only wanted the thought of him."

A tear rolled down her face.

"So why did you bring us here?" Ryder held his arms out. "Did you just want to flaunt what your percentage of everything we made since that night bought you?"

"Maybe I wanted to show you what the future could look like." Once more he took in the view. "This is my future. Right here. I wanted to start it off right."

"You want your future without us." Ryder shook his head. "Toss us out when you don't need us anymore."

"I don't see why anything has to change." Erin backed up.

"The only things that would change would be your bank accounts. The old rules would remain in effect." He attempted to be reasonable.

"So the only one giving up something would be you?" Ryder took a deep breath.

"Well, you wouldn't have me to do your dirty work anymore. You can all speak for yourselves, fight your own battles, and handle your own disasters."

"I'm not ready to make a decision. I don't know." Erin continued her retreat toward her car.

"I have to say, I'm with my costar. I don't think making a snap decision is a good idea." With a bit of a grin at having one-upped him, Ryder shrugged.

"You made the decision to pay me for two decades in less than an hour." He walked to the edge of his property. The kitchen window should face the view as should the master bedroom. Yes, once he and Ivy chose a contractor, they would have to be extremely specific about what they wanted.

Of all the property he had bought, he had never purchased a home. He barely remembered having a house, but he could have one with her, and he wouldn't let anyone taint what should be incredible for him or especially Ivy. "Don't contact me until you have an answer. If you need something, tell Brian."

"What if our answer is no?" Ryder's voice fell flat.

"Then I'll keep collecting the checks, but I don't think I'll be funding any more films, and I'm certain Drew would agree with me. Not that either of you would ever talk to him." He slid his phone out of his pocket.

"Is that a threat?"

"No, a threat is telling you that you will no longer have your pretty little face if you ever hit on Ivy again." He didn't even bother glancing in Ryder's direction. "She's smarter than Erin and saw right though you."

"Logan."

"Get off my land."

"When you want out, that's it, right?" Ryder raised his voice.

Logan didn't move. "The last time I checked it was the other way around."

At last, the sound of footsteps followed by the slamming of doors and a car driving away let him know they abided by at least one of his wishes.

Once more he found himself staring out at his property. The situation almost proved to be laughable. When Ryder and Erin wanted out, they got their wish and he was the genie, even though it meant giving up his acting career.

Hell, the situation seemed tailor-made for him. He was always the bad boy. The studio kept all four of them in character the entire time, so he would only be living up to his reputation.

At the time, it had seemed easy: he would be set, Wilson would be set, and he could still have it all.

Yes, it was easy. So easy. Life as an up-and-coming star is easy, especially when there seems as though there's no direction to go but up.

He remembered that night driving to the Beverly Garland hotel with the top down on his new little Italian sports car. He was at one with the stars, at one with the universe, and he was the leader. Yes, he called the meeting with Erin and Ryder. He would single-handedly fix all their ailments and make their acting careers.

The valet nodded at him as he pulled into the driveway, and as a reward, Logan tossed him his keys and a hundred dollar bill. Fine, the money was to spite his brother, but the valet was a cool dude. In a few short months, Wilson would no longer be his guardian, and he could spend his money as he wanted.

Upon walking up to the front desk, he was instantly handed a key to the suite they rented for their so-called meeting, but the space was more like the entire top floor of the hotel. Stardom had benefits. The Beverly Garland didn't even charge them. All they had to do to earn their keep was walk through the lobby a couple of times. They even had full run of room service. A few times they even let him into the kitchen.

Once the elevator opened into the suite, he froze as the scent of something other than cigarettes and the echoes of laughter wafted around him.

Every muscle in his body tensed, but he forced himself forward, through the living room area looking over all of Beverly Hills and into the master bedroom.

Like an ill-fated treasure hunt, he found his costars there. The room looked as if a dormitory of rich frat boys vomited up all their possessions inside and then they decided to make a mess. He balled his hand in a fist, preparing for the fight. In one corner, a shirtless Ryder, in the other Erin, in nothing but an oversize T-shirt. The ashtrays, the bottles, the other more hard-core drug paraphernalia, and the disarray told him everything. He was only thankful he didn't walk in on the middle of anything else.

"I told you he would show up." From his position reclining back on the bed, Ryder pointed at him. "In fact, he's early."

"If I know nothing else in this world, I know that I can rely on Logan." Erin downed a glass of something. She approached him, pressed her hand to his chest, and looked up at him with those big blue eyes. "If anyone knew the truth about you, it would ruin our reputation entirely."

"I told you we needed to talk." He grabbed her wrist. "We have decisions to make."

"Why don't you come and join us?" She slid her hand up and wrapped her arms around his neck.

No matter if she was all done up for a media event or a tipsy mess, Erin was universally gorgeous and he swore not to be pulled into her vortex of crap again. He put her hands on her waist to push her back.

She resisted and stood on her tiptoes. "You know it's you."

Ryder stretched and stood, ran his hands through his hair, and disappeared into the bathroom.

"Is that what you told Mr. Scott before I got here?" With a bit more force, he managed to get her off him.

"That's not fair." She backed away.

"That's the truth."

"You could have brought him, you know." Her eyes narrowed.

"What? So he could walk into this?" To prove his point, he motioned toward the tangled bedding. "I can see how brokenhearted you are."

"I don't know what I'm doing anymore." As if instantly going into a role, she waved her hand in her own face in a mock attempt to abate the tears.

"Then let me tell you." He pointed behind him. "We are going to go have a meeting about the sequel and then you are going to clean up this mess before housekeeping decides to sell photos of this to the *National Reporter*."

Redressed and as cocky as ever, Ryder joined them. "Remember we're supposed to live our roles. Well, here we are, the triangle." He walked across the room and patted Logan on the shoulder. "Let's give our girl a moment to collect herself and then have our meeting."

After shrugging Ryder off him, he returned to the living room and went to the bar, grabbing a bottle of club soda.

"You need something to mix in that, my friend." Ryder took a seat on the couch, spreading his legs in the need to take up as much space as humanly possible.

Logan opened his drink. In truth, he thought Ryder only sat that way to air himself out. With that image in his mind, he took a long swig of the bubbling liquid in hopes it would work its magic and get rid of the nausea. "Looks like you cleaned out the bar."

Ryder simply shrugged.

Without a word, in a new set of clothes, Erin entered the room and sat by Ryder. So this was how it was going to go down. Normally she had the decency to sit in a neutral location.

"You called this meeting. Let's get going." Ryder put his hand around the back of the couch.

Erin only stared at Logan, her eyes still wet from her faux tears.

Well, he might as well get right to the point. "They want to recast the part of Charles since Drew won't sign the contract."

"No." Erin shook her head.

As if this was nothing more than a bother, Ryder stared up at the ceiling.

"I think we need to make a stand and demand Drew, but there's some work we have to do first." After taking another gulp of his drink, he came forward and sat on the chair facing the couch.

"What do you mean?" Playing her role of innocent to the bitter end, Erin's voice came out more of a sad whisper.

"Erin." Ryder growled.

"I think you know exactly what I'm talking about." Logan leaned forward. "You got what you wanted. Everything centers on you."

"I have begged for him to talk to me, but he won't take my calls. I even wrote a letter." Her true fiery attitude blazed, melting away Erin's sweet veneer. "We can't do the movie without him."

"Erin!" Ryder spun toward her. "What are you talking about?"

She pressed her lips together and sat back, turning away.

Right below the surface something brewed between the two of them. Seemed all signs pointed to the fact they were doing something more than screwing and getting high before he arrived. "What're you talking about?"

Ryder faced him. "Erin and I want out of the sequel."

Before responding, he made sure he heard the words correctly. The way his stomach knotted told him his ears were functioning to perfection. Without them, there would be no movie. "You have signed contracts."

"We also have other offers on the table. Good ones." Ryder's tone reminded him of when Wilson tried to explain his parents' divorce.

"So do I, and they are waiting until after the filming." He attempted to remain calm, but he needed the movie, wanted the movie. "*Hollywood Stardust* created us."

"*Hollywood Stardust* created you. *Hollywood Stardust* created Drew." Ryder lifted his head up high. "*Hollywood Stardust* did not create me or Erin."

Almost every day of filming, he had to hear about how Ryder was classically trained, a seasoned actor. Heat burned through him until he broke out into a sweat. Erin wouldn't even look in his direction, and he remained silent waiting for the rest.

Ryder stood and took his time walking around the coffee table. "Here's the deal. We need your help in breaking the contracts. If Erin and I are seen as people who go back on our word, it could ruin our careers and the roles we have lined up."

"You want me to take the fall?" Refusing to look up at Ryder, he stood and stared him down.

"Logan." From her hiding place at the corner of the couch, Erin squeaked out his name.

"Let's face it, you're going to do an indie film or two and that's all. Drew was smarter than all of us and walked away. Erin and I need to move on. We don't want to be stuck as Roxy and William our whole lives. That may be okay for you, but not for us." Ryder held out his hand to shake. "Come on. Work with us, and I'll make sure we get you some parts in real films."

"Go to hell." He shoved Ryder away from him.

Ryder stumbled back, tripping on the side table that held a huge decorative vase. The entire collection crashed to the marble floor, sending shards of pottery and pieces of furniture shooting through the room.

Erin screamed.

"I'm done with both of you. If you're such great actors, you get out of your own contracts." He made his way toward the door.

"What? Are you afraid to finish the fight?" From behind, Ryder yelled at him.

Logan turned with enough time to catch his enemy charging toward him, but before Ryder collided with him, he pulled back his fist and swung. The sick vibration of his fist connecting with Ryder's jaw rang through him.

"No!" Erin burst into tears

"You will forever pay for this." Wiping his face, Ryder charged toward him.

The next moments whirled by in a blur. An angry storm, the two of them raged, throwing punches and shoving the other, and leaving a path of destruction in their wake. Together, they knocked pictures down, broke every knickknack in the room, and when Ryder grabbed him by the collar and thrust him against one of the walls, a huge mirror came crashing down, shattering and shooting sharp glass everywhere.

The pain throbbing through his body from Ryder's blows was only overshadowed by the sharp stabs in his arms and back of his neck from the pieces of mirror embedding in his flesh.

Erin sobbed. Amid the shards, he and Ryder panted and then the phone rang.

The three of them turned toward the intruder.

On the third ring, Erin lunged for the phone. "Hello?"

Both he and Ryder stood still as Erin nodded at whomever dared call them.

"Thank you. Good-bye." Her hands shook, but she managed to hang up the phone. "That was the valet. He wanted to warn us. People are complaining about the ruckus. The police are on the way."

"Shit!" Ryder ran toward her and grabbed her shoulders and glanced around the ruined room littered with booze and illegal substances. "It's too late to run. We're ruined. They're going to find everything. Do you know what that means?"

Erin's eyes widened. "We have to hide it."

At the turn in events, Logan couldn't stop his smile. "Well, the sequel is done, but so are you." He added, wiggling his fingers at them.

"We only wanted you to help." Erin scrunched up her face.

"We thought we could take you with us. We're the ones with the potential and you know it." In a sad attempt to fix the situation, he picked up a bottle and an ashtray and dumped it in the one trash can that wasn't knocked over.

Only the fact law enforcement would break down the door at any second stopped Logan from going after his foe once more.

"Wait!" Erin pressed her hands to her chest and ran to him, her shoes grinding the pieces of mirror into the overpriced floor. "Wait. Don't you see? We only wanted to take you with us."

Not following and not caring, he crossed his arms.

"Logan." She took his arm. "Logan, please hear me out."

He glanced down at her, hating that even through the mess she was still beautiful. "Every word you say may be held against you. Don't worry. You'll hear that soon enough."

"Listen. Help us, please." She held on to him for dear life. "Take the rap. Say it's all yours. You're seventeen, you're a minor, and you'll get off without a scratch."

"Are you insane?" He tried to pry her off him.

"Look, either way the sequel is through. The minute they see what's in the other room, the studio will drop the movie. Let us have our future." Tears streamed down her eyes. "I promise we will take care of you."

Ryder came forward. "I swear on everything I have, we will take care of you."

The possibilities ran through his head. Erin was right. The sequel was over no matter what. They had sure things, and he could have everything. "I don't need you to take me with you. I need a vested interest."

Both his dollar signs stood before him, hanging on his every word. He held their future and therefore he held the power. "A percentage of everything you make and I want a contract."

"For how long?" Ryder asked the most important question.

He took his time looking at each one of them. "For as long

as the career I'm giving you lasts."

"Done." Erin shook his hand. "I'll have Brian draw up the contracts, but no one else can ever know."

Like earlier, Ryder held out his hand, but the attitude, the entitlement had left him.

"*Hollywood Stardust* may have created me, but never forget who created you." Logan took the gesture and stared out the window overlooking Beverly Hills and waited.

He took a breath and looked out on his property once more. Two handshakes and a contract later, he had given Erin and Ryder their careers and thought he had given himself freedom.

Well, this was over. That night needed to vanish, and with it, the foolish agreement among three desperate people who hadn't been close to being adults but had needed to act like it anyway.

With or without their contract, he was through. He would have a life with Ivy, and she would never know what had happened. He only wished he could tell her about his heroics tonight. Maybe some stories were better left untold. Funny what happened when he tried to be the good guy. The role of villain always suited him better. At least this time he got the girl.

<hr />

"So let me get this straight, you hacked into Erin Holland's e-mail?" Matt chomped down on his chocolate.

"*Hack* is a very strong word." Ivy pushed her candy bar aside. All the nougat in the world wouldn't take away the swirl of nausea in her stomach at even thinking such a heinous thing. "I just started typing different passwords and on the third time." She motioned toward the machine. "Oh my God, I'm going to go to jail. Please fix it."

He swallowed and took a swig of his soda. "You know, if you would have asked me this before I almost asked you to marry me, I would have given you the answers you seek in a heartbeat."

"What do you say now?" She tried to smile, but was sure her upturned lips appeared more like a person who just got something shoved up their backside with no lubricant.

"Before I give you my official answer, I have a question of my own." He met her smile with one of his own, only much more genuine.

"All right." She sat up a little straighter.

"If it weren't for Logan, would you have said yes?"

If nothing else, she owed it to him to pause and honestly consider his question. She rewound her life, the one before Logan, or at least personally knowing the teen idol turned true love. With Matt, that special pit-of-her-stomach breathless feeling didn't exist. Her amazing friend and confidant never changed. "I love you too much to do you the disservice of giving you less than the best. I could have never been what you deserve, Logan or not." The woman who ended up with the man in front of her would be lucky, and she prayed whoever that ended up being would know it.

"Thank you." His eyes glossed over, and he nodded. "For that, we will resume our normal relationship." With a little bit of bravado, he raised his arms, mock cracked his knuckles, and leaned over the desk. "Since you logged in with her password, you are pretty much fine. All you need to do is log out and no one will know the wiser."

"So just log out and it's like it didn't happen?" She glanced between him and the computer.

"Yeah, our e-mail is made for remote users. As long as you didn't reset anything, you're fine. It's not like a bank where you get a notice that a different computer was used to log in to an account. The Chargge.com e-mail is made for users on the go. They have a history of logging in from multiple locations." He sat back. "Just log out and take a breath."

Once again, her gaze traveled between the screen and her friend. "It must be illegal to log in to someone's e-mail and then sift through them, right?"

"There's no *must* about it. It's illegal. E-mail is like your underwear drawer. No one really wants anyone sifting through it."

"Yeah, it is very wrong." She never did anything wrong. In

fact, she was barely bad.

"All you need to do is log out and eat your candy bar."

Stuck in limbo, she didn't move.

"Are you going to log out?"

"Well, I'm not going to stay logged in to her account forever." She wrung her hands together.

"Ivy." His voice rang out a warning.

"I'm logging out." She turned to her computer and took hold of the mouse. The "Log Off" button loomed at the top of the screen.

Matt cleared his throat.

"If one glanced through the e-mails but didn't change anything, it wouldn't show, right?" Her finger hovered above the mouse. One click and it would be over. She wouldn't betray Logan, but then if she didn't have all the facts, she couldn't save him either. "She probably deleted them all anyway."

"Well, I think I'll leave you and your conscience alone." Her friend pushed out of his chair and backed up toward the exit. "Whatever you do, make sure you log out when you're done." He closed her office door behind him.

"Thanks." Alone, she inhaled, filling her lungs to capacity, and then let the breath loose.

Her mind swirled. In those e-mails there had to be at least some of the answers she sought—about Logan, their relationship, what happened the unmentionable night, Drew. How did Logan expect them to move forward without ever telling her the truth? What was hidden?

One look.

She stared down at the screen. The list of incoming e-mails were mostly unopened advertisements.

As she moved the mouse pointer up to the search bar, her hand shook. She still had time to log out and chock the whole experience up to a jealous mistake.

Though some would call it an opportunity.

All her life she had been told she didn't have what it took to make it in this business. Fear. Fear of failure, fear of success, or fear of appearing as a fool stopped her from doing what she dreamed. Stories about her grandfather's antics filled her mind since she could remember. His motto—take a chance.

"I have to do this for Logan." At last, she clicked in the box, typed his name, and hit "Enter."

The screen flashed. Her heartbeat reverberated through her ears, and she was 100 percent certain she would throw up all over her keyboard, but finally the e-mails appeared, lined up in a perfect column.

No, Erin didn't delete e-mails—in fact, quite the opposite. If there were some sort e-mail hoarding, Erin would need to go into rehab.

At least fifteen years of messages scrawled out before her, both sent and received, and she scrolled to the last one.

The first few were simply mentions of Logan, a lunch date or his name in combination with others in conjunction with a party or event.

A trickle of sweat made its way down her spine, and she scrolled to the next e-mail, one to Ryder.

> *Hello Love,*
> *Got a residual check today and made sure to make a payment right into Logan's account. It's almost like we are parents giving our child his allowance. Do you ever wonder what he does with the money? When do you get back from location? I miss the nights. With you, things feel normal. We need to figure out how to get on the same project.*
> *Wren*

Deposit to Logan's account?

Her throat dried out, and she continued her way through the e-mails. Next came Ryder's response.

> *Hey. I think Logan uses the money we send to buy more cars. One day we will open up his garage and a million vehicles will come tumbling out. I sent him a check that I swear was more than I made, but I guess since I get to make movies, I should be happy. His career tanked.*
> *You're just bored 'cause you're between*

projects, but don't worry, I'll be back next week
and be right there as long as you promise to do
what you did the night before I left. Get on your
hands and knees and get ready, but make sure
you take your pills. Make no mistake, you and I
would make the worst parents ever. The only
one who deserves us is Logan.
    Later,
    Ry

Bile rose in the back of her throat, but she couldn't stop. She scrolled through several of Erin's and Ryder's exchanges of the same nature and stopped at an e-mail from Erin to Logan with the subject of Drew.

I saw him. He looked so different, not at all
like he did that night. He lost weight, looked
older with a sadness surrounding him.
    I ran after him, but in a move I can only
assume he learned from you, he shooed me
away, got in his car, and left.
    Why does it feel like I'll never see him again?
    Why does everyone leave?
    He doesn't want to hear me. No one does.
    I don't want these feelings. I'm in pain all the
time, and it's easier just to put myself in a place
where I can forget it or at least not think about it
all the time.
    When you see him, tell him I'll never forgive
him for not speaking to me even if it was just to
say good-bye.
    Erin

Minutes later, Logan had responded.

Don't do anything or take anything. I'm on
my way there.
    L

The pain in Erin's words was tangible. Logan's loyalty to his costars dripped off the computer screen. What on earth happened between them to make Drew walk away from everything? Ivy swallowed back the tears and continued her quest, stopping at an e-mail from Brian.

> *Just got a call from Smithstein. You didn't get the part even with the strings I pulled. Director complained you seemed distracted and messed up your lines. Did you even read the script? Are you on something? I'm not doing this with you again. Next time there won't be a Logan to clean up your mess. You complain about me, you complain about him, but remember without the two of us, you would probably be a junkie with your costar in the gutter.*
>
> *Don't bother showing up at my place with nothing but diamonds and perfume on again. The diamonds are fake, and the perfume cheap. Get it together, I am running out of balls of twine to make strings from.*
> —*Your agent for now*

The next e-mail wasn't Erin's reply, but instead an e-mail to Logan.

> *Lost a part today. Thought I should let you know you lost a revenue source. Maybe you should be my agent. Brian is furious. The director accused me of being distracted, and Brian accused me of being high. I did the audition on Drew's birthday. Probably no one but you or me even realized the date. Though while I suffered, I'm sure you got to see him. Do you bother giving him my messages or is it all a big joke to you? I know the answer. I sometimes think I should have sided with you and done the sequel. At least I would have had more time, but you managed to get us out because I begged you. Maybe one day you will deliver on what I really want. Don't bother replying. Needed to vent.*

Apparently Erin had been on a roll. Only a couple of minutes later, she had written a message to Ryder. The first part of the e-mail consisted of a similar rant to him, but the last part of the message caught her attention.

> *Do you ever think about it? Do you ever just want to go into that little magic place? Remember how we would go lock ourselves away with our stash? Smoke, eat, and make love for what seemed like an eternity? Too bad we got caught. It was so good back then.*
> *You know I love you,*
> *Wren*

As if she were addicted to a soap opera, Ivy rushed to the next message.

Logan's response had come about two hours later.

> *Temper tantrums and stomping your feet won't get you what you want this time. Go running to Ryder to make it better. Remember this: there is a clause you stay clean in our contract. I swear I'll stand there and watch you pee in a cup myself. Stop your tears about the one you can't have. Just like the rest, you would toss him in the trash once you achieved your goal. Well, in your case, you recycle, but that's as much my fault as yours.*
> *Don't give me your tears about the sequel. You and Ryder wanted an out and you got it. You're welcome.*
> *Get to work. Your true love is not any of us. It's your image on the screen, so go make it happen.*
> *LA*

Ivy tried not to shudder at the reference to Erin and her man together and went to Ryder's reply.

> *Baby, you and I are one destructive pair. If left to our devices, we would have been a mess.*

*We both know it. We were too high on our
careers, our drugs, and ourselves to notice how
badly we failed. The percentage taken out of
each and every check I receive—not to an agent
or a publicist, but for a screwup mistake—only
reminds me of what I have lost. I suppose I will
fall back on my mantra and say I hope I make
Logan a very rich man because I will be even
wealthier.*

> *I need to tell you something, but I want you
to promise me you won't get upset.*

> *I met someone. She's not in the industry. I
want to see what happens if I leave my baggage
at the door, and I wanted to be straight with
you.*

> *Don't dwell on Drew. If you were meant to
be, your paths will cross one day.*

> *As Drew once said, you know I'm always
here for you, but in my case I mean it.*

> *Ryder*

Even though the e-mails were exchanged a few years ago,
at Ryder's news, Ivy's chest tightened all the same. She blinked
away the tears for the woman she mostly disliked. What
happened with Drew? Did Erin really love him?

She went to the next e-mail from Erin to Brian.

> *My love,*

> *I've been sitting in my bungalow for hours
trying to think of what to do, who to call, where
to go. All paths always lead to you.*

> *I swear I'm not on anything. I was off that
day thinking of things I lost, when I should have
remembered I found you, or you discovered me.
Not that it matters.*

> *I know you love me, though it would be nice
to hear the words.*

> *I won't show up at your home to make it all
better, but remember my fake diamonds and
cheap perfume left you panting and begging for*

more.

*If you come to me, I promise to leave you
panting, no begging required.*

Years of e-mails told a story of a troubled woman, one who
wanted love, but didn't know where to look besides her history.

More importantly, the mist that surrounded that night,
that awful night that seemed to define them, began to clear.

She glanced at the time and went to an e-mail sent only
days before Logan walked into her office for an interview.

Logan,

*It's been a while. The anniversary is upon us.
I can't believe it's been twenty years since the
premier of the movie that changed all of us
forever. Funny, I still feel like the eighteen-year-
old on that screen. At the time I thought you
were so young. The gap between seventeen and
eighteen seemed as large as the Pacific Ocean.
Who knew that the fact you were underage
would later save me and Ryder?*

*You may have been the youngest, but you
were the smartest and the most talented. Don't
think that every day I'm not reminded that you
should have been a star. I will speak for Ryder
and say we hope that giving you a piece of our
careers made up for the fact you lost the sequel
and the other parts you wanted. Unfortunately,
Logan Alexander became typecast. Maybe in a
way we all did.*

*As per our agreement (look at how official I
sound), Ryder and I will continue to not speak
about the movie, the night you were arrested, or
the sequel. You were always the one to take care
of us. You know what needs to be done and
remember all the details. Hell, at this point, I can
only remember the name of the movie.*

*I have started to get phone calls and such
asking to break my silence. I would like to know,
how do you want to handle this? I'm done*

making mistakes in my life. Seems they last decades.

When I decided to write to you, I swore I wouldn't mention the unmentionable, but I can't stop myself. Will you tell Drew I need to see him? Do you think that maybe twenty years is penance enough? How many times do I have to beg? Is the fact that I never moved on enough, or do you still think I'm the world's greatest actress? If so, you better figure out a way to get me a goddamned Academy Award.

Since I'm not allowed to talk about this with anyone but you, I will say this. If I had one thing to change about that night, or the days leading up to that night, I only regret not getting the chance to talk to him and plead my case. Everything else, I take responsibility for, though in the end you took the blame.

I will ask one more time.

Attached are the places that already contacted me.

Wren

Ivy clicked on his response.

Erin,
As always, I will hold up my end of the deal. Continue to give me any information.
I'll see about that Oscar.
Logan

The only e-mails after that were ones forwarding Logan media contacts.

Finally, she did as she should have done before and logged out of Erin's e-mail. Her prediction was spot on. The answers were all there. Somehow the two of them had roped Logan, the underage teenager, into taking the fall for their drug use and getting the sequel canceled. In turn, the guilty parties had paid him for his silence, leaving him the villain in the movie and in real life.

"I seem to be low on what has now become my basic sustenance for life and I need my IV." Logan knocked on the doorjamb.

No matter how many times he showed up for her, her breath caught at the sight of him. "You're here."

"Always." He pulled a long-stemmed red rose out from behind his back.

As if on automatic, she stood and went straight for him. Rather than taking the gift, she wrapped her arms around him, burying her face in his chest and breathing in the scent of his soap and bit of cologne.

"Are you all right? You seem a little spooked." He ran his hand through her hair.

"Is it all right to tell you I missed you?"

"Only if it's all right to tell you that you didn't miss me one fraction of the amount I missed you."

She tilted her face up to him. "How was your meeting?" Her stomach twisted at the thought, though somewhere along the way her jealousy seemed to have vanished.

He bent down and gave her a soft but lingering kiss. "You know, throughout the years the three of us have sort of waxed and waned. We were sort of thrown together and just stayed that way, but I think after this gala, I need to wane."

"I understand." She pressed her palm to his face. A little stubble tickled her skin.

"You always do." He kissed her wrist. "However, I didn't spend my entire time with them. I had to do a little planning, and tomorrow night I have something sort of special planned for the grand finale before the gala."

"What is it?"

"I'll be the director, and you'll be my leading lady. It will involve a very apropos reenactment, as well as some sweeping romance, and some shocking reveals and plot twists, and that is all you're going to find out." He winked. "How about we go home? I thought I would make love to you and then make dinner."

"Isn't it supposed to be dinner then making love?" She raised her voice to sound coy.

"No, I need you first." He kissed her. "I love you, baby."

"I love you. Let me get my things." With a sigh, she separated from him, returned to her desk, and peeked over at him. The world needed to know who the villain was and who the hero was. They needed to know they got it wrong.

She turned back to her computer staring at the Chargge.com home page before turning it off. Of course if the world knew, then Logan would know she had betrayed him. She didn't know if she was ready to write that script.

HOLLYWOOD STARDUST

                                    CUT TO:

INT. STEVEN'S ROOM — GRANDPARENTS' HOUSE —
FLAGSTAFF, AZ – NIGHT

ROXY sneaks into STEVEN'S room.

                ROXY
          Can I come in?

                STEVEN
          Looks like you already
          did.

STEVEN slides over in the bed and pulls the
covers back.

ROXY checks the door and joins STEVEN in bed.

                ROXY
          Tomorrow we will get to
          Hollywood Stardust.

                STEVEN
          Aren't you celebrating
          with the wrong person?

ROXY turns on her side and faces him.

                STEVEN
          Or maybe it's the right
          person after all.

STEVEN kisses her. ROXY pulls back and gasps.

                STEVEN
          So what happens after we

reach Hollywood Stardust?

     ROXY
I don't know. All the
rest.

Chapter Twenty

"Logan." Ivy held her arm out in front of her in a vain attempt to navigate where he led her. "When can I take the blindfold off?"

"When we're at our destination and Wilson can film your reaction." He chuckled and wrapped his arm around her shoulders, pulling her in tight. "We're almost there."

Thus far, Logan had made her wear the blindfold from leaving their apartment to wherever they stopped the car, and now it seemed as if they had walked several miles. In preparation for what she assumed was going to be his quote unquote sweeping romance, she wore a halter-style 1950s maroon dress, complete with matching heels. The heels! She also didn't expect to be accompanied by her best friend and Logan's brother, but they were filling in as the production crew for their final shoot before the twentieth-anniversary gala.

"Hold on. We're right there and Wilson just needs to set up." He positioned her and gave her a light kiss on the top of her head. "Are you ready? This could be life changing."

Her stomach filled with flutters. Before Logan had hid her eyes, she had caught sight of him in black pants, a white shirt, and a black blazer, a bit dressier than his normal shoot attire. "What's going on?"

"Ivy, I thought you wanted me to take the blindfold off," he crooned in her ear.

She tried to use her other senses to take in her surroundings, but wherever he had brought her was pretty silent. "Where are we?"

"Why don't you take a peek?" He pulled the tie on the blindfold.

Once her vision cleared, she gasped. "Oh my God!" For fear her knees would buckle, she grabbed on to Logan's arm.

Before her, in all its grandeur, stood the Hollywood Stardust theater, well facade. The straight lines, the triangles, and the squares done in rich blues, reds, and metallic gold exemplified the art deco styling of the famed theater that never truly existed.

She glanced around. Logan had brought her to the movie studio lot. Other buildings, or pieces of buildings, littered the area, and she smiled.

"I felt it only fitting we do our last shoot where the movie ended." He guided her closer.

"It's so amazing." She stared up at the slice of building that meant so much to her and pictured the last scene of the movie. How Steven drove away. The moment Roxy opened her eyes and watched him go. Maybe the moment wasn't life changing, but it was certainly one she would never forget. More life changing was what she knew about Logan's past but didn't know how to tell him. "Thank you."

"Wait, we are not close to done." His low, robust voice reverberated around her. He led her to the front of the theater and turned them toward Wilson. "I'm going to tell you a secret."

"What would that be?" Though she knew they were filming, the only jitters she felt were for the man in front of her.

He pointed back at the building. "Even though every moment of the movie leads up to arriving at this spot, I have never been filmed outside this set piece."

All right, maybe the moment was life changing. She couldn't stop the smile. Only the two of them would have this moment. If the sequel were ever filmed, maybe he would have had his chance in the limelight in front of the facade on a much bigger screen. At the thought, her heart ached.

"In fact, Miss Ivy, you may or may not know this, but you've been instrumental in many firsts in my life." He turned to her and took both her hands. "The first time I trusted someone, the first time I honestly couldn't wait to see someone so bad it hurt, the first person I fell in love with."

The energy around them seemed to change, sizzle with pent-up anticipation. Unsure of what would happen next, she held her breath.

"You are the only person I will ever love—maybe that's a first and a last." Out of nowhere, he got down on one knee and reached into his jacket pocket.

She froze and watched Logan as if she were watching a movie. No way could this be happening to her.

"All I know is we are finally at the point where I am losing count of the days and I never want it to end. Will you marry me?" Like magic, he produced a diamond ring and held it up to her.

Marry Logan?

Marry Logan.

Tears blurred her vision.

Mrs. Logan Alexander.

Ivy Alexander.

She swore if she looked in some old prepubescent diary she could find where she practiced writing her name that way. They would always be together. "I've never wanted anything more."

"I love you." He slipped the most amazing ring on her finger, a huge pear-shaped diamond surrounded by a halo of smaller stones. "I chose something timeless, yet unique, like you."

At seeing his ring on her finger, she succumbed to the tears. "I love you."

He stood, took her into his arms, and leaned her back.

"I'm going to be your wife." Her eyes searched his.

"That you are." As only Logan Alexander could, he treated her to a kiss fit for any movie screen, yet one that would live in her heart for all time. "Once Wilson stops filming, I have one more surprise for you, future Mrs. Alexander."

"There's more?" All she could do was hold on. No doubt being married to Logan would be a ride of a lifetime. Yes, tonight changed everything.

"Yes, we need to plan our future." He motioned to Wilson.

"We'll see you in a while. Now we'll peruse the studio." His brother saluted them, rushed over, and handed Logan a duffel bag. "Excellent grand finale."

"Congratulations!" Giselle blew them a kiss and the two walked away.

"I want to show you something." He kept a tight hold on her and they went around to the back.

The facade had nothing on the flip side, only some scaffolding and supports, nothing too spectacular.

"First things first." With a little flourish, he took a blanket out of the bag and spread it out on the ground. "I take it you like your engagement ring."

Her cheeks heated at being caught staring at her ring as the last rays of sunlight sparkled off each facet. "What?"

He motioned for her to come over. "Before I reveal your surprise, I want to show you something."

She joined him on the blanket, crouching down next to him.

"I hope it's still here." He nestled her beside him and opened up a little panel. "Bingo."

They leaned forward and her breath caught.

Written on the back of the wood door to be protected from the years and weather were their four names, their signatures, and a date. By each of their names, they put a dash and a word. "What is this?"

"This was the wrap date." His voice was almost reverent as he pointed to the date. "And of course our names and autographs."

"What are the words for?" She stared at what few others had ever seen.

"We all chose the occupation we would have in the real world when this ended."

They were both silent as she read the list, smiling at their different handwritings.

Ryder's writing was more of a scrawl. "Rock star. That's not surprising."

Logan let out a laugh. "He can't sing."

A shudder ran through her at recalling what the man could do, especially with his costar. Erin came next, her writing that of a schoolgirl, big, neat, and bubbly. "Actress."

He nodded. "She always got what she wanted."

Well, she almost got everything she wanted. The third person on the list, Drew, eluded the woman.

Next down the line, their missing member, Drew, his writing precise and neat almost like what one would expect from an architect. "Astronomer."

"He put the star in *Hollywood Stardust*."

"Look who's next." Avoiding any talk of their missing member, she hugged him.

"Yours truly." Logan tapped his own name.

"Director." She took in his writing, jagged and slanted, cool even if it wasn't meant to be cool. "I didn't know you wanted to be a director." As the words left her mouth, she wrinkled her nose. Maybe in the back of her mind she had an inkling he wanted to direct, especially in the bedroom. Actually, the man was born to direct, be in charge, and tell others what to do. "I take that back. I mean, we just never voiced that you wanted to be a director." Again, she wondered if his dream would have come true if he hadn't taken the fall for his friends.

"As you know, I've helped produce some projects, even Ryder's little film, but that only involves me forking over a check." Once more, he reached inside the duffel bag. "I never had a project that excited me, or a soon-to-be wife to share it with, but I think you'll understand when I say this is perfect for us." He pulled out a thick spiral-bound book and placed it on her lap.

"*Hollywood Starburst*?" She put her hands over her mouth and read the simple typewritten cover page once more. *Hollywood Starburst*—Sequel to *Hollywood Stardust*.

"I'm going to give you the story you have wanted all along."

Her heart took off at such a rapid rate that she found it almost hard to breathe. Was he finally going to tell her? If he revealed the truth, she could tell him what had happened with little fallout.

"Have you ever heard stories about producers or directors

who destroy sets so they won't end up in other movies?" He put his arm around her.

She turned to him.

"For about five years, I listened off and on to rumblings about the sequel being made with a different cast. At first I didn't care, but as time went on, the thought of either not being in it or having it ruined in some other way grated on me. So I purchased the story and the rights. What you have in your lap is the original sequel. I own it, and now we own it, and you know everything there is to know." He leaned in until they were nose to nose. "Should we make a movie?"

Was that all he was going to tell her? Were they going to start their official lives together without ever addressing the rest? Did he still not trust her? "Logan." She inhaled. "I know you wanted to do the sequel. I know you weren't the reason it was canceled, and I would be more than honored to help make this happen with you."

"What are you talking about? You know the sequel was canceled because of me and my indiscretions. Back then I wanted to move on to other projects." His eyes widened.

"Please, don't lie to me. I know the truth. I know everything. Let's just lay it on the line and move on." Her body broke out in trembles, but maybe it was better this way.

"Ivy." He moved back and stared her down. "I demand to know what is going on right now. What have you done?"

She swallowed. At the moment, she was certain someone coated her throat with sandpaper. "You have to understand."

"Tell me!" He pounded his fist into the ground. "Tell me now. Tell me everything."

"I was upset when you left for the meeting with Ryder and Erin without me. I guess I was jealous." His expression didn't change, and she looked down at the blanket, tracing her nail over the plaid pattern, and forced herself to continue. "I was sitting there stewing and took out the card Erin gave me with her Chargge.com e-mail. Then I started fooling around, and by accident, I hacked into her account."

"By accident you broke into Erin Holland's account?" he hissed the question at her. "There are some who say there are no accidents."

"Her password is *Hollywood Stardust*." In an attempt to hold the tears back, she shut her eyes. "I know you took the blame for the drugs that night. I know they wanted out of the sequel, and you made it easy for them. I know you lost a part you wanted, and I know that for all these years those two fools paid you off."

When he didn't speak, she opened her eyes and peeked up at him.

He glared at her, narrowed eyes, set jaw, pale complexion included.

In all the times they had bickered, even in their fight when she'd said she was relieved about the drugs, he had never glared at her.

"I knew you were never the true villain. I could feel it in my heart." She pressed her hand to her chest. "I knew it, and the world can know as well."

"Are you that blind? Don't you think there was a reason I never told you?" He scratched his hands through his hair. "No matter how bad you want me to be, I'm not a hero. I am the one who orchestrated that night. I am the one who extorted money from them."

"What?" She shook her head.

"Yes!" He stood up, towering over her. "I walked in that night to beg them to do the sequel and caught them in the act of not only screwing each other, but also doing drugs. We got in a fight, and the police were called. I was seventeen and knew I could manipulate them."

"Logan." Somehow she managed to get on her feet and reached out for him.

He swiped her hand away. "I took the blame, I got the sequel canceled, and I made sure they would never do another project without thinking about how I helped them. The script I wanted to share with you, the ring I bought thinking we were going to spend the rest of our lives together, even the land I was going to have our house built on, was all bought and paid for with money I made from them."

Wanted? Thinking? Was going? Why was everything

suddenly past tense? "What are you saying?"

"I asked you one thing. I asked you not to pry. I begged you to leave it alone. I have contracts that now by telling you, I have broken. I could lose everything because you were bound and determined to not fall in love with the bad guy." He held his hands up. "What were you going to do? Prove your point and broadcast it to the world?"

"Not if you didn't want me to." Her tears fell freely. "I just thought—"

"Thought you were helping me." He finished her sentence. "Honey, I have news for you, I'm as bad as they come. I thought I could change, but instead I changed you. Now you're a villain too. You better keep your mouth shut. Breaking into someone else's e-mail is illegal."

"If you want to write up a contract, I'll sign it." She crossed her arms. "Did you really expect to marry me and not tell me the truth?"

"No, I expected to have a wife who trusted her husband." With his head high, he walked past her.

For a moment, she waited and simply listened to his soft footsteps echoing away from her. Did he really just leave? She spun around to find him way off in the distance. Instinct took over, and with the script still in her hands, she ran after him, catching up to him in the parking lot. "Logan?"

He stopped at the side of his car.

"You're leaving?" She didn't know why she asked the obvious question.

"Wilson's here. You'll get home." He opened the door.

"You just asked me to marry you." Her voice broke.

"Can you tell me you didn't do what you did?"

She shook her head.

"Keep the ring, keep the script, and keep your mouth shut." He slipped inside his car.

When the engine started, she shut her eyes. He couldn't leave. He promised he would talk to her. "Please."

At the sound of his tires screeching on the asphalt, she opened her eyes and watched him drive away.

Well, he didn't lie when he told her tonight would be life

changing. She would never be the same.

                                        CUT TO:

INT. RESTAURANT — NEEDLES, CA - DAY

The last pit stop before arriving at Hollywood
Stardust. CHARLES is on a payphone trying to
get home. ROXY, WILLIAM, and STEVEN finish up
their lunch.

WILLIAM turns to Roxy and takes her hand.

                    WILLIAM
               Maybe after graduation we
               can come back to
               California and see if we
               can make it here.

                    STEVEN
               So says every waiter and
               waitress in La La Land.

STEVEN stares down at WILLIAM holding ROXY'S
hand. ROXY looks between WILLIAM and STEVEN
and pulls her hand away.

                    WILLIAM
               Isn't it about time he
               knows?

ROXY shakes her head.

                    STEVEN
               If I take your hand, would
               you pull away?

STEVEN reaches across the table and holds his
hand out. ROXY doesn't move.

                    WILLIAM
          Why would that even be an
          option?

When no one speaks, WILLIAM hits the table.

                    WILLIAM
          Roxy, I thought we were
          together. What happened to
          the other night?

                    STEVEN
          You mean last night when
          she was in my bed?

                    ROXY
          Everything is a mess.

ROXY stands from the table and runs off.

Chapter Twenty-One

Right before he turned onto the main street from the studio parking lot, Logan took hold of his rearview mirror and tilted it. Ivy still stood by the gates, a gorgeous statue, the wind blowing the skirt on her dress and the sunset backlighting her. He prayed that one day he could remember that image rather than his first thought of how the only woman he loved, the only woman he ever would love, looking up at him and explaining how she blatantly betrayed him in the worst possible way.

She continued to watch him, and then lowered her head into her hands, no doubt crying. Did she honestly think any good would come of searching into things that didn't concern her?

"Damn everything!" If he continued to watch, he would turn the car around. But what use would it do? He could never trust her. What else would she break into? Any time things got tough, would she conduct her own investigation rather than come to him?

Once more, he grabbed the mirror and practically tore it off the top of the car before getting her into view again.

While she remained in the same spot, now she crouched down with her face in her hands. "Don't go back." He tore his phone out of his pocket, texted his brother, then finally gave in, and managed to rip the mirror off the goddamned car. No more backward glances, no more women, no more *Hollywood Stardust*. He threw the mirror into the passenger seat and skidded out into the street.

Not caring if he drove off a cliff, he bobbed and weaved through the traffic, cut people off, and stopped short, finding little amusement in the honks and middle fingers thrust at him.

At a light, he slammed on his brakes and realized he had nowhere to go. Everywhere was intertwined with her.

The light turned green, and he sat there, even with horns blaring at him. With only one option left, he made a U-turn. Some time later, he autopiloted to Pasadena, right into Isaac's driveway, and threw the car in park.

As he got out of the car, Isaac opened the door, and his black Labrador, Beaker, ran to him with his ball. On any other day, he would have shown up to play with the dog, but even the sight of the animal they helped rescue from the local shelter did nothing for him. He gave the dog a pat on his head and didn't bother shutting his car door, choosing to drag himself to the doorway and to his friend.

Isaac stepped back to let him in. "What happened to the engagement party?"

"I think I'll plan my funeral instead." With an overwhelming exhaustion suddenly encompassing him, he trudged through Isaac's perfectly designed craftsman-style home and made a beeline right to the couch.

He stared straight ahead, wishing his mind would clear instead of replaying that horrible scene at the studio over and over again.

Isaac joined him, and put two glasses and a decanter in front of him. He poured some of the blood red liquid into each glass and took his and sat across from him. "I take it she didn't say no."

He picked up the glass, glanced inside, and downed it, wincing as the liquid hit his throat. "What is this?"

"Port. It sounded like something a sophisticated man should drink, and it looks cool when you hold it." As if to demonstrate, Isaac sat back, crossed his arms, and held the glass out. Beaker came and sat by his side.

"All you need is a robe and a pipe." He poured himself another shot of the cough medicine and gulped it down.

"Logan." Isaac leaned forward.

"Let's just be glad she never put you and Drew together." He shook his head.

"Continue."

"Somehow, she broke into Erin's e-mail, and she knows everything."

"How did she break into Erin's e-mail?" Isaac took a sip of his drink and shuddered.

"She said she was fooling around and stumbled on her password."

"It's Hollywood Stardust." With a sneer, Isaac put the glass aside.

After pouring and swigging down his third helping of glorified cough syrup, he faced his friend. "And you know that because?"

"It's Erin. She'd choose something she wouldn't forget, but thought it was smart she didn't choose *password* or one, two, three, four, five, six.."

"Have you looked at her e-mails?" For the villain of the bunch, was he the only one who didn't commit e-mail fraud or know Erin's password?

"Let me put it this way, I know exactly what Ivy found, and may I say I'm glad? Maybe you can sleep at night once you get her back in your bed."

"You, of anyone, should know why I can't get her back." Simply saying the words aloud made his stomach churn. "Do you still love Erin?"

"I changed my identity to force myself away from her. I had you put it in your contract that she wouldn't try to find me except through you. There isn't a day I don't wonder what would have happened if I could have forgiven her." He turned away.

"Maybe love is too toxic." At the moment, his entire body felt as if it were cut open and someone had squeezed lemon juice on the sores.

"Maybe you should be thankful she told you what happened. Maybe you should choose not to live your life with a huge hole where you know someone fits."

"She told me after the fact." His phone vibrated, his heart

seized, and he stood. "I can't trust her."

"Logan. Don't do this. Go get her. Don't let this be her engagement day."

"You know what's funny?"

Isaac shook his head. "Nothing at the moment."

"After reading the e-mails, she dubbed me this great hero. I had to set her straight and let her know I was the bad guy who orchestrated the whole thing." His phone went off once more.

"There's at least one other person on the planet who knows the truth, and he thinks you're pretty cool." Isaac shrugged. "That would be me by the way."

"You know, once you cook an egg, you can't undo it. The egg's forever changed."

"That doesn't mean the egg isn't worth something. Maybe it comes out better in the end."

He backed up. "Can I take the guest room? I may need to stay for a while."

"It's all yours."

Without looking, he tossed his phone on the couch. "Will you do me a favor and make sure Wilson got her home?" For the first time since his mother had died, an unwelcome, unfamiliar, and unwanted pressure built behind his eyes, and he needed to get away from everyone.

Isaac gave him a thumbs-up. "For the record, except for tonight, you make a lousy villain."

He walked toward the stairs. While he might make a lousy villain, he didn't make a hero either, and now she could never see him that way. Not that it mattered. It was over, and he didn't get the girl. Why was he even surprised?

"I was engaged to Logan Alexander." With her mother on one side, Giselle on the other, and her father across from her, Ivy stared at her laptop and looked down at her left hand. For less than two hours, her fourth finger held the most incredible, beautiful, amazing ring she had ever seen.

Of course she didn't need a ring, or a script, or anything

else. All she wanted was Logan. The tears began again. Actually, she wasn't sure they had ever stopped.

"I think you should try to talk to him." Her mother wrapped her arm around her.

"It won't do any good." If nothing else, she knew that much. After Logan had driven away, she'd watched him stop in the driveway. For a fleeting moment, she'd thought he was going to back up the car and tell her he promised he wouldn't leave, that he just needed a breath, and they could talk about what happened. However, he left, and she knew there was no hope once Wilson and Giselle came for her. She gave his brother back the ring and the script, telling him twice she never even peeked at it, and then she broke down. After two days of crying, Giselle had finally called her parents.

"He's not even at the bar," Giselle whispered to her mother even though Ivy was practically sitting in her lap. "He won't answer the phone. He won't speak to anyone. Will called him an ass and said he would resurface once he got over it all or had something else to focus his attention on."

"Well, at least I provided him a distraction. Deep down in my heart, I knew it wouldn't last, I just didn't want to face it." She hid her face in her hands. Her eyes ached. Her tear ducts wanted relief.

"You can't just leave it like this." Her mother rubbed her back.

Somewhere, somehow, she needed to locate her backbone. She sniffed and raised her head. "I really didn't want to end up in a tabloid under the 'Why is he with her?' category.'" Being with Logan relegated her to a life of always wondering what he was doing, where he was going, who he was with.

"Ivy, don't speak that way," her mother chided.

"I always thought you guys made an adorable couple." Giselle nodded. "It was like the unexpected, but not unbelievable."

She turned to her friend. At least she still had an Alexander man.

"I thought it would be cool 'cause if you married Logan and I married Wilson, we would have the same last name."

For fear she would throw up, Ivy put her hand over her mouth and turned back to her mother.

"Giselle, why don't you go get that tray of sandwiches I made? Take your time." Her mother shook her head.

"Okay." Giselle hopped off the couch and walked away.

"I can't eat." The thought of eating made her want to cry. "Logan cooked." Maybe her stomach still held the contents of the turkey sandwich he'd made her before they left on their surprise expedition. He had told her he wanted to have a light lunch because he had a special dinner planned. She would never know where they were going to go, what was going to happen. Did he make the meal or were they going to go to one of his friend's restaurants? If she could turn back the clock, she would have taken a hamburger from the local fast-food joint.

"You're going to make yourself sick."

"Listen here, young lady." Her father stood from the side chair, took Giselle's spot, and patted her on the knee. "I know this hurts. I know your heart is broken. I know right now it feels as if things are never going to be okay."

She really prayed her father wasn't citing some line he spewed onstage. "Daddy."

"I'm not going to tell you to get over it. Healing will take time, but I think you need to face your career, decide what is important, and immerse yourself in your work." He opened her laptop and slid it over to her lap. "Now that you have had time in front of the camera, you can finish up your gig, and I'll help you with some other opportunities. We always knew your time at the Internet company was a jumping-off point to your dream. Didn't Ryder Scott offer you a part? There's a perfect place as any to start."

She stared straight ahead. Her sister wouldn't have as much let her mascara run down her face before dialing Ryder's number for some minor role. When this whole thing started, Ivy's only dream was to be in front of the camera and follow in her family's footsteps. Hell, she even took the job at Chargge.com just to have a chance. "I would never do that to Logan." He might have left her, but she wouldn't be the person who ran to Ryder. She wasn't Erin.

"Also, remember you got the story your boss asked you for, everything except for the information on that Drew fellow. With or without Logan, once you report that story, you can write your ticket to any broadcast news team." Her mother glanced at her watch. "Don't you have a deadline? You better call in."

"Damn story!" She shoved her laptop over to her father and stood up. Her head spun, but she made sure to stay on her own two feet. "This story ruined my life. I finally found a man I love and he loved me, and he didn't care if I wasn't on camera, and he didn't care that I liked to watch the same movie over and over again, and he liked it when I would give him the parsley off my plate, and he treated me like a princess, and in return he asked for one thing!"

"Ivy, you need to get control over yourself." Her mother went to her.

"No, let her emote," her father chimed in. "It's good for her. What did he ask for?"

"He asked that I leave the past where he left it. He asked that I trust him. He asked that I come to him if I had questions. He said the story would be amazing without all that, and it was. The numbers were growing. We had fans." Had she been able to give the finale of the series to Craig, they would have blown the top off the Internet. Not that it mattered, but she would have had the perfect video log of her relationship and of the most incredible proposal.

With a new goal clearly in mind, she spun around to her father. "In turn I doubted him, broke a law, and blindsided him with what I had done. I took something sacred and ruined it."

"He left you at a movie studio in tears. He promised you he wouldn't leave, yet he did." Her mother put her hands on her hips.

"I left him no choice." She swiped her computer back from her father. "I'm done being a slave to wanting something I wasn't meant to have, and I'm not using anything Logan taught me to get ahead without him."

She plopped down on the chair opposite them and gave a quick scan to her e-mail account. The e-mails from Craig piled up. One thing was certain, she wouldn't want anyone looking through her messages, least of all Erin, and her e-mails weren't nearly as interesting.

Without opening any of the e-mails, she composed one of her own.

"What are you doing?" Her father came over and peered over her shoulder.

"The only thing I can do. I have decided ruining an important story for the website and breaking into someone's e-mail is an offense worthy of losing one's job." She doled out her own brand of justice and began typing.

> *Dear Craig,*
>
> *I know this is not the most professional way to act, and I promise when I am in a better state of mind I will talk to you in person, but as of today, I am officially resigning from my job at Chargge.com. As you know, I was in a very personal and romantic relationship with Logan Alexander, which unfortunately ended two days ago. I find myself unable to cover the Hollywood Stardust story any longer, and I have decided I must pursue another career track. I apologize for the abrupt notice, but at the moment my life is not at the point where I could do the story any justice. In the end, I was unable to uncover any earth shattering news, but the opportunity to spend time with the stars from the movie will be something I will always remember.*
>
> *Thank you for everything,*
> *Ivy R. Vermont*

Before second-guessing her next action, she hit "Send."

"My quest to make it cost me everything. It's not even my quest anymore."

"You just quit." Her father raised his voice.

"Are you scared of having to cover the gala on your own?" Her mother rushed over.

"You know, fear is a warning sign." She looked between her

parents. "It tells you when something isn't right. I'm going to stop fighting the fear. I'm terrified of the camera, and I shouldn't be in front of it, and if I was terrified of being in love with Logan and having him leave me, well then, I shouldn't have him." With the words out, the truth out, the tears started afresh. Just because someone shouldn't have something, couldn't have something or someone, didn't mean they didn't want them.

HOLLYWOOD STARDUST

CUT TO:

EXT. STREET - NEEDLES, CA - DAY

WILLIAM and STEVEN search for ROXY.

> WILLIAM
> Did you sleep with her?

STEVEN glances at him.

> WILLIAM
> I was her first.

> STEVEN
> Well, I was her last.

They face each other.

> WILLIAM
> You're still my best
> friend.

> STEVEN
> We still need to find her.

Chapter Twenty-Two

"I'm going to say this one more time, and since I know you're speaking on a landline, don't give me any of your bullshit about you not being able to hear me." Logan paced the length of Isaac's kitchen, walked to the stove to check his sauce, and leaned back on the counter. "I am not going to the anniversary gala."

"And what is your reasoning?" As if he was put out, Brian exhaled into the phone.

"I have something in the oven." He bent down and peered through the window into Isaac's double oven. "Really, I have something in two ovens. I didn't want to lie to you."

"You know as well as I do you have to go."

"I just washed my hair, and I can't do a thing with it." He ran his hand through his hair and winced. Fine, he lied. He didn't just wash his hair. He didn't remember when he had washed it. In fact, he didn't do much of anything but cook and think about Ivy. For the first time in his life, he was ready to take a razor blade to his head and just throw in the towel on all counts.

"Logan." Brian lowered his voice.

"I'm no longer dealing with the minions. I don't want their money or their baggage. There's no more 'all for one and one for all.' I want out. They know this. They don't have to talk if they don't want to. They can just be eccentric, and I can be left alone."

"So after all these years, you just want to walk away, say

thank you very much, and they have no repercussions?"

"That's what I'm saying." He walked to the refrigerator and stopped. Refrigerators reminded him of Ivy and their first kiss. He pressed his forehead against the cold, unforgiving stainless steel that mocked him.

"Well, since we have no formal agreement and they are on their way to the gala, you, my friend, are still under contract and you need to get there."

"We are not friends." Before his life had imploded, he had gone with Ivy to pick out her dress for tonight, a gorgeous 1920s floor-length, form-fitted beaded dress in shimmering copper. Once it was on her, she looked like a gorgeous flame. Her new ring would have set the whole look off to perfection. While they had shopped, she had also told him she'd started dressing in vintage clothes because maybe she had been searching for her time and place, but now she had it with him.

Of course, before he'd lost everything that mattered, he was finally going to show up to something important with someone who mattered. Now everything seemed pointless. Though he thought about staying in his contract and letting his life continue as before, for him and for Ivy, he needed to end it. Even if she didn't know, he had to be a good guy.

"Well, maybe you'll like me better once I tell you to go look in today's *National Reporter*." Brian punctuated his sentence with an evil chuckle.

"At least you did something." While he wanted to enjoy the moment, it would have been made all the sweeter with his love there to wrinkle her nose in disapproval but secretly love it.

"Get to the gala and do your job. You are still a kept man." Brian ended the call.

In the last twenty years, he had been called every name in the book, he had been blamed for the cancellation of the sequel for a beloved movie, and he had even been vandalized. And he would go through it all again if only he didn't have to walk in without Ivy. The questions would begin immediately and he wasn't prepared to answer them. Hell, he wasn't prepared for anything except answering questions about Ivy's ring.

"All right, I found an old tuxedo, but you and I are not the same size." Isaac came bounding down the stairs.

His stomach churned at the sight of the outfit. "We are not even in the same decade."

"Well, you can go with the sweats." Isaac tilted his head. "You've had them on so long they could go as your plus one."

He stomped over and grabbed the tuxedo. "I'll need some underwear. I threw mine out the day after I moved in with you."

Isaac's focus landed on the front of Logan's loose pants. "You can keep both outfits."

"I'm a disaster." He returned to the kitchen and opened the refrigerator. At the sight of the raspberries, he insisted Isaac pick up at the store, his knees almost gave out.

"Also, I think flies are starting to swarm around you." Isaac snuck a look in one of the pots. "Oh, you made chicken and dumplings. Yes!"

"Don't eat that." He rushed over, slammed the lid down, and put his hand over his eyes. "Never mind, go ahead and eat it."

"I would not dare eat Ivy's chicken and dumplings, or Ivy's vanilla cake, or Ivy's meat loaf, but do you think we could get Ivy back before all the food goes to waste?" Isaac leaned back on the counter and crossed his arms. "She read some e-mails. You would've done the same thing if given the opportunity."

"I told her to come to me. The trust is gone. If you don't have that, what do you have?" The two of them were beginning to sound like one of those shows they played over and over on cable television where everyone sat around and argued. "She even said she wanted the world to know."

"But she didn't tell the world. She came to you." Isaac pointed at him. "Obviously, she didn't do a press release or you would have heard about it."

"Has she done any updates on the show?" He turned away.

"You banned looking at Chargge.com."

"At least someone listens." All he wanted to do was pound his fist through something.

"No, I only said you banned looking, but I looked anyway."

"*Et tu*, Drew?" He snarled.

"I deserved that." Isaac laughed.

"Well, are you going to tell me?"

Before Isaac could answer, someone pounded at the door. Beaker barked and ran to the front of the house.

"I'm going to get the door." On his way, Isaac flicked him on the head. "You should really take a shower."

"Hey, asshole!" Wilson screamed through the house. "When the going gets tough, my brother takes off."

"Why are you here?" He didn't bother to turn around.

"I had some things to deliver to you, and once again, I had to make sure you didn't screw your life up." Wilson came up behind him, grabbed his shoulder, and pulled him around.

He tensed and lifted his chin.

Wilson twisted his fist in his sweatshirt and held him fast. "I thought you would emerge once you realized what an idiot you are, but since it's the day of the gala and you didn't show up for clothes, I figured I'd come to the mountain."

"I'm fine." He attempted to jerk away from his monstrous brother.

"You look like crap and you have a shindig to get to." With a garment bag and backpack slung over one arm, Wilson kept hold of him and yanked him toward the stairs. "Is he in the guest bedroom?"

"Yep, the towels in there are clean." Isaac laughed.

"Let go of me." He tried to push his brother away, but Wilson was always gargantuan, and he managed to literally drag him up the stairs and into Drew's guest room.

"You go take a shower and don't make me get in with you." Wilson thrust him toward the bathroom door.

He tripped and caught himself on the doorknob. "You are just like everyone else. You just want to make sure the money keeps rolling in."

Wilson tossed his items on the bed. "After the last four days, and after what I've seen, I'm telling you that after I finish what I have to say, we're off each other's payrolls. I made some mistakes. I made you feel indebted to me because I was there for you. Well, I was wrong. You held up your end of the deal and now we need to be brothers."

Unsure of how to deal with Wilson's admission, he stared his big brother down.

"I came with your clothes, not for the money. I came because you are not a quitter, and you need to see your commitments through to the end, because you're different than all of them." His brother got up in his face. "Get cleaned up, now."

"What did you see the last four days?" His mind went to instantly to Ivy.

Wilson lifted his chin.

Knowing he would get nothing more, he entered the bathroom and slammed the door. He had watched enough movies to know he could climb out the bathroom window and escape, but it would do no good. They would find him. With or without Ivy, he would have to go to the gala and do the job he, himself, had put into place.

He turned on the water and tore off his pity ensemble. Not caring if the water was hot or cold, he went through the motions of getting cleaned up and tried not to think of anything.

As if on automatic, he finished washing and rinsing his hair, stepped out, and dried off, returning to the bedroom buck-naked.

"Lord, have some dignity." Wilson threw him a pair of underwear.

"I lost my dignity when I used a bar of soap to wash my hair." He got into the tuxedo. In truth, he lost it way before that, but now wasn't the time for details.

"You put it in a ponytail. It's not like you need to style it." His brother pointed to the door.

At this point all he could do was continue to go through the motions. Make his appearance at the gala, deal with Erin and Ryder, walk the red carpet alone. He went downstairs.

"Don't lose your glass slipper." Drew opened the door for him. "Actually, maybe you should go find your princess."

"I'll be back before midnight, and fairy tales don't exist." He shook his head. "Take the food out in twenty minutes."

Wilson pushed him outside. "We'll take my car."

Though he wanted to get in the backseat and have Wilson chauffeur him, his brother's late model SUV didn't lend itself to a grand entrance. He got in the passenger seat and stared out the window as once again Logan drove away.

"Are you going to speak?" Wilson got on the freeway in the dead of rush hour.

"Are you going to tell me what you saw the last four days?" He took a pair of dusty sunglasses off his brother's dashboard.

"First, I have something for you." With the car going no faster than a crawl, Wilson reached into the backseat and handed him a brown grocery bag.

He reached inside and pulled out Ivy's ring and the *Hollywood Starburst* script. A weight settled right in the center of his chest.

"Those were returned to me the night I took your sobbing, almost fiancée to her apartment. I was the one who sat with her. I was the one who let her cry until my shirt was soaking wet. I was the one who tucked her in when she fell asleep from exhaustion." Wilson squeezed the steering wheel.

At the image his brother described, he exhaled and broke out in a sweat.

"She wanted me to tell you she didn't read any of it, not one word."

He knew if Ivy had said she didn't read it then she didn't, and he also knew what it meant. "How is she?" The question just happened—he couldn't stop it.

"How do you think she is?" Wilson gave him a quick look.

"Tell me." He closed his hand around the ring.

"I don't know. She was engaged to the man of her dreams for all of five minutes before he went postal on her for telling the truth. Her whole life is in shambles because the so-called man who loved her ditched her." His brother hit the steering wheel, and the car lurched forward the few inches they managed to move in the gridlock.

He sat up in the seat. "She broke our trust. I told her not to go looking. She didn't come to me."

"Maybe because she knew what would happen." Wilson took a breath. "In case it means anything to you, while Ivy freely admitted to doing things she shouldn't, she never told Giselle what she found out."

He ground his teeth together. Of course she wouldn't tell Giselle. She wouldn't tell anyone. The woman practically threw herself in front of a crazy fan to protect him, and she came to him on the night of her engagement to tell him what she discovered. She never said she was going to tell the world. She only wanted to discuss it with him, which was what he told her to do. "What else?"

"She quit her job two days ago. Right before your engagement piece should have aired. And just so that you can sleep at night knowing your stupid precious little secret is kept safe, Giselle looked at the e-mail after Ivy went to sleep. She point-blank told her boss there was no story beyond what the media already knew, and she failed at her assignment." Wilson reached into his pocket and tossed a folded piece of paper to him. "Here, she printed it."

"After tonight, I am changing every password on every account. Nothing is sacred." He opened the paper and scanned the words. Her loyalty to him dripped off the page. What had he done?

"Now you just committed the same offense Ivy did. Are you going to tell her or hide it?" Wilson spat the words at him. "Better yet, why don't you just stay gone? She's better off without you if she has to live in fear that anytime she tells you something you'll disappear."

He froze. "I drove away."

Wilson stared out the windshield.

"I promised her I wouldn't drive away, and I drove away." He looked down at the script.

"You suck," Wilson hissed.

"Will you get to this shindig already?" He pointed ahead.

"What are you going to do?" Once more Wilson glanced at him.

"I have to get to that party and deal with my minions."

"Then what are you going to do?" Wilson pulled into the emergency lane and sped down the freeway.

"Right now I just need to not be the villain." He pushed the sunglasses up on his nose and sat back. "I'm not walking the red carpet."

⌒⌒⌒

Alone.

For the first time since she had watched Logan's taillights take off, Ivy found herself alone in her apartment. It was a strange kind of alone, one she hadn't felt for a long time. Lately, and most especially since Logan, any alone time was met with a sense of urgency of something she needed to do or anxiety over Logan's whereabouts. However, this solitude came with nothing, no anticipation, no sense she wouldn't be alone again sometime soon. Simply nothing.

In a world where she didn't break into a movie star's e-mail and was still gainfully employed, she would have been ready to go to the gala and waiting for Logan to do whatever it was he did when he made himself look like a dream.

After admitting she lived in the real world, she took a deep breath and put her dress away on the far side of her closet along with Logan's clothes, which she promised she would give to Giselle to give to Wilson tomorrow.

Yes, tomorrow she would finally accept it was over, down to Logan's last sock. When their project began, they were only meant to last until this night.

Though she wondered if anyone from Chargge.com went to the gala in her place, and how Logan and all the rest were faring, she promised herself to stay away from any form of media until it was over. She didn't need Julia flaunting her victory on the step and repeat backdrop with the people she built relationships with. She definitely didn't need to see Logan in a tuxedo. Acid burned the back of her throat at the thought he might have chosen to bring another date.

In her bathrobe with a diet frozen dinner waiting for her and a stack of DVDs that were not *Hollywood Stardust*, she plopped down on the couch right as a knock came at the door.

Since home cooking was out of the question, hopefully the pizza gods took kindly on her. She forced herself up and made the hike a few feet to the door. A delivery didn't constitute not being alone. It only made for a brief interruption of her solitude. "Who is it?"

"Isaac."

A quick glance through the peephole revealed Logan's friend, and she opened the door. "Hi." What on earth was he doing here? The anxiety that bubbled just below the surface all day, that nagging ache that told her something was wrong but she couldn't fix it, amplified and demanded to be heard.

"Did you see today's *National Reporter*?" He leaned against the doorjamb and held the paper out to her.

She backed up. "Please."

"I promise, it's nothing to do with the obvious."

"Come in." The magazine had already been turned to the page he wanted her to look at, and she returned to the couch and read the article.

Internet Hookups

Online personality, Julia Davis, has given the world of Internet porn a whole new meaning when it was uncovered that she has slept her way through some of the most successful and most notorious start-ups since Silicon Valley became more than a pinprick on the map. In an exclusive exposé, we have uncovered how she slept with, and blackmailed, some of the digital age's top executives, amassing hundreds of thousands of dollars only to lose it in the stock market. Ms. Davis secured her job at her latest victim, Chargge.com, through "a connection" with a vice president. Since then, she has earned quite the reputation as being a bully to the other females at the successful Internet portal. We hope this little piece of information will be dealt with quickly at the company headed by one of the youngest and most successful female CEOs in the world. We can only hope the girls gang up and run her out of town. We won't stand for bullying anymore.

She put the paper down. The story had Logan written all

over it. If they were together, she would have scolded him, but it would have gone no further than that because she would have known he did it to protect her.

"Is this why you came here?" In a truth she could admit only to herself, she sort of wished the story would have been about how bad Logan was doing without her.

"No." He leaned forward and took a breath. "I came to tell you that I am Drew Fulton."

"I know." Her heart sped with something other than an ache for her ex. With the two of them alone and with no fear of being barged in on by anyone, she revealed what she'd discovered and looked him right in the eye.

His mouth fell open, and he flopped back on the chair. "You know?"

"I do. I'm sorry." For the first time since Logan had driven away, she smiled.

He stared at her. "Is it that obvious?"

"No, I figured it out the night of the party, with some words you said and then the way you disappeared the moment Ryder and Erin showed up and—" Tears blurred her vision. Logan had told her he loved her that night.

"What is it?"

She swallowed. "That night when Erin came in she said she thought you would be there. She almost sensed you."

"She said that?" His tone came out with a twinge of excitement or maybe hope.

"Yes." With no point fighting the tears, she allowed them to fall. "I don't know what you do or don't know about what happened with Logan and me, but I never told anyone I figured it out, not him, not anyone."

"Ivy." He moved next to her on the couch, popped a tissue out of the box on the table, and handed it to her. "Will you go to the anniversary gala with me?"

"I can't." She shoved the tissue to the corner of her eye.

"You'll have your story." He bent down.

"I don't care about the story. After I fell in love with Logan, I didn't care at all about the story. I quit my job. Logan was right all along, when he said the story was fine the way it was."

Heat and the sensation of being closed in overtook her and she stood. "I can't go there."

"Ivy, I came to tell you who I was because I need to take you to that gala. The minute I walk in with you, there are people who are going to recognize me, and I didn't want you to be blindsided." Drew came up behind her.

"You know, I have an entire evening planned." She tightened her bathrobe around her, ran to the kitchen, and pulled her dinner out of the freezer. The ice-crystal-covered box must have been there for at least a year.

Again, Drew followed her. "Well, if we are going to eat ourselves into oblivion, can we go back to my place? Before I came here, I spent thirty minutes putting away all the food Logan has cooked for you today."

Thankful for the blast of cold air from the refrigerator, she didn't move.

"Yep." He snatched the box out of her hand and shoved it back in the freezer. "Some guys troll for chicks when they're upset, some play video games, some drink. Logan, he cooks. Normally, I benefit, but he wouldn't let me touch one bite. Of course, they weren't my favorites."

She went to the sink, but forgot what she wanted once she took the two steps to her destination.

"We have pasta sauce, chicken and dumplings, meat loaf, pot roast with those pearl onions that he bitches about peeling the entire time. We even have something like four containers of raspberry sauce he made from scratch. I watched him strain the seeds myself."

"Do you like raspberries?" She stared down the drain wondering when her life fell in there. All she needed to do was turn on the garbage disposal.

"It's a give or take. Fruit is not a dessert. Only you and Logan think it can pass." He made a noise of disgust. "Always been a chocolate man myself. Chocolate and peanut butter. Logan knows this. He likes to swoop in and control things and make things better. I think it comes from lacking control when he needed it most. Sometimes things get out of hand, and you control everything so much that it ends up taking control. I think he found that out after he fell in love with you. Up until then, the whole deal with Ryder and Erin, and even helping keep me under wraps, was no big deal."

She glanced over her shoulder at him.

"Then he found someone to live for." He joined her at the sink.

"He drove away. Didn't let me explain." She clutched the edge of the counter.

"Yeah, and you pushed his buttons and went for the one thing he didn't want you to know. He wanted to be perfect for you."

With someone to finally really talk to who knew Logan maybe even better than her, she let everything out. "I don't think he really wants me. I'm just easy for him. One day he'll realize he could've had someone else."

Drew laughed. "Why is it that every woman on the planet thinks that an actor has to be with another actor? Oh, and if it's a guy, then he must have to be with some sort of model, right?"

She ground her teeth together.

"Well, the stereotype is there for a reason." He elbowed her. "We all start out thinking we're going to get these babes dripping off us, and it happens, especially for Logan and Ryder."

"See."

"I'm not done. You know, I lecture over at UCLA, and I always tell my students not to interrupt until I'm done with my anecdote." He opened up a cabinet and took down a glass. "Anyway, for some actors that may work and that's fine, but I think you've forgotten two very important points."

She watched him return to the sink and fill his glass with water.

"First, Logan isn't an actor. He hasn't been for many years, and even if he ever ended up acting again, he's a businessman. They can get babes too, you know. Women dig money." He held the glass out for her. "This is for you."

"Thank you." She furrowed her brow and took the glass.

"Shh, not done." He put his finger over his lips. "Second, he loves you. He doesn't love a model or an actress, or some ideal you have stuck in your head."

Rather than speak, she took a sip of the tap water and winced. Logan would have never allowed water from the faucet. He would have gotten her a club soda to settle her stomach. She could use some now.

"Oh, it doesn't have bubbles in it. I apologize for my grave error." With a bit of sarcasm, he over exaggerated his movements as he put his hand to his chest. "You know, one day he's going to drive away again. One day when you have a couple of kids, and your house is built around a kitchen in Los Feliz, the two of you are going to get into a tiff, and he's going to get in his car and drive away. He's going to wind his way around the streets and probably end up at my house for a few hours. Then he'll come back, because that's what he's going to do. Just like you're going to peek around and do your research and ask him the tough questions that no one else dares."

She put the glass down, went to the refrigerator, and got a bottle of club soda she bought herself.

"He needs to know that he could drive away and you'll come for him." Drew closed the refrigerator. "You have to go to the gala, because as bad as everything is for you right now, let me tell you that Logan is one hundred times worse."

She shook her head.

"If nothing else, he needs to know you knew about me and never said a word." He took her by the shoulders. "He needs to know you quit, and he needs to know you love him, and then you need to hear what he's trying to do to be worthy of you."

Worthy of her? Her heart hurt. It didn't want to be cut open yet again. "Why are you doing this?" She stared into his face for the first time without feeling guilty for knowing the truth. The Drew from the movie was there, hidden away.

"He's my best friend. He's always been there for me. You belong together and you need each other." He shrugged. "Maybe I should have talked to Erin and not disappeared."

"You're going to have to zip up my dress." She thrust the bottle of water at him and walked to her bedroom. Worse than any stage fright was the fear of facing him. Yes, fear was a warning, a sign, but she also had a small glimmer of hope trying to shine through, and she would never forgive herself if she snuffed it out.

HOLLYWOOD STARDUST

CUT TO:

EXT. HOLLYWOOD STARDUST - HOLLYWOOD, CA - DAY

After dropping CHARLES at the airport, they make it to Hollywood Stardust. WILLIAM gets out of the car.

> STEVEN
> Here we are, the end of the line.

STEVEN motions toward the door.

> ROXY
> Aren't you coming?

> STEVEN
> Go live your happily ever after.

ROXY gets out of the car. WILLIAM guides her to the front of the theater and takes her in his arms.

> WILLIAM
> It's just you and me.

ROXY opens her eyes and watches STEVEN drive away.

FADE OUT
ROLL CREDITS

Chapter Twenty-Three

Over twenty years ago, the Hollywood Stardust facade had been erected on the studio back lot along with other building parts and pieces. Erin and Ryder had taken their marks by the theater entrance and Logan had driven down the fake rendition of Hollywood Boulevard on his way out of the city.

With his hands in his pockets, and trying to stay away from the red carpet leading into the gala party and screening of the *Hollywood Stardust* movie, he watched the guests pose in front of the facade. They would never know about the hidden message the four stars had written behind a hidden panel, they didn't understand what that spot meant to the one person he loved, and they didn't realize only last week he had proposed to her in that exact location.

After seeing, and more importantly, understanding, the movie with Ivy, he knew Erin's character had opened her eyes and watched him go. Her one last look opened the door to the sequel.

Eyes wide open, Ivy had watched him go. In fact, he had watched her watch him go. The screen faded to black. The music played.

She had watched him go.

She had also quit her job and returned the ring and cried on his brother until his shirt was soaked.

Most importantly, she hadn't read the script.

Had Ivy taken her chance, she would have found *Hollywood Starburst* contained her Hollywood ending.

Trust was a two-way street. People made mistakes, but in the end, she had done the right thing and told him.

He had driven away and, as she'd predicted from day one, broke her heart.

Still, she'd opened her eyes and given way to the sequel.

If he did nothing else, he had to give her a Hollywood ending if she would allow it.

Though his agreements with the dynamic duo might state he had to attend the function, it didn't specify how he entered, whom he spoke to, or how long he stayed. He waited until the last of the guests entered the studio and photographers dispersed and made his way around to the side entrance, nodding at the guard who let him inside.

A lump formed in his throat the moment he entered and got a look at the main room. They had set the inside up as the interior of the Hollywood Stardust theater, had there ever been an interior. The art deco theme ran throughout the room, plush red velvet chairs were set up for the screening of the newly remastered movie, and they even had people dressed as old-fashioned ushers guiding the guests to their seats.

Ivy needed to see this. She deserved it more than anyone. He glanced at his watch. If it took only ten minutes to deal with his costars, he could leave, get Ivy, grovel and beg, and drive her back before Steven drove away. Of course, his entire plan hinged on whether she took him back.

Needing to hurry things along, he ventured inside and scanned the room. He found his stars smack-dab in the middle of a large group holding court and decided to join them.

"There's Logan!" A woman thrust one of the collector's programs and a pen in his direction.

In an instant, a throng of other women surrounded him.

"I need to get one of these." He signed his name on top of Ryder's autograph, and much bigger, just because he could, and then signed a few more.

"Where's Ivy?" One of the women tiptoed up to him with her book.

"You know her name?" He put his autograph on the cover and didn't answer the question.

"I've been watching you since the first time you were on the Internet." She smiled and hugged her program. "I love the two of you together. You're not who everyone used to think you were."

"What's your name?" He plucked the program away from her.

"Mary." She leaned over.

"Mary." While he rarely, if ever, personalized an autograph, he figured he owed her something special. He put her name on the program and added the words "thank you." "Here you are."

"Thank you!" Once more, she hugged the book and then went to show her friends.

"Well, well, look who missed his photo opportunity." Ryder came up beside him, patted his shoulder, and leaned in. "We have media wanting interviews—also some newspapers insisted you and Ivy be interviewed. What're you doing? Where's your girl?"

"Logan." In a yellow floor-length gown, chosen no doubt for her to stand out in the crowd, Erin joined them. "I need you to talk to some people. Did you leave the little woman at home and decide to make it about us for a change? There's a man here who wants to do a story. How could you be late to this?"

Some of the onlookers started taking pictures of the three of them together.

In an effort to stop the flashes and demands, he held up his hand. If nothing else, he succeeded in ruining a few pictures.

The lights flashed, and an announcer's voice came through the speakers announcing the screening would start in two minutes. The crowd began to disperse to their seats.

"Where is Ivy?" Ryder elbowed him.

"Logan." Erin grabbed his arm.

He jerked his arm away and turned toward them. "The two of you are the most selfish, inconsiderate people I have ever met, and you are in good company because I'm the third. I just went through the worst four days of my life, and all you can think about is if we get an interview or a photo, or if you're the center of attention."

Ryder jutted his jaw out.

Erin wrung her hands. "I thought for sure Drew would have come tonight."

"Listen to you. Look at you. Drew is the smartest of us all. I should have joined him." He shook his head. Ivy knew everything. Every selfish move, every bribe, every deal, and she had still said yes when he'd asked her to marry him. Yet he had driven away. If she allowed it, he would spend the rest of his life making it up to her, but first he needed to go to her as a hero. "We all need to face the fact that times have changed. I want an answer to my question now, and I need to get out of here."

Almost as if they had planned it, the lights lowered, and the room shimmered in the distinctive flicker of a movie projection.

"Did Ivy leave you?" Erin touched his shoulder.

Her question seemed to echo through the space and suddenly every guest there let out a collective gasp.

"No." Ryder hit him. "She's up on stage."

The lights came up, the movie stopped, and he turned. Only the magic could produce what he saw on the stage. Ivy, his love, the woman he wanted to marry, stood in front of the screen. Had he passed out? Was this a hallucination?

"What's she doing?" Erin growled.

Ivy put her hands over her mouth and, like an actor who had forgotten her lines, turned toward stage right and shook her head. At last, she faced forward again. "I need help."

Never one to miss his cue, Logan went running.

❧

With her mouth open, her heart threatening to explode, and the real threat she might vomit any second, Ivy stood in the middle of a soundstage in front of no less than five hundred people. For her grand finale, she also managed to interrupt the screening of her favorite movie. If anyone would go down as the villain, she would.

She and Drew had raced to the gala and, not wanting to make a scene, snuck into the back with the help of a guard. Her plan was to lead where Drew followed and pray Logan would come to her. One wrong turn landed her exactly where she didn't want to be, and the only words she could utter were that she needed help.

Somehow, she thought Logan would magically come to her and carry her off the stage. Instead, she stood there with people staring and glaring at her, and finally she realized a greater fear than stage fright.

The fear Logan wouldn't appear.

She used her father's old trick and stared into the lights. Through the glare, she couldn't make out the individual people, and she didn't care because what she had to say only one person needed to hear. Of course, she made sure to follow Logan's rule and tilted her head to ensure she looked her best.

"I'm sorry to interrupt your evening." Her voice seemed to bounce back at her, but she forced herself to continue. "You know, I studied the movie you're about to see, or really were seeing until I arrived. I wrote my master's thesis on it. I barely remember a time when this movie wasn't a part of my life."

The crowed whispered and grumbled.

She swallowed. "I was and still am a fan, and then in what I would call the most incredible plot twist never written, I met and fell in love with one of the stars while doing a story. Even more amazing is he fell in love with me."

"That's Ivy!" someone yelled out.

"Guilty." She lifted her hand in a weak wave. "I'm also guilty of making some really bad mistakes. I realize now I should have gone to him and trusted him."

The crowd let out a collective *aww*.

"When we first got together, he told me he wanted to be with me until we lost track of the days. I just wanted to tell him that we've been apart for four days, and I can keep track of every minute."

She waited, looked down, and wondered if anyone would notice if she tiptoed away. If her heart didn't break before, it shattered with the utter and complete silence in the room.

"That's funny because I can also count every second we've been apart, and it feels like torture."

At the sound of Logan's voice, she turned. There would never be a day when the man didn't enter the room and take over.

The crowd broke out in applause.

"Ivy." With his hands out, he approached her. "I made the mistakes. I should have never driven away. I was on my way to get you now. I wanted to be what you deserved when I came to beg you to take me back, but this is all I am."

"Don't you get it?" She stared into his eyes. "No matter what, you're always my hero. I don't care if the world knows or not. I do."

"Four days ago, I asked you to marry me and you accepted." In a sudden move, he got down on his knee, reached into his jacket pocket, and held up her ring. "I'm asking you again to be my wife. If I ever drive away again, I promise to turn around and get you in the front seat with me."

"I promise to always come to you first." She took her first full breath and held her hand out. "Yes, I'll marry you."

He pressed his lips to the back of her hand and slipped the ring on her finger.

The crowd cheered, and Logan stood, nodded to their fans, and picked her up. "To be continued."

As they made their way off stage, she wrapped her arms around his neck. "I can walk."

"But you don't have to. I am more than thrilled to be your personal mode of transportation, future Mrs. Alexander." He stopped and lowered his face to kiss her.

"Congratulations." Ryder interrupted them.

She tightened her hold on Logan at the sight of both Ryder and Erin.

Logan took a step back. "I think we have nothing more to say. I'm off duty."

"You can be off duty forever," Erin whispered. "It's over."

Ryder nodded. "It's time."

"We all need to do the right thing." Logan exhaled.

"You should stay. Everyone really wanted to talk to Ivy." Ryder let out a laugh. "How did you end up on stage anyway?"

"We took a wrong turn." From behind some crates, Drew

appeared.

"Oh my God." Erin put her hand over her mouth and dashed away.

"You know, I always thought no one could make me out, but your fiancée figured out my identity at Wilson's opening and never said a word." He lifted his chin in Logan's direction.

"I know who I can trust." Logan tightened his hold on her.

Ryder shook Drew's hand.

"Why don't I do the media thing tonight, and you and your fiancée can get out of here?" Drew tilted his head toward the exit. "I think I'm a pretty good distraction."

Logan bowed his head, and with her still in his arms, he walked away. "Let's go walk the red carpet, shall we?"

"I think I finally got over my stage fright." She pulled him down.

He brushed his lips over hers. "Well, it looks like I finally got the girl."

The End

AN EXCERPT

Limelight

BOOK TWO IN THE HOLLYWOOD STARDUST SERIES

By

Kim Carmichael

Chapter One

Flashes from the cameras created lingering, silver, glowing starbursts in Drew Fulton's eyes. The media frenzy started almost instantly, derailing the twentieth-anniversary screening of the one and only movie he had filmed, *Hollywood Stardust*. For someone who had successfully remained hidden for two decades, he chose the ideal subtle moment to come out of his self-imposed exile—or maybe not.

"Drew, where have you been all these years?" called out one of the reporters gathered for the gala.

Once the studio executives had realized what had happened, they'd stopped all the festivities and, with a bit of movie magic, had made the stage into a spot fit for a press conference in record time.

Before showing up at the shindig, he had promised himself to go for it. Now was the time for full disclosure, and he leaned down to the microphone. "To encapsulate two decades into one sentence, I changed my name, went to school, earned my doctorate, and opened up a small nutraceutical laboratory." All right, it wasn't the world's best sentence, but it would suffice. In the next two days, he would have to show up at his business and do a lot of explaining, something he sort of pushed aside when he made his snap decision to come here to find her.

A woman waved her hand. "Why did you feel the need to change your name and disappear?"

Drew wasn't sure if she was part of the media or not, but if he didn't answer her, someone else would force the issue.

He searched for her in the studio set converted to look like the inside of the Hollywood Stardust theater, the destination for the four characters in the movie. In the film, their quest took them across country. The road was a metaphor for the trip one takes to transition between adolescence and adulthood.

In real life, he and the other actors had faced the same challenges.

Once more, he looked for her. With her knowledge of all things smoke and mirrors, no doubt she managed to squirrel away where she could watch everything, yet not be seen. For the first time since he had met her, she'd shied away from the limelight.

He swallowed and took hold of the microphone stand. While he wanted to offer the fans of the movie the truth they sought for all these years, the answer as to why he disappeared was better left unspoken, at least in public.

"Sometimes you need to just get away from everything and everyone and start over." More lights went off, leaving him blinking to see.

"But how did you hide your identity?" The question came from a male in the crowd.

An easy one. "During the movie I wore prosthetics to appear more like the producers wanted the character, and they asked me to stay in costume for public appearances. It was very easy to fade away once the costume came off . . . and the weight came off."

Some chuckles went through the audience.

Yes, he was the chubby kid. During filming he had lost weight, causing a whole host of issues for the movie. They had to keep adding padding to his costume to keep the consistency. He hid for a while, let the fanfare of the movie die down, and then went abroad for college. By the time he returned with a different name, no one ever put it together. He still found it incredible that he had pulled it off at all. Maybe he was a real actor after all.

"Have you kept in touch with your cast mates?" Another question barreled toward him.

He glanced off to the side. While he might not be able to find her, his best friend, Logan Alexander, was always there. Logan nodded, giving him the okay to answer. "Only Logan Alexander." The quote unquote villain of both the movie and of real life was one of the best people he knew. One might even say a hero.

Some mumbles went through the crowd.

"Drew, why did you decide to come back now?"

Again, he looked for her. Where did she hide herself? On the other side of the stage, he located Ryder Scott, their leading man. The poster boy for a movie star, he always had everything. After the film, Ryder went on to a successful career and now also dabbled in directing and producing. However, he couldn't locate the last of their four. The reason he came out of hiding.

"I have some unfinished business." He needed to go find her. "I can take one more question before we should probably let you all get back to the movie."

"Can we get a picture of the four of you together?"

Well, the promise of a picture that would be all over the world should bring her out. He turned left and right. Ryder joined him first, shaking his hand and taking center stage to thunderous applause. Logan, who only moments before proposed to his fiancée on this exact stage, came out next, and the clapping grew to the point where it vibrated the building.

Logan shook his hand and raised his eyebrows.

"Where is she?" Drew attempted to ask the question without moving his lips.

"She'll be here." Logan patted his back and took his place.

The crowd stilled as if holding its collective breath, waiting for the one female of the group.

He ground his teeth together. After everything he just did, would she not reveal herself?

And then she appeared.

Damn him to hell for his breath catching at the sight of her. Though he followed her career and watched her in her movies, her television appearances, even clips of her in a stage play, nothing compared to her in person.

She stepped to the edge of the stage, and the applause began once more. Yes, even with his news of showing up after twenty years, Erin Holland would always steal the spotlight.

The color that overtook her cheeks would be gorgeous in the pictures, but he knew better. He knew the blush came from her being flustered, unsure, and taken off guard. If they were alone, away from the scrutiny of the public, she would be crying. Not that it mattered. Crying, flush, with or without makeup, and even with twenty years behind them, he had never seen a more beautiful woman.

Instead, she nodded toward the audience and made her way to them. Her silver form-fitting dress moved like liquid metal, fluid and flowing. She wore her blonde hair down, smooth and cascading over one shoulder, but pulled back from her picture-perfect face. Her doelike blue eyes and heart-shaped lips were all natural and the envy of many a teenage girl way back when.

She stared into his eyes, asking questions, shooting accusations. In short, being Erin through and through. The one woman he couldn't stand, but couldn't get out of his mind. He could never move forward if he only looked back, and the second she came within reach, he held his hand out to her.

"Drew." She licked her lips, put her hand in his, and gave him a hug. Her trembling betrayed her cool outward demeanor.

"I came here for you." He inhaled. Her perfume might have changed, but the aroma enveloping him was the same. It was just her. "We need to talk."

Without a word, she pulled back and took her position between Logan and Ryder. The three made up the love triangle of *Hollywood Stardust*, while Drew's character was always left standing on the edge, just like him.

Again, the flashes went off, and he found himself posing with the rest of them. Old habits returned—subtle changes in his position to catch the light, show off a better angle, allow the photographers to get the ever-important shot.

He needed to get to the person he came here for and raised his hand, the universal signal for stopping the show.

"Drew, one more question before you leave," a woman called over the mumbles, the claps, and the oohs and ahhs.

He waited.

"What unfinished business brought you back? Is this a publicity stunt for the movie or was it something, or someone, else?"

"It wasn't a stunt. In fact, I didn't even know I was going to do this until about an hour before I arrived." He turned, wanting to catch her before she ran away licking her self-perceived wounds.

As usual, he was too late. Erin had already vanished, and he almost fought a laugh. Once more, he changed his life for her, and again she wasn't around. "As for the rest, stay tuned."

TO BE CONTINUED . . .

About the Author
Kim Carmichael

Kim Carmichael began writing nine years ago when her love of happy endings inspired her to create her own.

A Southern California native, Kim's contemporary romance combines Hollywood magic with pop culture to create quirky characters set against some of most unique and colorful settings in the world.

With a weakness for designer purses, bad boys, and techno geeks, Kim married her own computer whiz after he proved he could keep all her gadgets running and finally admitted handbags were an investment.

Kim is a PAN member of the Romance Writers of America, as well as some small specialty chapters. A multi-published author, Kim's books can be found on Amazon as well as in Barnes & Noble.

When not writing, she can usually be found slathered in sunscreen trolling Los Angeles and helping top doctors build their practices.

To find out more about Kim Carmichael visit:

Website: www.kimcarmichaelnovels.com

Facebook:
http://www.facebook.com/kimcarmichaelnovels

Twitter: @kimcarmichael4

CH⚡RGGE

get plugged in...

Visit http://www.chargge.com/ to get the latest about the *Hollywood Stardust* crew.

Now Available from Amazon

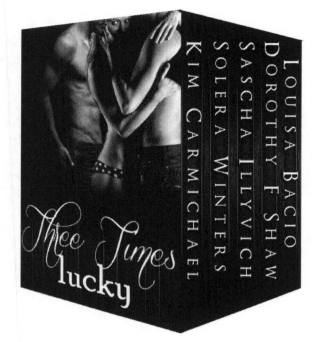

Now Available from Amazon

Made in the USA
Charleston, SC
21 June 2015